1780

A Time to Live Free or Die

HARRISON NEESE

The HayeCountry Collection
Farmerville, Louisiana

1780—A Time to Live Free or Die

Publisher's Cataloging-in-Publication Data

Neese, Harrison.
  1780 : a time to live free or die / Harrison Neese.
  pages cm
  ISBN: 978-0-9864050-2-0 (pbk.)
  1. United States—History—Revolution, 1775-1783—Fiction. 2. South Carolina—History—Revolution, 1775-1783—Fiction. 3. Women—United States—History—18th century—Fiction. 4. Family life—Fiction. 5. Loyalty—Fiction. I. Title.
PS3614.E367 A72 2015
813.6—dc23   2015900996

Published by: *The HayeCountry Collection*
Cover Design: *Book Cover Design by Judy Bullard*
Interior Design: *The HayeCountry Collection*
Editing: Foster-Akin Editing Services by Jean Foster Akin

10 9 8 7 6 5 4 3 2 1

Printed and Bound in the United States of America

The HayeCountry Collection
Farmerville, Louisiana

To my beautiful wife, Bonnie,
for your love, patience, friendship, suggestions, and
willingness to read every draft until we got it right.

Table of Contents

"Never give up, for that is just the place and time that the tide will turn"   *- Harriet Beecher Stowe*

1780, A Time to Live Free or Die.

It was their darkest hour . . . when the British captured Charleston, South Carolina and with it, the entire southern American Army. Patriots everywhere gave up, ready to accept defeat as the flame of liberty bent and flickered against the cold relentless winds of tyranny.

Yet, there remained small bands of patriots—men and women—who would not quit. Without orders and without hope of reward, men like John Hamilton led eager volunteers throughout South Carolina bedeviling the enemy to keep alive the patriot cause.

Herein lies my story of the fictional family of John and Rachel Hamilton of South Carolina, the colony where more battles were fought than any other of the original thirteen colonies.

Rachel Hamilton opens our story at a moment in time when the outcome of our revolution was most in doubt. When the men left their homes to engage the enemy, their wives, sisters, and daughters were left alone to carry on the home duties of their men. Here these unsung heroes were exposed to risks that women living alone have always faced. Calling themselves 'Daughters of Liberty', patriot women endured much suffering during the years of the conflict between Great Britain and her American colonies, and more than a few didn't live to see the victory they so longed for.

The patriotic efforts of the women in this story were drawn from real events in the lives of women of that period as found in historical records. Even before the colonies declared their independence from Great Britain, patriot women were boycotting British goods, spying on the British, and delivering secret messages.

Only a few generations have passed since that time when battles were fought on the front lawns of homes, on farms, and in the streets of nearly every village, town, and city in America.

The patriot blood of those who came before us flows through our veins, and that should give us pause to wonder: If we had lived alongside them, would we have done as well for freedom's sake?

Harrison Neese
December 2014

CHAPTER ONE

DAUGHTERS OF LIBERTY

"We may destroy all the men in America, and we shall still have all we can do to defeat their women."
　　　　—attributed to British General Lord Charles Cornwallis

Spring 1779, at the Hamilton Farm, South Carolina

Rachel Hamilton held her long rifle loosely in the crook of her arm and stepped down from the veranda of her sprawling, two-story clapboard house. It had been an hour since Caleb, the overseer of Hamilton Farm, had come to her to say that the house was being watched. This wasn't the first time and surely wouldn't be the last, but today none of the men of her family were home. Her husband, John, and eldest son, Gideon, were off fighting with the militia, and son, Daniel, was in town tending their leatherworks store.

She breathed an audible sigh. *Just a pack of good-for-nothings, who aren't afraid of attacking defenseless women and children.*

She gripped her long rifle a little tighter. *But I'm not defenseless, and they should know it.*

Rachel was in her mid-thirties, and after giving birth to five children, two of which were lost in infancy, she was still a most attractive woman. She had an oval face, a straight delicate nose, and dark brown eyes. Her dress was of her own homespun linen that came from the four acres of flax planted by her husband and her sons. Rachel was known throughout the South Carolina backcountry for her flawless needlework and the flattering fit of her dresses. A competent seamstress, she dressed her family in linen that was the envy of the district.

Even though her family could afford the fashionable fabrics brought over from England, she boycotted all imports of food and merchandise from the mother country. There'd been no British tea brewed in the Hamilton home since the now famous tea protest in Boston Harbor in '73.

Though women of her time usually remained inconspicuously in the background, Rachel was a woman on a mission and was generally outspoken. Much to her husband's chagrin, men like General Sumter often sought her counsel.

Something caught her eye; a movement in the shadows of the woods. Trespassers profaning her sanctuary of oaks, black walnut, white ash, and a smattering of pines that stretched from her orchard of peaches and kitchen vegetable garden to the edge of the flowing waters of the Wateree River.

Rachel moved back to the veranda steps and looked toward the trees, shading her eyes with her hand; whoever was out there was still watching. If they would come out of hiding, she was certain she'd know every one of them.

She was about to go back inside, when she saw Caleb coming toward her from the barn. She dropped her hand and waited to hear what he had to say.

"Miz Rachel, you ought to go back in with the other ladies and do your spinning. I'll keep watch on those heathens; it's likely to be Mister Rufus and his bunch."

Caleb looked back toward the trees. "Whoever's out there is tryin' to figure out how many folks is inside your house, probably countin' these here buggies and wagons."

Rachel nodded, looking over at the various wagons, carriages and buggies parked on the front lawn.

"I'm sure you're right, Caleb, but if that's true, then it's not Rufus. He knows each of these vehicles have brought the *Daughters of Liberty* ladies here for our regular spinning bee."

"Mister Rufus is just plain ornery," Caleb said, "He wants y'all to know he's watching you, but he ain't likely to bother us 'cause he figures some of the ladies might be armed."

"Poof, Rufus Sherman's not afraid of getting shot by any of the women here," Rachel said, standing her rifle by her side.

Caleb grinned. "He sees you and knows you're likely to shoot him, if he gets close enough." Chuckling, he pointed to her rifle, "Yessir, Mister Rufus knows what he can expect from you, and that's keeping him out yonder behind them walnut trees."

"Be that as it may, but I'll feel better if you'd send someone to town and fetch Daniel—tell him to bring help if he can, but don't delay."

"I've already done that, ma'am."

She nodded. "I'm going back in, Rufus or not. You holler if they start this way. The ladies are probably wondering why I'm not in there with them doing my part."

With a wave of his arm, he left to finish tending the horses and mules. Rachel turned as the front door opened. It was Emma Garrison, wife of the township's only attorney. And the other women of the sewing circle were right behind her.

Emma shielded her eyes and looked out toward the trees. "Rachel, what's keeping you out here, and with your rifle, no less?"

The rest of the women murmured and came forward, pressing around Rachel and Emma.

Rachel hushed them. "Please ladies, back away from the steps, and I'll tell you what's going on."

The women moved back, giving Rachel some room, but Emma, hands on her hips, stayed where she was. She hadn't taken her eyes from the tree line.

"Caleb came to me nearly an hour ago," Rachel said. "He tells me someone is out there at the edge of the woods. How many of you brought a firearm with you today?"

All of the women raised their hands. "How many long rifles do we have?" Only two lowered their hands.

Rachel stared across the front of her farm home, and then she looked over her shoulder. "Emma, they've been out there near an hour now. If they've come here to do us harm, they should be about ready."

Emma hadn't moved, her eyes remained fixed on the shadowy edge of the woods. "I agree, but what're we going to do if they decide to attack?"

The grimly determined expression on Rachel's face underlined her words. "Do? Why we're going to show them how well we shoot . . . that's what we're going to do."

Rachel paused and looked into the eyes of the women now gathered around her. She had known most of them since she and

John had settled here. To a woman, they'd proved their mettle by enduring the hardships of making homes and communities from the backcountry wilderness. Now left alone when their men went to war, these women were managing farms and running businesses, as well as surviving the pillaging and plundering of occupying soldiers.

Rachel knew these women had the backbone to face whoever was out there. Pointing to three of the wagons, she said, "We need these three wagons turned parallel to the woods and we'll split up into three groups, and take cover behind the side boards of each wagon.

The women moved quickly and kept their eyes on the tree line. Although it was too far for a musket ball to reach them, they were careful to expose themselves as little as possible.

"Get to the wagons, ladies," Rachel called. "You with rifles, rest them on the top of the sideboard to steady your aim. Wait until you hear the command to fire . . . no early shots."

Rachel took a deep breath to calm her nerves, and swallowed hard. She didn't see Emma with the women behind the wagons.

"Emma . . . Emma, where are you?"

"Right behind you, Rachel dear, I'm afraid my stays prevent me from crouching behind one of those narrow sideboards. I'm a better shot standing, anyway."

Emma stood on the veranda, using one of the posts to steady her rifle. Stepping up to Emma's side, Rachel whispered, "Caleb thinks it's Rufus Sherman out there—if it comes to it, I want you to shoot him or whoever is leading the trespassers."

Emma looked at her with melancholy eyes and nodded her head. "I'll do it—for Ezra—my dear sister's husband."

"Mizz Rachel!" shouted Caleb, from his end of the porch. "Here they come!"

A red-coated soldier astride a large gray came out from the shadows of the wood, followed almost immediately by another redcoat carrying a white flag tied on the barrel of his musket. The women, their mouths slack, watched as the two riders headed toward them.

Liza Fulton, in her sixth month awaiting her first child, almost shouted. "It's not Rufus and his men, its redcoats!"

Rachel choked back a gasp at the sight of the uniformed men riding towards them. She could see their bright red coats reflecting rays of the morning sun. She felt the stares of the women as they waited for her reaction.

"Nothing's changed, ladies. 'Tis no matter the color of their coats; they're our sworn enemy. Evidently, they want to talk, but keep alert and your eyes watchful, there's not a fair-minded man among them."

Rachel warily watched the man riding the large gray. He sat upright and resolute in his saddle and was head and shoulders above his cohort. Stopping his horse a short distance from her and the women, the apparent leader rested a hand on his sabre handle and took a deep breath. His eyes were busy assessing the line of women.

Now that they were only a few feet away, Rachel noticed the men's boots and uniforms were dust covered and streaked with mud and sweat—both appeared weary to the bone. There were dark circles under their bloodshot eyes, and the white flag bearer's head was crudely bandaged with a blood soaked cloth.

The tall soldier cleared his throat, his voice as cold as steel, disaffirming any trace of fatigue. "Madam, are there no men about today?"

Rachel recognized the epaulette on his right shoulder signifying he was an infantry officer of some rank. "Nay, but we expect our husbands to return any day now—they're riding with Colonel Picket in pursuit of men wearing uniforms such as yours."

At the mention of Colonel Picket, the muscles at the corner of his mouth twitched.

Ignoring her remarks, he made a sweeping gesture with his arm and said, his voice dripping with disdain, "What is the purpose of this uh---gathering before me?"

Rachel looked at him sharply, her voice held a ring of impatience. "I'm not accustomed to conversing with strangers, sir, if you have a name; please state it with *your* purpose for trespassing on my husband's property."

The officer had been focused on the women behind Rachel, but he suddenly turned back to her. Narrowed to mere slits, his glare perused her slowly. Holding his response for a moment, he studied this petite woman before him. Rachel knew, as both a man and British officer, he was not about to allow her or any woman to gain the upper hand.

He leaned forward in the saddle, his voice hostile and threatening now. Gone was the weariness and exhaustion he presented when he'd first ridden up.

"Madam, I have neither the time nor desire to engage in the social mores to which you may be accustomed. My men are in need of a temporary place of respite. Some will die without the services of a doctor. We shall be here only to—"

Raising her hand in protest, Rachel said, "We've reached an impasse, sir. I'll not allow one of you to remain on my husband's property. For all we know, you've come from an engagement with our men."

"I shouldn't be concerned, madam, for Colonel Picket's men," he snapped angrily. "We were ambushed by him and his primitive band at Grindal's Shoals. We were afforded few targets while they hid themselves among the trees and rocks like the wild savages they are."

Unable to conceal her offense at his remarks, Rachel countered, "I know well you British believe we Americans are ill bred and your social inferiors, but that's of no consequence at the moment. What matters is that you're the enemy of our country, and anywhere you stand in America, you're trespassing and unwelcome." Lifting her voice for emphasis, she said, "Now, for the last time, get off my property."

The officer's eyes rolled back in his head, and the reins slipped from his grasp.

"Oh," Rachel gasped as the man slipped from the saddle and landed heavily on the ground in a crumpled heap.

His aide jumped from his saddle and ran to him. "He's got lead in him, but won't allow anyone to help him."

Rachel saw Florence Crandall jump from a wagon and run towards the fallen officer. Florence quickly unbuttoned his uniform coat, then his shirt, revealing a rough bandage that bound his abdomen.

Looking at the aide, Florence snapped, "Sit him up and help me get his coat and shirt off."

The aide cast a hard glare at Florence. "And who might you be? The Major needs a doctor."

"I go by Florence Crandall, and I'm a midwife. I'm the nearest to a doctor you'll find between here and Charles Town. Now, your officer has lost a lot of blood judging by his shirt and coat. I'll need your assistance if I'm to help him."

Her eyes darting to Rachel, she pointed to her wagon. "Please fetch my bag while I examine this man's wounds—it's under the seat." Over her shoulder, she called to another woman, "I'll need bandages and water."

Rachel saw that the women's eyes were riveted on the wounded officer. "All right, ladies, let's get back to business. Florence can take care of the officer."

⟶•◆•⟶ ⟶•◆•⟶ ⟶•◆•⟶

Taking the veranda steps two at a time, Rachel went to Emma. Speaking in a low voice, she said, "I think you and I should interview the officer's aide, what do you think?"

Emma nodded. "It wouldn't hurt for us to know how many of these rascals are out there. Maybe he'll tell us."

Rachel and Emma knelt beside Florence. Rachel watched Florence's busy hands as she tended the man's wounds. "What does it look like, Florence? Will he live?"

Florence shrugged and answered, "I can't say just yet. He's lost a lot of blood and there's no exit wound, so he still has the ball in him. I can clean and dress the wound, but he needs to be put in a bed for me to probe for the ball."

Rachel looked out toward the woods before she answered. *In my home? John would never allow a Loyalist, let alone a British officer, in our home.* "Can it wait until Emma and I have a talk with his aide?"

Florence shrugged her shoulders. "Don't take too long."

Emma motioned to the aide kneeling beside his wounded officer. He sucked in a sharp breath and stood, pain brimming in his eyes. He looked exhausted and ready to give up and place himself at the women's mercy. He stumbled behind Rachel and Emma a few feet away and waited, staring at nothing.

Rachel, feeling the officer's life was uncertain, decided to get right to the point. With her arms folded across her chest, she asked sternly, "How many soldiers are out there in the woods?"

"Only five, madam—with serious wounds, like myself. The rest are scattered or captured. The Major took the worst of it."

"Seven of you altogether? How many of you were there when Picket and his men engaged you?"

The man was clearly suffering from the effects of his wound and distressed about their losses to such an inferior enemy. "We left Fort Guilford—with fifty men and two waggoners—driving much needed gunpowder to Fort Ninety Six."

The man looked like he was ready to drop. "Would you like to sit for awhile," Emma asked.

Without acknowledging her question, the soldier settled on the ground, his arms trembling to support him in a sitting position.

"Do you feel you can tell us how there's only seven of you left?" Rachel asked in a low tone.

He nodded. His breathing had become labored. "Th-they gave no warning before attacking—it seemed a sharpshooter— was behind every blade of grass. It was over in just a few minutes. A good many prisoners were taken . . . but th' dead and dying were left where they lay."

The officer groaned as they knelt beside him and Florence. Rachel glanced at him, her forehead furrowing in consternation.

"Emma, what are we to do with these men? Just yesterday, they were in a shooting war with our men, and now they're at my door asking for help." Rachel's eyes were glued to the erratic rise and fall of the wounded officer's chest.

Leaning on the rifle she still carried, Emma looked on as Florence wiped the forehead of the unconscious officer. "There's no doubt in my mind that, if any of the seven were able, they would take our lives and sleep soundly with no regrets after it."

Inhaling a deep breath and blowing it out audibly, Emma said, "Only moments ago, we were ready to kill them all and now that we have them dying at our feet . . ."

Florence looked up at the two women. "Do you want to know what I think?"

Rachel looked her friend. "Of course we do, Florence."

Pushing her knees to stand, Florence arched her back and stretched. "There's no need for either of you to fret over what to do with these men. I can take them home with me and care for them until our men return. Then, they can decide what should be done with them."

"You would do that, Florence? Won't you need help caring for them?" Rachel asked.

"I have good neighbors who will help me get them situated in my barn, but I may not need much help," she said, with a wave of her arm. "The officer here is not likely to live until morning, and his aide is burning up with fever, which means infection has set in."

Her voice tinged with relief, Rachel said, "Caleb can help us get the men into your wagon."

Emma nudged Rachel. "Your son has arrived."

Looking toward the long drive, Rachel saw Daniel riding fast. He was leaning forward, holding the reins in one hand with his long rifle held high in the other.

Bringing his mount to an abrupt stop, he jumped down assuming the women had been in a shooting skirmish with the wounded redcoats.

Rachel hurriedly explained the situation and he took charge of retrieving the wounded and getting them loaded in Florence's wagon.

CHAPTER TWO

THE DARING HAMILTON WOMEN

A month passed before Rachel and her family learned that the officer had died the next morning and two of the redcoats died later. Florence's father and uncle transported the remaining soldiers to the patriot prison at Fort Charlotte.

The sound of galloping hooves interrupted the morning stillness. Rachel looked up from her mending and saw it was Lottie astride her roan, riding like a man, her heels dug deeply in her horse's flanks. *What am I to do with that girl? Has she no pride?*

Rachel could only watch as her daughter rode her mount straight for the veranda where she sat. Then, at the last second, Lottie pulled back on the reins to bring the horse to a jarring stop, sending a scattering of grassy clods of dirt in every direction.

She slid from the saddle with practiced ease, sucking in a lungful of air. "Mama, wait 'til you hear what I overheard at the Smithery!"

Rachel knew it was useless for her to say anything about her daughter's manner of riding, not to mention her recklessness. It would have to come from Lottie's father to do any good, but that wasn't likely to happen since he had always encouraged her to ride like her brothers.

"Slow down girl, and watch your step, you'll be stepping on my sewing notions. Now what's got you in such a stir?'"

"I overheard some Tories talking about a courier coming through Camden tonight, heading for Fort Ninety Six."

Rachel rose to her feet and placed her hands on her hips. Her voice hardened, "Lottie, how many times have you been told to stay away from the Smithery? Have you no regard for your reputation, or that of mine by you hanging around where men congregate? It would be no different if you were to frequent a tavern."

Rolling her eyes in exasperation, Lottie responded, "I wasn't alone, Ma, Sarah was with me and we were on an errand for her father; he needed some nails."

Rachel felt the argument was slipping away from her. "Is there more to this business of a loyalist courier?"

Lottie nodded, "Well, one of the men mentioned Colonel Sumter was in for a surprise tomorrow night."

Looking off into the distance, Rachel considered this bit of news from her daughter. The mention of Colonel Sumter's name could mean many things, but the only way to find out was to intercept the courier and take the message to Sumter himself.

"Ma, someone's got to intercept the courier before he reaches the fort," Lottie said, drawing her mother out of her reverie.

Eyeing the lather-streaked flanks of Lottie's horse, Rachel said, "Take care of your horse, and we'll decide if there's anything we can do."

Lottie's eyes lit up, and her face broke into an enthusiastic grin. "We'll dress ourselves as men, and—"

Rachel interrupted, her voice rising. "Whoa! I haven't said the two of us are going to hold up an armed British soldier—especially not you! Now, do as I've already said, and we'll meet in the parlor."

⎯⊶⊙⊷⎯ ⎯⊶⊙⊷⎯ ⎯⊶⊙⊷⎯

Lottie found her mother sitting on the couch, her hands loosely folded in her lap. Rachel looked up and motioned for her to sit beside her on the couch. Lottie felt her mother's eyes follow her across the room as she made her way to the couch.

Rachel waited until Lottie settled down beside her. "Lottie, I want you to think back to the conversation you and Sarah overheard this morning and try to remember everything that was said—it's very important that we know if it's one man or more than one."

"Oh, Mama, does this mean we're going to ambush the courier?" Lottie said, her face flushed with enthusiasm. "The men talked about one man; in fact, they kept referring to him as 'boy'."

Chagrin crept in Rachel's tone as she spoke. "Lottie this isn't a game. Do you remember those wounded redcoats that collapsed at our stoop? Did you get a good look at them and their comrades?" Rachel saw the crestfallen look on her daughter's face. "Can you picture yourself as one of those with one or more musket balls inside you? Maybe it will be me who takes a ball of lead tonight. Will you be able to stop the bleeding and get me home?"

Lottie screamed, her hands covering her ears. "Stop, Mama, stop it! You're trying to scare me!"

All of a sudden, they heard footsteps running from the hallway. Belle, the cook, rushed through the door. "Have mercy on me! Why's you ladies shouting and screaming?" Stepping closer, she exclaimed, "And why's th' room so dark? I'm fixing to open the curtains."

Covering her daughter's hand with hers, Rachel said, "Lottie, you should know I wasn't trying to frighten you. I wanted only to help you see the seriousness of war, and that there are risks—real risks—ahead for us in confronting the courier."

Her eyes locked with her mother's gaze, Lottie said, "I'm sorry I reacted so terribly. That's not really me, Mama. It's just that I've wanted so long to be a part of the effort I believe in. I know I can contribute something besides spinning thread and weaving cloth."

"I understand, dear, and I'm glad you feel the way you do. Now, let's decide on how we can safely do this."

<hr />

A curtain of clouds hid the quarter moon, darkening the road leading into Camden, South Carolina. It was at the east side of the one lane bridge over the Wateree River that Rachel and Lottie were hiding among the brush and tall reeds of grass. Hot and humid, the night was buzzing with mosquitoes, yet neither protested the constant stinging bites. A few yards behind them stood a live oak whose far-reaching limbs deepened the darkness where they hid. Their horses, tethered nearby, grazed quietly in the blackness of midnight. Both women carried a pistol that was simple and smooth in design and sized for their hands; nonetheless, both guns were accurate and deadly at close range.

The mother and daughter wore the loose tan smocks and brown breeches that were the common attire of the farming men of South Carolina. Their hair was tucked under shapeless black hats with wide brims that they'd pulled low over their brows.

The night was quiet, but for the music of crickets; the women's eyes searched intensely toward the shadowy distance. An hour crawled by without any rider passing their place of hiding.

"I need to move my legs; both feel tingly like they're asleep," said Lottie.

Sighing, Rachel breathed, "All right, but do it quietly. The courier should've already been here."

Lottie's eyelids were becoming heavy from want of sleep. "Maybe he started his run later than usual."

"Maybe—just change positions and settle down—you're making me nervous. If he's coming tonight, we won't have much longer to wait."

Neither moved nor spoke for the next long moments. Then, the faint sound of hooves pounding the packed dirt of the road reached their ears. Rising to their feet, the pair listened hard to gauge the distance of the rider. The hooves were getting louder.

Appearing suddenly out of the darkness, the rider was almost upon them before both stepped into the middle of the road with their pistols drawn.

The courier, his horse at a canter, looked to be asleep in the saddle as Rachel yelled, "Stop, sir, and dismount!"

On its own, his horse came to an abrupt stop, nearly throwing the rider from the saddle.

Rachel stood with her feet apart, held her pistol steady, and aimed at the rider's chest. Her mouth was dry and her chest tight with tense anticipation. She was afraid to take her eye off the man to see where Lottie was.

Keeping her voice flat and deeper than usual, Rachel said, "I said dismount, sir, and I mean now!"

The courier, foggy headed from sleep, shuffled down from the saddle and stood by his horse. He was a tall, scruffy looking man. Even in the dark, Rachel could see that he was unshaven and careless about his appearance. He brought to her mind the image of a pirate, even though she'd never seen one.

Without removing her eyes from him, Rachel said to Lottie, "Take his horse and see if he's carrying saddlebags or weapons."

Her voice lowered, Rachel said roughly, "Hand over the message you carry, and be quick about it."

Blinking sleep from his eyes, the young man said defiantly, "I carry no messages. I'm on my way to visit my brother and his family in Camden."

"What's your brother's name and where does he live?" asked Rachel bluntly.

"My brother—uh—his name is Charles," he replied slowly.

"And?" snapped Rachel.

He stared at her as if he didn't understand what she was asking.

Peeved, Rachel motioned with her gun and said, "Never mind, remove your coat and boots, then lay flat on the ground with your face down, and arms spread out."

Unnoticed by Rachel, the courier had stealthily inched closer to her. When he removed his cloak, he flung it toward her, striking her in the face and knocking her off balance. Immediately, he threw himself into her, taking them both to the ground.

Rachel, with the cloak about her head, let out a muffled scream. Being much stronger than she, he pinned her gun arm to the ground and began to wrest it from her grasp. She gasped for breath, her blood pounding in her ears; she knew he was moments from taking her weapon from her. With her free hand, she made a fist and slammed his nose as hard as she could. He grunted and shook his head, but kept struggling for the pistol. Pulling her arm back farther, she struck him again, and this time he yelped, but still didn't stop trying to get control of the pistol.

Suddenly, Lottie appeared with his saddlebags, and swinging in a wide arc, she hit him full in the face. Without uttering a sound, his body fell limp, and Rachel shoved him to the side.

Quickly, Rachel sprung to her feet, holding tightly to her pistol, and grinning crookedly at her daughter. "I thought you'd never come."

"I hit him pretty hard, didn't I?" Lottie said, timidly staring at the prostrate figure, "Did I kill him?"

"No, he's not dead, just dazed a bit. You just let him know we mean business." Then Rachel kicked the courier in the knee. "Off with your waistcoat and boots, and then lay there and don't move, if you expect to see the morning's sun."

Laying flat on the cool road, the courier watched as the women expertly examined his garments. They deftly removed stitching in his waistcoat to reveal a hidden pocket with a coded letter meant for the leader of the Loyalist militia headquartered near Camden.

Leaving the young man bound on the side of the road, the women set out to deliver the message to Colonel Sumter's camp on the Broad River. The women knew every shortcut and every trail in the district, so they would be avoiding the main roads. Time was against them for they had to be home before first light. If they were seen and identified, it would mean certain death. There would be no trial, just a British hangman's rope around their necks.

Rachel pulled up where the trail veered off toward the river and twisted in the saddle. "I leave you here, Lottie. You know the way home. Approach the house from the creek, so you can see how things look before riding in. I'll be along as quick as I can."

"I'm going with you, Mama. I won't slow you up, and besides you may need me again before you're done tonight."

Sighing heavily, Rachel said, "Lottie, we've already decided this, and you agreed: if I let you come with me tonight, I would deliver the message alone. My horse is faster than yours, and we're running out of time. Now just do as I say."

Lottie was quiet for a moment, then she handed her mother her pistol. "I'll go then, but take my pistol, I won't need it. Hurry home, I shan't be able to sleep until I know you're home, safe and sound."

Rachel took the pistol, kicked her heels hard in the flanks of her horse, and leaned over his neck as he lunged forward. Lottie watched until her mother disappeared into the misty darkness and then turned her horse toward home.

Rachel approached the patriot camp cautiously. She couldn't make out the shape of a sentry, but she sensed he was close. Of a sudden, a crusty voice came from the shapeless darkness. "Halt right there, mister. Put your hands on top of your head and state your business."

After a few minutes of answering the sentry's questions, he called for an escort to take Rachel to Colonel Sumter who took her for a boy. Without dismounting, she handed him the message packet, took her leave, and was soon careening through the night, racing against the approaching sun. It had taken her longer to reach the patriot camp than she figured; now she had to push her tired horse to get her home before first light.

Rachel knew her horse was exhausted, dangerously close to being winded, but she had no choice. Leaning close to his neck, she whispered encouragement, hoping he had enough run left in him to carry her home. She shuddered to think what would happen if anyone saw her out and wearing men's clothing.

Quicker than she expected, the familiar landscape came in view. She was almost home. Her horse, anticipating the rest and food ahead, suddenly found untapped energy to carry them on.

Rachel entered the stables just as the edge of morning pushed its way through the fading darkness.

Caleb was waiting for her. "You know me 'n Belle ain't slept much with you and Miss Lottie out all night. If Mister John finds out I let you go off like you did, he's liable to—"

"Caleb, quit your worrying. John, himself, would've had a hard time stopping us from going last night. I pray Colonel Sumter can use the information."

Rachel dismounted. "Take care of my horse, Caleb. I rode him hard last night. I'll be down in time for breakfast."

As Rachel hurried across the dew-laden lawn, she noted the thin ribbon of smoke winding its way skyward from the farm's kitchen. She could almost feel the warmth that the kitchen offered where Belle would have breakfast well underway. Entering through a side door, Rachel headed for the back stairs that would take her directly to her room without going through the main part of the house.

"Now, don't you be trying to sneak past me, Miss Rachel, you know I can hear the footsteps of a cat."

Belle's eyes roamed over Rachel, standing in her disguise. "And you ain't fooling nobody with Mister John's breeches and hat. You're too much of a woman to pass for a man, anyhow."

Rachel grinned, "You know I wasn't avoiding you, Belle, and as for my disguise, I fooled the courier last night and that's all I wanted to do.

Pausing, she asked, "Has Daniel come down for breakfast?"

Belle shook her head.

Her eyes fastened on Belle. "I must be in my room before Daniel gets up. Tell him I'll be down for breakfast."

Upstairs in her room, Rachel went to the wash stand to pour water in the basin. She scrubbed as best she could, promising herself a warm bath as soon as Daniel was off to the leatherworks shop. She shivered in the early morning air as she removed the smock and then began to unwind the wide strip of cloth around her chest that hid her feminine shape.

Rachel moved quickly until she had rid herself of last night's disguise, and for the sake of time, she would wear only one petticoat under the skirt and bodice. Lastly, she brushed her shoulder length hair up, pinning it quickly, and fitted it all under a linen bonnet laced with a blue ribbon. Standing before her full-length looking glass, she was confident no one could possibly connect her and Lottie to the highwaymen who held up the Tory courier.

Heavy footsteps running down the hallway meant Daniel was up and headed for the dining room. Of her three children, Daniel was the most predictable, especially where food was concerned—he was always hungry.

Rachel stopped at Lottie's room on her way to the kitchen. Noiselessly, she eased the bedroom door open and lingered a moment to marvel at the angelic face of her youngest child. A shudder rose in her as she recalled the danger and risk she had allowed to come near her daughter only the night before. Tears filled her eyes, but she tightened her lips and silently backed out of the room and closed the door.

Her hand on the door, Rachel whispered a prayer. "Thank you Lord for your protection . . ."

Rachel entered the sunny dining room to find Daniel where she expected, fully engaged with his breakfast. "Good morning, Daniel," she said as she took her seat at the end of the table.

Coming to his feet, Daniel replied, "Good morning, Ma." On retaking his seat, he lifted a buttered biscuit and took a hefty bite. "Just out of the oven," he said, chewing.

Belle came in with Rachel's plate. "I 'spect you'll be wanting coffee this morning, Miss Rachel. I'll be right back with you a steaming cup of my strong coffee." Without waiting for an answer, Belle was through the door heading to the kitchen.

"When did you start drinking coffee, Ma?" asked Daniel with raised eyebrows. "I thought you couldn't stand the stuff."

Caught off guard by her son's directness, Rachel replied, "Well, I—uh, I drink a cup now and then with your father. You can't pay any attention to what Belle might say."

Belle came through the door with a cup of coffee. Tendrils of steam curled upward as Belle placed the cup near Rachel's plate.

Daniel watched his mother stir cream into her coffee. "What time did you get back, Ma?"

Rachel nearly dropped her cup of hot coffee. She raised an eyebrow and met her son's inquisitive gaze. "What are you talking about—get back from where?"

Shrugging his shoulders, Daniel answered, "Your secret's out, Ma. I was awake when Lottie came in, and with just a bit of help, she told me all about it." His face beaming, he said, "I think it's about the biggest thing to ever happen in our family. Just ask yourself, how many women in the colonies have done anything like what my mother and my sister did last night? I'm famous!"

He looked at her with frank admiration. "When did you two decide to do something like that? Pa's going to have a fit when he finds out Lottie went with you—she's still his baby!"

Rachel came around to sit beside her son. "You're nearing nineteen, Daniel, and you are old enough to understand the consequences of what your sister and I did. If you don't, I shall tell you. The moment we're found out, we'll be marked for death by hanging. There'll be no trial, no judge, or jury, we'll just simply be taken to the public square and hung by our necks until we choke to death. And that includes Caleb and Belle as well because they helped us last night."

Looking his mother in the eye, Daniel replied, "Ma, I'm not stupid. I know the seriousness of what you and sis did, and I'm proud of you both. I never discuss our family's business outside of our home . . . ever."

Taking her son's hand, Rachel said, "I'm sorry I reacted so strongly to what you said, son. I suppose I'm having second thoughts about allowing Lottie come with me. I should never have done that."

Laying his fork down, he said, "It wouldn't have been fair to sis if you'd left her home. She's wanted to be a part of the struggle for a long time. Besides she shoots as well as me or Gideon."

She looked thoughtfully at her son noting the serious look of his face. "We'll just put this behind us and not speak of it anymore, agreed?"

"Yes ma'am, it's forgotten."

Standing, she went back to her chair. "And just so you know, I'll tell your father about last night when he returns. Now stop by the kitchen and pick up your lunch. You'll be late in opening the shop."

After Daniel had left for the shop in town, Rachel went back upstairs to find Sally, the housekeeper. She found Sally in the laundry room sorting the items for the week's washing. Rachel smiled at the sight of this small woman of boundless energy. She was the twin sister of Belle, but that was as far as it went, for they neither resembled the other nor shared the same temperament. While Belle shared the spontaneous thoughts of her mind with everyone, Sally was timid and reserved; she rarely spoke more than a few words to anyone, and then only in response to a question.

"Good morning, Sally. I see you're starting your washing early. If you'll draw me a bucket of water, I'll heat it and take it up to my room for my bath."

Looking down at the floor, Sally responded quietly, "Your bath's waiting, Miss Rachel. Belle done told me already."

"Well, thank you, Sally, and I must thank Belle, too."

Rachel turned to leave, and she heard Sally whisper, "Miss Rachel?"

Taken aback at Sally's unprompted voice, Rachel turned back to her. "Yes, Sally, do you have a question?"

Hesitantly, Sally breathed, "No ma'am, but I do have a burden that's worrying me something awful."

Stepping closer to her, Rachel touched Sally's shoulder. "Don't be afraid to tell me what's worrying you, Sally, and don't be afraid of me, ever. Now, share with me this thing that has you upset."

Taking a deep breath, Sally's eyes darted upward to Rachel's face, and then fell again as she began to speak. "I'm afraid for you and Miss Lottie. You shouldn't be going out in the night.

There ain't nobody good scurrying around in the dark. They just lay out there waiting to pounce on good folks like yourself and Miss Lottie."

Rachel's heart sank. She hugged Sally while tears filled her eyes and spilled down her face. "Oh, Sally, don't worry. Last night was such a foolish venture. I can see it clearly now. I'm sorry I caused you to worry. Please know I'll never do anything like that again."

Back in her room, Rachel sat on the edge of her bed and wondered. *Lord, who else knows?*

A PROPOSAL

John and Gideon made camp in a wooded area of spreading live oaks. These giant trees spread for many miles along the Wateree River before giving way to the even larger cypress trees of Beaver Swamp.

Huddled around their small fire that barely kept the damp chill of the night away, neither felt the need to talk. They were nearing home and both men were bone-tired from three months of riding hard through the South Carolina backcountry.

Gideon stood and stretched his arms above his head. "I guess I'll turn in, Pa. I'll be headed to see Sarah in the morning. I hope Ma understands."

Grinning, John replied, "Your mother understands, but she'll be anxious to see you, so don't tarry."

The next morning, the two broke camp early with John headed in the direction of home and Gideon toward the Sherman homestead.

━━◦◦◉◦◦━━ ━━◦◦◉◦◦━━ ━━◦◦◉◦◦━━

Keeping his horse, Shadow, at a canter, Gideon looked forward to seeing Sarah this morning. He knew the time had come for him to ask her *the* question. A smile creased his mouth. *I can see it in her eyes and hear it in her voice; I certainly can feel it in her kisses. If I don't ask her to marry me soon, she's likely going to ask me!* The image of Sarah on bended knee gave him a long chuckle and brought another smile to his face.

A slight rise in the road lay just ahead, and as he crested the ridge, Gideon scanned the hickory grove ahead. It had been their private meeting place since they were old enough to ride horses.

A movement from the grove startled him, and he instantly yanked the reins back, bringing Shadow to an abrupt stop.

Then he saw her as she stepped out from the trees leading her lilac roan gelding. She was wearing a dark blue linen cloak with a hood that hid her features but failed to confine her coppery, auburn hair. Her hair brushed her cheeks and fell softly across the breast of her cloak.

Her breath-taking emerald eyes followed him as he dismounted and reached for her. She didn't resist but met him as if her very life depended on hearing the beating of his heart.

She laid her head against his chest. "S-sometimes the pain in my heart hurts so—"

"Shhh," he said, lifting her face to his, his lips finding hers. For just a moment, there was no sound, but the beating of their hearts, and there was no earth, but for the small spot under their feet.

They parted slowly and Gideon held her at arm's length. He reached to push the hood of her cloak back, but she pulled away with such a frantic movement, he was startled. She pulled the hood forward and buried her face against his coat.

"I-I'm sorry, but the hood helps keep me warm," she whispered.

Gently taking her by her shoulders, he said, "What brings you here this morning? You couldn't have known I'd pass this way. "

He felt her trembling. "Please look at me, I want to see your beautiful face, darling."

Gideon lifted her chin and pushed back her hood. She raised her hand to cover part of her face, but he pulled it away. It was then he saw why she was hiding her face. Gideon's lips grew tense as his eyes fell on the big raw welt on her cheek.

"Look at me, Sarah. Your Pa did this?" He knew the answer.

Nodding her head, she murmured, "Y-yes."

Titus Sherman, Sarah's father, was the brother of Rufus Sherman, the latter a notorious Tory renegade who terrorized patriots living in the Piedmont backcountry from Virginia to Georgia. Titus, one of Camden's earliest settlers, had become wealthy through his trade as a hatter.

Unlike his brother, Titus gained a reputation of fairness throughout the South Carolina colony. His shop was open to all, regardless of their politics, but Titus had a dark side that he kept hidden from everyone outside of his own family. Titus was an avowed Tory with an unshakable allegiance to King George III. Influenced by his brother's twisted mind, Titus became a silent partner with Rufus. From before the beginning of the fighting, his money bribed the Indians into committing atrocities, and paid off the ruthless mercenaries who rode with Rufus.

Titus prided himself on his respectability and wealth, but within the walls of his home, he didn't pretend respectability. His wife, Lydia, had delivered two stillborn sons after giving him Sarah as their firstborn. Now, Lydia was coming to the end of her childbearing years, and Titus knew she would never give him sons. He'd come to despise her and could barely tolerate the presence of his only child, Sarah. From the time she could carry full milk buckets, he had forced Sarah to do the work of the son he never had.

Gideon's stomach churned and he felt anger welling up in his throat, but he knew he must remain calm. He leaned over and lightly kissed her wound and pulled her close to him.

For a time, neither spoke, but each listened to the other's heartbeats—something they had done since the tender age of nine when he'd declared they would one day marry. As the years passed, this special 'quiet time' evolved with them.

Gideon ran his fingers tenderly over her bruised cheek. The gentleness in her eyes nearly took his breath away. A shudder went through him. Oh, how he loved her.

Stepping back, his hands rested on her shoulders. "Why did he do this, Sarah? Was it about us—me?"

She nodded. "Pa doesn't need a reason, but yes, it's about you and your family's stand against the king. He's forbidden me to see you again." Slowly, she added, "I'm supposed to be milking. By now he knows I've left, but I needed to get away from him—home and everything. I didn't know where I was going, until I found myself here. He's said he'll shoot you the next time he sees you."

Gideon held her as she began to sob. "You can't go back. You'll come to stay with us."

Sarah stiffened and replied, "I can do no such thing, Gideon Hamilton! Surely you don't expect me to live in the same house with the man I'm to marry—and what would your mother think if I should do such a thing."

Stepping back, Gideon looked as if she'd slapped him. "But, I meant only to protect you from your father; I didn't—"

Wiping the tears from her face, Sarah interrupted him. "I can stay with my mother's sister in Camden. Now, I must go back and get what's mine. I'm not leaving with only the clothes on my back."

Gideon helped Sarah into the saddle and they rode to her home. Neither spoke until they approached the house. Sarah pulled back on the reins. "Do you see Pa anywhere? His wagon is gone. He could've put it up and be waiting inside."

Sarah's mother came out on the porch and waved to them. "You two come on in. Sarah, your pa left just a short while ago to find you."

Sarah ran up the steps and hugged her mother. "Mama, I didn't come back to stay. I'm here to get my things and I'll be at Aunt Margaret's. I wish—"

Her mother interrupted. "Never mind wishing, child, I've wished enough over the years for both of us. And mostly, I've wished I could've been stronger and stood up for you against your pa, but it's too late for wishing."

Taking Sarah by the hand, she led them to Sarah's room. "I knew it would come to this between you and your pa someday, so after he left, I started putting your clothes and such in this trunk. You can finish and take what you'll need. I've put your dowry in the bottom. I 'spect your pa will have another one of his fits when he finds out about it, but by then, it'll be too late."

Sarah and her mother finished packing while Gideon hitched up his horse to the Sherman buggy. By the time he was back to the house, they were waiting for him. With the trunk loaded, Sarah and her mother said their tearful goodbyes.

Sarah leaned against Gideon's shoulder as he set his horse at a good pace. With Sarah's home miles behind them, Gideon pulled back on the reins, stopping the carriage. Jumping down, he held out his hand for her to follow. Sarah looked at him with questioning eyes.

Holding both her hands, he went on bended knee at her feet. Sarah's sky-blue eyes glistened in the morning light as she fixed her gaze on his.

His eyes locked with hers. "Sarah, I can't imagine my life without you by my side. I want to be with you for the rest of my life as your husband and the father of the children you bring to our lives. Will you marry me?"

"Yes." A radiant smile spread across her face. "I will marry you."

For a moment, neither spoke until Sarah broke the spell. "Gideon, I want us to get married right away—before your enlistment in the army starts. I want our child. If you do not come back to me, I will always have our child to remember you."

He wrapped his arms around her and touched her lips with his. "I'm not sure how we can get married on such short notice."

Sarah grabbed his arm and said, "I don't either, but let's ask your father; he'll know how it can be done."

He lifted the reins and brought them down in a snapping motion and the carriage lurched into motion.

A touch of mist hung over the river and clung to the trees and bushes that lined the carriage drive up to the elegant, sprawling two-story Hamilton home. Sitting on a high crest overlooking a view of the Wateree River and their peach orchard, their home rivaled the prestigious mansions of the elite coastal low country of South Carolina.

Rachel had risen early to await the first notes of the songbirds of the Wateree River Valley. The springtime dawn chorus was a pleasant reminder for her that life was a treasure, truly a gift from a loving God. She relished this peaceful and quiet time when it seemed everywhere she turned there was nothing but strife and conflict.

Weeks had passed since Rachel's impulsive hold-up venture. Unbridled interest had risen throughout the district about the identity of the men who had intercepted the Loyalist message and delivered it to Colonel Sumter. The Colonel said he didn't get a good look at the courier, but the message forewarned him in time to thwart a surprise Loyalist attack, bringing about a much-needed Patriot victory.

Rachel removed her shoes and sat back in her favorite chair on the veranda. Clutching her steaming cup of hot chocolate in both hands, she gently blew the rising steam into the chilly morning air. John and her oldest son, Gideon, had returned and now, with her man and her children around her, she was happy and contented. She was proud of the man Gideon had become. Smiling, she recalled the afternoon when he brought Sarah to stay with them because of her father, and how she and John had acted surprised at the news of their engagement.

Rachel was an energetic woman whose first priority was maintaining a clean and orderly home for her family. Barely fifteen when she eloped to marry her childhood sweetheart, she became a mother ten months later. Motherhood brought maturity and discipline to her young life early.

She was proud of John, and his courageous stand for his impassioned belief that liberty was a God-given bequest to all men, and from his example, their three surviving children were impassioned patriots. Nevertheless, at the same time, she chafed under the injustice of being born a woman in a male dominated society that relegated women to the world of having babies, without the ability to reason and think on anything beyond the walls of their homes.

God forbid that I could be courageous enough to take a stand for the cause of Liberty!

Determined to do something for the cause, Rachel had organized a 'spinning bee' attended by women of the district and Camden, calling themselves the Daughters of Liberty. She had opened her home to these women and together, working from sunup until sundown, they would produce more than thirty skeins of linen to make clothing for the patriot soldiers.

Granted, this work was important to keeping the soldiers properly clothed, and as the war wore on from one frustrating year to the next, Rachel found it nigh impossible to keep her feelings about the war hidden within her. She had developed a deepening interest in politics, much to John's displeasure.

She had not yet told him of her actions during his absence, but today she would tell him. *He's a sensible man, and come what may, I'll tell him today . . .*

Sighing deeply, she sipped gingerly from her hot chocolate, waiting for the man who was the first and only love of her life. *If John doesn't hurry, he'll be too late to hear the birds.*

She looked back at the door. Then, she heard him approaching. She heard the front door open and close and then the comforting, heavy tread of his footsteps.

John placed his coffee on a table and walked to the edge of the porch. Leaning against a column, he sighed heavily and gazed toward the moonless starlit sky. For a time, neither of them spoke.

Rachel's eyes lingered on the man standing near her. After twenty-one years of marriage, he was, in some ways, still a mystery to her. He'd mellowed after their youngest child, Lottie, was born, openly doting on her, yet he remained demanding of their two sons, expecting them to measure up to his standard of masculinity. He stood out in a crowd, head and shoulders above most men, and when he smiled, which was often, his pearl-white teeth shone, and his dark hair was always combed neatly and tied in a queue. The deep timbre of his voice set him apart and gave him an air of authority that was palpable—men listened when he spoke.

After the citizens of Boston had dumped British tea in the harbor, John decided to send his account books, land titles, notes, and hard cash to his friend Haym Solomon, a well-established patriot financial broker in New York City, for safekeeping.

"Your coffee's getting cold," Rachel said softly.

He picked up his cup. "Have you ever tried to count the stars?"

Rachel smiled as she got up and padded barefoot across the porch to him. John held out his arm and gathered her close to him, and she leaned against his chest.

Whispering, she said, "Not in a long time—not since I was a little girl."

This time was precious, and she didn't want it to end. Pulling him to the swing, she sat facing him, tucking her feet under her and spreading her skirt over them.

She took hold of one of his hands and said, "John, I have such a sense of foreboding about this war. Do you realize the time will soon be here when Gideon will be leaving?"

The mention of their twenty-year-old son's name brought a stirring to his heart. Gideon had started riding with John and his men when he was eighteen and had become increasingly restless about wanting to fight as a regular soldier.

Rachel had resigned herself that her sons were at the threshold of becoming men, ready to test themselves in the world that lay just beyond the road that passed their home. How much longer they would remain home with her was something that occupied her mind more than she cared to admit.

Caressing his calloused palm, she said wistfully, "I've worried enough when Gideon rode with you and your men, but now he's signed to serve in the regular army."

Sighing, John said, "By most anybody's reckoning, he's a man, Rachel. We couldn't keep him with us forever . . . and there's Daniel and Lottie coming along right behind him. We'll have to rely on our faith in God to take care of our children as their time comes to leave the nest."

John took both her hands in his and gazed into her eyes. She knew he was about to quote a passage of scripture.

"There're some verses from the book of Philippians that might help you. I may not remember all the words, but it goes something like this. *'Don't worry about anything, but in everything, through prayer and petition with thanksgiving; let your requests be made known to God.'* "

Leaning her head on his shoulder, she said, "Thank you, John. It's times like now that my faith seems so weak, but you seem to be stronger in trials."

"That's not how I see myself," he responded. "Any strength you see in me comes from God."

The medley of music from the songbirds began, and Rachel looked out toward the river. Leaning back, she looked at her husband. "How will we hear from Gideon? Will he have any way to post letters?"

"The Sons of Liberty have couriers that are able to come and go, almost at will," John replied. "His letters will find their way to us."

He touched her cheek lightly. "Thanks to you, our children can read, write, and cipher to make their way in this world. That's a legacy from your father, but I doubt he ever considered that when he sent you abroad to school."

The night slowly gave way to morning light. The dawn chorus of songbirds had built to its full melodious crescendo and was now fading away. Sitting together, the war seemed so far from them, but as surely as the brilliant hues of today's morning sun would gradually give way to the full light of day, war was coming to South Carolina—to their town—even to their home.

Rachel tried to think of some way to bring up her part in intercepting the information that helped Colonel Sumter win the skirmish with the Loyalists.

She took another swallow from her now cooled cup of chocolate. "John, have you seen Colonel Sumter recently? I mean since his skirmish with the Loyalists."

"No, but I did hear Sumter just barely avoided a deadly trap the Loyalists had set for him that would have taken the lives of most of Sumter's men. I was told a Loyalist courier was waylaid by a militia of burly patriots who delivered the message to Sumter."

Rachel laughed, and John looked at her quizzically. "What's funny about that?"

John's face reflected the seriousness of his question. It was enough to bring on another round of laughter, but Rachel knew she had to tread softly until she was done with her confession.

Straightening her back, Rachel began by answering John's question. "It's funny because it wasn't a militia of burly men."

John's brow furrowed deeply. He stared at her for a long moment before he said, "I'm almost afraid to ask how you would know anything about the men, whatever their number."

Here goes. Projecting her words with crisp precision, Rachel said, "The Loyalist courier was intercepted by me and Lottie. We were disguised as men, and I delivered the message to Colonel Sumter myself, after I'd sent Lottie home."

He was clearly dumfounded. John's mouth slackened, but it was apparent he wasn't trying to speak. For nearly a full minute, he didn't move or make a sound, but his eyes never left her.

Rachel knew one of them had to say something. "John, you must—"

Her voice brought him to life. He brought his hand up to stop her in mid-sentence. "Who else knows about this?"

Shifting her position so she could more directly face him, she said, "Only those who live under this roof."

His dark eyes studied her face for several seconds. "You're aware that you and my daughter are no longer spectators in this struggle. You've stepped out from the shadows and set yourself at odds with the king."

Taking her hand, he pulled her to him. "You must never speak of this again—ever. Can you do that? No one outside of our family can ever know of this, even if we win this war."

"You're not upset or angry with me? I've been so worried that you would be offended or outraged that I would do something so unladylike."

He took both her hands in his. "In the world before the revolution, what you and Lottie did would have been scandalous and shamed our family name for as long as you and I lived. But today, our fighting men depend heavily on the support and participation of our women."

He leaned toward her and kissed her lightly on her forehead. "I'm very proud of my wife and daughter. Because of the two of you, Sumter was warned in time to get ready for the Loyalists. There's no way to know how many, of course, but your action saved many patriot lives—it was no small thing what you did."

"We were so scared," Rachel said. "My hands shook so, I was afraid I would drop my pistol."

"Yes, and every boy and man who has faced the enemy shares that feeling with you," John said, pulling her close to him.

Suddenly, Lottie came bursting through the door, letting it slam behind her. "Breakfast is served, m'lord and m'lady," she announced, with a showy curtsey.

Skipping across the porch, Lottie grabbed her father by his arm and said proudly, "Come to breakfast, Papa. I cooked it all by myself."

John grinned and cast an eye toward his wife. "That's quite an accomplishment, daughter. What're we having?"

Beaming, she answered, "Eggs, biscuits, and ham with honey and butter, Papa. You may have either your cider or another coffee—or both."

Lottie, not waiting for them, hurried back inside. John held Rachel's hand. "Hereafter, dear wife, I ask that you confine your patriotic efforts to spinning bees and quilting bees . . . such service traditionally expected from our women."

Rachel only nodded her head, and walked with her husband to the kitchen with its wide hearth and polished oak table. They found Sarah sipping her coffee, and Gideon, by her side, was nearly finished with his breakfast. Looking up, he said, "Milking is done Ma. His eyes caught Sarah's. "And we've transferred the fresh milk to the jugs in the cellar."

Daniel came bursting through the door, his eyes on the platters of food on the table. "Kitchen firewood is stacked, Ma. What're we having for breakfast?"

Beaming with pride, Lottie said, "I cooked this morning's breakfast, and we're having eggs, biscuits, and ham with honey and butter."

Looking shocked, Daniel said, "All by herself, Ma? Belle didn't help?"

Rachel smiled at her son's reaction. "All by herself, Daniel, and from the scant crumbs left on Gideon's plate, she did quite well."

Shrugging his shoulders, Daniel said with a big grin, "Well, if it didn't kill Gideon, I think I'll try some, too."

The children's banter during this morning's breakfast brought Rachel and John out of their melancholy mood.

After his second biscuit, John said, "Would you just look at her, Rachel? Our daughter has grown up before our very eyes. And not only is she a beautiful young woman, she cooks as well as her mother."

Her face crimson, Lottie said, "Oh, Papa! Stop it! I'll never be able to cook as well as Mama."

She hurried around the table to her father, and hugged him tightly. "I love you, Papa, more than words can tell."

For the next several minutes, the talk was light and lively, and the war seemed to be forgotten. But only one hundred-forty miles away, the roar of many cannons was raining chaos and destruction on Charles Town. British General Clinton's second in command, Major General Lord Charles Cornwallis, was, at that moment, crossing the Ashley River at Bee's Ferry toward the South Carolina mainland with British forces.

CHAPTER FOUR

WAR HASTENS MARRIAGE

The hall clock struck a quarter past the hour, and John swallowed the last of his coffee and rose from his chair. "I must take my leave if I expect to greet our first customers today."

Gideon looked at his mother. "Ma, would it be all right for Sarah and me to go for a walk to the creek where Pa built your bench?"

Rachel glanced at her husband. She remembered the day he brought her to that place. He'd built an old-fashioned love seat bench and cleared the area so she could plant her roses. She answered tenderly, "Yes, it's lovely there, but you shouldn't be unchaperoned. Lottie can go with you."

Gideon and Sarah left by the back door; Lottie followed some distance behind. The young couple slowly walked hand in hand, whispering. A smile touched Sarah's lips as they drew near the small garden.

The gentle slope toward the creek had taken them out of sight of the house, and Gideon circled her waist with one arm and pulled her close to him.

Lottie came running to them. "Wait up, you two! I'm not going with you any farther. I'm going back to the house; Ma will have to understand. This is your time, and it will be more memorable if you're alone. For the rest of your lives, you'll remember everything about it."

Gideon hugged his sister and said, "I love you Lottie. No man could have a more loving and understanding sister. Thank you."

Sarah and Lottie embraced and then Lottie left.

Watching Lottie run up the path, Sarah said, "That was a nice gesture; your sister is strong-willed to go against her mother."

Nodding his head, he lifted her chin with the crook of his finger. It was a moment when words could not carry the love from his heart to hers. Their eyes met, and he kissed her.

He clasped her hands in his. "This morning will be a good time to discuss our wedding plans with Pa. We have enough time for me to show you Ma's private garden and still catch him before he leaves for the shop."

After Lottie had returned to the house, she sat down with her mother and told her why she came back to the house. Rachel thought about scolding her, but finally gave in and reluctantly agreed today was a special day; an uncommon time, and as much as she wanted Gideon close to her, she knew he needed Sarah even more. Rachel went to the window, her eyes not really focused, and gazed toward the path the couple had taken.

Lottie absently stacked the plates left on the table. "Ma, do you remember Robert?"

"The Alcott boy?" Rachel answered without turning from the window.

"He's almost twenty and a sergeant in the army; he's not a boy, mother," Lottie responded, rolling her eyes.

Wiping her hands on her apron, Rachel turned to face her daughter. "Forgive me, dear, I didn't mean it like it sounded. Of course Robert's a man."

Gazing at her daughter, Rachel could see she was bothered about something. "Do you still think of him? He was only here a short time before he left for the army. I haven't heard you mention his name recently."

Lottie traced the rim of a plate with a finger. She wasn't ready to meet her mother's eyes. "Yes, I still think of Robert. After the way you and Papa treated him, I thought it would be best if I didn't mention his name anymore."

Rachel looked at her daughter whose figure belied her young age. Her perfect face with large sea-blue eyes and small, straight nose complemented her blonde and full-bodied hair which fell in ringlets about her shoulders. *Where have the years gone?*

"Look at me, dear," Rachel said, her voice tender and loving. "When Robert stopped by to visit us on his way to North Carolina, you were only fourteen and were planning to elope with him. Your Papa and I only did what we thought was best for you."

Lottie's eyes brimmed with tears. "But Ma, if you could've—"

Shaking her head, Rachel said, "Let me share with you what your father and I decided the day we stopped your elopement—"

"Papa ran him off!" Lottie injected sharply.

Rachel sighed deeply, "You and Robert have our blessing to marry, if your love for him and his love for you endures to this war's end. We only meant to protect you. If we did anything else, we pray for your forgiveness."

Rachel wanted to reach out to her daughter, but hesitated when Lottie didn't respond. Their eyes remained locked as the moment lingered. Rachel knew she couldn't leave the table without some word of reconciliation with her youngest child.

The moment strained to near its breaking before Lottie fell into her mother's arms sobbing. It was a moment when no words were needed, and none were offered.

Lottie took a handkerchief and gently dabbed at her eyes and nose, sniffling and coughing a little. "There've been moments I thought my heart would burst inside me, and I had no one to help me—no one to talk to."

She folded the handkerchief along its creases. "I've written Robert two letters, but he hasn't replied to either, and that's added to my heartache and worry. He may've been killed or taken prisoner . . . Oh, how I hate this war."

Rachel tucked a stray tendril of hair under Lottie's bonnet and fluffed the ribbon. "Darling, I must see about your father before he leaves for work. I want us to talk some more, would you like that?"

A smile spread quickly across Lottie's face. "Yes, Mama, I would like that very much. Now go see about Papa, I'm all right, now."

Rachel smiled, removed her apron, and went to their bedroom where John was dressing for his day at the store. She found him sitting on the side of the bed pulling on his boots.

She sat beside him. "Lottie left Gideon and Sarah alone; she felt she had no right to infringe upon her brother's last days at home."

Grimacing as he thrust a foot into its boot, John responded, "She's a smart girl."

She brushed an imaginary speck of dust from his waistcoat. "There's something else you should be aware of concerning your daughter. She still insists she's in love with Robert Alcott, and she has written letters to him—"

"Has he written to her? I thought he understood our agreement. Evidently, he's not a man of his word. I'll have a talk with her this evening."

Rachel sighed audibly and gave him his coat. "Please, John, before you decide to do anything, allow me to finish. This is something very real to her, and we must treat it differently than before. Although she's written Robert, she hasn't received any letters from him."

John buttoned his waistcoat and stood with his eyes on the floor. Rachel couldn't guess what was going through his mind. Lottie was his treasure, the dearest to his heart of his three children.

Rachel tugged on her husband's coat. "There's nothing for us to do now, John, but comfort Lottie. She needs her loving Papa now more than ever."

John grinned, nodded his head, and leaned to kiss her gently. "That, I shall do."

Motioning for him to sit at the dressing table, Rachel took his hairbrush from him and said, "I'll do your hair."

Gathering his hair in the back, she braided a ponytail, attaching a ribbon to match his suit. "You need to visit the barber, your queue falls below your shoulders. I think it needs to be shorter, especially for a successful businessman."

A series of rapid knocks at the door interrupted John before he could answer her. Opening the door, Rachel was surprised to see it was Gideon and Sarah.

With a fragile smile on his face, Gideon said, "Mother, we would like a word with Father and you. May we come in?"

Hesitating only slightly, Rachel stepped through the door. "We can wait in the parlor while your father finishes dressing."

John soon joined them in the parlor. His eyes scanned the faces of his son and future daughter-in-law for clues as to what this was about. He went to the wingback chair Rachel had taken and stood by her, his arm resting on the back.

"What is it son?"

Standing, Gideon began, "Please hear me out, Father. Since our future is so unsettled, Sarah and I wish to be married as soon as we can—before I leave. Will you help us?"

John's brow furrowed deeply, he should have seen this coming. It was only natural, and he knew he would have to help them. Rachel watched her husband, anxiously awaiting his decision. She held her breath and clasped her hands tightly to a fold in her apron.

"Marriage, even in normal times, is a weighty matter," John said, as the seriousness of his face faded, and his mouth stretched into a smile. "We must think of someone who will act as your guardian, now that your father has taken steps to disown you."

Sarah rose from her chair and stood by Gideon. "My father will not deter us. If I'm an orphan . . . are there no provisions for orphans to marry? Why can't Mother serve as my guardian? In God's sight, who could come before a person's birth mother?"

Scratching his head, John replied, "Sarah, you've asked questions only Judge Trimble can answer."

Placing his hand on Gideon's shoulder, John said, "I'll see Judge Trimble today and ask his advice about a civil wedding for the two of you." His eyebrows raised, he added, "He's a traditionalist, he may not marry you without the approval of a guardian."

Rachel turned to look up at John. "There'll be little traditional about this wedding, but there's nothing orthodox about our lives anymore. You must find Judge Trimble." Her eyes grew focused and her words crisp. "Be temperate, but insistent, when you find him. You might remind him that it was you who put him in his esteemed office."

Locating the Judge proved to be a problem. Trimble was a well known Whig and outspoken member of South Carolina's patriot governing Council of Safety. His whereabouts, on any particular day, was generally known by only a few trusted associates. To see him about performing a marriage ceremony, John found would not be possible.

The day was ending, and John was preparing to close when he heard someone enter the shop. At first glance, John saw only a nondescript businessman walking toward him; the man's face was obscured enough by his tricorne hat that he was unrecognizable.

After a few steps toward the counter, John recognized the Judge's singular stride. Grinning, he extended his hand, "Hello, Judge."

"Hello, John. I fool most folks, but I would've been disappointed if you hadn't seen past my disguise. I'm told one of your sons wishes to be married, and there's a problem with the young woman not having a legal guardian."

John replied, "That's right Judge, I—"

With a wave of his hand, Trimble injected, "Not to worry, I'll appoint one of my associates as her temporary guardian, and we'll have'em wed proper."

Dropping his voice to nearly a whisper, he said, "Now, I must tell you that my schedule these days is tight and unpredictable. I must be in Charles Town a fortnight from yesterday, so we must wed these young folks tomorrow—at ten o'clock a.m. in my chambers. It's the best I can do."

Without hesitating, John nodded, "Tomorrow morning it is, Judge. I'll have them there."

<hr />

It was a few minutes before ten o'clock when the Hamilton's carriage pulled up at the courthouse. A small crowd of friends was gathered on the portico. John had paid some boys to pass the word around town that Gideon and Sarah were to be married at the courthouse this afternoon.

Gideon was waiting inside with the judge when they heard the clatter of the carriage wheels followed by the friendly voices coming from the crowd. Trimble went to the front entrance and peeked outside.

Turning to Gideon, he said, "She's here."

Gideon rushed for the door, but Judge Trimble stopped him. "Hold on, there! You'll see her soon enough. Stand with me."

Gideon's face burned crimson as he sheepishly retook his place. The Judge placed his hand on Gideon's shoulder. "All in good time, young Gideon—all in good time."

The door opened, and Sarah stepped into the courtroom. Golden sunbeams fell through the tall, uncovered windows bringing a golden radiance to her chestnut hair and fair complexion. Her sky-blue eyes widened in search of Gideon, and then she saw him. Their eyes met and held for a long moment. Gideon felt his chest tighten; he was mesmerized by her beauty.

She slowly came to him, and he extended his hand. She whispered, "You look very handsome."

His mind was a fog. His eyes could see only her. He heard her laugh, but wouldn't know until later that he had responded by saying that she too was very handsome. His father, nudging his arm, brought him back to the reality of the moment.

The ceremony began, and Gideon held her hand and squeezed gently. The balding judge intoned the customary words that Gideon would barely remember. Then, he heard the judge pronounce them man and wife. Gideon kissed his wife tenderly, and they turned around to the applause of their friends and family.

CHAPTER FIVE

PATRIOTS ALL

"If there must be trouble, let it be in my day, that my child may have peace." — Tom Paine

<u>Winter 1779, at Trenton Farm, South Carolina</u>

John Hamilton stepped down from the veranda of his house and stood silently on the wide stone pathway that led to the circle drive. There was a strange quietness as the snow muffled ordinary sounds of the morning. His hands were clasped tightly behind his back, and his breath sent clouds of vapor swirling above his head.

Everything had changed this morning. Snow covered the fields and meadow for as far as he could see, and snow was still falling. He became suddenly uneasy and found himself shivering as a light layer of snow covered his wool coat.

The sound of crunching footsteps broke into his reverie, and he turned toward the side of the house. Swallowing the lump in his throat, John watched as Gideon and Daniel came into view.

A keen sense of pride surged through him as he watched the two young men walk toward him. It was plain to see they were his sons. Both had the same lean and wiry build their father had when he was a young man, with the same dark, wavy hair. Gideon, at just over six feet, was as tall as his father, and Daniel was poised to surpass them both.

Gideon was leading Shadow, his roan gelding, while he listened to his younger brother. Their conversation was still out of their father's earshot as they walked along the path, but John, not wanting to intrude, remained where he was.

The older man's jaw was set hard, but his deep, clear gray-blue eyes mirrored the stirrings he felt in his heart. Gideon had volunteered to deliver John's message to Colonel Andrew Pickens now garrisoned near Orangeburg.

Gideon, at twenty, and older than Daniel by a year and a half, had always been very protective of his brother. Now, both were at the threshold of manhood, and it was Daniel who sought to give counsel to his older brother.

Gideon's ride would be less than seventy miles but would take him through the heart of Tory country. If he was wounded or needed shelter, he would be alone, without help, until he reached Orangeburg.

Taking his brother's arm, Daniel said, ". . . and if you don't know'em, assume they're Tories. And stay off the Orangeburg Road, especially at night, you—"

"Thank you, brother, but Shadow will outrun any of the Tory nags I should chance upon." Gideon knew his brother was concerned for his safety and meant well. "Catching me on Shadow would be akin to catching the wind."

Daniel held to his brother's arm, slowing their pace. "I'm serious brother, God's hand of protection may not always be there for you, and Shadow's match might show up just at the wrong time."

Daniel saw his brother's knitted brow and instantly regretted saying that Shadow could possibly be beaten.

Gideon stopped and stroked along Shadow's long neck and whispered into his ear. Shadow's ears pricked forward, his big eyes softened, and he nuzzled Gideon's shoulder.

Gideon's expression changed to a look of sheer love.

"Daniel, you're beginning to sound like Pa. You've been there for every race Shadow's run." Gideon shook his head. "I don't know how you could ever doubt Shadow's ability. There's not a horse alive that can match him; it doesn't matter what their bloodline may be, or what fancy English stable they're from."

As they reached their father, Daniel placed a hand on Gideon's shoulder and with the other shook his hand. "Godspeed, brother, I wish I could ride along with you."

Gideon's gaze lingered on his brother. "There'll be other times, brother."

John's quiet nature sometimes came across as aloofness, but this wasn't evident this morning. He stood with his sons as they waited for him to speak. Absent was the authoritative Colonel, and in his place was a proud and loving father about to send his son on a journey that could cost him his life.

"You have everything?" John asked, his eyes on the rifle and brace of pistols secured across Shadow's saddle.

Before Gideon could answer, Sarah and Lottie came through the front door of the house. Lottie carried saddlebags stuffed with food.

She extended the bags to Gideon. "Here brother, I think your bride outdid herself, there's enough food in those bags for a month's trip."

Sarah's face reddened as she went to him. "It's not so much, but I did fit in a jar of fig preserves for you."

He secured the bags and bent over and kissed his mother's cheek, and cupped her chin in the palm of his hand. "You'll be on my mind, until I return, Ma."

Lottie lunged toward Gideon and wrapped her arms around him. "Oh, Gideon, I love you, and I'll miss you terribly. Please hurry home."

Gideon kissed his sister lightly on her cheek. "Thank you, little sister. I'll miss you, but don't worry, I'm going to be all right—me and Shadow."

Pulling John's arm, Rachel stepped back to the veranda. Daniel and Lottie followed. All was quiet.

Sarah stood before him, her eyes brimming. She felt a sadness cloak her heart at the thought of his leaving. Gideon's gaze traced the contours of her face, and then he pulled her to him and closed his eyes, trying to hold onto the quiet heartbeat in her chest. She looked up into his face, his expression solemn and she whispered, "Come back to me."

Then he tenderly held her face in his hands and they kissed.

He gave his mother another hug, shook hands with his father, and then saddled up, ready to ride. Gathering the reins, he saluted his father and dug his heels into Shadow's flanks. Billows of vapor blew from the gelding's nostrils as he dug his hind legs into the hard earth beneath him and leaped forward into a gallop, sending clods of snow-covered sandy soil hurtling backward from his pounding hooves.

⊶⊷⊶ ⊶⊷⊶ ⊶⊷⊶

The family stood together in the solemn quietness while the snow fell from the low hanging clouds, and watched until

Gideon reached the end of the long drive and turned south on the main road.

John, his face cryptic and his jaw set in a hard line, absently removed his gold watch from a pocket in his woolen biscuit-colored waistcoat and looked at the time. He turned to re-enter his house, with the women following. Daniel turned back to finish his morning chores.

John went directly to the parlor fireplace and stood by the mantle, rubbing his hands together briskly from the cold. He stared into the flames that danced and weaved their bright blazing orange and yellow. A charred log shifted and fell, scattering fiery embers spiraling upward. His musings broken by the crackling and popping, he repositioned the log and stirred the embers with the iron poker, moving the biggest pieces together.

Rachel watched as Sarah slowly made her way up the stairs. Hesitantly, Rachel followed Lottie to the kitchen where Belle was clearing away the breakfast dishes. "Lottie, help Belle finish the kitchen, and then help Sarah strip the beds in all the bedrooms, and take them to Sally for washing. I'll be with your father this morning, and then I'll see to finishing your dress this afternoon."

Lottie tied her apron around her waist. "Yes ma'am. I can't wait to wear my new dress when we go to Charles Town."

Rachel poured coffee for her and John and left for the parlor. She found John in an introspective mood, standing before the fireplace. She extended the tray. "Would you like another cup of coffee?" she said, "Belle just made it."

Without hearing her question, John took the nearest cup and blew softly across the tendrils of steam rising from the cup.

Rachel placed the tray on a nearby table and sat on the sofa facing the radiating heat from the fireplace. Cradling her cup in her hands, she watched her husband. She knew it bothered him to send Gideon on such a perilous journey, but Gideon had pressed his father for the courier duty until John gave in. Couriers on either side, if they escaped death, expected to be eventually captured, but the patriots seemed never to lack for volunteers to take up this dangerous job.

Patting the couch beside her, Rachel said wistfully, "Come sit beside me, John. It shan't be long 'til *you're* gone too."

John stood impassively before the fireplace. Rachel sighed silently; she knew he hadn't heard her. He would be this way until he actually left to join Colonel Pickens, but she was so proud of him. The number of defeats suffered by the Patriot Cause hadn't dented his resolve; if anything, he'd gained strength from being part of something larger than himself. "Freedom," he'd told her, "is universal in the heart of every man and woman, and it beats in the heart of their children. It will never die. If our generation doesn't win it, the next will pick it up; it will never fade from the hearts of mankind."

She tried again to break his meditative silence. "What did you say in your message, John?" she asked, smoothing wrinkles from her skirt. "Can you tell me?"

John came to her, sat on the couch, and touched his finger to her lips. "My dear Rachel, after more than twenty years, I'd be surprised if you couldn't already recite my note, word for word." He leaned back and laughed heartily.

She knew he was referring to her way of finishing his sentences, and apparently reading his mind. She laughed with him, wanting to keep this moment with him in her heart and relive it during the lonely days that lay ahead for her.

"If we expect to win," he said, after hesitating a moment, "we'll have to keep our Tory neighbor, James Boyd, guessing. If he even suspects Pickens is trailing him, it'll take away our only advantage. Boyd has us outnumbered almost two to one, so we must catch them off guard if we're to beat them. From the latest dispatch from Colonel Pickens, Boyd's militia has already crossed the Saluda River on his way to meet up with the British army at Augusta."

"This war has turned the world upside down, John," Rachel said wistfully. "The Boyds' are—or were—our good friends. James was one of our first customers, but now . . ."

John rose and again took his place by the fireplace. "Uh-huh, and no matter how it all ends, I doubt we can ever return to the way it was." He sighed. "I've thought some about what I'll do if James and I come face to face in the heat of the skirmish."

Rachel came across the room to stand beside him. "I don't like to hear you talk about such things, John. The heat of battle is no time for reflection."

She pulled him around to face her. "I want you to come back to me and our three children. You'll not be facing your friends when you catch up with James and his men. Just remember his work at the Williamson's farm last winter. He allowed his men to burn them out of their home, kidnap their slaves, and to sell them in Charles Town. Then they forced Agatha and the children to watch as they hung poor Ezra."

Wrapping his arms around her, John kissed her lovingly. "Shhh, let's not talk anymore about this. I shouldn't have brought it up. It's not at all like it sounded. There'll be no hesitation from me when we meet up with him and his marauders.

━━◆◇◈◇◆━━ ━━◆◇◈◇◆━━ ━━◆◇◈◇◆━━

Two days later, Gideon rode on the road toward Orangeburg, the headquarters of Colonel Pickens. The wintry wind that cut through his heavy coat was bone chilling cold. He tried to keep his gun hand protected from the wind, in case he had to use his pistol.

Riding at night and sleeping during the day, Gideon had hoped to avoid most of the British and Tory patrols. This night would be his last before he reached Pickens' camp. All that remained for him was to cut through Socastee Swamp, and he would be home free.

This last stretch before the safety of the swamp would take him past a crossroads. About a quarter-mile from the junction, he slowed Shadow to a trot and peered ahead into the predawn darkness. Seeing nothing, he hoped Shadow would alert him in time to outrun any patrol that might challenge him.

He had ridden Shadow since he was a colt, and his stamina was unmatched. Not only was Shadow always the fastest, but he always had a little more run left when other horses became winded and quit.

Shadow's ears pricked up suddenly, and out of the misty darkness Gideon saw the shapes of horsemen spread out across the road thirty yards ahead. It was too late to avoid being seen.

"Advance slowly, and keep your hands visible," a voice called out.

The accent was unmistakable. *British!*

Gideon's throat tightened, as he pondered what he might do. Only one thing came to mind, make a run for it! Socastee Swamp lay somewhere ahead, and it would soon be light, but he'd been riding for several hours, and he could only hope that Shadow had enough left to get them to the swamp.

Determination fueled by plain grit sent him forward to the waiting redcoats. His plan was simple; he would lunge Shadow through the line and make a run for it.

He approached the redcoats slowly, and the leader's horse stepped toward him, leaving an opening in the line. The British officer veered slightly to approach Gideon; it was all Gideon needed. Digging his heels into Shadow's sides, his horse lunged past the officer and through the line before anyone could react. As Gideon went by the stunned officer, he shoved him hard with his hand. The surprised officer slipped from his saddle with his right boot caught in the stirrup.

Gideon heard the officer yell as he was left hanging from his saddle.

The officer's aide responded quickly. "You men go after him! I'll attend to the Captain."

Gideon leaned over Shadow's neck. "It's a race, boy! Don't let'em catch us!"

He knew Shadow loved to race, but he also knew the horse must be exhausted. Gideon shook those thoughts from his mind. He knew his beloved horse would run until he fell.

CHAPTER SIX

DEATH IN THE SWAMP

The British patrol stayed close behind him, and from the pounding of their horse's hooves, he judged they hadn't gained on him since he'd run their blockade.

Suddenly, the crack of a pistol shot sounded behind him. The musket ball sang past his ear. Gideon leaned forward with his head laid close to Shadow's neck.

"C'mon boy, let's go!"

Shadow must be about to give out, Gideon thought. They'd not stopped for food, water, or rest since leaving Fort Tyler last evening, and now that they were nearing Socastee Swamp, his horse might not make it. Gideon knew, even if he killed him doing it, he had to keep his heels to Shadow's flanks. As long as his faithful mount was able to respond, he needed every gallop the horse had left.

Night was giving way to the pale edge of a mist-shrouded dawn when he again looked back over his shoulder. He could now see a small company of his British pursuers with a single rider out front, and the redcoat was closing the gap. That soldier must have been the one who fired the pistol, because he was carrying his unsheathed sabre high.

Gideon fumbled beneath his greatcoat for the handle of his pistol. His near frozen hand shook, but he freed the weapon from the waistband of his breeches and brought the hammer fully back. Another turn of his head and the young man saw that his pursuer was indeed closer. The others hadn't gained on him, but they hadn't fallen behind, either. Gideon saw his pursuer was closing in for the kill.

I can't outrun him; Shadow's too near gone. I'll have only one chance, so I have to do this right.

Looming in the distance ahead was Socastee Swamp. "If you can get us into the swamp, boy, we'll have a chance."

"Stop, you bloody rebel!"

The shout startled him. He glanced over his shoulder and saw the soldier was coming up alongside him. The redcoat was now leaning from his saddle toward Gideon with his sabre poised for its lethal stroke. He was almost within striking distance. Gideon leveled his pistol directly at the soldier and fired.

The musket ball slammed into the man's chest, almost knocking him from his saddle. His horse immediately slowed and stopped.

Ahead, the old live oaks gave way to the even larger cypress trees of the swamp. Like a heavy curtain, clinging Spanish moss hung from the foliage of the huge cypress trees, leaving only smoky bits of the emerging morning light here and there to reach the black swamp waters.

Shadow dutifully carried Gideon into the swamp until the sounds of his pursuers faded. Gideon slowed the horse and looked back. The patrol must have stopped to see about their stricken comrade, but he knew they weren't done with him yet, not after one of them had been wounded or possibly killed.

The curtains of hanging moss filtered the morning sunlight, and a pair of pileated woodpeckers, as big as crows, lit on the trunk of a tree and began their incessant drumming. He guided Shadow into the deepening shadows, following a faint trail that would lead him to his destination.

The British had never learned to discern the subtle differences in swamp ground; to them the soggy black loam all looked the same. No matter how much they wanted to capture him, Gideon knew the patrol wouldn't venture very far into the labyrinth of the swamp in hopes of catching up with him.

It wasn't long until he heard his red-coated pursuers closing in. Gideon stopped and eased down from the saddle. He laid his hand lightly over Shadow's nostrils hoping to conceal any sound his horse might make. He decided now would be a good time to reload his pistol.

He heard one of them call out, "This way, he came this way!" The voice sounded American.

Gideon held his breath and listened intently to determine how close they might be. *They're coming this way.* He stroked Shadow's neck. *He did his part, I asked him to get us into the swamp, and he did it.* Gideon looked into his horse's weary eyes, and he could see only exhaustion.

Suddenly, he heard a shout, "Everybody out—everybody out, now! Captain's order!"

He could hear movement and, in a few moments, it began to grow faint. They were leaving, but Gideon still didn't move. He felt an uneasiness spread through his body, raising goosebumps on his skin—someone might still be close, maybe the tracker.

A minute—two minutes slipped by as Gideon listened for any sound from his adversary. His gut tightened; he was barely breathing in the misty morning stillness of the ancient swamp.

Then Shadow's ears pricked, and the horse's nostrils flared, but he still made no sound.

One of them is still there!

Gideon held his breath and cocked his head to listen. He listened carefully, but there was no more movement, no sound—nothing but silence.

You're there, mister. You can't fool Shadow; he's already heard you or smelled you.

Then Gideon heard the barely audible sound of a boot squishing through muck. Shadow turned his head in the direction of the sound, and Gideon's hand tensed around the handle of his pistol. It was then that Gideon spotted the man, kneeling with his back to Gideon, looking at swirls of steam rising from droppings left by Shadow.

The man's back was wide at the shoulders, tapering to a trim waist. Gideon hadn't moved, but he saw the muscles in the man's back tighten—the man knew he was being watched.

Then Gideon pulled the hammer back to its full position. The sound echoed in the morning stillness. The man sprang to his feet and spun to face Gideon. There was no panic in his deep-set eyes, only the deadly look of a hunter.

The man's mouth creased in a twisted and wicked smile, exposing yellowed, tobacco-stained teeth. "Hmm, looks like I've found one of John Hamilton's stinking sons. You be Gideon, I think."

Gideon stared at the young man whose hair was queued at his neck. For a moment, he was taken aback that the man knew his name.

"Do I know you?" Gideon asked.

Hate clouded the man's features. "Nah, I doubt it, but your Pa and mine are slightly acquainted, you might say. I'm Zeke Sherman."

Gideon recoiled when the man said his name. The menacing figure before him was Sarah's cousin, the eldest son of Rufus Sherman.

The father, Rufus Sherman and his three sons ran with a band of renegade Cherokee Indians. Hiding behind the pretense of loyalty to the crown of England, they cut a wide swath of murderous raids and destruction behind them.

Zeke lowered himself into a crouching position and with his right hand, unsheathed a wicked looking knife.

Gideon thrust his pistol toward him. "Stay as you are. Another move and it'll be your last."

Flashing his irregular, stained teeth, Zeke grinned. "What's your business this far south, Hamilton?" he demanded.

"I would ask you the same question," Gideon said calmly.

"Humph, it wouldn't be some treasonous business against your king, now would it?"

Gideon watched the subtle move of Zeke's knife hand, as he held it away from his body in the manner of a skilled knife fighter.

"Unless you want to die this morning, drop the knife," Gideon said grimly.

"It's not me that's about to die, Hamilton. I'm going to do a nice Indian job on you."

Zeke had barely finished speaking when he lunged forward. Gideon, leaner and stronger, sidestepped him and fell back, firing his pistol. Off balance, he just nicked Zeke's shoulder. Zeke hit the muddy ground with a splat, but he was up in an instant and spun around quickly.

"That's about it for your little pea shooter, ain't it?" Zeke said darkly. "Just one shot, and if you miss . . . well, I think you know what's about to happen."

His teeth bared in a predatory grin, Zeke leaped toward him with his hunting knife in his hand. Gideon attempted to grab Zeke's knife hand, but managed only to deflect his arm. However, he was able to hit him solidly in the face with his pistol. Zeke was stunned and fell to his knees, but not before he plunged his knife deep into the flesh and muscles just above Gideon's hip.

Gideon thought he'd been punched.

Zeke's face was bloody and his nose, looking bent, was bleeding profusely. Still, he had plenty of fight left in him. He staggered to his feet and wiped the blood from his eyes with the sleeve of his dirty buckskin shirt.

Then he spotted Gideon leaning against an ancient cypress tree. He glared at Gideon with dark eyes. "You ought not to have done that, Hamilton. Now you've made me mad, for sure."

Gideon had become vaguely aware of a burning sensation in his lower side, and when he'd looked down, he saw Zeke's knife buried deep just above his hip. When Zeke moved, Gideon knew what he had to do. He took a deep breath and gripped the knife handle tightly. With one swift pull, the knife came free.

Zeke charged him with his face down, hitting Gideon like a battering ram. Both men went down and began a desperate struggle for the knife. Zeke grabbed Gideon by his wrist and twisted viciously and Gideon nearly dropped the knife. The ground was slippery, and neither man could get traction to overpower the other.

Grappling to gain an advantage, the men made it to their feet, struggling and twisting until Zeke was able to grab Gideon in a chokehold with his free arm. Right away, Gideon felt lightheaded. Zeke kept up the pressure on Gideon's throat; Gideon knew he would soon pass out if he couldn't break free. With his life at stake, Gideon came down hard on Zeke's instep with the heel of his heavy boot.

Zeke let out a cry of pain and relaxed his hold on Gideon's neck. Gideon hammered his boot down a second time, and he was able to break free from Zeke's choke-hold. Pivoting, Gideon caught Zeke full in his face with a looping left-handed punch.

Zeke fell back releasing his hold on Gideon's knife hand. He stood unsteadily, his breathing heavy and irregular. Blood was dripping from his crushed nose. Gideon's heart pounded in his chest as he struggled to regain his balance. Just a few steps from him was his adversary. Zeke looked to be in a bad way, but Gideon had seen men look worse and yet fight on to overcome their foe.

Suddenly, with a move that disaffirmed any weariness he might have felt, Zeke came at Gideon, wrapping his powerful arms tightly around him. His hands interlocked, and he squeezed until Gideon felt his ribs would break.

Then Gideon remembered the knife in his hand. Unable to free his arm, he brought the knife to Zeke's side and thrust it into his rib cage. Zeke shuddered, but kept up the crushing pressure on Gideon's upper body.

Then Gideon stabbed him again, twisting the blade as he thrust it to the hilt. Gideon saw the killing rage wane from his assailant's dark eyes; Zeke's arms weakened and fell limp at his sides—it was over.

Glassy eyed, Zeke gasped and sank to his knees. Gideon stood over him, his own side bleeding. "It didn't have to end this way, you have only your own murderous heart to blame."

Dying, Zeke nodded. His voice a fragile whisper, he said, "Aye, but there's no taking it back now—your cause is a just one—but I couldn't turn my back on family . . ."

Gideon lingered until Zeke breathed his last. He watched Zeke's chest fall and become still. Among the many men in the Carolinas who were known as habitual plunderers, even murderers, Rufus and his sons were about the worst. Gideon shuddered to think what Rufus would do when he learned his son had been killed by a son of John Hamilton. Gideon sighed and mounted his horse, nudging him toward the other side of the swamp.

Daybreak was three hours past when Colonel Pickens's headquarters came into view. Gideon rode flat out and brought his horse to a sliding stop before the sentry.

Panting for breath, he said, "I bring word—from Colonel Hamilton—for Colonel Pickens."

Limping, he led his horse to the hitching rack; he looped the reins loosely over the rail. Another sentry escorted him to Colonel's tent.

Someone had already alerted the Colonel, and he had stepped outside to wait for Gideon's arrival.

"Well, my young Gideon, what news from your father do you bring?"

Gideon saluted the Colonel. "By now, he and his men are on their way here, sir."

"Did he send a written message?" asked the Colonel.

"Aye, he did sir," slipping the packet from his inside coat pocket.

Pickens's face relaxed, and he accepted the packet, noting Gideon's blood soaked breeches. "Have you been wounded, young man?"

Gideon grimaced. "Yessir, stabbed in my hip, but it's stopped bleeding."

Turning to his aide, the Colonel said, "Send a man to Doc Fuller's farm and bring the doctor back with him. Tell him it's a knife wound."

The Colonel took Gideon by his arm. "Come with me. I'll find you a place to lie down while we wait for Doctor Fuller."

Seeing that Gideon was comfortable, Pickens carried the packet inside his tent where his adjutant stood waiting.

"Get on this, Lieutenant. I've asked John to join us in our skirmish with Colonel Boyd. He has a number of sharpshooters that'll make the difference when we meet up with him."

The Lieutenant brought the dispatch to his table and began the exacting task of decoding the dispatch.

Colonel Pickens anxiously watched as the young officer skillfully, letter by letter, made sense of the garbled code. Pickens had waited for a week to hear whether John and his men could join him before Boyd left for Augusta.

Tearing off the decoded page from his tablet, the young officer handed it to Pickens.

With message in hand, the Colonel went outside where his officers and sergeants gathered about a fire. Holding the message above his head, he said, "Colonel Hamilton and his boys are on the way."

Immediately upon hearing this good news, the men cheered with three huzzahs.

He waited for the men to quiet down before he said, "I figure they'll get here the day after tomorrow, or sooner, if I know John."

"Can we tell the men, Colonel?" asked a sergeant.

Pickens nodded his head. "Yes, sergeant, and you can tell them to be ready to ride Friday next at sunup. We won't be able to wait any longer for John. Boyd's a cautious man, and if he gets wind that we're after him, we'll have a tough time catching him."

⊷⊶ ⊷⊶ ⊷⊶

John's men were ready for a fight. At daybreak, the morning following Gideon's departure, John started south with two hundred and fifty men. They rode hard, stopping only to allow their mounts to feed and rest; they didn't want to take any chances they might miss Boyd and his militia.

Riding fast through the backcountry was second nature to John and his company—a part of their daily life. Crossing creeks, ravines, and threading the dense woods posed no difficulty for these men. Riding off the roads, John figured they would cut considerable time, maybe half a day in rendezvousing with Pickens.

Late the second day of hard riding, they reached a timbered ridge, a half mile from Pickens' camp. Following the ridge south past an abandoned gristmill, they came upon the camp. They rode in very tired, hungry, and most of all, cold after being drenched in freezing water when they forded Breed's Creek.

Colonel Pickens told John right away about Gideon's wound. "He's over at Doc Fuller's house, about an hour ride from here. The doc says your son is all right, but he took him back to his house for a week or so for Gideon's own safekeeping."

A smile crept across Pickens's face. "Seems Gideon got into an argument with the doc about laying up awhile and giving himself time to heal. Gideon felt he'd just need a bandage to be ready for our upcoming skirmish."

Cradling his cup of coffee in his hands, John nodded. "I hope Gideon calmed down after he got to the doctor's house. After you lay out my orders for the fight, I'll ride over to the doctor's place and see that young man who argues with doctors."

Pickens smoothed out a roughly-drawn map and described the plan of action. "Boyd's camped near Kettle Creek at a place called 'The Bend'. I want us to be in place an hour before sunup. The creek is flooded right now, and if we hit him from the southwest, he'll have no retreat route."

"How many men does he have?"

Sighing heavily, Pickens responded, "Our scouts have told me we'll be facing about six hundred men, and we have no more than three hundred and fifty, but I'm counting on your sharpshooters to cut deep into their number during the first few volleys." He looked John in the eye. "Can they do it?"

Not wanting to sound boastful, John nodded his head. "They've never failed me before, Andy. How do you want to use them?"

Pointing to the map, Pickens drew an imaginary line. "There's a ridge along here about a hundred yards from Boyd's camp. If we place your shooters along this high ground, they can stop or slow down any bayonet charge. Splitting the other men into three units, we'll hit'em from both flanks and head on. We'll keep pushing until we get their backs wet in the creek."

"I like your plan, Andy. If we hit'em before they get up, it shouldn't take long, but if they have time to get ready, we'll be in for a struggle, for sure." John stood. "Now, I want to check on my son, before I talk to my men. I'll see you in the morning."

John rode at a canter and arrived at the frame house just as the sun was disappearing below the horizon. A woman opened the door only enough for John to see her face, and right away, he saw her eyes were filled with fear.

"If you've come for the doctor, he's not here. Some of those cowardly Loyalists kidnapped him." Her voice broke with grief and fear. "By now, they've likely hung him."

Speaking evenly, but firmly, John said, "I'm sorry, madam about the doctor. My name is John Hamilton, and I've come to see my son, Gideon. I'm told the doctor is, or was, treating his knife wound."

She held the door in place. "And do you have anyone with you?"

"I'm alone, and I assure you, I mean you no harm. I just want to see my son."

She looked at John thoughtfully for a moment, and then slowly opened the door. "Well, come in, then. I'm Maggie, the doctor's wife. Your son is in the attic. Come with me, and we'll help him down. His wound is close to his hip, and it's painful for him to stand very long."

Gideon was white-faced by the time he was down from the attic hideout. Concern etched John's face. "Feel like telling me about your ride, son?"

Gideon took a deep breath. "It was dull until I run into a Redcoat patrol about five miles east of Socastee Swamp. I'd ridden Shadow hard most of the night, and he couldn't outrun'em, but we made it to the swamp, and the Redcoats turned back—except for one—Zeke Sherman. Getting knife-stuck was my fault, Pa; I should've shot him when he told me his name, but I hesitated, and he came at me with his knife before I could get off a shot."

John looked questioningly at his son, but didn't say anything, only waited for him to go on.

The vision of the death struggle in the swamp was vividly embedded in Gideon's memory. "We struggled for awhile, me with his knife in my side, but at the time, I couldn't feel it. I don't have a clear recollection of pulling the knife out, but I'll never forget the look in his eyes when I stabbed him in his chest . . . he died pretty quick."

CHAPTER SEVEN

A BRIDE FOLLOWS HER HUSBAND

Spring 1780, Camden, South Carolina

C olonel Boyd's camp lay wrapped in deep silence shortly before dawn. John's sharpshooters were in place waiting on the signal from Colonel Pickens.

Suddenly, the morning stillness was broken as Pickens shouted, "Let's go!"

Instantly the air filled with a roaring racket and clamor of battle. Boyd, one of the first casualties, was shot from his horse as he tried to rally his men. The tide turned quickly in favor of the patriots when the leaderless Loyalists rioted and ran for the safety of the swamp.

Emerging from the skirmish with only nine men killed and twenty wounded, the Patriots quickly disbursed to their homes to await further word from Colonel Pickens. John remained for a time until Gideon was able to travel.

━◈━ ━◈━ ━◈━

Sarah and Rachel were in the orchard when they heard someone shouting. Looking toward the house, they saw John and Gideon riding up. The women caught up their skirts and began running. They reached their men as John was helping Gideon down.

Gideon found himself wrapped in the arms of his wife and mother. Both were talking at the same time. Finally, John was able to calm the women down. "Here now, he's all right. It was a knife wound in his hip, but he's about well now. The ride was a bit hard for him, but now that he's home . . ."

Months passed and Gideon had fully recovered. One morning, just as the barest hint of sunlight peeped through the sheer curtained window, Sarah nudged Gideon awake. He squeezed his eyes tight and turned toward her.

"Wake up, sleepy," she said cheerily, "I want to talk to you about something important."

He looked at her with pleasant, half-closed eyes. "Uh-uh, I'm not awake yet . . . can't think this early."

Propping herself on one elbow, she said, "You don't have to think, just listen to what I have to say, and you'll wake up."

Gideon moaned and fluffed his pillow into shape. Turning on his back, with his arms folded behind his head, he said half-grumpily, "What's so important that you have to wake me so early?"

Sarah took a deep breath and laid her hand on his chest. "I'll be going with you when the army leaves for Charles Town."

Gideon's eyes fluttered open, and he stared at his wife. A moment passed before he could respond. "You don't know what you're saying Sarah. War is no place for women. No, you can't come with me. It's out of the question."

"The British Army allows the wives, even encourages them, to follow their husbands, and Caroline Bridger is going with her husband when all of you leave. I doubt she's the only wife that'll be going; I'm sure there'll be more."

Gideon sat up with his back against the headboard. "Since we were small children playing along the river, you've been headstrong and stubborn. Man or woman, there's not another in the territory who can best your courage and resolve."

Shaking his head, he took her hand, "But I'm serious when I say war is no place for women. Your doggedness and heart may not be enough to see you through this. Besides, past Monck's Corner, I don't know where we'll be going or how long the war will last. I may fall in the first battle or the last; I could be crippled for the rest of my life. I know it's going to be painful while we're apart, but we'll endure it like everyone else."

"'Tis as you say, husband. I'm headstrong, but that's just who I am. My place is with you." Moving to sit by him, she said, "You're willing to leave me here, and expect me to suffer the loneliness and heartache of not knowing where you are or if you be alive or dead."

Shaking her head, she went on, "Nay, I'll take my chances just as you shall. God willing, we'll come through this together and look back on this time with pride, knowing we helped birth our country."

Gideon looked at her. He knew he'd lost this battle of wills. Unyielding determination was written all over her face. "How will you travel? You can't very well march alongside us."

She smiled, and her whole face lit up. "By wagon, of course— I'm sure we can find one for sale, and we'll need flour, meal, bacon, pots, pans, and a good skillet for a start. I'll add to that as I think of it."

"Well, let's get dressed, and we'll talk to the Bridgers," he said. "Then we'll tell our folks, but don't be surprised when Ma and Pa stand against this."

⚬⚬⚬ ⚬⚬⚬ ⚬⚬⚬

Gideon hired a buggy from the livery, and they drove the five miles to the Bridger's farm north of town near Rumney's Mill. Ethan Bridger was coming from the barn when they approached the house.

Ethan reached them as Gideon was helping Sarah step down. "Congratulations Mr. and Mrs. Hamilton, we heard you two were married! This is a surprise, indeed. We don't get many visitors from Camden. Most folks coming by are traveling south looking for the road to Charles Town."

Caroline came running from the porch. "Oh Sarah, how lovely you are! You and your handsome husband! Please come inside for tea."

As they entered the house, Caroline said, "You'll have to excuse the disarray, Sarah. We've sold the farm and nearly all the furniture. I'm sorting what we'll need to take with us from the things we'll have to leave behind."

Ethan and Gideon settled themselves on the floor, while the women took the only chairs. "Well, what brings you two up this way?" asked Ethan.

Glancing at his wife, Gideon said, "We wanted to tell you that Sarah will be coming with me when the army leaves for Charles Town."

Turning to Sarah, Caroline exclaimed, "Oh, wonderful! We haven't heard from any of the others, and we thought I might be the only wife going."

Sitting on the edge of her chair, Sarah said, "We thought the two of you would tell us how you'll be traveling. Perhaps we can do something similar."

Ethan stood and said, "Let's take a walk out to the barn, and you can take a look at what will be Caroline's home for some time."

Outside, Ethan proudly showed them a small but sturdy-looking covered wagon he'd outfitted for his wife. "I'm about finished with the caulking of the wagon box, and then I'll treat the bonnet with linseed oil. We've decided to use a pair of oxen to pull the wagon, since they're more reliable and tougher than mules or horses. Oxen will eat poor grass and only require the yoke to hitch to the wagon."

Lowering the rear gate, Caroline said, "This will be my all-purpose table. From here, I'll be able to prepare our meals. I'll set everything up so the things I use most will be within arm's reach"."

Ethan knelt on one knee. "Gideon, take a look underneath. You'll see I've fitted a place for a front spare wheel as well as one for the back."

By mid-afternoon, Gideon and Sarah were on their way to return the rented carriage. "Did you happen to ask Ethan when he expects the army to leave?" she asked.

Gideon's hands were loose upon the reins. "He says we have a fortnight, and not much more, to find you a wagon and get it ready.

It was late afternoon when they pulled up in front of the livery. The owner, Amos Boone, came out and helped Sarah step down. "I hope you folks enjoyed the day. Since you left this morning, the town received a few copies of the Charles Town Gazette and the main headline was about the British laying siege to Charles Town."

Stunned for a moment, Gideon said, "Could I read your paper?"

Amos went back to his office and returned with the paper. "I'm done with it; pass it on when you're finished." He took the reins from Gideon and led the carriage horse inside the livery barn.

Gideon called to him, "Sir, would you wait up?"

Amos stopped and turned back to the couple. "Yessir, is there anything else I can do for you?"

Stepping around the carriage, Gideon went over to Amos. "I certainly hope you can, sir. My wife and I are in need of a sturdy wagon. She'll be doing the driving, so we'd prefer one that's not too large."

Rubbing his chin whiskers and staring thoughtfully at the couple, Amos replied, "Sounds like this little woman is going to be following your camp." He shook his head. "Can't say that I'd recommend that, madam. Nossir, I wouldn't advise the young lady to do that at all. Fields of battle are not pretty, and round balls kill and maim women and children just as easily as they do the men."

Gideon could see the determination in Sarah's face. "Thank you for your advice, sir, but do you have a wagon for sale?"

"Hmph, I should've kept quiet. Young people are all alike," he muttered, "I might have something that'll serve your purpose."

He took them to the back lot where he kept carriages for rent and showed them his only wagon. "I don't get much call for wagons. It'll need some work on it; the tires will likely need some attention from the smithy, but the box is solid and tight."

Gideon looked the wagon over and turned to Sarah, "What do you think?"

Her face beaming; she replied, "It's perfect. It already has the bows; I'll make a cover. Yes, it will do just fine."

Gideon scratched his forearm. "Name your price, Mr. Amos, but remember the shape it's in."

Amos studied the ground at his feet and ran his fingers through his thinning hair. "Well . . . it doesn't seem right to make a profit off folks heading into harm's way, so I'll just loan you the wagon. You can keep it until you come home, and I expect to see both of you sitting on the seat when that day comes."

Two days passed before Gideon, and Sarah had their wagon inspected and repaired by the smithy. Locating a healthy pair of oxen took up the following morning. That afternoon, Sarah guided the oxen in pulling the wagon to the Hamilton's mercantile store while Gideon was bartering for flour and salt near Grindal's Shoals. Major Thomas Franklin, commander of the new army recruits, met her as he was leaving the store. Holding the door open, he bowed gallantly and said, "Good afternoon Mrs. Hamilton. I see you are preparing for our departure."

"Aye Major, and I'm about done, too," she responded, cordially. "And will Mrs. Franklin be a member of our party?"

Franklin's features darkened, and he said tersely, "There's no Mrs. Franklin; I'm a widower."

Sarah saw his gaze harden and his back stiffen. "Oh! Please forgive me, Major, I just assumed . . . I mean I—"

Seeing his reaction had unsettled Sarah, Franklin managed a smile. "Nay, Mrs. Hamilton. You've brought no injury to me. 'Tis I who is in need of *your* forgiveness for my boorish manners in the presence of a lady. Since I'm a stranger to the backcountry, you couldn't have known of my recent loss."

Sarah could now see the dark circles beneath his eyes and it pained her heart to know she had awakened his grief. She was afraid of saying anything more for fear of intruding further.

A moment's silence hung in the air before the Major spoke: "Please, Mrs. Hamilton, let's put this behind us. You had no way of knowing, and I should have taken your gracious inquiry as you intended." Bowing deeply, he said further, "Now, I must beg your leave, as I have much to do before the sun sets today if the brigade is to depart as scheduled."

Without waiting for her reply, he turned toward the hitching post for his horse.

⊸⧫⊷ ⊸⧫⊷ ⊸⧫⊷

It was dawn of the appointed day, and a sergeant had just finished the company's roll call. He headed for Major Franklin, who was conferring with his aide.

"Major, we have five missing," said the sergeant gruffly.

"Give me the names, sergeant."

The sergeant read off the names of the absent soldiers.

"All right, sergeant, have the company stand by. We'll give the stragglers a few minutes. I'll be at the rear conferring with the women."

He trotted his horse to the area where the women had gathered. He took note that the number included only two children, and one of the women looked ready to deliver at any moment.

Deciding not to dismount, he tipped his hat while his eyes slowly scanned the group. "Ladies, time is of the essence, so I'll be brief. The company is standing by ready to march. I want to remind you that I am the senior officer and am in absolute command of the company. I shall expect your group to follow behind the supply wagons at a safe distance. What constitutes a safe distance will be determined according to the circumstances of the day. Finally, you must keep up; I cannot allow you to delay or slow the company. If difficulty arises among you, I expect you to solve it. I cannot spare a man to help you."

Then his voice softened. "God willing, we shall be victorious and free our country. How long that shall take is not known to me, but I believe that God is on our side. May God speed each of you and this company on its way."

With that, he returned to the head of the company. The atmosphere was subdued. Three men approached the sergeant and apologized for their tardiness. He took their names and turned to the Major. "We've got three of the five, Major—whatta you say?"

Franklin stood and said crisply, "Let's go. We're headed for the northern fork of Milton's Creek."

Motioning to a corporal, the sergeant said, "You lead out, we're goin' to the northern fork of Milton's Creek . . . on your feet, men—by twos. Let's move out!"

The company moved out along the road to Charles Town that paralleled the north bank of the Wateree River. Twenty women had come to follow their husbands. Most were milling about when the company began moving. Caroline went to her lead ox, tugged on the lead rope, and said, "Giddyup!" Sarah held back a moment before starting her team behind Caroline.

Into the night, the company trekked; their women followed at some distance behind them.

It was nearing noon the next day when the company approached Gunter Shoals, a village of Quakers. They stopped for water and rest while Major Franklin went to look for the village elder. Several of the Quaker women brought out fresh bread for the company.

A sergeant came back to the women's area and doled out some of the bread. In less than an hour, the company moved on southward toward Monck's Corner, South Carolina.

CHAPTER EIGHT

THE CALL OF THE WHIPPOORWILL

Major Franklin chose the sandy terrain of the High Hills of Santee for their first camp. The new recruits, all at home in the backwoods of their colony, set up camp quickly.

Caroline saw Sarah coming from the river with water for her team. "Sarah, there's a woman in our group whose husband is the sergeant who gave us some bread back in Gunter Shoals. She's invited the women to her wagon. Her name is Vivian, and she's followed her husband since '77."

"I heard some women at the river talking about her. It seems her husband was in Washington's army that winter at Valley Forge," Sarah said.

Vivian was giving instructions when Caroline and Sarah arrived at her wagon. ". . . For you ladies who don't have the utensils or provisions for cooking, you'll be able to sign up to do work like washing, mending, and cooking for the soldiers in exchange for your own food."

She talked on for a while and answered a few questions until the sun began to set. "If any of you think of a question you'd like to ask me, I'm never far from my wagon. And you're free to call on my son, Edward, for any chores you might have. He's twelve, but stout for his age. We're likely to get more rules from General Isaac Huger when we get to Monck's Corner. Not likely to be much more than to tell us to stay out of their business—you know how men are" A ripple of laughter passed through the group of women, prompting Vivian to grin.

"One more thing, ladies, before you go," Vivian said, raising her voice, "My man's given name is Reuben, but he answers to 'sergeant' as well. He's here to help us, so don't be afraid of him. He makes a lot of noise sometimes, but he's really a gentle soul." She paused and said with a grin, "But don't any of you tell him I said that. . . .

This brought hoots and more laughter from the women. "Well, good night, ladies. Get your rest, we'll be moving out early I imagine."

Vivian was right. Major Franklin led the men out early, much before daylight and except for stopping for two rest breaks, the company pushed on until they arrived at Lynch's Ferry on the Santee River.

Franklin decided to make camp there on the east side of the river and reach Biggin Bridge near Monck's Corner by mid-afternoon the next day.

⸻ ⸻ ⸻

Brigadier General Huger, himself, welcomed Major Franklin's recruits. By nightfall, the new company was assimilated into the camp with their women joining the women's camp already set up. By the end of the week, the soldiers had settled into a routine and Gideon was able to visit Sarah in the evenings when he was free. Most of the time, he brought some food from the cook tent.

Sitting before the fire cross-legged, Gideon said, "The talk around camp is Clinton is pounding Charles Town hard. I hope my family is all right. They should be on their way to Fairview Plantation, my uncle's home, for his wedding. It's on the peninsula neck just north of the city."

"Maybe your uncle will protect them." Sarah looked up at him. "Isn't he a redcoat officer or something?"

"Hmph, I don't know much about him, except he hates Pa."

"The Biggin Bridge is very important to General Lincoln. Nearly all the men and supplies from the interior come down the Cooper River to Charles Town." Gideon looked at her wrinkled brow. "Major Franklin says if we lose the bridge, Lincoln will be cut off with no line of communication in or out of Charles Town."

Sarah studied her husband's words. "Then the British must have Monck's Corner in order to capture Charles Town." She watched his face while he stared at the light cast by the flames that twisted and curled in cryptic shapes along the sides of the wagons.

Minutes passed until she broke the silence. "Oh Gideon, we must hold on to the bridge. Charles Town can't survive without food, supplies, and ammunition. General Huger needs more men. Does he feel we'll be attacked?"

———

"I don't know the answer to that, but what I do know is this. If we *are* attacked, you stay put," he said, giving her a serious look. "Get under your wagon and stay there. It'll be like a calamitous storm, loud and frightening. If something should happen to me, I want you to—"

Touching her finger to his lips, she said, "Shhh, nothing's going to happen to you. Now kiss me before you leave."

He kissed her several times, and they hugged each other tightly. He said, "I have charge of the pickets tonight beginning at midnight, but I'll be on the south side near the bridge. I'll try to see you tomorrow about this time."

She watched him jump the rope that separated the women's camp from the main camp. Then she began tidying up her area before turning in. Afterwards, staring out the back of her wagon, she lay still while dusk gathered and listened to the whippoorwill's haunting, insistent call. Startled, Sarah sat upright. She remembered one of her grandmother's superstitious sayings about the call of a whippoorwill. *If a whippoorwill sings near a house, it is a sign of impending death!*

A cold shudder passed through her, and she pressed her hands tightly over her ears to silence the nerve-wracking birdsong. *I must stop this! I'm not superstitious; I've heard the whippoorwill's call all my life without anyone near me dying. Besides, this wagon is not a house!*

The sounds of the women's camp grew faint and fainter, until quiet settled over the area. Sarah didn't know when she fell asleep. Her breathing became regular, and the evening became still.

The predawn stillness covered the camp. Gideon smothered a yawn. *This would be a perfect morning for the British to hit us . . . why did I allow Sarah to come? Tomorrow, she goes home; I'll—*

An unnatural sound reached his ears, but before his hand could reach his gun, he was overrun by a thundering line of charging, yelling, swearing, and shouting horsemen. Directly in their path, Gideon was knocked unconscious in the first wave of the charge.

During the time he lay crumpled on the ground, the redcoats had rushed straight at the sleeping Americans. Pandemonium reigned for only a short time as the British immediately sent the Americans into a rout. Gideon and most of his company were herded to the edge of the swamp while the British rounded up nearly two hundred much needed horses, half of which were trained cavalry mounts. By the time the shadowy edge of dawn appeared, Tarleton and his officers had control of the area. Tarleton quickly left the area astride one of the prized cavalry mounts captured. A third of his infantry would remain to hold the bridge until Charles Town was defeated.

Left to themselves, the dispirited women had looked on from some distance away in horror as their men were overwhelmed by the attack. In the midst of the fighting, Sarah had done as Gideon told her. She had lain still under her wagon; her fingers gripped her pistol tightly. She couldn't see much, but from her relative safety, she could hear the booming of the muskets and rifles mixed with the calamitous shouting. Finally, she buried her head in her arms, squeezed her eyes shut, and prayed for Gideon and the rest of his company.

In the midst of the shouting and gunshots, there came the anguished cries of wounded men. Sarah heard movement behind her and someone whispered her name. "Sarah . . . where are you? It's me—Caroline. Help me with Ethan, he's been wounded."

Twisting around, Sarah saw the shadowy outline of her friend. She couldn't see enough of her face, but her voice sounded strangled, desperate in the dark.

"I'm right here under the wagon, where's Ethan?" Sarah said, hoping to keep her voice steady.

Caroline tugged anxiously at her arm. "In our wagon, I was able to help him get in, but now he's unconscious."

The two women crawled across the ground toward Caroline's wagon and through the acrid smell of smoke that hovered in the air over their heads. Sarah's eyes burned from the stinging smoke, but she could make out Ethan's form. He was barely in the wagon with his feet extending past the gate. Sarah bent over him and studied his face. "Ethan," she whispered. "Can you hear me? It's Sarah. Can you open your eyes?"

Ethan didn't respond.

Caroline was pressed against her shoulder. Sarah touched her friend's shaking hand and said, "We'll have to risk a candle, so we can tell where he's been wounded."

Caroline fumbled for the flint she carried in her apron and lit a candle. Sarah reached for Ethan's muslin shirt and began unbuttoning it. "Hold the candle over him, and I'll see if I can find where he's hurt."

Caroline held the lamp high, and when Sarah had opened the blood-soaked shirt, she swallowed hard and breathed, "He's been hit in his chest—"

Suddenly, deadly musket balls ripped the muslin canopy. Sarah heard the angry whistling lead missiles whizzing past her ears like angry wasps. The candle fell to Ethan's chest and smoldered on his bloody wet shirt a moment before it went out. At the same time, Sarah felt Caroline's full weight fall on her back.

Turning, she was able to get her arms around Caroline and lay her against the side of the wagon. "Caroline! Say something, what's wrong?"

There, as the dimness of dawn approached, Sarah pressed her fingers on Caroline's neck. She felt no pulse, and her fingers came away wet. Sarah fell back and let out a blood curdling primal scream of agony. Her body shook and trembled, as she sobbed with uncontrollable emotion.

Some time passed before Sarah's emotions ebbed. A solemn stillness hung over the camp and in the dawn's light, Sarah's heart stirred. There was no noise of battle, no gunfire, and no screams of pain. Faint morning light touched Caroline's face, and Sarah saw a dark, ugly hole just under her friend's left eye.

Caroline, who had become like a sister to her, was dead. Sarah sat there wistfully, staring out the front of the wagon for a while, before sighing and looking back at Ethan. She could see he was still breathing, if only barely. His bleeding had subsided, so she went back to examining him further. Seeing no other wounds, Sarah went to find Vivian to help her with dressing his wound and burying Caroline.

Sarah stumbled over the uneven ground and found Vivian at the river's edge cleaning pans that had been used for dressing wounds. When Vivian saw Sarah, she said, "Well Sarah, my man and yours will soon be on their way to some British prison. Of course, as bad as that is, they're alive, and there's some with us who lost their men this morning."

Looking at Sarah's stunned expression, Vivian asked, "Are you all right? Sit down here and let me look at you."

Stumbling for words, Sarah said, "—can't sit down just yet, Vivian—it's Ethan Bridger; he's wounded in the chest . . . it looks bad. The bleeding's stopped, but I can't turn him to clean and bandage the wound."

Then Sarah's chin quivered, and her eyes spilled warm tears down her face. She struggled to say what she knew she must. "And Caroline's dead—shot—w-while we were tending her husband."

Vivian's face whitened. "Let's go, Sarah. No need for you to hold it in now, if tears come, let them fall. I know the two of you were close."

On the way, Vivian stopped at her wagon to pick up more cloth. Sarah suddenly realized how disoriented her mind had been since the battled started. She'd been in a muddled daze and hadn't been able to focus on Gideon's plight.

As Vivian climbed down from her wagon, Sarah said, "Tell me what you know of Gideon. Did you see him this morning? Did he say anything? Was he wounded?"

Vivian pulled Sarah along in the direction of the Bridger wagon. "Whoa now girl, slow down, and I'll tell you what I saw. First off, I saw the redcoats rounding up a bunch of our men, and I saw my man—he gave me a sign that he was all right," she said, "He even threw me a kiss, and that's not like that man at all. About that time, your Gideon was at my husband's side and shouted for me to tell you he was all right and to wait for him at home."

Sarah let out a big sigh. "Do you have any idea where they'll be taken, Vivian?"

"No, I don't, but it doesn't matter much, dear." She responded, shrugging her shoulders. "Prisoners on both sides of this war don't fare so well, but my man's a tough old rooster and Gideon strikes me as a man that can take care of himself. We'll just have to pray that they'll survive and come home again."

Sarah had to force herself to climb back in the Bridger's wagon. Vivian first looked at Ethan, and her shoulders sagged. Looking at Sarah, she shook her head.

Vivian whispered, "It doesn't look good Sarah. He's been shot awfully close to his heart. He looks to be in the throes of dying. I've seen more of these wounds than I care to recollect, but we'll clean him up and bind his wound anyhow. We'll know, one way or the other, before the day's gone."

Ethan's breath came in short, ragged gasps, and the women got the job done. Vivian then turned her attention to Caroline.

With her thumbs, she delicately closed Caroline's eyelids and said, "At least, she didn't suffer."

Fatigue had settled on Sarah's shoulders, almost crushing her. *Caroline is dead, and it could've been me. We were only inches apart; I heard the bullet that killed her whistle past my ear. How could it have missed me, yet killed her?*

Ethan died without waking, and he was buried alongside his wife. A spot under a giant red oak was chosen, away from where the carnage had taken place. The women identified each of the men killed and buried them near Ethan and Caroline. They stayed in camp another day before heading back north to their homes around the Camden area.

Vivian was the obvious one to be in charge of their little wagon train. The first night around the campfire, she spoke to the group. "Ladies, I need to know what firearms we have amongst us. Let's see a show of hands for ones with long rifles."

Most of the women raised their hands. "I assume you with rifles have sufficient powder and round balls in case we have trouble."

The women all nodded.

"How about pistols?" Vivian asked. "How many of you carry one?"

Almost half raised their hands.

Finally, Vivian said, "We'll be pulling out around daybreak, so make sure you've got everything packed and ready for travel. I, for one, am anxious to get away from the stench of those red coated devils down by the bridge."

Surrounded by the soft whisper of rippling water and repetitious throating of frogs accompanied with chirping crickets, the women slept fitfully, while around them in all directions, near and far, were turmoil and bloodshed. Morning came with threatening clouds. It looked like their first day on the road would be wet and muddy. Two of the women who'd followed their husbands on foot would be taking the Bridger wagon home.

After a cold breakfast, they were on their way. All of them left something of themselves at Monck's Corner that morning. More than a few looked toward the ancient red oak with so many fresh mounds under its canopy.

Sarah trudged along beside her lead ox, reliving the last moments with Gideon. She wanted to keep that memory alive. *How could this have happened? I don't want to go home; I want to go to Charles Town and find where they're holding Gideon.*

By mid-afternoon, Vivian figured they had come about ten miles. "We'll make the High Hills of the Santee by evening and camp near the river."

That evening, Sarah cooked the last of the bacon. "We should be close to James Mackenzie's store. I seem to recollect it being near the Santee River."

She looked over at Vivian. "We ought to get there by tomorrow afternoon. Don't you agree?"

Vivian nodded as she hobbled the front legs of the oxen. Standing, she said, "We can stay a day at Mackenzie's and get ourselves some hot baths, even sleep on real beds if we want."

CHAPTER NINE

RUN FOR YOUR LIFE

It was dusk when the women pulled up in front of the store. A portly, balding middle-aged man came out to greet them. "Hello and welcome, good people, I'm James Mackenzie, owner of this establishment. Come in and rest a while. If you're hungry, my wife offers a repast suitable for King George himself." He chuckled so hard his belly shook.

Vivian extended her hand toward Mackenzie. "I'm Vivian Sanderson from Camden, Mr. Mackenzie. These ladies and I are headed home to Kershaw County. Our men were overrun at Monck's Corner just two days past. Some of the ladies lost their loved ones in the skirmish, but many of the other men were taken as prisoners."

Mackenzie nodded and removed his hat. "For each of you brave ladies, I offer my sincere condolences. You all are welcome to come in and have your meal on the house."

Inside, James's wife met them and escorted them to a back room away from the tavern. Seated at one of the tables were three British soldiers, all showing the rank of sergeant. Their conversation ebbed as each of them noticed the women taking their seats on the other side of the room, but it was Vivian's son, Edward, who came under their particular scrutiny.

After a few minutes of boisterous talk among themselves, one of the soldiers slid his chair back, the legs scraping loudly on the floor. His heavy boots sounded on the wooden floor. He stopped beside the table where Edward sat with his mother, Vivian.

"Stand, you rebellious cur. You dare come near members of his majesty's 63rd Regiment of Foot, showing your rebel's coat of armor?"

The sergeant smelled of sweat and tobacco. His breath reeked of old ale. Trying not to breathe deeply, the young boy answered, showing no fear in his voice. "I wear no coat of armor. This hunting shirt is common dress for men of South Carolina, from Charles Town to beyond the Blue Ridge Mountains."

Anger spread over the sergeant's face like a coming flash storm. "Your own congress established the fringed hunting shirt as a symbolic garment not only for American liberty, but as a garment worn in outward defiance against the crown." Turning to his comrades, he said loudly, "We've bloodied the likes of this rebel aplenty, haven't we lads?"

The other redcoats cried in unison, "Aye that we have!"

His eyes fixed on the boy, he said gruffly, "I'm taking you prisoner, and if you're found to be a rebel spy, it'll be the gallows for you, lad."

Vivian screamed, "Can't you see he's but a boy? He's done nothing against your king. Only two days past, he watched as his father was taken prisoner at Monck's Corner. I beg you— don't take my son."

Mackenzie made his way to where the sergeant stood. "See here now, Sergeant Campbell. Surely, you don't—"

Spinning around and pointing his finger angrily at Mackenzie, Campbell said, "Do you really want to interfere, innkeeper? It would be a feather in our caps to bring you in for aiding and abetting a rebel. Now stand away or we'll take you along, too."

Campbell turned and thrust the boy toward the others. "Finish your ale. Then take him outside and bind him, we're leaving."

Vivian held the arm of the soldier and pleaded, "Let me speak to my son before you take him away. Surely, you can grant that to his mother."

The sergeant jerked his arm from her grasp. "Hold on. His mother wants a word with him." Turning to the Vivian, he growled, "Hurry on now, woman. Be brief."

Vivian pulled her son aside away from the group of soldiers, and she held him close. Hugging him to her, she whispered in his ear. "Listen carefully, Edward. You must save yourself by running. I can't save you. Before I release you, we'll take a step or two toward the door. When I say the word '*now*', you run as fast as you possibly can for the river, and head north to Indian Town. We'll meet up there."

Edward looked into his mother's eyes and whispered, "They won't catch me Ma; they're too fat."

She held his face in her hands and looked at him tenderly. "Your Pa tells everybody that you run like the wind; that's what you must do today." She hugged him again and they eased toward the door.

The sergeant, drinking the last of his ale, saw them moving and shouted. "Hold on there!" He stumbled toward them, spilling his drink on himself.

"Now!" Vivian cried, giving her son a push toward the door. Edward plunged out the door and ran headlong toward the river. The three soldiers lumbered out the door after him, but after a brief chase, gave up.

Edward ran toward the Santee River. Once he was across the road from the inn, he came to a well-worn trail that led straight to the river's edge, but he flung himself headlong into the tangled undergrowth that grew along the untamed riverbanks of South Carolina. He ran and ran until his lungs burned, his knees wobbled, and he felt he was going to faint. He ran until he fell and couldn't take another step. His chest heaved, as he took in short, quick gulps of sweet fresh air. Young Edward lay on the lush grassy river bottom ground; his heart pounding. He listened for any noise, any movement. His ears picked up the breeze wafting through the tops of the trees. He picked himself up and brushed his pants with his hands; he knew he'd escaped the red-coated devils.

—◆◇◆— —◆◇◆— —◆◇◆—

Red-faced and panting for breath, the soldiers lurched back inside, shoving Mackenzie aside.

"Well, the little nit got away." He grabbed Vivian roughly by her arm. "You madam, just committed a treasonous act. It'll be the gallows for you or prison for the rest of your miserable life."

His bloodshot eyes scanned the women at the other tables. "Now, everybody stay calm while we take our leave. This woman will—"

Hearing an ominous click, the sergeant's face lost its color. His eyes darted to his men, but they had already raised their hands and were staring past him at whomever was behind him with the musket.

With his rifle at the ready, Mackenzie said crisply, "Loose the lady."

The sergeant spun around, dragging Vivian with him. Holding her as a shield, he said, "You'll hang for this Mackenzie, just for threatening one of his majesty's finest. Now put your rifle down and stand aside."

Mackenzie stepped to stand in the doorway. "You don't understand, sergeant. You've bullied your last victim. Shortly, you and your companions will be on your way to one of our hospitable prisons. The war's over for the three of you."

The sergeant's face twitched as his eyes darted around the room. He heard the rustling of skirts and turned in time to see Sarah and the others come to their feet with their pistols drawn.

A smile etched its way across Mackenzie's face. "Thank you ladies, my wife should be here any moment now. She left after you all first came in to get help from friends who live nearby. "

⊷•◍•⊶ ⊷•◍•⊶ ⊷•◍•⊶

Gideon was surprised to find he wasn't wounded. He'd just come off picket duty and was walking to the small tent he shared with the major's aide when the attack begun. It seemed like only seconds from the first musket blasts and screams of the attackers until he was lying on the ground without his musket. Vaguely, he recalled being knocked to the ground and trampled on by many feet, but he couldn't be sure because he'd lost consciousness soon after he fell. That fall saved his life, since the attackers thought he was dead or dying.

He was looking around for his musket when he heard a rough voice. "Stand where you are, Rebel, and put your hands on your head."

Two redcoats jumped toward him with their bayonets to the front. Gideon's eyes were riveted on the bayonets and he stood very still with his hands on his head before they reached him.

Gideon was taken to a roped off area where several other of his men were milling around under the close watch of several redcoats. He found Reuben, his sergeant, sitting down cross-legged, Indian style, with a few of the Camden recruits. Gideon eased down near the sergeant who was whispering to the recruits.

Reuben noticed Gideon and leaned toward him. "Come closer, Captain. Some of us want to make a run for it, what do you think?"

Gideon looked around at his friends. In their faces, he saw grit and determination, and a refusal to accept defeat. These men had already decided if they were to die, they would rather it be on the field of battle than in some British death camp.

"I think we'll have a better chance of surviving this war if we do make a run for it, sergeant. How far along are you with a plan?"

The sergeant shook his head. "We'd just started talking when you found us. How do you think we can pull it off?"

Gideon felt the stares of the men. They weren't defeated, they weren't ready to quit, and they certainly weren't going willingly to one of the prison ships to die a slow death. These men were ready to follow Gideon; all he had to do was say the word.

A guard, his face black with powder and dirt, pushed his bayoneted musket towards the group. "Let's break it up; you look like you're up to something."

The men grumbled, but began to split into smaller groups. Gideon grabbed Reuben's arm and motioned for him to follow him.

In a spot away from the others, Gideon and Reuben worked out the plan. Speaking in a whisper, Gideon said, "I think most of the men can make it to the swamp from here. We'll have a better chance once we're in the swamp, and from there we should be able to shake the redcoats. Once on the other side, we're home free. Those that make it will meet up on the north bank of the Santee at Murry's Ferry."

Pausing, Gideon said, "What do you think, Sergeant?"

Nodding, Reuben said, "I'm in. When do we go, and what'll be our signal to make our move?"

Gideon leaned in closer. "Since the odds won't be getting any better than they are now, I'm for running before we begin the march to Charles Town. The enemy's a bit disorganized at the moment with gathering up their prize horses and extra gunpowder. Only a small number is watching us, so let's pass the word around to jump the guards and start running for the trees. The signal to make our move will be when you see me jump yon guard."

Reuben nodded. "Let's get the word around. You start that way and I'll go this way. When we meet up, we'll be watching for your move."

"All right," said Gideon, "Tell the men to give it everything they've got, and if God wills, we'll all meet at Murry's Ferry."

The men slowly made their way around to their fellow prisoners, whispering the instructions to their compatriots.

Gideon spied a guard near him and eased closer. His hand went to his belt for his knife, but came up empty.

Already on edge, the guard suddenly thrust his bayonet toward Gideon. "Back away, you scum or I'll run you through!" Swinging his musket around, he yelled, "And that goes for all of you stinking rebels. Keep your distance; I'll not be saying it again."

Gideon could tell by the expressions on their faces that most of the men had made up their minds to run. Every man was poised to take out a guard when Gideon made his move.

Gideon was mentally ready; he gauged the distance between him and the nearest guard. It was now or never. Rubbing the stubble on his chin, he leaped toward the nearest guard, throwing him to the ground.

Almost simultaneously, the men made their moves on the guards. Gideon found himself in a fray with the help of two of his fellow patriots as they quickly overpowered their man. Grabbing the socket of the bayonet, Gideon twisted and pulled it from the barrel end of the musket. With little wasted movement, he plunged the seventeen inch blade into the soldier's chest just above the cross belt.

With his foot on the redcoat's chest, Gideon jerked the bayonet free. What seemed like long minutes had only taken a few seconds. Without speaking, the three patriots began running for the trees.

There was only the faint pre-dawn light to guide them over the unfamiliar ground, but the prisoners ran headlong for their lives. In later years, these men would remember this morning when they ran for their lives.

Then Gideon could see the stand of trees drawing nearer. Behind him, he heard someone yell, "The prisoners are escaping! Muskets to the ready!"

Intent on reaching the woods, Gideon hadn't looked around to see how many of his friends were also running. The tree line was getting closer when the booming crash of a volley sent a barrage of deadly musket balls toward the runners. He heard someone cry out, but he couldn't afford to stop. Another loud volley of lead was shot, this time in his direction. Gideon flinched when the whistling missiles came whizzing by, but he was almost at the trees, and he knew he would make the swamp before the soldiers reloaded.

CHAPTER TEN

TRAVELING IN HARM'S WAY

John Hamilton eased his horse around a fallen tree and gently urged his gelding to step away from the edge of the woods. Away from the shadow of the trees, he spied a red tail hawk soaring effortlessly before gently settling down to perch high in a majestic loblolly pine.

Suddenly, his horse raised his head and snapped his ears forward, and the muscles in his neck tightened. John tugged his hat down tight on his head and pulled up, then leaned forward to stroke his mount's withers. His right hand rested on the well-polished handle of his flintlock pistol while his eyes swept the carefully tilled fields and grassy pastureland that ran to the sparkling clear water's edge.

Whispering, John said, "I see'em, boy."

Across the creek, three men were standing by their horses and watching him. He nudged his horse to back away into the shadows. He studied the three men as they led their horses to the water's edge. Their eyes never left him as their horses drank their fill.

This looked to be the first of many British patrols he and his family would encounter on their way to Charles Town, but this lonely stretch was also known as a favorite of roadside bandits. John was taking the measure of them when Daniel eased his black mare beside him.

"What is it, Pa?" he whispered.

Without turning his head, John replied, "Straight yonder are three men watering their mounts. They've already seen us. How far back are your mother and sister?"

Staring across the creek toward the three men, Daniel said, "Not far. We should hear the wagon any moment."

John figured the creek was about one hundred yards away, and it would be no more than twenty feet to the other side of the creek where the men stood with their horses. From this distance, he could recognize nothing about the men or their horses.

The noisy wagon, carrying Rachel and Lottie, came to a stop behind them.

Rachel, called out, "What's the matter, John? Why've we stopped?"

He twisted in the saddle and looked back to see her standing in the wagon. Rachel had wrapped the reins around the brake lever and was standing with her flintlock rifle at the ready. Her piercing brown eyes met his with a questioning look.

"I see three men across yon creek. Fetch the spyglass, and see if you recognize'em. Your eyes are better than mine," John said.

She opened a box under the seat and took out a leather pouch. From it, she removed a brass spyglass. Rachel telescoped the brass tube out to its full length and studied the open field beyond her husband. Grunting, she wiped the front and rear lenses with one of her sleeves and looked again.

"Well, do we know'em or not?" John asked, with a hint of impatience.

"They're loyalist militia—wearing their green regimental coats," she said, offering the spyglass to her husband. "I've never seen them before."

Shaking his head, John said, "I don't need to look. If you don't recognize'em; they're sure to be strangers to me."

Rachel put the glass to her eye once more and peered through the brass tube. She was about to put it away when movement in the shadows of the tree line behind the riders caught her eye.

"Wait—another is hanging back at the edge of the trees. He must be talking to the three watering their horses, because they've turned to face him."

Steadying the glass, she followed their movements. "Now, they're mounting their horses and—he has a glass on us, John—aimed right at us!"

John had moved nearer the wagon. "Give me the glass. Quickly!"

He snatched the spyglass from her hand and hastily tried to find the men. Peering through the eyepiece, he saw the glint of sun from the observer's glass now aimed at them.

"Redcoat dragoon," John muttered under his breath, focusing on the figure clad in the scarlet uniform jacket and leather boots. He heard Rachel sigh heavily.

"I'm wondering why His Majesty's intrepid agent is reluctant to show himself?" he said, aloud.

Rachel pulled her coat tighter around herself. Her chill came more from the emptiness in her heart than from the wind. She recalled the afternoon she'd received a personal letter from British Major General John Burgoyne telling her of her older brother's death and his brave and gallant service for the crown at the Battle of Saratoga.

Some of her feelings of grief, she knew, came from the division within her family over her deep feelings that the colonies should be separate and independent from their mother country. Roger, her older brother by eighteen months, had been a major in the British cavalry. He'd always supported her in what he lovingly called *your misguided heart.* It had been his belief that, someday, she would give up the notion of the colonies' independence.

Sighing softly, thoughts of her younger brother Thomas brought no warmth to her chilled heart. Thomas, a colonel in the British Infantry, was the opposite of his older brother. Even as children, Rachel remembered Thomas as a skulking and sneaky boy who, as he grew to manhood, bore enduring grudges. Adding to her sorrow was his refusal to accept her husband, John, as a member of the family.

Now, with the war in its fifth year, an intuitive sense of impending disaster had stolen any joy she might have felt on this special visit with her brother and friends.

John nudged her shoulder. "You're thinking much too deeply, dear. Do you have our passes?"

Her lips drawn thin in a tight frown, Rachel responded, "Yes, they're in my handbag. Now, we're losing daylight just staring at one another, John. If you'll lead the way, we can ford the creek and soon be on our way."

John folded the glass and returned it to his wife. "Let's keep our wits about us then, we must be convincing. Nowadays, with Cornwallis about to take Charles Town, it doesn't take much to rile these heathen intruders. If you can manage it, your pretty smile will be enough to get us along our way."

Rachel shot her husband a sidewise look. "Nay, I've no mirth in my heart for neither this red-coated devil nor the cowardly Tories who side with him."

John looked at his wife and daughter. In addition to their long rifles, each of them carried a pistol sheathed in a scabbard held by a shoulder sling. John and his son each carried long rifles and pistols in scabbards hanging from the pommels of their saddles.

Prodding his horse forward, John rode into the shallow water. Daniel followed at his side. Rachel snapped the reins, and the wagon clattered across the rocky shoals of the creek.

John studied the men with carefully disguised interest. The red-coated officer rode a dapple-gray horse. Atop his head, he wore a brass helmet with his regimental death's head insignia with the motto '*Or Glory*' in white metal. He noticed the fringed epaulette on his left shoulder to be the rank of Lieutenant. The man's right hand was near the grip of his sword, which remained sheathed in its brass and black leather scabbard.

British Seventeenth Regiment of Light Dragoons! John's throat tightened. *What's an officer of the only British cavalry regiment in America doing so far from Charles Town?*

John's eyes scanned the area. If this officer was with the infamous 'Tarleton's Raiders', that meant Cornwallis would not be far away. This would be bad news for Camden and the surrounding backcountry.

His eyes finally settled on the militiamen. Dressed in well-fitted buckskins and moccasins, they looked to be Overmountain men from beyond the Blue Ridge. The nearest of the three watched them with black, soulless eyes. John knew if there were any threat to come from these three, it would first come from this man.

Suddenly, a shock went through John. *I know this man! It's Wesley Morton!* Wesley was a renegade, who was suspected of inciting the Cherokees to attack isolated settlers across the Blue Ridge Mountains. He'd been run out of Camden awhile back.

Maybe he won't remember me.

John and his family were met by the lieutenant after they were across. A tense silence stretched between them until the lieutenant spoke. With a conceited tone of command in his voice, he said, "State your name and your business on this road."

Speaking evenly and deliberately, without looking at Wesley, John answered, "I'm John Hamilton, and these people are my family. We've just come from Camden on the Wateree River, and are on our way to Charles Town to visit my wife's brother.

The lieutenant's eyes narrowed while he studied John's answer. "You're not aware that Charles Town is under siege? You can't just saunter in as if you're on an afternoon Sunday drive. Moreover, by the time you get there, the city may be sealed against civilian traffic."

Momentarily, his attention turned to Rachel. "And you madam, what is the loyalty of you and your family in Charles Town?"

Rachel looked directly toward the officer and said haughtily, "To our king, of course. My oldest brother lost his life during the battle of Saratoga serving with General Burgoyne, and my younger brother, a Colonel, is serving with the 64th Regiment of Foot."

John smiled inwardly; his wife's imperious manner was actually her way of mocking the snobbishness of her British heritage. After all these years of living on the western frontier of South Carolina, she could, in the blink of an eye, still speak with the inflection and tone of the British gentry.

The lieutenant's manner relaxed enough that John could see he was considering letting them pass.

Before the officer could reply, John saw Wesley's eyes widen.

He recognizes me!

John hesitated, and Wesley prodded his horse forward, slamming into John's mount. John's horse snorted loudly, lunged with his teeth bared, and sunk them deep into Wesley's leg, just above his knee. Crying out in pain, the man fell from his horse and sprawled on his back.

While the British officer struggled to calm his own skittish horse, John had cocked pistols in either hand. Motioning with his head, John said to the officer, "Step down and lay your sword on the ground."

Staring hard at John, the officer dismounted and lay his sword down.

John's eyes darted in the direction of the remaining riders, and he said gruffly, "You two stand beside your man and keep your hands in view."

Visibly upset at the turn of events, the lieutenant said, "You sir, have taken matters to the extreme. Holding one of his majesty's officers at gunpoint is a hanging offense. Have you forgotten a state of war exists between the crown and the colonies?"

Red-faced, John came back, "How can I forget when I'm accosted by the likes of you when I'm traveling with my family to visit her relatives? Your man drove his horse into mine, and he now suffers the consequences. My horse was only defending himself."

The lieutenant dismissed the incident with a wave of his hand. "It happened as you say, sir, but nowadays, the countryside is full of traitors. If you are whom you say, you shall receive no further mistreatment from us, you have my guarantee. Now, please lower your weapons. My man on the ground seems to be unconscious. When he awakes, he will find himself under arrest."

John shook his head, no. "I trust you would take care of the matter properly, sir, but I'll keep my pistols in hand until I and my family are safely on our way. Now, I see no further business for us here, so we must take our leave."

Before John could leave, Wesley came up on one elbow. His eyes full of hate, he pointed to John. "He's a rebel—a militia leader—there's a reward on him."

John nudged his horse to back away; his pistols steady on the group of men. "Well, I see the game is up." His eyes directed at the officer, John said, "How shall we resolve this?"

The lieutenant's face was contorted in anger. "You're under arrest! Step down in the name of the crown and surrender your weapons! I—"

John couldn't prevent the contemptuous tone of his voice. "You have no authority nor does your king to arrest any American. As you so kindly reminded me, a state of war exists between our countries. As a militiaman, I can shoot you all here and now and likely receive a commendation. However, I believe it would be more fitting to place you in one of our hospitable prisons to rot for the duration."

To his family, John said, "We'll secure them to their mounts and turn them over to James Mackenzie."

Rachel reached for her husband's arm. "Can't we just bind them to a tree? I'm afraid they'll overpower us on the way."

Leaning from his saddle, John kissed Rachel. "Nay, we'll get these ne'er-do-wells to their new lodgings. You and Lottie hold them at bay, while Daniel and I bind them."

Daniel fetched a length of rope from the wagon, and then he and his father bound the men hand and foot and lay each man across his saddle like sacks of grain.

The family was soon on its way, leading the men's horses. It was after midnight when they reached Mackenzie's store.

John noticed several wagons and the animals hobbled as he rode up.

Turning to his family, he said, "Wait here while I awaken Mackenzie. It looks as though he might be full up."

It took several minutes to rouse the innkeeper, and while they were waiting, Daniel noticed Sarah's wagon. "Ma, I believe Sarah's here. I see her wagon—"

Rachel jumped down and followed Daniel to the wagons. "Oh! I think it is son. Something has happened to Gideon or she wouldn't be here."

Throwing the back cover aside, Rachel peered into the dark interior, but couldn't see anything. A touch of worry edged into her voice. Speaking plainly, she said, "Sarah, are you in there? Can you hear me, this is Rachel."

From the darkness, they heard Sarah's voice, thick with sleep. "Is that really you Mama Rachel?" A moment passed before Sarah found her shoes and cape. In the midst of the hugs and tears, she told them of the fight at Monck's Corner.

"Gideon wasn't hurt Mama Rachel, but they took him prisoner with a lot of others. I'm told prisoners are mistreated so badly that most of them die there."

Rachel swallowed past the painful lump in her throat, but words wouldn't form on her lips. She took Sarah in her arms and held her close.

When John saw his wife and daughter-in-law weeping, he anxiously asked, "Did something happen to Gideon?"

Sarah looked at him with heartache in her eyes. "Gideon has been taken prisoner, Papa."

Letting go of a long sigh, John hung his head and stood quietly by the women.

After some minutes passed, Lottie whispered, "Where's Caroline's wagon, Sarah? Is Ethan also a prisoner?"

A sob escaped Sarah's throat. Her knees began to buckle; she became limp and sagged toward the ground. Her arms fell to her sides. Vivian came hurrying around the wagon and tried to catch her before she collapsed, but Daniel had already grabbed her arms to keep her from falling. Sarah dropped her head and leaned heavily on her brother-in-law.

Vivian held Sarah's opposite arm and said, "Folks, I'm Vivian Sanderson. My husband was one of the men captured. The Bridger couple was killed in the battle. For about an hour, there was absolute bedlam around that bridge. Early in the fighting, young Ethan was mortally wounded."

Vivian, visibly bothered by recalling this story, paused to clear her throat. "He was able to get over to our camp where Caroline helped him in their wagon before he lost consciousness. Sarah went to help Caroline, and they had just started to see about Ethan, when their wagon was hit by a barrage of musket fire. I counted eight holes in the cover; I don't know how Sarah was missed, but Caroline was killed instantly and fell across Sarah's back. She's plagued with guilt; I've seen it before. Sarah can't understand why she's alive, and her friend is not."

⸺◦◦◦⸺ ⸺◦◦◦⸺ ⸺◦◦◦⸺

John and Mackenzie went to retrieve the prisoners. Even in the dim light, John saw right away that one of them was missing. A quick inspection told him what he first suspected. The missing captive was Wesley Morton.

"I should've double checked his bonds. Wesley's one hard man to hold," John said, ruefully.

Snatching one of the remaining captives from his horse, Mackenzie said, "You had Wesley Morton in this bunch? Few people can say they got the jump on that wily rascal."

Standing off to the side with his rifle at the ready, Daniel said, "Actually it was Pa's horse that gets the credit. He nearly bit Wesley's leg off."

"You don't say," Mackenzie guffawed.

The men herded the prisoners around to the rear of the inn where they were left in the cellar.

John stopped the officer before thrusting him in the cellar. "Are you carrying any correspondence?"

With disgrace written across his face, the lieutenant responded, "Nay, my men and I were simply on patrol."

John looked at him with contempt. "You're lying. Why would you have hidden yourself back at the Wateree River unless you were a courier? Where's your regiment?"

The officer returned John's stare. Suddenly John grabbed him by his coat and threw him to the ground. With his hands bound, the young officer fell heavily. John quickly searched his coat pockets. Opening his coat, he saw a letter in the woolen waistcoat pocket.

Breaking the seal, John held the parchment near Mackenzie's lamp. "I see this is addressed to his commander, General Clinton," John said with a sneer.

The officer glared at John. "'Tis only a personal letter, as you will see, between two old friends."

"I'm afraid you've been found out, sir. There's no need to continue your feeble attempt at deception. We have talented people waiting to unravel letters such as this. You've failed your king."

John shoved him into the cellar, and Mackenzie barricaded the door and stepped back. "There's no way of escape except through this door, John. No man has ever escaped from my custody; a record I'm proud of and aim to keep."

The next morning, Sarah joined her family when they continued their journey to the home of Rachel's brother Thomas. Mr. Mackenzie took charge of her wagon and would see that it was returned to Amos Boone in Camden.

Sarah was excited to be traveling toward Charles Town. "Mama Rachel, maybe Uncle Thomas can help us find out where Gideon is being held."

Rachel, her own heart heavy with anguish, took a moment to consider Sarah's question. "I can't answer that with any certainty, dear. It's been years since I last saw my brother, and you must remember he is in service to his king—a very devoted and loyal servant."

From the look in Sarah's face, Rachel knew she had to say something positive—something for Sarah to cling to. "But I do feel my brother will do what he can for us."

CHAPTER ELEVEN

MY BROTHER, MY ENEMY

Colonel Thomas Covington held back the curtain from his upstairs bedroom. At the far end of the quarter-mile drive, he watched his sister and her family approaching his home.

His eyebrows knitted tightly together, while his free hand rubbed his chin methodically. Since awakening this morning, he felt a vague angst of impending calamity.

Could it be the anticipation of my marriage to Meg? Why is she willing to marry a man who's never said the words 'I love you' to her? He mused, dropping the curtain.

He pushed his feet into his boots. *Or could the dark cloud that hovers over me be from the anticipation of having my quarrelsome sister and her rebel husband in my house?*

The corner of his mouth twisted with hatred as he came downstairs. He was dreading even the formality of greeting his estranged sister's family.

With his brother's death, Thomas had inherited Fairview plantation consisting of more than three thousand acres. Since the war, Thomas had been an absentee owner, but had been allowed leave from Savannah for his wedding to Margaret

Turnwell, the daughter of one of the prominent families in the South Carolina Low Country.

Her family behind her, Rachel watched her brother as she approached the stately mansion.

He won't even pretend, but then why should he? He wound up with everything, she thought, *he no longer has to feign his love for me . . . he can just be Thomas.*

Stiffly, Thomas cleared his throat and said, "It's good to see you, Rachel, and for all here at Fairview, I extend a hearty welcome."

"Thomas, may I present Sarah, Gideon's wife. Sarah this is Thomas, my younger brother."

When it looked as though shaking hands was as far as he would extend himself, Rachel reached up, hugged him tightly, and kissed him on his cheek.

"There were times when we were young, and sometimes quarreled, that Father would make us hug and kiss to make up," she said, with a laugh. "Do you remember those times, brother?"

Clearly ill at ease, Thomas settled his arrogant gaze on his sister. "I-I- . . ."

She grinned and could see he was taken aback as he fumbled for his composure.

"Oh, I'm afraid I've embarrassed you!" She took him by his arm. "Let's go inside. I want to see how you've changed the house."

The distant rumbling of cannons sounded like the thunder of an approaching storm. Charles Town, only a few miles distant, was only days from surrender after nearly six weeks of siege.

Galvanized by the sound of British artillery, Thomas recovered his voice. He turned to look directly at John. "Your visit comes at a significant turning point. Sir Henry Clinton has delivered his offer to accept your General Lincoln's surrender. The rebels have until midnight to reply. I'm sure, John, a man of your competence and distinction can grasp the significance of the fall of Charles Town. It will be the merciful deathblow to your rebellion. A few months of rounding up the fringe criminals will bring your insurrection to a close."

Rachel saw her husband's face reddening as anger took hold of him, and she grabbed his arm and pulled him into the house. She knew she couldn't prevent some heated debating from occurring during their stay, but it wasn't going to happen during the first few minutes of their arrival.

In a whisper, she said to John, "I thank you, husband, for your strength of character, and I know your children appreciate their father, too."

Stepping inside the entry hall, Rachel breathed deeply and her hand, involuntarily, went to her throat. This was the first time she had been home since the death of her parents. Her mother had taken ill one summer and by fall, she had died. Her father never recovered from her death and slowly wasted away. He joined his wife before winter was over.

Thomas led them into the parlor. Eight wingback chairs and two couches were arranged in the spacious room with the mantled brick fireplace as the focal point.

After everyone was seated, he stood with his back to the fireplace. "The siege of Charles Town goes on round the clock; the cannons are seldom silent. General Clinton has already landed a substantial number of men and artillery on the peninsula and is only days away from having the city completely sealed off.

"With that in mind, I must advise you that, during your stay here at Fairview, I cannot vouch for John's safety. Nonetheless, you have my sworn word; I shall not reveal your presence to my superiors during your stay. Actually, I'm afraid, John, you shouldn't have come."

John's voice was flat, but stern. "I appreciate your honesty, brother-in-law. I didn't come expecting any consideration for me, but it goes without saying, your sister and her children must be under your protection in all circumstances."

⟨∘⟩ ⟨∘⟩ ⟨∘⟩

The feelings of hostility Sarah felt being this near a British soldier were intense. It didn't matter that he was Gideon's uncle, he and his kind were the enemy. Even the smartness of his uniform sickened her, but her feelings were not important, especially if she was to help Gideon.

Sarah swallowed to ease the painful knot in her throat and joined Thomas at the fireplace, curtseying appropriately. "Uncle Thomas, do you have any knowledge of where the prisoners from Monck's Corner were taken?" she asked with as much politeness as she could muster.

His hands clasped tightly behind him; Thomas felt a bit ill at ease with Sarah standing so near. He cleared his throat and stepped back. "Word has only just reached me today of Colonel Tarleton's victory, so what I know is very sketchy."

His eyes narrowed on Sarah's face. "Was Gideon among those captured, my dear?"

She nodded expectantly. "Yes sir and I'm told he wasn't wounded."

Thomas paused a moment before he said, "That's in his favor, of course. The enemy wounded generally receives no attention from his majesty's surgeons."

Thomas stiffened when Sarah laid her fingers on his arm. "Is there any way I can see Gideon, Uncle Thomas? Or maybe, take him some clean clothes and shoes?"

Rubbing his chin, Thomas said dryly, "I shall look into it, it's sometimes allowed, but I'll first have to locate Gideon since there are three prison ships in the harbor."

Stepping over to the large window that overlooked the expansive flower garden, he turned his back to the window and cast his eyes disdainfully over his family, finally coming to rest on John.

"It seems the king's American colonies have little stomach for fighting a war, but then I may be unfair since you've only farmers and planters for leaders." He cocked an eyebrow just enough so John would know he was challenging him.

John quickly came to his feet, but Rachel was faster. "Thomas, we plan to make our stay at Fairview as brief as we possibly can. During that time, I ask only this from you: stop your taunts and insults. It's a pity brother; you don't recognize your king can't win this war. It was lost to him in '76; the United States of America was born that summer. You think a battle won here and there means you've won the war."

With her hands on her hips, she said, "Your king's now in a world war against every nation with a navy, with a very real threat of attack on the hallowed ground of England itself— French soldiers are poised to camp on your precious soil and attack your cities."

John eased by his wife to stand face to face with his brother-in-law and said, "Since your statement was meant as a challenge to me, I would like to add to my wife's inspiring words."

Returning his brother-in-law's penetrating stare, John said, "Answer me, if you can, Colonel. If the British army is so powerful and invincible, why has it taken you five years just to reach Charles Town?"

Sarah and Rachel returned to the couch. The room grew almost unbearably pin-drop silent as everyone stared at Thomas. No one spoke, and tension mounted by the minute.

Thomas stood rigidly intimidating in his bright red coat and shiny black boots. He clenched his teeth and bit back a furious retort. "Yes, well, I suppose I must defer to my sister and her husband. It seems, after fourteen years of military service, I still have much to learn."

The tension lessened, but the room remained quiet.

After some moments of awkward silence, Thomas added with a bland smile, "I'll not go with you upstairs since Rachel is already familiar with where the bedrooms are. I've taken our parents' former bedroom, and with the exception of that room, you're free to choose where you sleep."

He was about to leave, but he whirled about and said pointedly, "I've scheduled a meeting of my fellow officers here this evening, and due to time constraints, we cannot reschedule the meeting. We shall be in the parlor promptly at seven and may not finish our business until rather late. I want your word, dear sister and brother-in-law that you will remain in your room until morning."

Rachel and John both nodded and said they wouldn't leave their room until morning.

Thomas studied their faces and said, "After tonight, you may have the run of the house. I'll have the maid prepare baths for you before supper."

—◦◦◉◦◦— —◦◦◉◦◦— —◦◦◉◦◦—

It was not until they were bathed and dressed for supper that John and Rachel sat down to figure out a plan to eavesdrop on Thomas's meeting.

John slowly traced his lips with his finger while he considered the problem of getting within earshot of the parlor tonight. His eyes narrowed. "What room is above the parlor?"

"It's Thomas's bedroom. Why?" Rachel responded.

"I'll go there tonight. With my ear to the floor, I should be able to hear enough of their conversations to learn why they're this far from Charles Town."

Rachel's whole body tensed. "No, I won't let you do that; it's too dangerous. You'll be trapped if Thomas should return to his room while you're there."

For a moment, he looked at her, and she seemed so fragile. He could see the fear in her eyes. "I wish I could reassure you that won't happen, but I can't. It's possible the information we gather tonight will save many lives, and I cannot turn my back from it. He looked around the room. "Does his room have a balcony like ours or another connecting room?"

Apprehension still lingering in her voice, she answered, "All the rooms have identical balconies, and there's a connecting room. It was mother's sewing room."

He smiled confidently at her. "If he returns before I can dash back to you, then I shall make my exit from his balcony or into the next room."

Shaking her head, she said, "I'm not sure I could survive any bloodshed, John. Tell me you'll not linger once you learn what my brother is up to."

He crossed the room to where she was standing in front of a full-length mirror and wrapped his arms around her waist. Her head fell back against his chest; she could feel the rhythmic beat of his heart.

He gazed at her reflection in the mirror and whispered, "'Tis a risk for sure, but one we must take. We're not in a war like other generations before us. We're not fighting to gain territory or to conquer any other people. Nay, we fight for the freedom that comes from God, and whether or not we attain it rests with people such as you and me—"

Unexpectedly, they heard Daniel's voice from the hall, followed by light tapping at their door. "Hurry up in there. I'm starving!"

⬥◦◦⬥ ⬥◦◦⬥ ⬥◦◦⬥

After supper, Rachel watched the sun sink below the horizon from their balcony door. Behind her, lying across the bed, fully dressed, John was fast asleep, snoring lightly. Without warning, Rachel heard thundering hooves. She gazed out the window toward the widespread lawn and open field that lay beyond, and she could see the faint outline of several riders approaching.

Their room suddenly went dark and she jumped. John had heard the approaching horses and snuffed the candle.

"Stand away from the door a bit," he said quietly, "the light from the entrance lanterns will give us a view."

The red-coated riders pulled their horses up short, some forcing them to sliding stops. The moon was hidden behind clouds, and the lanterns eerie light cast harsh shadows against the young officers' faces.

The soldiers dismounted, and John and Rachel heard Thomas congratulating them on their horsemanship. They watched as the men postured and strutted like peacocks, each attempting to stand straighter than his comrades.

"There was a time when I thought my brothers were so dashing in their bright uniforms, but now I feel only revulsion," Rachel said, a sad look in her eyes.

The men disappeared from view as they entered the mansion. John sat in a chair to wait for the party of men downstairs to settle down for their meeting.

Suddenly, John touched his lips with his index finger and pointed to the door. Rachel nodded. Nimbly crossing the room, he drew the door open.

Thomas immediately straightened and backed away from the door. Red-faced, he was clearly embarrassed to be caught eavesdropping.

Rachel glared at her brother. "Still up to your sneaky habits, little brother? I should think Papa's discipline would have cured you of such deceitful behavior, but evidently not."

Grim faced, John stood at the threshold. "Is there something you need brother-in-law before you leave?"

Thomas wheeled around and stormed down the hall, disappearing down the stairs.

Taking Rachel in his arms, John said, "Your brother has no sister."

Looking up at her husband, tears welling in her eyes, she said, "But I shall never give him up, John. The same blood flows in our veins, and if he should ever need me, I would be compelled to help him."

John kissed her lightly. "I'm going to his room. You'll need to leave our door ajar slightly and watch the stairs. If Thomas should return while I'm in his room, you must delay him in some natural manner. Engage him in conversation; just be yourself so as not to raise his suspicions. I'll only need a minute to make my exit."

"I'm so unsettled. Just watching those soldiers has shaken my nerves, but I'll manage somehow," she replied.

"I'll need a pin from your lovely hair," he said, "in case his door is locked."

In his stocking feet, John eased into the dim hallway. He stood listening for a moment before treading toward Thomas's room. He crouched before the locked door, took Rachel's pin from his hair, and began to probe the lock. He could feel his heart beating as he maneuvered the pin.

Downstairs, a door opened and closed, and then footsteps were coming up the stairs, so soft they were barely audible. John looked around; he was trapped with nowhere to hide. He'd never make it to his room before Thomas reached the landing. His hand gripped his pistol.

CHAPTER TWELVE

SPYING ON FAMILY

H's *coming back!* John crept back toward the next door. *If the door's locked, I won't have time to pick it open. . . .* Then he heard someone call out to Thomas, and the footsteps stopped briefly. John kept moving away from Thomas's bedroom door and tried the knob on the next door down. It was unlocked!

Silently exhaling the pent-up air in his lungs, John wondered why he'd thought this was a good idea to begin with. He eased the door shut. Enough moonlight spilled through the window for him to see the room was sparsely furnished, apparently unused. While he was taking stock of the room, he heard a key turn in a lock next door. Thomas's bedroom door opened and then shut. He could hear Thomas moving around in that room, and watched the movement of the shaft of light under the adjoining door between the rooms.

That was close! John thought. What's he doing in there?

John dared not move as he listened intensely. He was sweating, feeling overwhelming regret for ever thinking he would be able to pull this off without getting caught by Thomas. He knew if he had been in Thomas's room, he would not have had time to reach the balcony before Thomas entered the room. His life or that of Thomas would hang in the balance unless Rachel could delay her brother in the hallway.

Still, I'm this close; I can't turn back now, John thought.

John watched the light under the door disappear and heard Thomas's key turn the lock closed. He waited until he was certain Thomas was back downstairs with his friends before he moved to the door that led to Thomas's bedroom.

Once inside, he lay prone in the middle of the room and placed his ear against a plank, moving several times to find the spot where he could understand what was being said below him. After several attempts, he was ready to give up. The conversation coming from the parlor was too muffled for him to make any sense of it.

Sighing, John brought his knees under him to stand, and he felt a board move. Squatting back on his heels, he felt around with his hand until he found a board that moved slightly. In the dark room, he was finally able to lift the board up. It was hinged on one side and he carefully laid it back.

The voices from the parlor below were now much clearer, and he was able to understand the conversation. He wondered if it was Thomas or his father before him who eavesdropped on conversations. John eased back in position, and began listening intently.

As John expected, his brother-in-law was the dominant speaker, likely the others were of lesser rank. Listening to Thomas speak, John had to admit, though grudgingly, that Thomas was a good tactically-minded leader.

Safely back in his room, John decided to write down what he'd heard in a cipher based on symbols, with each letter corresponding to a specific symbol. Using the paper he used to make his rifle cartridges, he meticulously wrote the odd-looking characters vertically in a neat line. When he was finished, the work resembled Egyptian hieroglyphics.

Rachel looked on as her husband penned the message. When he was done, she helped him cut the paper into four parts to make four paper cartridges.

John held the finished cartridges in his hand. "Perfect, these will do nicely."

"How will these be recognized when they're mixed in with real cartridges?" Rachel asked.

"Well, these *are* real cartridges, but for the difference in the way I've tied the string about them. He held one out to her so she could inspect it. "Look closely and you'll see I tied the ends with two loops of string, and on the regular cartridges only one loop secures the ends."

Rachel took the cartridge from his hand and examined it closely. "How devious of you!"

He sat on the bed and slipped on his moccasins. "I can leave these cartridges with an aide if the General is unavailable. It's dark, so I should be able to get in undetected. If I leave now, I ought to be back before daylight, and your brother will be none the wiser."

Rachel moved to sit by him. "Do be careful, John. You'll find no one but ne'er-do-wells about this time of night."

Once outside, John stealthily made his way to the barn and retrieved his horse. Walking him until they was out of earshot, John rode off in a fast gallop.

⚬⚬⚬⚬⚬⚬

Sarah found sleep to be elusive now that she was so near Gideon. She'd neglected to throw her cape around her but stood in only her shift on her balcony. The night air felt chilly, but she was lost in the moment of scanning the numberless stars that spread across the night sky.

Suddenly, she heard a soft whisper of sound. To her right, she saw a figure that looked like a man running toward the stables. Another movement brought her eyes to the balcony of Gideon's parents. *It's Mama Rachel! Was that Papa running toward the stables? What are they doing?*

Sarah started back into her room to slip on her robe. She'd make a visit to Rachel's room and find out for herself where Papa was going. Perhaps he was heading to Charles Town. Rachel would know.

Slipping into the dark hallway, Sarah tip-toed to Rachel's room and knocked lightly on the door.

Rachel opened the door and whispered, "Sarah! Come in. Is there something wrong?"

"No, I'm fine," Sarah whispered back, entering the room and closing the door. "But was that Papa I saw running toward the stables, just now?"

"Yes, and if you saw him, I hope no one else did," Rachel responded.

"Is this concerning his militia?" asked Sarah. "I wish there was something Papa could do to free Gideon."

Smiling in spite of her own sadness, Rachel said in a quiet voice, "John will do everything in his power to rescue Gideon, dear. He's gone now to deliver information to General Lincoln. When he returns and has time to rest a bit, we'll sit down and talk with him about Gideon."

Sarah looked at her mother-in-law. "Mama Rachel, I want to be strong because, in my heart, I know Gideon is strong, but it's so hard for me. There are moments when I just want to curl up in some corner and go to sleep. How do you handle your feelings so well? You're the strong anchor for this family."

Rachel stroked Sarah's hair and looked at the anguish and heartbreak in her face. "I'm not what you make me to be, dear. Right now, my heart is heavy for my son who's in the hands of those who hate him, as well as for my husband, who is in even greater danger tonight. To get from one day to another, sometimes from one minute to the next, I immerse myself in the routine day to day activities at hand."

Rachel sighed audibly, "That's not the picture of a strong anchor is it, dear? Nevertheless, it's me . . . it's who your mother-in-law really is. I hope I haven't made it worse for you." She moved to her bedside table and picked up a leather-bound book there. "Let me read one of my favorite verses from the Bible that helps me."

Rachel opened her bible to Isaiah, chapter forty-one, verse ten, and read: "'*Do not fear, for I am with you; do not be afraid, for I am your God. I will strengthen you; I will help you; I will hold on to you with My righteous right hand.*'"

When she'd finished, she looked up into Sarah's eyes and smiled. "Now, you go back to your room and try to sleep, and I'll do the same. Before we know it a new day will be here."

⚬⚬⚬ ⚬⚬⚬ ⚬⚬⚬

From the back trail he was riding, John could see the orange flashes from British cannons in the distance, near the Ashley River. From the roar, he figured they were likely using sixteen pounders, and that they were raining down cannon balls indiscriminately on Tories and Patriots alike.

He wondered aloud, "The general better have a good evacuation plan ready, because it looks like Clinton remembers his retreat of '76 and has come to win this time."

When he arrived at Lincoln's headquarters, he found the general still up.

An aide brought John to the general's office, and the general greeted him heartily. "Sir, your arrival is an act of Providence! I have men searching the countryside for you at this moment, and you come to me. What else could it be other than a blessing from the Almighty?"

Not knowing what to make of Lincoln's high spirits, John said, "I cannot answer that, General, but Providence may indeed have protected me in acquiring the news I bring."

"Then I shall wait until I hear what you have before giving your new orders to you."

John's eyebrows went up as he looked at the general. *New orders? Something big may be in the air. Could it be connected with Cornwallis, or Clinton . . . or maybe both?*

The General went around to his desk, motioning for John to sit in a nearby chair. "What word do you have for me, John. Could it be good news?"

Taking his seat, John looked directly at Lincoln and said, "I was able to get close enough to a meeting of Cornwallis's aides and hear that Sir Henry Clinton is about to move most of his fleet into the harbor opposite the city. The officer holding the meeting is my wife's brother, Colonel Thomas Covington."

Stone-faced, Lincoln began to pace. The loyalty of John's brother-in-law was something he already knew. "Suddenly, I find myself brought from the backwaters of the conflict to the very center."

The contempt clear in his voice and posture, he said, "I am presently in command of only 1,400 Continentals and 1,000 North Carolina militia, and your governor has refused to supply even a company of this state's militia. To add insult to injury, your colony's legislature has ignored my request to create black regiments, and the plantation owners have refused to allow their slaves to work on the defenses of their city."

"What you're saying is new to me, sir. I had no idea the situation was as bad as you're describing. Do you plan to defend the city?"

Lincoln stopped and faced John. "Yes"—he pounded his desk with a heavy fist—"I'm under explicit orders to defend Charles Town. Under no circumstances, shall I abandon the city as we did in Philadelphia."

Grim faced, John said, "What can I do, General?"

Lincoln tilted his head and looked toward John. "General Gates has requested, nay ordered, that I put someone in place to head a network of covert agents in South Carolina. Your name naturally came to my mind as a man to fill that position."

John's eyes narrowed. "Could you be a little more specific? What network of covert agents?"

Coming around to sit at his desk, Lincoln answered, "A web of spies, John. The general wants people who can get close to the enemy and gather intelligence for him. He didn't lay out any explicit instructions for you to do this, so you have free rein to get the job done."

John shook his head. "General, I'm a merchant—a business man. I don't know anything about spying."

"I understand your reluctance, John, but I know of no other man who could take your place. The information you bring me this night proves to me that you're the man for the job."

Placing his beefy hand on John's shoulder, Lincoln said, "John, I'm making you a Colonel in the South Carolina Militia. The pay is nothing to speak of, especially since it's issued by Congress, but it's the best I can do. I expect you to continue harassing the enemy wherever you find the opportunity."

There was a long pause, and then John rose to his feet and let out a long sigh, buttoned his waistcoat, and said, "I'll do it. Thank you for the promotion. I suppose it's good that I know little about the intelligence business, for if I did, it's likely I'd refuse your request."

"Never you mind about your experience. For twenty-five years, I was a town clerk, and today, I command the Patriot forces, meager as they are, that are now in harm's way.

<hr />

John beat the sun by only a few minutes, reaching the balcony to his room just before the dark edge of morning twilight yielded to dawn.

Rachel eased the door open and pulled him inside. "What delayed you?" she breathed, "I've worried so."

"Shhh! We'll talk later. This has been a hard night. Let's sleep while we can."

Although red-coated officers were still downstairs, John was asleep as soon as his head rested on his pillow. Rachel watched the rhythmic rise and fall of his chest, marveling at her husband's ability to fall asleep so quickly. She slipped under the cover beside him, rested her head upon his chest, and listened to the steady beating of his heart. Her eyes grew heavy, and she was soon asleep.

CHAPTER THIRTEEN

A FRIEND FROM THE PAST

Sunlight poured in through the open window as Rachel carefully eased from the bed to dress and make her way downstairs. John hadn't moved since he had lain down.

Her children stood when she entered the dining room, and she hugged them before taking a seat. Thomas remained seated and didn't look up, seemingly preoccupied with his breakfast.

The silence at the table was deafening. Rachel gave Lottie and Sarah, seated across the table, questioning looks. Lottie scowled and rolled her deep blue eyes in a show of exasperation. Focusing again on her mother, she made a subtle tilt of her head toward her uncle. Sarah managed an anemic smile, while Daniel rested his chin on his hand and nodded.

Rachel looked at her brother at the end of the table as he pushed a small piece of bacon around with his fork, mixing the bacon with his sweet potatoes. He occupied the place where her father had always sat. *You live in a house you did not build, you sleep in the bed of your father, you eat from your father's table, you sit in the chair of your father, but you will never, dear brother, be half the man he was.*

Another moment passed before she could bring herself to speak. She wanted to reach out and touch him, in some way to bring him back from the unrecognizable place where he now lived. Rachel felt her heart would break. Memories flooded her mind of their endless childhood dreams, where they had played together near the creek that ran through their home's property, and challenged each other to stone-skipping contests.

"Good morning, brother." She said, her voice flat as cold coffee. "I trust you had a good night's rest."

He slowly looked up; she noticed his bloodshot eyes and the shadow of the dark circles from lack of sleep. His face closed in a caustic scowl, he said, "The business of last evening's meeting took longer than I anticipated. Dawn was breaking when my men were able to leave."

"Business you say?" she said, stifling the urge to laugh. "Are all British officers as raucous as your men in their conduct of business? My husband and I were kept awake most of the night by the noise and discordant singing coming from the parlor."

Thomas was silent, looking off to one side, avoiding his sister's direct stare. When she finished speaking, he stood awkwardly. A muscle tightened in his jaw, and his voice remained brusque.

"I shall take my leave, now. As I've already said, you may have free use of the house and grounds. Meg should be here today, if she's able to avoid our patrols. She should encounter little difficulty, in any case, carrying my signed paper identifying her as my betrothed. The two of you will enjoy renewing your friendship, I'm sure."

Laying his napkin on the table, he raised his gaze to meet the stare of his sister. "I shan't be taking my meals with you for the rest of your stay. I'm sorry, but it's best that I don't."

Rachel came to her feet. "Wait, Thomas! Why did you invite us to your wedding, if we're unwelcome in this house? I'm your sister," she said ardently, "and these are my children—your nieces and nephew. You're their only uncle. We all share the same blood of kinship. What has changed you, Thomas; do you owe your king such loyalty that you deny the only family you have of your love and nurture?"

She paused to collect her thoughts and said, "All I can do is watch as you leave, dear brother. You've caused me such pain and heartache, but I'll always love you and cherish you for all the remaining days of my life. You'll not be taking that with you, and I'll always be ready to help you."

Thomas couldn't raise his head from his chest. With a slight nod of his head, he walked quickly from the room, and Rachel collapsed in her chair and sobbed uncontrollably.

Lottie and Sarah came around the table to sit beside Rachel. With her children's arms around her, she cried and cried until no more tears would come. Shortly, John came in to find his children hovering close to their mother. Daniel and the young women stood as their father came to them.

The situation became clear to John quickly. He knelt beside Rachel's chair and pulled her close. She rested her head on his shoulder and sighed heavily.

Looking up at Daniel, John asked in a low voice, "Did her brother cause this?"

Daniel nodded, but before he could speak, Rachel said, "I'm all right, John. I'd held this heartache inside for as long as I could, and now I have no more tears to shed for my brother." Sitting up, she gazed into her husband's eyes and said, "You and my children have helped me more than I could ever tell you. I feel lighter, as though a weight has been lifted from me. It's time I just let it go."

Gradually, the chilliness in the room gave way as the young people engaged in their usual banter. By the time John was finishing his breakfast; Rachel was smiling and nibbling at food from John's plate.

In mock seriousness, he said, "You really should take a plate if you're hungry."

"Oh, I'm not really hungry," she said casually while cutting off another part of his remaining biscuit with her fork.

Breaking off her teasing of her brother, Lottie said, "What's there for us to do today, Mother? Does Uncle Thomas own horses we may ride?"

"When papa was alive, we had several thoroughbreds. Your father will take you to the stables and see if Thomas has kept them."

Turning to her husband, she said, "John, I want you to take careful measure of the horses that my brother has, and don't allow the children to pick their own. And maybe you should ride with them since you know the grounds."

A dejected grimace spread across Daniel's face. "Mother, I'm quite capable of choosing my own horse. Have you forgotten I'm almost nineteen?"

Suppressing a laugh, Rachel took his arm. "How could I ever forget? Please allow me this small indulgence just for today. Now, put a smile on your face and enjoy your ride."

<hr>

After her family had left, Rachel had a hot bath. She wanted to look her best when Meg arrived. Rachel and Meg had known each other since they were small children. Their fathers had been close friends, and their mothers were childhood playmates, too. Meg had been in England when Rachel came home for her father's funeral, so today would be their first reunion in nearly twenty years.

Rachel remembered the bittersweet day when she left home and family for the backcountry frontier town of Camden. Meg had come to see her off; she could still see her best friend, brokenhearted, waving goodbye.

It's been twenty years. I wonder if she will recognize me. Will I know her? I'm so thankful she's marrying again. Mother, in her letters, told of how everyone feared Meg would take her life after the death of her husband.

Rachel looked over the clothes she brought from home. It took her only a minute to select the one she would wear. It was her favorite because John always complimented her when she wore it. The gown wasn't new; it was a simple gown of red and green plaid taffeta. The neckline was trimmed with a narrow frill, and the waist was encircled by a wide sash.

After several attempts, Rachel felt her hair was at least presentable. Standing before the full-length mirror, she thought she could see a glimpse of the young girl who had run away from home.

She heard a carriage pull up. Looking from her window, she saw Thomas assisting two women from the carriage. One, the taller of the two, was unmistakably Meg. It was plain to see that she'd matured, but she was still a stunning woman. Her hair highlighted the delicate features of her face and gown.

Thomas embraced Meg, and they kissed briefly. Meg's face was lit with a radiant smile. Rachel wanted to see the other woman, but Thomas stood in her line of vision. Then, the three started for the house, and Rachel could see her. Without a doubt, she was Meg's daughter. It was like looking back in time to a young Meg. Her hair was golden, silky, and shining, perfectly styled to enhance the delicate bones of her face. She wore a fashionable gown of blue silk that accentuated her blue eyes.

Rachel hesitated, trying to decide if she should just rush downstairs now, or wait until Thomas sent someone to fetch her. *Why am I worrying how my brother will react if I choose to come down now?* She took one last look at her reflection in the mirror and left the room.

Rachel made her way down the wide hallway toward the stairs. Approaching her brother's room, she noticed the door was ajar. Out of curiosity, she looked into the dimly lighted room. Her eyes widened as she saw several papers strewn across her brother's bed. She could feel her heart pounding; Meg was forgotten for the moment. She could hear her brother's voice coming from the parlor downstairs.

She took a deep breath and slipped into the room. Her nerves were taut to breaking as she shuffled through the papers. The papers were all written in a numeric code. She hurriedly replaced them as she had found them and made her way back to the stairs.

Rachel paused to catch her breath and wait for her nerves to settle down before she went to meet Meg and her daughter. Breathing deeply and exhaling, she descended the stairs. She stopped at the parlor door. Meg was sitting on the couch. Her daughter was at the piano playing some light aria that Rachel recognized from her days of piano lessons. Then Meg saw Rachel and, squealing with delight, she rushed across the room to her.

Startled, Meg's daughter stood at the piano, ending her informal recital. Stunned by her mother's outburst, her hand went unconsciously to her lips.

Thomas, taken aback by his fiancée's sudden exuberance, jumped to his feet and spun around. From across the room, he watched as they embraced and cried, both trying to talk at the same time. For a twinkling moment, his heart ached. It ached for the time that once was, but was never to be again. He choked back the lump in his throat, shutting off all thoughts but the present and his duty as a British soldier.

Rachel watched Meg's daughter cross the room. Nothing could have prepared her for the up-close vision now walking toward her. It was as though she was a young girl again herself, and Meg was walking toward her.

Her reverie was broken when Meg took her arm and said, "Eleanor, this is my dearest and closest friend, Rachel Hamilton."

Eleanor curtsied and said, "I'm very pleased to meet you at last, Mrs. Hamilton. Mother has kept you before us with delightful stories that I could hardly believe are true. Please call me Ellie, all of my friends do."

Rachel laughed aloud. "Yes, Ellie fits you nicely, and we must set aside some time for us to reminisce before we return home."

As the three settled on the couch, Thomas stood and made a cursory bow. "I shall be in my room, ladies, until dinner."

Her brother's remark sent a flutter of dread in Rachel's stomach. *Will he notice his papers have been moved? Did I—"*

"Rachel, dear, you seem preoccupied. Are you well?" asked Meg.

Jolted out of her pensiveness, Rachel said, "I'm sorry, I thought I heard my children arriving. They went riding with John, earlier and I'm concerned they haven't returned already."

"They'll return soon, I'm sure. I shouldn't worry if John is with them."

Rachel had been fighting to suppress feelings of guilt for spying on her brother, and now she just lied to Meg, the only person in the world other than John to whom she had never lied. If there was anything in her life she hated, it was this war. Families, on both sides, were suffering.

Hardly a person had not lost a close relative on the fields of battle and no less terrible was the painful upheavals within families caused by sworn allegiances for one cause or the other. Brothers fought against brothers, and in some instances, fathers fought against sons and daughters.

The housekeeper came in and bobbed a curtsey. "Mr. Hamilton and the children are coming in."

Rachel rose from the couch and said, "Thank you Mollie, please send them here."

Lottie, Sarah, and John noisily entered the entrance hall. That they had enjoyed themselves was evident by their high-spirited laughter and conversation.

John was the first to enter the parlor followed by Lottie and Sarah. He bowed and kissed Meg's outstretched hand lightly. "Dear Meg, your beauty has remained untouched by time."

"Thank you, John. We both know you're such an accomplished liar, but I love hearing it anyway," she replied, adding, "John, this is Ellie, my daughter."

"I'm pleased to meet you, Ellie," Turning, he placed his hand on Lottie's shoulder. "Meg and Ellie, this is Charlotte, our daughter" He reached a hand to Sarah and brought her forward. "And this is Sarah, Gideon's wife."

Sarah and Lottie curtsied politely.

Meg, with a twinkle in her eye, said, "John, you're as handsome as ever." Seeing he was taken aback, Meg gleefully raised her voice, "John was not only good-looking, but he was so personable; all the girls on the peninsula were in love with him. It was at my fifteenth birthday party that he first met Rachel and all—"

Lottie ran to her father and took his arm. "Ohhh, Papa is that true?" Her eyes darted to her mother. "Mama, did you know Papa was so popular? Who were these girls?"

Rachel, with the barest hint of a smile, her eyebrows arched as she looked at her husband, said, "Yes, I knew all about the young maidens who purred around him. However, you should ask you father how he remembers those times."

<hr />

John saw that this wasn't going away anytime soon. Every eye seemed to be directed at him, especially his daughter's and Ellie's. To him, women were an unfathomable mystery, so he had to think of some polite way to excuse himself.

Then, in a moment of inspiration, he said, "A true gentleman never mentions a lady's name in idle conversation."

Turning slightly to face Rachel, he said, "However, I will tell you that the days of my youth have dimmed considerably, and any recollection would likely not be accurate. But the memory of the first time my eyes beheld Rachel remains clear and unblemished as if it happened yesterday."

Suddenly, Daniel burst into the parlor and said vigorously, "Mother, you'll never believe—"

It was then he saw Ellie. Her vision of loveliness before him struck him speechless. Try as he might, he couldn't finish his thought. He felt his throat tighten and his tongue had stuck to the roof of his mouth.

His mother saved him further embarrassment by standing and taking him by the arm. "Daniel, I want you to meet Meg Turnwell, my childhood friend and her daughter, Ellie."

Making a quick recovery, Daniel made a proper bow before Meg and said, "I'm so pleased to meet you, Mrs. Turnwell. Mother has spoken of you many times."

Meg responded, "Thank you, Daniel. It's indeed my pleasure to meet you. You're a handsome young man; it's easy to see you're John's son. You must be all of eighteen by now, are you not?"

He regretted the warmth building in his cheeks. "Yes ma'am. Actually, I'm nearing my nineteenth birthday."

Daniel turned to Ellie. He took her offered hand, kissed it lightly, and bowed crisply. He had been aware of Ellie's gaze upon him as he spoke with her mother. Now, he looked directly into the startling turquoise blue eyes of this very pretty young woman with a compelling resemblance to her mother.

Before releasing her hand, he lingered for an impetuous moment to admire her elegantly arranged honey-gold hair that fell over one shoulder in three long ringlets. "And I'm so pleased to meet you, Ellie."

Ellie felt her face grow warm under his gaze. "Thank you, I'm pleased to meet you, Daniel."

Daniel stepped back to stand beside his father, conscious that Ellie's eyes subtly followed him.

CHAPTER FOURTEEN

YOUNG LOVE

Knowing he and his sister had made no plans for the afternoon, Daniel decided, impulsively, to ask, "My sister Lottie and I have planned an afternoon ride. Would you care to join us, Ellie?"

Ellie's eyes sparkled with enthusiasm. "Yes, I would love that." Her eyes moved to her mother, and she said, "Do you approve, Mother?"

Waiting nervously for Meg's response, Daniel felt a tightening in his chest that was like nothing he'd ever felt before. He glanced toward Ellie and found her eyes were locked on his face. *She has no idea how lovely she looks.*

Daniel's reverie was broken when Meg said, "Yes, of course, dear, today is a perfect day for riding, and Daniel has not only displayed himself as a gentleman, but he comes from a good family. However, Daniel, you must have her back an hour before sundown to give us time to get home before dark." Then an almost imperceptible smile appeared across Meg's face. "And will you assure me, Daniel, the three of you will remain together?"

Startled by the implication of her question, Daniel felt color coming to his cheeks again. "Oh yes, Mrs. Turnwell, and you have my word nothing untoward will happen to Ellie while she's in my care."

Mollie came in and announced she had tea for those who wanted it. Rachel took Meg's arm and said, "Please excuse us. Meg and I will be in the study for a while." Turning to Mollie, she added, "Mollie, you can serve us where you always found us when we hid from Papa."

Mollie smothered a laugh and curtsied. "Yes ma'am. I know where you two will be."

Mollie brought a platter with the silver tea set into the study where Meg and Rachel sat together on the window seat. "Hmm, you two are still trim, nice looking ladies, but I didn't think you'd be fitting behind that corner couch . . . it's not here any longer anyway. Mr. Thomas gave it to one of his officer men."

They all laughed, and Mollie hugged them both and dabbed tears from her eyes before she poured two cups of tea and handed them to the ladies. Then she offered them milk, sugar, and biscuits.

Rachel waited until Mollie had left and closed the door. "I feel a bit guilty, even though this is my brother's tea. I haven't tasted a drop of British tea since '73." She took a small sip from her cup. "This is much better than the whorled loosestrife leaves the ladies of Camden use to make their 'Liberty Tea'.

Meg stared into her cup of tea. "Can you remember the day when we sat in this room, and you told me that there was something very serious you needed to tell me?"

"I remember many days like that very well, but I'm sure the one you're talking about was the day before I eloped with John—the end of our childhood."

Sipping from her cup, Meg said, "Yes, that was a devastating day for me. I felt so alone with you leaving. Today, it's my turn. I have something serious to say, and you're the only person in the world I can tell."

Rachel looked at her best friend, searched her face for a clue that would tell her what this might be about. "What is it, Meg? Is there something I can do?"

Meg drained her cup and set it aside. She took a deep breath and let it out. "There will be no wedding."

For one of the few times in her life, Rachel found herself unable to form a sentence. The only thing left was to wait for Meg to continue.

As though she was discussing an appointment with her seamstress, Meg said, "This has been building inside of me for some time. Although it may sound odd, Ellie has been such a pillar of support for me. She's wise beyond her years, and I'm grateful for the help she's been, even though she's my daughter."

Recovered from her initial shock, Rachel said, "Have you told Thomas you want to call the wedding off??"

"Not in so many words, but we've had numerous heated debates, mostly over the issues of the war. I'd be shocked if he cares one way or the other, except losing my fortune which has been of great interest to him."

"When do you plan to tell him?" Rachel said.

Meg nodded her head. "I'd planned to tell him today before I knew definitely you and your family would be here. Now that you're here, I'll not be anxious about how he'll react."

"What do you mean by 'how he'll react'? Are you afraid of him?" asked Rachel, her brows creased across her forehead. "Has he ever struck you?"

Meg became interested in her hands, avoiding looking directly at her friend. In a soft voice, she muttered, "Yes."

Bending toward Meg, Rachel said, "Look at me, Meg. I want to know what my brother has done."

Meg raised her eyes to look at her friend. Rachel's heart nearly broke as she gazed deeply into her eyes, past the beautiful color and sparkle that was there most of the time. Rachel saw the pain of embarrassment and shame that now marred her friend's beautiful features.

Quietly Rachel asked, "How many times has this happened?"

Meg sighed deeply and dropped her eyes.

Rachel placed her arm around Meg's shoulders and said, " Oh, I shouldn't have asked such a question, please forgive me."

The beginning of a smile appeared on Meg's lips. "It's all right. It'll never happen again."

❦ ❦ ❦

Daniel and Lottie were leading their saddled horses from the stables when Ellie arrived. It was a clear spring day with little chill and white puffs of clouds floating in the blue sky. A warmish breeze gently blew a scattering of leaves into the pasture behind the stables.

Ellie's eyes were on Daniel as she walked up. "Thank you for asking me to ride with you and Lottie. Do you think me forward for saying yes so quickly?"

Daniel grinned. "Not at all, 'tis I who should worry about that. I nearly swallowed my tongue when I blurted out my request after only just meeting you."

"'Twas a bit brassy of my brother, I'll admit, but I'm glad he did it," Lottie said with a laugh.

Daniel led the way to the stalls. "Have you ridden any of these before, Ellie?"

"Yes, I usually ride during our visits here."

He felt her arm brush against his as she leaned into a stall, sending a tingling sensation down to his toes. He moved his arm and immediately regretted it. She felt something too, because he saw a look in her eyes that wasn't there a moment ago. They grew quiet, and he became very still, feeling whatever the moment had been, it had passed.

She said, "Would you saddle this bay for me, Daniel? I've ridden him before. Although it's been a while, I believe he'll remember me. By the way, I must tell you, I'm not an accomplished horsewoman."

She watched as Daniel expertly bridled and saddled her horse. "How long are you and your family staying, Daniel?"

Looking over his shoulder, he said, "I'm not sure, but I imagine only a day or so after the wedding."

She looked at him with her alluring blue eyes. "There's not much time for us to become better acquainted. I do so want to know more about you—and Lottie."

In taking the reins from Daniel, her hand touched his, and she didn't remove it. Their eyes met and locked, and the world seemed to fade away.

Daniel suddenly felt an urge to kiss her, but he'd never kissed a girl. He'd die of embarrassment if he did it all wrong, and she'd probably laugh. Lottie coughed, and it broke the spell.

"Didn't we saddle these horses to ride?" Lottie asked. "Surely brother, you can find a place more suitable for staring than a smelly stable."

Daniel looked at Ellie, and they all broke into laughter. "Let's go for a ride."

He stood to the side of Ellie's horse, ready to help her mount. She took the reins from him and set her left foot in his interlaced hands. He boosted her up with barely any effort. Ellie hooked her knee over the sidesaddle's pommel before securing the foot of her opposite leg in the stirrup and draping her skirts to cover her legs.

Ellie's eyes caught Lottie already in the saddle. "Y-you're riding like a man?"

Lottie laughed aloud. "Side saddles aren't very suitable in the backcountry. Actually, it's becoming fashionable in the Camden district for women to ride this way."

Ellie's mouth slackened as she searched for words to say. Daniel saw the look of astonishment on her face. "Lottie tends to stretch the truth on this subject. She's one of only a handful of women at home who sit a man's saddle. And only when she thinks Ma isn't around."

He swung himself onto his saddle and said, "Shall we go?"

"Daniel, can we go to the old mill on Sparrow Creek?" asked Ellie.

He twisted in the saddle. "Yes, if you know the way."

Turning her horse, she said, pointing, "It's this way. We just follow yon trail."

The trail was wide enough to allow Daniel to ride along side Ellie. Lottie slowed her horse until they were some distance ahead.

At first neither of them spoke. Ellie was as nervous as Daniel, who so wanted to get to know this lovely young lady. He looked at her, and she met his gaze with a smile that caused his heart to flutter. Returning her smile with one of his own felt as natural as anything he had ever done.

"Is it true, Daniel, that your father is a patriot?" she said easily, as if she was inquiring how he made a living.

Her face reflected no animosity, and he could detect nothing in her voice that told him about her allegiance. Daniel decided to answer her candidly.

"Not only my father, but my brother, myself, my mother, and my sister as well," he said.

He watched her for a reaction, but she didn't respond, and that puzzled him.

The old gristmill came into view. It had been abandoned when the family that owned it had migrated to Kentucky territory that lay west of the Blue Ridge Mountains. Dismounting, he hurried to help Ellie down from her horse.

He reached up to grasp Ellie around her waist. Lifting her off, they found themselves face to face, and his hands still resting on her hips. Daniel looked down into her crystal blue eyes.

A moment passed without a sound other than the water rushing over the rocky bed of the creek. Then something happened. Neither would be able to recall later what that something was, but they would always remember this day and this place.

"Will you . . ." Ellie hesitated and took another breath. "Will you kiss me, Daniel? I've never kissed a boy."

His throat tightened, and his legs felt as though they were about to fold under him, but at least she wouldn't know if he did it wrong. They would teach each other.

Taking her in his arms, his lips met hers. He released her, and they remained close and quiet for a few moments.

Then Ellie touched his cheek and said, "Daniel that was wonderful. Was it for you?"

Swallowing hard, he replied, "Yes . . . yes it was, and I must confess that was my first time, too."

Lottie walked up with a smirk, "I'm going upstream for a while. Are we still on Uncle Thomas's land?"

"Yes, follow the creek and you will come to a stone marker. That's the northern boundary of your uncle's estate," Ellie said.

He led Ellie to a low stone wall that extended over the creek's edge. He wiped away debris from the stones so she could sit down without soiling her skirts. He looked away for a moment before his gaze returned to her. *Her face is so perfect and so pure . . . an angel's face,* he thought. He fought the urge to kiss her again; to take her in his arms . . . *Stop! I must stop these thoughts. We've just met!*

Aware that he must have been staring, he wiped an area of the ledge and sat beside her. "Why did you ask about the loyalty of my father a moment ago? Is it important to you?" he asked.

She slowly shook her head. "I'm not sure, Daniel. I can't think of a reason other than I've overheard Thomas speaking badly about your father."

"Does it matter to you," he asked gently, "that I'm a patriot?"

"I am a daughter of Liberty," she said, resolutely, "Were I a man, no hazard could deter me from service on the fields of battle for our sacred cause."

He watched her face as she spoke, and he knew her words came from her heart. "Does your mother know of your patriotism? Where do her loyalties rest?"

"My mother's heart and mine beat as one on this issue."

A deep furrow appeared on his forehead. "But why is she—"

She cut him off. "Why is she marrying Thomas? 'Tis not for love, I can tell you. Mother has convinced herself to do this for the social status that she would enjoy as the wife of the Fourth Earl of Hayecrest." All feeling had drained from Ellie's voice. "Mother is about to live the rest of her life in a lie for the sake of a dying tradition."

Daniel studied the ground at his feet and then locked his eyes on Ellie's face. "I believe your mother lives in a make-believe world if she believes she can be a true patriot as the Countess of Hayecrest. Do you live in that world, too? What are your plans for your life after your mother marries?"

<hr />

Rachel found John napping after talking with Meg. "Wake up you sleepy head, today is too pretty to stay inside. Come walk with me to the pond."

Rachel and John came to a shaded area near the pond, and John spread a colorful quilt under the massive spreading canopy of an ancient live oak's limbs. Rachel sat and beckoned John to join her. He kissed her lightly and lay down with his head in her lap.

Over them was the bluest of cloudless blue skies. She looked at the intricate design of the quilt beneath them and ran her hand over the stitched pattern. This was her favorite because she had helped her mother cut the patterns.

Even with the shadow of Gideon and Sarah in the back of her mind, Rachel felt blessed to have this peaceful moment with her husband. She knew Meg was not looking forward to a possible confrontation with Thomas. As bad as it was, she also knew she couldn't tell John about Thomas striking Meg, at least for the time being.

Then there was the business of Thomas going out of his way to antagonize John over the politics of the war. Her brother seldom let an opportunity pass without berating John for his stand as a patriot. John had promised her that he would be restrained in his conversations and not take up any political talk, especially with Thomas.

Rachel glanced at her husband; he seemed deeply absorbed in thought. His dark hair ruffled by the occasional breeze. Neither of them had spoken for a few minutes. She ran her fingers tenderly over his face.

With an edge of feigned reprimand in her voice, she said, "My, you're so romantic this afternoon. Have you forgotten this place . . . are there no memories here that stir you?"

He slowly opened his eyes and gave her an impish grin. "Yes, I remember. This is where we—"

Touching his lips with her finger, she said, "Shhh, lower your voice, Meg and Thomas may be somewhere near, and I was referring to the afternoon when you asked me to marry you."

He was silent for a moment. Then he drew in a deep breath. "Aye, that day is yet branded in my heart. I carry it still within me. You said yes in rebellion against your father, and I stole you away in the dark of night a fortnight later."

"You know it was never about you. It was Papa's disapproval of your family's social station," she said with feeling, "Although your father was wealthy, my father considered him a commoner, and no amount of wealth could ever change that. Papa lived his whole life believing that his heritage as the son of the Earl of Hayecrest set him apart and above the merchant class."

"Do you sometimes regret marrying a 'commoner'?" John asked candidly.

"Is that how you think of yourself, my dashing husband?" she answered coquettishly, "You're a most uncommon man of peerless perfection. Tell me now, what is there about you that I should regret?"

His mouth opened, but before he could speak, she said, "Shhh, I see Thomas and Meg heading this way."

Closing his eyes, he said, "Tell them I'm asleep."

Rachel studied her brother as they drew nearer. He was holding Meg's hand as they walked. He was dressed in his finest starched military clothes. His uniform was immaculate from his bright scarlet coat down to the white ruffled sleeves of his beautifully starched shirt. Even the buttons and buckles were all polished and sparkling in the sunlight.

Evidently, she hasn't told him.

CHAPTER FIFTEEN

NO WEDDING FOR THE WIDOW

is face stuck in a contentious scowl, Thomas glared at Meg as if she were something repulsive. She remained mute, and with her hands on her hips, she returned his hard gaze.

He'd given in at the last minute and agreed to stroll around the pond with her. Now the immaculate shine of his knee-high leather boots was splotched in mud.

"Does the sight of my boots render you speechless?" he said, his words dripping with sarcasm. "Since you forced the issue of this outing, I think it would be proper for you to restore my boots to their original luster."

Meg turned her eyes on the trail ahead. "The condition of your boots is your responsibility. As you can see, I slipped on my patten overshoes before we started our walk."

Thomas decided to ignore her response when he spotted John and Rachel just ahead.

In the haughty, aristocratic manner of an English officer, Thomas said, "Ah, there you are brother-in-law—napping! It seems to be a habit among you rebels. Colonel Tarleton regales in telling how he came upon your stalwart rebel brothers at Monck's Corner while they were still asleep."

John yawned and slowly stirred. Sitting upright, he touched Rachel's lips with his fingers and kissed her lightly.

Standing, he said, "Humph! 'tis only the esteemed brother of my lovely wife disturbing my rest. How long has it been, brother-in-law; this game you play—it's been years, now hasn't it? Yet, you've never tired of it. I assure you, I have."

John stepped closer to Thomas. "I stand here as your equal, man to man, and challenge you to make your charge; arrest me if you have proof of my treason. Leave your sister out of it. I don't stand behind her skirt for protection, and she can't save you from my musket."

Thomas stiffened and pulled away from Meg. Her eyes widened as she stepped back with her hand to her mouth. Thomas tipped his head back slightly and looked down his nose at John with undisguised hatred.

The two men stared at one another for an awkward moment before Rachel held out her hand to John and led him away to the house. Thomas turned his back on John and Rachel as they left.

Meg watched her best friend go, and her tear-filled eyes followed her and her husband down the path. "Thomas, go to her. She's your sister. The two of you are all who remain in your family."

With just the faintest grimace, he said, "That I can never do. My oath as an officer in the king's service supersedes every loyalty I have. My sister and her husband have made their choice freely and now must accept that they will suffer the worse for it."

"Please take me back to the house," Meg said, after hesitating for a moment, "the afternoon is ruined."

Thomas turned to look at her; his mouth thinned into a hard, straight line and his dark brown eyes burned with silent indignation.

He managed a mock smile. "Yes, it would seem so."

Neither said a word until they were inside the house, and he flung open the parlor door and thrust her inside.

He followed her in and slammed the door behind him. He stood facing her, a menacing spark of anger rising in his eyes.

"Just what were you thinking out there when you asked me to overlook the sins of my sister? Not to mention the unprincipled degenerate she claims is her husband. Are you siding with rebels against your future husband?"

Meg came closer and stood inches from him. The rage within her strangled any fear that might have surfaced when she and Rachel talked earlier.

Forcing her breakfast to stay down, she said, "You are, without any doubt, the most self-centered, egotistical, and pompous man I've ever met. How is it that God has placed you in such a lofty place to be the judge of us all?"

He looked as if he was about to speak, but she said, "I have something to say, Thomas, and I want it said before you have one of your tantrums."

She watched him for any telltale signs he might be about to hit her. Without any feelings of nervousness, she said matter-of-factly, "There will be no wedding for you and me. It was a mistake for me to accept your proposal when I knew you were only after my money."

He looked down at his hands, which he clenched and unclenched nervously, his face reddening. Slowly, his eyebrows furrowed, his lips pressed together, and then his hands were gripping her upper arms. He squeezed so tightly, she felt hot arrows of pain to race up and down them and cried out.

He glared at her, his dark eyes brimming with anger and hatred. "My superiors have warned me not to marry you, my dear. Your outspoken views supporting the rebels' cause have brought you to their attention. Lord General Cornwallis, no less, takes a dim view of your spoken fondness of the rebel's cause. As my wife, he expects you to sign an oath of loyalty to the king."

Meg stiffened her back and gazed hard into his eyes. "Never!"

"I can no longer look the other way and pretend, my dear Meg," he said, lowering his voice to a menacing softness. "You've become a burden to me. I had hoped you could rise above your station, that you could carry the title, Countess of Hayecrest, in the manner of my blessed mother."

Thomas's jaw muscles tightened as he hardened his steely grip on her arms. Meg winced, but was determined not to make another sound. She could see the evil pleasure in his face as he watched her in pain. Her heart pounded in her ears and her arms felt distant and weak.

Finally, he pushed her away from him in disgust. She fell back, striking her head against a chair. The chair flipped and came down on her back. Her head was reeling, and she struggled to regain her feet.

Raising herself to her elbows, she gathered her skirt, and with some effort, managed to get her trembling legs under her. The floor seemed to be moving beneath her feet. She held to the back of a chair and glared at Thomas. Her arms burned from his crushing grip, and her heart pounded like a battering ram against her chest, but she held his unyielding stare, her eyes filled with fiery defiance. His expression hadn't changed.

I could have broken my neck in the fall, and he would have reacted no differently, she thought.

Her anger began to rise, and she unconsciously clenched her teeth. She managed to take a few faltering steps toward him and looked up into his face. She couldn't believe that he had ever intimidated her. She knew that contemptuous glare; she'd seen it many times before.

Meg's face flushed, and her eyes blazed with fierceness. Then she slapped him hard with the full force of her body behind it. The blow snapped Thomas's head to one side. Her hand felt as if thousands of needles were piercing her palm. She hadn't intended to hit him; it just came from somewhere inside her, and now she could scarcely believe she'd actually done it.

The force of her slap had knocked him off balance, and now about three feet separated them. She watched as an angry red welt began to rise on his cheek.

Touching his cheek with the palm of his left hand, Meg saw him ball his other hand into a fist. She stumbled to the hearth and grabbed the iron poker.

She held it with both hands in front of her. Then she said, "You'll pay a cost before you lay your hands on me again, Thomas. Now stand away from the door."

She saw his fist relax, and the fingers of that hand unfurl.

With his arms extended to either side, Thomas made a show of slowly backing away. "'Twas your clumsiness that caused your fall, it was not of my doing."

He brought a hand to his face and stroked his cheek. "If you say otherwise, people will believe the word of a gentleman before that of a commoner."

Meg flung the poker to the floor and stormed past him, slamming the parlor door behind her. She found John and Rachel standing nearby.

"Oh, dear Rachel, I suppose you heard our quarrel," Meg said tremulously.

Rachel said tenderly, "We weren't eavesdropping. Your voices carried quite clearly upstairs to our room. We just now came down when the shouting stopped. We were afraid for you."

"Thank you both," Meg said, with a quivering voice, "Can we go upstairs?"

Upstairs in their room, Rachel and Meg sat together on a miniature couch by the window. For a moment, they were quiet. Meg looked downcast; her hands clasped tightly in her lap.

Rachel reached out and took one of her hands. "Sometimes tears are good for us," she said.

Sitting straighter, Meg replied, "I'd rather not, dear Rachel. That odious, self-centered man isn't worth *one* of my tears. I'm only upset because he physically attacked me, and I had to take the fireplace poker to defend myself."

Rachel gasped as she glanced at John who was sitting across the room. John started for the door, but Rachel stopped him. "Please John, stay here with us!"

John shook his head in frustration. "You're asking much of me—maybe too much. He needs to be dealt with."

Someone knocked softly on the door. Already there, John opened it to find their four children huddled with worried faces. He ushered them in and stepped into the hallway.

He could see Thomas standing by his door at the far end of the hallway. Thomas took a step toward him and motioned with his arm.

"I'd like a word with you," he said, curtly.

"I would think that's in order after what you've done," John said, after hesitating a moment. He closed the door behind him and walked toward Thomas.

Stopping a few feet from his brother-in-law, John said, his voice dripping with contempt, "What is it you want to say?"

Behind him, John heard a door ease open and muffled footsteps. He turned to see Rachel and Meg, with the children behind them, coming toward him. When they reached him, he came back around to face Thomas.

"We're waiting." John said.

"I want the lot of you out of my house," Thomas replied, his eyebrow raised imperiously, "I'll not furnish food and comfort to feckless rebels any longer."

"That's to be expected from a man who lays his hands on women," John said, clenching his fists. "You should enjoy Fairview while you can," he said, sneering. "For the day is approaching when your sister and I will live here."

Thomas's face convulsed with hatred, and he wheeled about and stormed to his room, slamming the door behind him.

Everyone's eyes were on John. His lop-sided grin exuded confidence. He looked at Rachel and Meg and touched both their faces tenderly.

"It seems we're no longer welcome at Fairview," he said, his voice no longer full of tension.

Meg touched Rachel's shoulder. "You all will stay with me at my townhouse in the city. I need your company right now, and I have plenty of room."

With raised eyebrows, Rachel glanced toward John and said, "Will it be safe for us in Charles Town, John? Do you think there's a way we can get in?"

John didn't answer right away. He shifted his gaze and became very pensive for a few moments. "The British now own the Cooper River, after taking Monck's Corner. They have effectively sealed Charles Town. There's no longer a sure way in or out of the city."

"But John, are you saying I can't go home?" asked Meg, alarm clearly in her voice.

"No, I just mean it will take some planning to avoid the patrols and checkpoints." He turned to Rachel, "Do you believe Thomas will be a man of his word and not reveal us to the enemy?"

"My brother is a man who stands by his word. He may be many things foreign to me, but I believed him when he said that he would not turn us in. He places a lot of value on an English officer's word."

"Our lives will be in your brother's hands for a while, he replied. "There's an old Cherokee trail that parallels the Cooper River that we can try. Gather our things while Daniel and I see to the carriages."

Sarah's heart leaped in her chest. *Maybe I'll be able to find where Gideon is being held. Papa John may know a way we can free him.*

The day was ending when the carriages were packed and loaded. John and Lottie, astride their horses, led the way.

Only Rachel, driving her carriage, looked back. She caught the glimpse of a shadow at Thomas's window. Tears welled up in her eyes, but she hid them from Meg seated by her.

The women remained quiet for some time on the upholstered bench before Meg twisted to face her friend. "Rachel, I know it will sound strange to you, but I was never in love with Thomas. I'm thirty-four years old and beyond any girlish infatuations.

Our relationship was doomed from the beginning. He wanted the wealth and prestige that my estate would bring to his gentry, and I wanted the status his peerage would bring."

Rachel shifted the reins to her left hand and looked at her. "You don't need to share any of this," she said gently, "especially if it's painful for you. I know who my brother is, and he can never come between us."

"The only pain I feel comes from the hurt I've inflicted upon my daughter," Meg said. "She's known almost from the beginning that I've felt nothing for Thomas."

"Maybe," Rachel said, with a grin, "Ellie is stronger than her mother believes."

Puzzled, Meg asked, "What do you mean?"

Tilting her head forward, Rachel answered, "Look ahead of us and tell me what you see."

Ahead, Ellie was sitting close to Daniel with her arm tucked inside his.

"Oh my, how did this happen, Rachel? I'm mortified! They just met this morning!" exclaimed Meg. "This could never have happened when we were girls. Ellie has never given me cause to think she would act this way."

Rachel smiled slowly. "Times have changed considerably since we were their age, and then there's the war. There seems to be an urgency about every part of our everyday lives now. Gideon and Sarah were married the same day he proposed. Besides they're only sitting close. They're aware we can see them, so there's no need to worry."

CHAPTER SIXTEEN

AN OLD FRIEND - A NEW ENEMY

The miles rolled by and neither Daniel nor Ellie had spoken until the silence was broken when they both spoke at once.

Blushing, Daniel said, "I'm sorry, what were you about to say?"

She shrugged her shoulders. "I just want you to know how much I've enjoyed being with you today, even with the rumpus brought on by Thomas."

"I feel the same about you," he said, after hesitating a moment. "Of course, you're aware our mothers' are watching us. I imagine they've discussed how close we're sitting and the fact that your arm is entwined with mine."

Ellie, a mischievous smile playing on her lips, and a twinkle in her eye, said, "Do you want me to move, Daniel?"

Jerking his head toward her, he said, "Oh no, don't move. At first, I was a bit uncomfortable, but now it feels very nice."

She looked at his face, her lips puckered in a mock pouty expression. "I'm sorry if I've made you uncomfortable, Daniel."

Sighing heavily, he breathed, "Please, I'm not uncomfortable. It was a poor choice of words on my part. I feel good, really I do."

She scrunched a little closer and watched the corners of his mouth lifting.

Then they were quiet again.

⟞❈⟝ ⟞❈⟝ ⟞❈⟝

John raised his arm for everyone to stop. Some distance ahead, he could see a crossroads where several riders were milling around. John squinted, but couldn't tell if they were Whigs or Tories. "Take a look with the glass, Rachel. Tell us who they are."

Rachel extended the spyglass to its full length and held it to her eye. Almost immediately, she whispered, the loathing clear in her voice, "Green coated Tories! And two of them are riding toward us at a gallop!"

John touched his waistcoat pocket where he carried a forged Tory pass that he hoped would help speed them on their way.

"Let's keep our wits about us, everyone. Just remember we're loyal Tories, and we'll get through this just fine," John said his voice deep and calm.

They didn't have long to wait. Both riders rode headlong and drew up at the last second to sliding stops.

"Good afternoon, sirs, did we just witness a race?" John's tone was friendly and casual. "Your mounts are well matched, and I believe it ended in a draw."

The nearest rider, a beefy man with broad shoulders and bulky arms and legs dismounted. With a wave of his hand, he motioned for John to dismount. "Stand down, so we can have a closer look at you, and while you're doing it, let me see your papers."

Standing before the bulky Tory, John looked every bit a merchant in his dark gray three-piece suit. His silver buckled shoes with their high shine were earmarks of his prosperity.

John produced his forged papers from his waistcoat pocket and said, "How is it the king's militia rides together this close to the city?"

The man didn't look up, but read quickly, and when he came to the 'signature' of General Charles Cornwallis, his eyes narrowed and he looked intently into John's eyes. "Just how would you be deserving a passport signed by none other than Lord Cornwallis himself?"

Looking bored, John said evenly, "My relationship with the General is stated plainly in the letter, sir. I'm a saddler and cobbler by trade, a maker of leather goods. The general wears my custom made boots."

Passing the documents back to John, the man said, "And what, specifically, brings you to Charles Town when the roads and rivers are clogged with citizens who are leaving?"

Sweeping his arm in the direction of Rachel and Meg, John replied strongly, "We are guests of Mrs. Turnwell, the lady in yellow."

The Tory, who hadn't dismounted, said, "All right, Mr. Hamilton, you and your ladies may pass, but I wouldn't remain in Charles Town past a fortnight."

"But we're Loyalists, sir. Are you saying we won't be safe?" John said skeptically.

Believing he was talking to loyalist friends, the Tory responded, "I'm saying the king's artillery is random and chaotic. Civilians within the city itself are encouraged to leave, and you can see many are on the roads today doing just that. Today, with your spyglass, you can see a goodly portion of his majesty's fleet off Fort Moultrie. General Clinton has offered General Lincoln the opportunity to surrender and is now waiting for his answer."

Sweeping his arm in a westerly direction, he said, "Across yonder beyond Hampstead Hill, there are ramparts being built for fifty cannons and several thousand troops. Three days ago, General Clinton landed a force to seal off the south bank of the Ashley River. The city will be surrounded, and Generals Clinton and Cornwallis will continue the siege in earnest. No one will be able to enter or leave the city until the rebel General Lincoln surrenders his army."

John felt his throat tighten, along with his stomach. He steeled himself to show no emotions of remorse. For a moment, he was speechless; then he heard himself say, "Mrs. Turnwell does not wish to leave her home during the siege, and we'll see that she reaches it safely."

The Tories allowed them to pass and for several minutes, they cantered steadily and were soon on Meeting Street.

Nudging his horse forward, he said, "Now, let's take a look at your townhouse, Meg. I'll leave you and Rachel there while I talk with a friend. I shan't be long."

———————

Riding up Meeting Street, they noted the crowded sidewalks on either side of the street. Everyone seemed to be in a hurry. The streets were jammed with wagons, carriages, even wheelbarrows, each loaded with all it could hold. Armed blue-coated soldiers on horseback as well as sailors seemed to be everywhere; everything was in a noisy frenzy.

All of a sudden, John stopped his horse. He sat very still, his gaze focused on the skyline. Lottie came alongside, and asked, "What is it, Papa?"

No words escaped his lips, but he pointed ahead to a structure, painted black, that loomed higher than any of the other buildings around it.

Behind them, Meg gasped as she recognized what it was. "It's the steeple of St. Michael's; they've painted it black!

A group of soldiers, on foot, was pushing through the crowded street headed west when one of them stopped. Tipping his cocked hat to Meg, he said, "Aye ma'am, 'twas myself that gave the order to cover our lovely spire in black and to remove the beacon's light that has guided so many to safe harbor. We'll not be providing the redcoats' guns with a target to flatten downtown."

They weaved their way through the crowded street until they reached Meg's house. By the time the animals had been stabled and the carriages put away, they saw a woman running down the walk toward them from the three story brick building on the corner.

Breathless, she exclaimed, "Meg, what a pleasant surprise! I saw you coming and couldn't believe it, but isn't tomorrow your wedding day?"

Forcing a smile, Meg answered crisply, "At this time tomorrow, Amelia, I shall still be a widow. I can only tell you the reasons are many, but I'm happy with my decision to remain a free woman."

Amelia wasn't able to mask her shock. Her fingers covered her mouth while her widened eyes remained on Meg.

Seeing Amelia had been taken aback with her unexpected answer, Meg adroitly changed the subject by introducing everyone.

———————

The family was asleep when Ellie padded barefoot down the hall to her mother's room. She knocked gently on the door and listened to the steady ticking of the longcase clock. It was almost midnight. She was about to knock again when she heard the latch turn, and her mother, looking sleepy-eyed, partially opened the door.

"Ellie, what is it? Are you sick?"

"No, I'm fine, Mother. Can I come in? It's freezing out here in the hall."

Meg added another stick of wood to the fireplace. The light blazed up and threw dancing shadows against the walls of the room. "Come to bed, I have my bed warmer under the covers. What is so important that it can't wait until morning?"

Settled in the warm bed, Ellie sat with her back against one of her mother's large down pillows. "Mother, I love Daniel. If he were to ask me to marry him, I would say yes."

Overwhelmed at this unexpected bit of news, Meg quickly sat up and fluffed her pillow behind her. Shaking her head in disbelief, she said, "Ellie—dear Ellie, three days ago you didn't know he existed. You're only eighteen and couldn't possibly understand the meaning of love."

Ellie felt the heat rise from her neck, but she was determined to control her temper. The times she failed to do that, her mother always got the upper hand. Not this time . . . she would remain in control.

"Weren't you barely sixteen when you married papa? I've heard you tell the story of eloping in the middle of the night, as if it were an adventure you'd never forget, and I'm two years older than you were."

Meg shook her hair back in frustration. "Ellie, you cannot compare my life to the situation you now bring to me! That was totally a different time and circumstances."

Ellie saw her mother's eyes fill with tears, but she swallowed hard and willed her eyes to remain dry. Neither of them said anything for what seemed like an eternity.

Finally Meg said quietly, "And what of Daniel? If he were a gentleman as he pretends, he wouldn't be seducing a child."

Ellie had expected that her mother would think badly of Daniel. "Daniel hasn't seduced me, mother. Please don't say things that you know aren't true. He loves me as much as I love him, but he's wise beyond his years. He believes his future is so uncertain as long as the war continues that we should put thoughts of marriage aside for now."

Shaking her head, she stared at her daughter. "Nothing could have prepared me for this, Ellie. Would you tell me if anything further happened between the two of you?"

"Yes Mother, I would, and it hasn't. And it should be encouraging to you that your question doesn't upset me." Ellie said, holding her mother's hand. "It's because I'm mature enough to understand it comes from your heart."

"And where does this leave Andrew?" asked Meg, curtly. "Have you given any thought to how he will feel when you tell him about Daniel?"

"Andrew has no claim on me, Mother." Ellie said hotly. "If you are referring to grandfather's arrangement with Andrew's family when I was only a child of twelve, then I will tell you, I do not consent to become Andrew's wife—ever."

Looking deeply into her mother's eyes, Ellie said, "Do you support me on this, Mother?"

Meg realized she was wrong and had been so for a long time. Perhaps she'd been blinded by her close friendship with Andrew's mother . . . perhaps she had still wanted to please her father who now lay buried beside her mother.

Tears spill down Meg's face. "You know that I do, precious, and I'm deeply sorry for the part I played in allowing it to happen. I could never stand up to my father, and I've carried that burden in my heart for a long time."

She reached out to Ellie. "Your grandfather had promised you a birthday celebration and when we arrived, it turned out to be a marriage arrangement ceremony. You should know your father refused to sign the document and got in a heated argument with your grandfather, but the attorney said only grandfather's signature was needed since he would be providing the dowry."

Feeling tension building within her, Ellie said defiantly "And there's something else, Mother—something you and I've discussed many, many times—Andrew and his entire family are dyed in the wool Tories. We've managed to hide our patriot feelings from them, but if I should be forced to marry Andrew, I would be married to someone with whom I could not share my beliefs."

She paused to catch her breath. "I cannot bear the thought of living a lie for the rest of my life. We just don't love each other. By this time, Andrew should have declared his love for me. He hasn't, and that tells me that he's been pushed into this as much as I."

Ellie's emerald eyes grew a shade darker. "Andrew and I likely would've never met socially were it not for grandfather—and you know I speak the truth. I don't wish to dishonor grandfather's memory, but when he was alive, he controlled every aspect of my life. He decided what time I should rise each day and when to go to bed. The food I ate, the people with whom I socialized, and even the opinions I could express were all his to decide by decree."

—⊷◉⊶— —⊷◉⊶— —⊷◉⊶—

Spasms of pain struck Meg's heart, listening to her daughter relive the hurtful past, a past when she was unable to stand up to her father in Ellie's defense. Meg recalled how overjoyed Andrew's parents were when her father had granted his approval for Andrew to pay Ellie court. Even after the death of Meg's father, Andrew's parents saw that Ellie was invited to attend their dinner parties and social functions. There were many occasions that Ellie and Meg were the only guests—there could be no mistaking that Andrew's parents expected their son to wed Ellie.

"Mother, I've no desire to hurt you by bringing the memory of grandfather into this, and I don't wish to hurt Andrew, although I suspect he'll be relieved more than hurt. I only know that I love Daniel and that he loves me, and someday we'll be man and wife."

Her mother's face softened, and her eyes were full of tenderness "You've taken me by surprise, dear, but you shouldn't be in a hurry to get married. It's common knowledge you shall be wealthy; there shall always be beaus coming to your parlor. Daniel is your first affair of the heart."

Pulling her knees under her chin, Ellie sighed deeply. "I'm not in love with the color of Daniel's eyes, the sound of his voice, or his face, as handsome as it is. Nor have his kisses befuddled me. I—"

"He's kissed you?" her mother blurted, raising her hand to her mouth in shock.

"Shhh, you'll wake everyone up!"

Lowering her voice, Meg asked apprehensively, "When, in heaven's name, did this take place?"

"Yesterday, during our afternoon ride, and before you think badly of Daniel, I asked *him* to kiss *me.*"

"Darling, ladies just don't ask to be kissed—I shouldn't have to tell you that. Whatever could you have been thinking?"

"I—well, I wanted to know what it was like to be kissed, Mother. I'm likely to be an old woman before Andrew gets around to it."

Meg was emotionally drained; she straightened her pillow and lay back. She watched the flames of the fireplace consume the new wood she'd just added. After some moments of silence, she reached for her daughter's hand. "We need our sleep; please stay here with me for the rest of the night."

Ellie kissed her mother on her cheek and lay down beside her.

Meg then snuffed the lone candle. "Good night, Ellie."

"Good night, Mama."

The soft light from the fireplace bathed the room, and the only sound was the random popping and crackling logs. Meg lay back, fully awake, to wait for sleep.

CHAPTER SEVENTEEN

BAD NEWS IS GOOD NEWS

At dawn, the British guns sounded from all directions bringing a hailstorm of fireballs. The firing was steady and lasted through breakfast. Shortly after the shelling stopped, thunder rolled in the distance.

Meg looked wistfully toward the window. *Thank you Lord! Maybe the rain will dampen the king's powder enough to stop the shelling.*

She knew that John and his family were anxious to leave Charles Town as quickly as possible. Rachel was clearly in an agitated state, especially when the house and grounds shook so violently from the British shelling.

Edging forward on her chair, Meg cleared her throat. *Where to begin when I don't know my own feelings?*

Reaching across the breakfast table for the hand of her dearest friend, Meg began, "Rachel, please forgive me for delaying our departure, but Ellie came to my room last night and made me aware of her feelings for your Daniel."

A gasp of shock escaped Rachel's lips and her eyes widened in a look of clear amazement. "Wh-what—"

Meg said tremulously, "Surely, you're aware of Daniel's intentions with Ellie."

Perplexed, Rachel looked at Meg and then at John and asked, "It's evident they've become friends, but if it's more than that, then we're not aware of it. What are you talking about, Meg?"

Seeing that she had upset them, Meg searched for words to make them feel better. After a moment's hesitation, she replied, "Oh, I meant nothing dreadful toward Daniel. He's a fine young man; a gentleman in all respects. I suppose the prospect of losing my home and property was just too much to hear at once."

Taking Rachel's hand, Meg said, "Last night, Ellie came to my room and confided that she and Daniel are in love. Of course, I couldn't get back to sleep after that, but by this morning, I've gotten past it. These last few days have been calamitous for me, but I'll manage."

A series of rapid knocks at the front door brought the housekeeper to answer it. She came hurrying into the parlor with a letter, neatly folded and sealed with the Hayecrest emblem, addressed to Rachel.

"It's from Thomas," Rachel whispered anxiously.

Hands shaking, she opened the letter and passed it to John, who began reading aloud.

Rachel,

The men captured from the skirmish at Monck's Corner have been transferred to ships offshore and will depart soon for Honduras. However, several of the rebels escaped to St. James swamp before reaching the ships, killing three British soldiers to gain their freedom. Gideon must have been among those who escaped, since he is not among those headed for Honduras. Nonetheless, Gideon, along with his counterparts, has a price on his head for the murder of one or more of his majesty's soldiers. Like father, like son wouldn't you say?

Colonel Thomas Covington

Earl of Hayecrest

His Majesty's 64th Regiment of Foot

Rachel sighed heavily and covered her face with her hands. John moved closer and comforted her.

"I'm going to fetch Sarah, she needs to know about her husband," he said.

John returned with Sarah, and Rachel opened her arms and held her while John and Meg looked on.

Meg moved to sit beside the women. "Surely your tears are ones of joy and hope," Meg said. "Gideon is free, and I'm sure he'll find a way to let you know of his whereabouts soon."

Sarah dabbed her eyes. "Aye, 'tis true, my tears are from a thankful heart that my husband managed to escape his captors, yet until the day he's once again in my arms, there'll be an empty place in my heart."

———

From their chairs on the veranda, Daniel and Ellie had overheard most of the conversation from the parlor. Daniel stood and took Ellie by the hand to lead her inside.

"I need to see about mother," he said grimly.

Inside, Daniel placed his hand on his mother's shoulder and said, "I knew Gideon would find a way to get free, Ma, and he'll find a way to get back home, too, Sarah. You just wait."

Rachel made an effort to smile and patted his hand. Sarah stood up and hugged Daniel. "Thank you, Daniel. My tears came from the shock of hearing Gideon was free. God willing, we'll hear from him soon."

She dabbed her reddened eyes. "I'm so fortunate to be a part of this family. God has blessed me many times over in giving me Gideon as my husband."

Daniel took her hand and looked directly at her. "Sarah, when Gideon was only twelve, and I was two years younger, we were kidnapped by Cherokee renegades. After three days of running, they took us to their main camp and sort of relaxed. I guess they thought two little boys would be too scared to give'em any trouble. They let us sleep without tying us up, and that's all Gideon needed. I don't remember everything that happened that night, but I do remember running until I couldn't take another step and my brother carrying me most of the way until we reached the settlement of Ninety Six."

Rachel grinned. "I'm glad you reminded us of that time, Daniel. You boys seem to have always been able to take care of yourselves. If there's a way home, he'll find it, and if not, he'll make a way."

Ellie pulled Daniel to the door. "You're a good son to your mother," she whispered.

With a somber expression on his face, he said, "I meant every word. None of what I said was just to cheer my mother and Sarah up. Gideon, if he can stay alive, will find his way back— no doubt about it."

"Let's sit on the swing," she breathed, pointing to the far end of the porch, "Mother kept the window open to eavesdrop on our conversation, but she didn't consider that we would also be able to hear the talk coming from the parlor."

Seating herself beside him, Ellie said, "Would you like for me to come to stay with your family?"

Daniel grasped her hand firmly. "Yes, I would. I can think of nothing that would please me more than to see you at the beginning of every day, but is that something you want, Ellie?"

"Oh yes, I've been so melancholy just thinking about you leaving me in a few days," she said buoyantly, "and now we're going to be together."

For a few minutes, they sat quietly, arm in arm, basking in the glow of their newfound love.

The quiet was broken when she took his hand and squeezed his fingers. "Tell me about your time in the militia. Were you gone for a long time?"

Sighing audibly, Daniel said, "War isn't a suitable topic for a man to discuss with a lady."

Ellie, sorry she'd unsettled him, decided to speak boldly from her heart. "Wouldn't a husband confide such a topic with his wife?" she replied.

Stunned, Daniel stared at her, his mind racing to sort out the meaning of what she had just said. "B-but, we're not . . . I mean—"

Holding back a giggle, Ellie said, "Oh Daniel, 'tis not that I'm thoughtless and loose with my words, surely you must know I love you."

"How old are you, Ellie?" he asked calmly.

She looked at him and wondered if she had revealed her heart too soon. "I'm eighteen and old enough to know my own heart. There will never be another man for me, Daniel Hamilton. I know I love you, and someday, I shall be Mrs. Daniel Hamilton."

Daniel gazed deeply into her blue-green eyes and drew a line down her slim and delicate nose with his finger. "You know my feelings. My heart yearns for the day when you shall carry my name, but I've seen a lot of life and too much death to pretend we're married. When Pa decides it's time again for the militia to ride and face the redcoats, I'll be with him."

Ellie exhaled deeply; his words had seared her heart, but she refused to let him go. "I don't believe you've seen so much of life, nor even death, that you can't confess your love for me."

She placed her hand on his chest, and the steady beating of his heart sent a shiver through her. "I now plant the seed of my love in your heart, and only I can remove it. Wherever you go, no matter how far, nor how long you shall be away, I'll be with you."

Neither spoke for a few moments until Ellie broke the silence. "Come, I want to speak with Mother."

They came into the parlor where their parents were still in conversation. "Excuse me for interrupting, but Daniel and I would like to go for a walk. Would that be all right, Mother?"

Glancing at Rachel before she answered, Meg said, "Yes, but don't go too far, nor be out too long. It'll be dark soon."

"Thank you, we'll walk as far as the State House and come back," Ellie said.

<hr />

Ellie and Daniel walked slowly down Meeting Street. Pointing to the unbroken line of border plants edging her mother's garden, Ellie said, "Aren't these camellias beautiful, Daniel? They like to show off their blaze of color during these dreary days."

Daniel noticed the flowers for the first time. "Yes, they are, it'll be a miracle if they survive the bombs and cannon shot."

"Shh," let's not talk about the war. It's too—"

With an abruptness that shattered the serenity of the afternoon, the British artillery came alive with an ear-splitting roar. Solid shot passed over their heads and slammed through roofs and walls of buildings and homes around them. Deadly splintered beams of wood, bricks, and shingles flew through the air around them. Daniel crouched and pulled Ellie to him in the covered doorway of a stuccoed brick mercantile building. Destruction and disarray was before them in every direction.

Screams and crying of women and children could be heard above the roar of the cannons. Over their heads, Daniel could see red-hot round shot and bombs streaking from every direction; it felt as if it was the end of the world. A whooshing sound passed directly over their heads as a fireball crashed into the roof of an empty building across the street. The roof ignited almost immediately and became a fiery inferno before their eyes.

The thought that they would not survive brought a feeling of desperation over him. He wanted to kiss her this time without thinking about whether he was doing it right or wrong. Pulling her to him, he slipped his other arm under hers, and leaned forward toward her beautiful upturned face until his lips pressed softly against hers.

Releasing her and holding her hands in his, Daniel said, "Whatever directions our lives take, Ellie, I plight thee my troth, now and forever."

The noise and commotion shook the ground around them, but went unnoticed as she responded, "As do I my dear Daniel, I plight thee my troth, now and forever."

There on Meeting Street amid the smoky clouds of spent gunpowder and chaotic destruction, the young couple held each other and witnessed the death throes of their beloved Charles Town.

As sudden and unexpected as it had started, the thunderous British artillery stopped and before the dust and smoke began to settle, a smattering of people began coming outside to view the destruction.

"We'd better get back, your mother will be worried about you," Daniel said pulling Ellie's arm.

Looking up at Daniel, she said, "Were you scared, Daniel?"

Touching her lips with his finger, he replied, "I must tell you I was scared, Ellie. We were at the mercy of a random shot. There was no place to hide; no place to run."

Leaning against his arm, she said, "I don't remember a time when I've been as scared as I was during that barrage, but it was different than when I was a little girl. This time, as I huddled in your arms, I knew you couldn't save us, but if we were hit by one of those hideous bombs, we'd be together forever."

Returning from their ordeal, Ellie saw a familiar horse at the gate to her house. She pulled her hand from Daniel's grasp.

Daniel sensed she was disturbed and said, "I see you have company."

"Yes, I do. It's Andrew, a family friend."

They found Andrew in the parlor with Meg and Daniel's family. Andrew came to his feet quickly when he saw her and came to greet her.

Ellie choked back the instinct to panic while she took a moment to pull her thoughts together. She extended her hand and pasted on a bright smile.

"Hello Ellie," he said, brushing her fingers lightly with his lips, "you look lovely today,"

"Thank you," she replied, in a quiet voice, not sure what more to say.

Andrew continued confidently, "I apologize for stopping by unannounced, but my parents are hosting a small affair tomorrow evening to celebrate my brother's commission as

Major in Lord Cornwallis's Legion. I would like for you to be there with me."

Ellie could barely manage a smile with so many eyes focused on her, and she was very much aware that Daniel had positioned himself close beside her.

It was Meg who saved the day when she came to her daughter's side and said, "Ellie, we all were about to have our coffee in the study; you and Andrew can join us shortly."

Meg took Daniel's arm and led the Hamiltons to the study. Andrew waited until no one was left in the parlor, before he again took Ellie's hand.

Ellie studied Andrew's face as he stared at the parlor door. It was apparent to her that he was upset. "Would you care to sit on the couch, Andrew?" she asked.

Struggling with emotions he couldn't explain, he nodded and took a seat beside her. He knew he didn't like seeing Ellie with Daniel. She seemed altogether too happy to be with him.

Is this jealousy I feel? Andrew asked himself. *Should I be jealous? I think not; he's nothing more than a backwoods saddler's son, yet he stood so close to Ellie, and her hand was tucked securely into the crook of his arm. That was surely her doing.*

Ellie fixed her gaze across the room toward the fireplace; her face a picture of composure, but she felt the intensity of his unsettling stare. He never took his unblinking eyes from her face.

She turned to look at him. "Andrew, I shan't be able to attend your brother's party tomorrow evening. Would you carry my congratulations to him?"

Ignoring her question, his jaw tightened as he looked at her with obvious resentment and anger. "Just as I figured, it's because of him—Daniel."

She opened her mouth to speak, but he interrupted. "Where did he take you?" he said with a tone of bitterness in his voice. Without waiting for an answer, he said, "I've been here almost an hour."

Ellie's stomach tightened as she examined her hands in her lap. A storm was approaching; she could see it in his eyes and hear it in his voice. She hadn't considered that Andrew would ever react with such possessiveness.

CHAPTER EIGHTEEN

A PARTING OF WAYS

Willing her emotions to quieten, Ellie said evenly, "Andrew, I'll answer your question, if you'll allow me the courtesy of asking a questions of you."

With a self-confident smile, he nodded. "Very well, I've nothing to hide."

Ellie paused to take a breath. "We went for a walk to the Exchange."

He tilted his head back and looked slightly down at her. "How callous of your frontiersman, a gentleman would never consider exposing a lady to such risk."

Andrew's face provided her with no clue as to what he was thinking. She studied his penetrating eyes until she had to avert her gaze. Thinking he might see that as weakness on her part, she decided it would be best to tell him of her feelings for Daniel straightaway.

She lifted her eyes again to his, and said, "Andrew, you've paid me court for almost one year. Yet, we've never gone beyond polite handholding, nor have you ever professed your intentions."

Getting up to stand by a window, "Can you tell me why you're behaving as you are now? Your conduct leads me to believe you're jealous."

He said, his voice trembling with frustration, "I've been careful in my in my courtship of you since your mother's open ties with the rebels' cause are so well known. By default you are suspect as well, and if I'm seen in your company, it reflects on my family—my father in particular."

Ellie felt her chest tighten, and her throat was dry. "Not that it would have changed anything, but why would you tell me of this now?"

Shaking his head, he replied, "I can't say."

He reached to take her hand because, more than anything, he wanted to touch her. She withdrew her hand from his grasp and reached for her handkerchief.

Andrew became silent and looked at his empty hand. His eyes turned to one side, avoiding her direct gaze.

Then he breathed a muted sigh. "Am I too late to pay you court, Ellie? You haven't told me of your feelings for Daniel. Is your heart already set on him, or have I a chance at winning your affections?"

Ellie was touched by the gentleness of his voice and his heartfelt words. She was silent for a lingering moment to think of some words that she might use to say what he didn't want to hear. Andrew was part of her childhood, and she didn't want that memory tarnished. He was honest and straightforward in his request, and she must honor that with a forthright answer.

"Andrew, I must tell you; Daniel is more than a friend," she said. "I love him, and he loves me. We have each declared our love for the other, and we look forward to marriage once this war is over."

He breathed deeply and stared past her for a brief moment of time. Then he brought both his hands together pressing hers between them.

"Ellie, I can't accept the finality of your words. From what your mother's told me, the two of you met just days ago. This can only be an infatuation, at best, so I feel I must protect you from your own foolish heart."

He moved closer to her, until his knees touched her gown. Although she was covered with several layers of petticoats under her skirt, Ellie moved back.

The set of his jaw gave him the look of a man frustrated, but not defeated. "Perhaps I *have* neglected to call on you recently, but in any case, you and I have a marriage contract agreed to by your grandfather and my father. I intend to uphold my end of the matter."

Ellie was stunned and yanked her hands back to free them from his grip, but he held her firmly. "Oh come now, surely you remember the occasion. It was on your twelfth birthday that your grandfather, with the benign approval of your parents, agreed to establish a rather large dowry for our marriage. You and I stood together as the legal document was signed in the presence of our family's attorney."

"Loose my hands Andrew. I'd hoped we would part friends. We share so many good memories, and our families have known each other since before we were born," she said, nostalgia reflected in her eyes. "But our union was never meant to be. I will never consent to become your wife."

Andrew kept her hands firmly clasped in his and stared at her.

Ellie felt heat rising up her neck. "There's denial written all over your face, Andrew. Well then, I shall remind you that the sole owner of my grandfather's estate, the dowry money included, is my Mother."

Watching his face as that bit of news sunk in, she said, "When you see your father again, break the news to him gently."

Andrew raised her hand to his lips and lightly pressed a kiss to her fingers. "A man must face the challenges life throws his way head-on."

"It's rumored that Daniel and his father have fought for the patriots," he said in a tone that chilled her heart. I look forward to the opportunity to meet my rival on the field of battle. Perhaps it *is* wise that you do not marry just now...."

Ellie felt the blood drain from her face. She willed the churning in the pit of her stomach to quieten. "Andrew, how could you come into my home and utter such vile words? You've just destroyed any feeling of friendship I may have had for you. Please leave—I never want to see you again."

She immediately left the room and ran upstairs to her room.

————————————

Andrew slammed the door behind him, but he was so blinded by rage, he didn't hear it. Standing on the veranda, anguish and jealously thundered in his chest. *How can she forsake all I can offer for a life on the edge of civilization? How can she turn her back on the only life she has ever known to live in a log cabin surrounded by Indians and renegades?*

He didn't hear the footsteps behind him until a voice called his name. Startled, he jumped and whirled around, coming face to face with Daniel.

Andrew's anger surged with renewed fervor. "You! Stay away from Ellie! She's not for the likes of you."

Daniel saw that Andrew was close to losing control of his anger. "By that, you mean she's for the likes of you. Is that it?"

"Yes, you ignorant backwoodsman, Ellie's a woman of cultured breeding, no doubt beyond your—"

Andrew never saw it coming. In fact, it was the last thing he was expecting. Daniel's fist caught Andrew flush on the jaw, sending him off the landing and into the street, unconscious.

Daniel rubbed the knuckles of his hand. *That's for sending her to her room crying.*

Flexing his hand, Daniel pondered whether he should help Andrew wake up. *He actually looks as if he's napping.*

Looking at Andrew with disgust, Daniel sighed and knelt beside him and gave him a good shaking. "Wake up, m'lord, wake up!"

⊷•◦•⊷ ⊷•◦•⊷ ⊷•◦•⊷

Andrew's eyes fluttered opened and he moaned. "W-what happened? W-who—"

Daniel came slowly in focus as Andrew's eyes narrowed, and his mind stopped spinning. Then he sprang up on his elbows and cried, "You struck me, you savage! Get back or I'll—"

A pounding headache cut any off any further talking. With both hands, he grabbed the sides of his head and groaned.

When the headache calmed enough for him to stand, he looked around for Daniel, but he was gone.

Andrew rode with no regard for his horse or himself; he had to escape the embarrassment and pain of Ellie's rejection. He whipped his horse on, faster and faster, until red lines of blood streamed down the animal's flanks; it was running its heart out.

Andrew was through with Ellie, and with her arrogant and high-handed mother, but Daniel was another matter. *I'm not through with that ignorant backwoodsman, no sir, not by a long shot.*

He reached home, threw the reins to the ground, and flung the bloodied and frayed whip onto the front lawn. Storming into his house, he started upstairs for his bedroom, but the doorman stopped him. "Mister Andrew, Mister William is waiting for you in his study—your mother is with him."

"Tell him I'm tired and will talk with him tomorrow," Andrew said, with a defiant edge to his voice.

Before Andrew could take another step, the old man said crisply, "Mister Andrew, you might ought to reconsider. I ain't never seen your father like he is tonight."

Andrew looked down at the scuff marks on his boots. *Another lecture! This will be the last, and if he dares to lay a hand on me. . . .*

Andrew knocked lightly on the door and went in. Closing the door behind him, he saw his father standing at the mantle before the fireplace and his mother seated in a nearby wingback chair. He could tell they had been in conversation before he came in.

"Do you want to see me, Father?" Andrew said, with a feigned smile.

Motioning for his son to take a seat, William said, "Yes, you may take a seat, if you wish."

"Thank you, sir, but I prefer to stand." Andrew replied, casting his eyes toward his mother whose eyes remained focused on her husband.

His father stood stiffly with his hands clasped tightly behind his back, his face unreadable. "I'll come right to the point, son. I don't intend to lecture you on any of your many transgressions. I've obtained a commission in the army for you. You have an appointment tomorrow morning with General Sir Henry Clinton at his headquarters on Simmons' Island."

Casting his eye toward his wife, William paused. "I don't know why Henry wants to meet with you, but an escort will meet you at Stono Inlet to take you to him. He's expecting you at 10 o'clock, so please be prompt."

Andrew's mind was reeling with this bit of news; he looked to his mother for some guidance, but her eyes remained fixed on her husband.

"Father, I must tell you I have other appointments—"

In two steps, his father was in his face. Andrew could see the veins on his neck standing out. "Not another word, Andrew! I called you here to tell you how things will be beginning tomorrow. I'll entertain no discussion about the matter. I'm through with your broken promises and shameful behavior. The girl from the King's Ale Tavern showing up here claiming you're the father of her mongrel child was the last straw."

Andrew stared sullenly at the window, watching the trees sway in the breeze. His father stepped back and straightened his waistcoat. "If you choose to not accept a commission, then I shall blot your name from any inheritance and immediately reduce your present allowance to one hundred pounds annually."

Bitterness turned to fury as Andrew stared into his father's cold eyes. His mother still had not looked at him; it was as if he no longer was her son. Andrew closed his eyes and dropped his head. There had been no warning; his mother had always shielded him from his father's wrath.

It's all because of the tavern girl, and I can't even remember her name!

Unsure of what to say, he sighed deeply, gritting his teeth. *He knows he's left me no choice, and my mother has united with him against me.*

Contempt was scrawled across Andrew's face, and he made no effort to hide it. "Very well, Father. I'll see Sir Henry tomorrow morning."

⬥ ⬥ ⬥

Ellie kicked off her shoes, collapsed across her bed fully clothed, and buried her head in a feather pillow. Her body shook with the unrestrained sobs. Twisting in the covers, she struggled to understand what had happened. When her sobs finally waned, she saw the sun had set, and the pillow was wet with her tears. She turned over and lay staring at the ceiling until sleep closed her eyes.

Her body jerked, and right away she was awake. A noise had awakened her, and she sat up and listened. Nothing—the only sound was the rhythmic crackling of the waning embers from her fireplace. She was about to relax, and there it was again. Now she recognized the sound—soft tapping at her door.

Thinking it might be her mother, she was tempted not to answer, but then she heard a voice whisper her name. *It's Daniel!*

She hurried to the door and cracked it open. He opened it farther and stepped past her.

"Daniel, you can't come into my bedroom," she said emphatically.

Shrugging, he said, "Hush, keep your voice down. I wanted to see you, and besides you look fully dressed to me." He eased the door closed and went to the fireplace. Stirring the embers a bit, he placed a couple of small pieces of wood over them to rekindle the fire.

He sat on the floor beside her chair and said, "Please sit here. I won't stay long, I promise. I just wanted to see you and make sure you were all right."

Sighing deeply, she settled in the chair and began straightening her crumpled skirt. Suddenly, she became conscious that her tiny stocking-clad feet were peeping out. She tugged briskly to straighten the wrinkled pleats and cover her feet. She glanced toward Daniel, and he was grinning from ear to ear.

Ellie's first impulse was to turn her head to conceal her embarrassment, but she found herself grinning with him.

Daniel looked at her in the growing firelight. Shining bright in the flickering flames, her honey-gold hair had fallen and spilled over her shoulders. Sparkles of light danced about in her turquoise eyes. She had the face of an angel, and he could never tire of just looking at her.

His reverie was sharply broken by her impassioned, exasperated voice. "You're quite bold, Daniel Hamilton! Did you come in here just to get warm? You have a fireplace in your bedroom. I suggest you go to it, sir."

Seeing the hurt expression on his face, she immediately regretted her outburst. He was getting to his feet, when she stopped him. "Oh please forgive me, Daniel. I've been so upset since Andrew's visit that I don't know from one minute until the next what to say or do. Please sit back down, and I'll tell you what happened."

Her bedroom door suddenly opened, and Meg came in. "I thought I heard talking in here." Her eyes, with the passionate glare that could only come from a mother protecting the virtue of a daughter, darted to Daniel. "You'd better have a believable reason for your presence in Ellie's bedroom, young man."

Daniel had risen to his feet and was now looking contrite and trying to avoid the glare of Meg's stare. "Mrs. Turnwell, I seem to keep finding a way to upset you, but I assure you my intentions, while on the surface may look ungentlemanly, are honorable at heart."

Courage came to his voice, and he stepped to Ellie's side and placed his hand on the back of her chair. "I came in, *without* Ellie's invitation, to assure myself that she was all right. I happened to see her earlier when she ran crying from the parlor to her bedroom, and I knew I couldn't sleep without knowing whether or not she was all right."

Ellie thought she could see her mother's expression softening. "Come sit, Mother, I want to tell you and Daniel about Andrew's visit."

⟡ ⟡ ⟡

An avalanche of morning light flooded through the tall dining room windows as Annie assembled hot breakfast dishes on the sunny table. Meg seated her guests and began lifting the covers off the dishes for everyone to serve themselves while Annie served steaming coffee. John sighed contentedly when he took his first sip of hot coffee.

Ellie had not yet come down for breakfast, and Meg noted Daniel kept a watchful eye on the door, but he seemed otherwise to be in a sociable mood. Their eyes met briefly, and she was encouraged more so by the engaging smile that creased his face. No doubts lingered in her mind about Daniel. She knew his love for Ellie was real and would stay real for a lifetime.

Meg was about to go see about her daughter when the young woman appeared at the door. Ellie was positively radiant. She was dressed in her favorite gown; a sky blue two-piece costume consisting of a hip-length jacket with split sleeves. Her hair was curled high to catch the full effect of the bright sunlight.

Her hesitation at the door was just long enough to halt the conversation. Daniel moved quickly to escort her to an empty chair next to him. Meg noted the apparent familiarity that had grown between Daniel and her daughter. He whispered, and Ellie smiled while their eyes never left each other. Ellie rested her hand on his as he led them to the table.

Ellie took her seat and smiled cheerily around the table, lingering to gently blow her mother a kiss. "Good morning everyone, I'm sorry I overslept."

The conversation resumed while the cook returned with the serving bowl and platter and waited while Ellie served her plate, and Daniel refilled his empty plate, as well.

Shortly, Meg stood and said, "I'm having coffee brought to the study, John, if you'd care to join Rachel and me." Swallowing the lump in her throat, she continued, "I've finished sorting through my possessions and am ready to leave."

John rubbed his chin and nodded his approval. "I must meet my friend, Patrick Hopkins this afternoon and when I return, we'll pack your wagon for an early start in the morning."

Looking elated, Meg said with enthusiasm, "Oh, I know Patrick, he's a baker, and I might add, a good one—very well known throughout Charles Town, but only a few close to him know that Patrick and Amelia are patriots and Quakers, albeit a bit unorthodox. He keeps a musket close at hand, and will defend himself and his family, when the time comes."

John nodded, "Yes, Patrick is very adept in his business dealings with the public. That's why I've chosen him to remain in Charles Town. He can play the part of a devout Tory baker and be a tremendous asset for our cause.

CHAPTER NINETEEN

A PERILOUS ESCAPE

The enticing aroma of fresh baked bread and tempting sweet rolls filled the air for blocks around Patrick's bakery. A small crowd waited outside for seating, and John drew a few frowns and stares when he weaved past the queue and went inside. Once in, he noticed a counter with seats for a dozen customers and five tables that accommodated twenty.

Two young girls were handling the tables and behind the counter was a round, chubby little woman whose cap was crooked on her head. All three women wore white starched aprons.

John caught a glimpse of Amelia in the backroom kitchen, but didn't see Patrick, and the women out front were too busy to stop and talk with him. He was about to leave to come back later when a shrill woman's voice shouted his name.

"John, don't leave. I'll be right there!" It was Amelia rushing toward him. She, too, wore a clean, starched apron, but with traces of flour on her forehead, he surmised she was the one responsible for the sweet smelling pastries that were being consumed by the contented shop guests.

"Good morning, John. Are you alone?" Not waiting for his answer, she looked around, "It seems all of our seats are taken." Then, she took him by his hand and led him back to the kitchen.

She motioned toward a desk in a corner. "Sit here John, and I'll get you some of my fresh apple pie to go with your coffee."

He sat back and marveled at the work being done here in the kitchen. There were two young women busily washing dishes, and two more who looked to be fortyish attending to the ovens and preparation tables.

Amelia was back with a large slice of pie and cup of steaming coffee. "We began our business from our home kitchen selling apple pies, and it just kept growing. That was five years ago. Now we also deliver bread, pies, and pastries all over Charles Town in three carriages. Patrick and the husbands of our dishwashers make the deliveries."

John sliced his fork into the pie and took his first taste. "Mmmm, Amelia, this is the best apple pie I've ever tasted!"

Her face beaming, she said, "Thank you, John. I would like to visit with you, but we have at least another hour before the crowd dwindles back to normal."

"Actually, I came by to see Patrick, but since he's out with the deliveries, would you and he stop by Meg's house this evening—about seven? It's very important that I speak with him before we return to Camden."

Her face turned serious, and she stared intently into his eyes. "Yes, we'll be there at seven this evening."

⋙⋘ ⋙⋘ ⋙⋘

Promptly at seven, Meg escorted Patrick and Amelia into the parlor. Patrick was a slender, clean-shaven man of average height. His three-piece suit, while not lavish, reflected his status as a successful merchant. At a passing glance, Patrick would seem to be a man accustomed to living in ease and affluence, but until he married, Patrick had lived west of the Blue Ridge Mountains.

By the time everyone was seated, John and Patrick were already in discussion about the ominous cloud hanging over Charles Town. Both men agreed General Lincoln would be unable to fend off a concerted attack by General Clinton.

"Clinton has the upper hand this time around, John," Patrick said. "I've heard he's negotiating with Lincoln about the terms of surrender."

"If Lincoln surrenders, there'll be no American army in South Carolina," John said, shaking his head. "Surrender makes no sense. Surely, Lincoln recognizes his surrender could possibly trigger the total collapse of our cause. The ripple effect would be felt all the way to Philadelphia."

"Someone I know who works out of Lincoln's headquarters is saying Lincoln isn't taking any counsel from his officers; his mind is made up."

John quietly observed his friend, the fire was in his eyes; he was not a quitter—he would be there trying until his dying breath.

After a few minutes of back and forth conversation, John said, "Patrick, I need someone who has a sharp eye for what's happening around them, someone with good hearing, and a good memory. This person must be able to remember what they've seen and heard and transfer that information to paper."

Patrick nodded his head and started to speak, but John held up his hand and said, "Wait, there's more. You must know that the risk of being caught is real and the penalty is always death by hanging. You'll be alone; no one will be able to help you."

Patrick had absorbed everything John was saying, and he had no doubts at all. "I want to work with you, John—to help in any way I can. I know the risks, and I know Charles Town cannot withstand the siege. If he won't retreat, then Lincoln will be forced to surrender."

He reached for Amelia's hand and gazed into her eyes. "My wife and I are fighters. We'll remain where we are after the inevitable and serve the redcoats. Our shop has always been a public meeting place where secrets are shared, sometimes overtly, sometimes not. Amelia and I expect the British and their friends will be just as forthcoming in their conversations. Among themselves, they're know-it-all boasters."

John, with his familiar lop-sided grin, stood up and everyone expected him to speak. He lingered until the grin was gone, and his face took on a determined look.

"I'm glad to have Patrick and Amelia as our newest 'soldiers'. They join an exclusive company. The men and women of our band each have a common strength, they're fighters; people who are eager to take the fight to the enemy."

John's eyes swept the room, and his shoulders squared away and his back became a bit straighter. "If this city is surrendered to Clinton, there will be a lot of people who've claimed to be patriots who'll give in and quit. Nevertheless, many won't give up, and I expect you, in this room, to be among the many that don't. We're in every colony, and there'll be more than a few of us in South Carolina."

Patrick cleared his throat. "I don't mind saying that the wife and I pick up a lot of information every day, and we've had occasion, once or twice, to send that to General Lincoln."

Looking a little sheepish, he said, "Once we sent a letter hidden in a loaf of fresh baked bread."

John slapped his palms together and exclaimed, "That's exactly what's needed! We must know what the British are doing and what they're planning to do next. Keep your ears open; it doesn't matter how you come across the information. Don't try to decide whether or not the information is important; just send it on."

Amelia leaned forward in her chair and said, "Patrick and I heard something yesterday from more than one of our Tory customers. Clinton has landed a force near Cummins Point on the Neck. Before sunset, we were able to get up to the attic and spotted them with Patrick's spyglass." Turning to her husband, she said, "You finish, Patrick. You know about cannons and such."

"We got a good look at'em. It looked to be at least a thousand soldiers building a long curving rampart and artillery emplacements. Just before we come over tonight, they had eight pieces set up. It looked like three howitzers, two mortars, and three big guns, looking to be sixteen pounders."

"Does that mean more shelling?" asked Meg with some apprehension in her voice.

"It's not going to let up until Lincoln surrenders," Patrick said. "Clinton's ships are getting past Fort Moultrie with ease, so they've got a good many big guns already in place. From what the wife and I've seen with our glass, there's more than two hundred big guns aimed at us."

Amelia nudged her husband. "If we stay much longer, there'll be no need for us to go to bed. Our day starts at four a.m., so we must say good night."

After Patrick and Amelia left, Meg begged her leave and went upstairs to bed.

Tugging her husband's arm, Rachel said, "Let's go upstairs, we don't know what tomorrow holds."

John resisted. "You go on to bed; I'll be along shortly."

She came back to sit in his lap. "There's no need for you to sit there and brood. No matter what happens, you need your rest."

He grinned crookedly. "I'll be up shortly."

She leaned over, kissed his forehead, and breathed, "Good night."

John drew the wingback chair closer to the fireplace. Stretching his long legs toward the heat, he settled back. Concern was written across his brow as he listened to the mesmerizing sounds of soft crackling from the fireplace and watched the remaining embers glowing and twinkling.

Maybe we've waited too long to leave for home. Is there a way to Camden that's open now? How am I going to keep everyone safe?

After a while, his eyes grew heavy, and his head began to nod. His breathing grew more regular, and then he was asleep. A shadow passed over him as Annie tiptoed by him to place the screen across the fireplace opening. She quietly gathered the cups and saucers and eased toward the door. The night passed in safety, and the sun, yet still below the horizon, eventually yielded its faint light over Charles Town. John had awakened sometime in the night and was now sleeping soundly in his bed.

<hr />

Just as dawn's light opened the day, the air itself seemed to explode. A deafening rolling boom reverberated up and down the streets and alleys. John felt the bed shake and the windowpanes shook. A candlestick on the bedside table quivered and fell to the floor. This time the booming sound was sustained without letup.

John and Rachel dressed hurriedly and made their way downstairs. Standing just outside the front door, John said, yelled over the booming, "It's too dangerous right now for us to leave. A good bit of this cannon fire is also coming from British ramparts near the Ashley River. I figure that when the British get full control of the Cooper River, they'll seal off all roads and waterways in and out of the city."

Rachel nodded. "There's nothing for us to do out here. We should go inside and see that all are ready to leave as soon as the cannons stop."

Inside they found everyone having breakfast. Pouring a cup of coffee, Rachel said, "Outside, everyone is running about in near panic, but I find the people I love sitting around the breakfast table."

"Dear Rachel, I saw you and John go out front," Meg said as she rang a bell for the cook, "but Patrick sent one of his delivery drivers over to see if we needed any help, and I stayed to thank him. He brought a loaf of fresh bread and explained what was happening in such a simple way that calmed us right away."

Rachel breathed a sigh of relief. "That's wonderful, Meg. I had no idea how I might find all of you. Patrick needs to go out on the streets and help those poor souls running about."

Daniel buttered a chunk of the still warm bread and took an enormous bite. "Just baked," he said, chewing. "What does Pa say about us leaving this morning? If we wait much longer, we'll not have a way out."

"Yes, we'll be leaving as quickly as the cannons stop, so as soon as you can, you need to help your father with the wagon and horses. Since room is scarce in the wagon, Lottie and Sarah will be riding horses with John and Daniel." Rachel said.

The sun imperceptibly had crept fully over the cloudless horizon, and John and Daniel were awaiting the women to gather the last of their bags. The cannons were now still, and the prevailing wind had quickly carried the smoke seaward. Patrick and Amelia were standing around to see their friends off.

Daniel led his horse around the wagon where Ellie and her mother were standing. "We really must get started," he said, softly. "We want enough daylight to reach our first stop before dark."

Ellie took Daniel's arm and he walked her to the wagon. After she and her mother were settled on the upholstered bench, he mounted his horse.

Patrick and Amelia stood quietly by. Patrick said softly, just above a whisper, "Goodbyes are hard, but this war can't last forever. Besides, Amelia and I will be only one hundred and fifty miles away."

Meg wasn't listening; it was an effort just to breathe. She hadn't reckoned leaving her beloved home would be so unsettling. The pain in her chest was so great; she felt that her heart would stop beating. Her father had this home built and waiting for him and her mother when they first settled in America so many years ago. Meg had been born in this house.

Patrick and Amelia watched them until they disappeared around a bend.

CHAPTER TWENTY

HOME AGAIN

John flinched in his saddle at the sounds of explosions close around them. He could see the gray smoke clouds of the artillery coming from the west near Gibbs Landing. He knew they were in a precarious position.

"Those are scatter-shot bombs," he called back to Rachel. "Let's go! We have to move fast."

Rachel released the brakes and slapped the reins across the backs of the pair of horses. The wagon bounced and careened wildly as Rachel tried to avoid the ruts and bumps. The deafening blasts from exploding bombs had frightened the wagon horses, but Daniel and John paced their mounts alongside to keep them from panicking and running away.

John looked back at Rachel and saw the determined look in her face and the firm grip she had on the reins. Pride surged through him as he saw how well she was handling the team. The incessant whistling was all around them now.

Suddenly, a bomb swooshed over the wagon, nearly hit Rachel, and landed just a short distance away from Daniel. The explosion nearly overturned the wagon. Daniel's horse was hit by several pieces of the flying metal; the animal quivered and swayed from the impact, but Daniel was able to pull him back to the road, and then he drove his heels into the animal's flanks and prodded it into a fast gallop toward the speeding wagon.

Daniel felt a burning sensation high on his forehead. Touching the area, he was startled to see blood on his hand. He knew then he'd been hit, but was unaware his horse was also wounded in several places. Blood dripped from his forehead down his face, his head began spinning, and the road ahead blurred. Daniel knew he was likely to lose consciousness, but he had to close the gap between himself and the wagon somehow— the rest of the family was pulling away from him.

Suddenly, his horse threw up his head, whinnied, and staggered. His pace slowed quickly from a fast gallop to an unsteady trot before exhaling one last blow and collapsed. Daniel felt himself falling forward over the animal's head. He landed on his back, stunned, with the breath knocked out of him. After a few seconds, he was able to prop himself on one elbow, and struggled to expand his lungs. By the time he was regaining his senses, he saw John and the others coming back for him.

John was the first to reach him, jumping off his horse before it had fully stopped. Daniel had gotten up to a sitting position and was wiping the blood from his cheeks.

Pushing hair back from the wound, John said, "Are you hit anywhere else, son?"

"I don't think so; at least I'm not bleeding anyplace I can see. How bad is my head?"

"It's a little deeper than a scratch. You've got a bloody furrow across the hairline." Hearing the clattering wagon returning, John said, "With five nurses, you're likely to live."

Rachel stopped the wagon, and Ellie leaped down and rushed to Daniel. Rachel and Lottie stepped down, and Rachel said in an urgent voice, "Bring some water from the barrel while I get my bag."

Ellie examined him thoroughly for any other wounds. The wound at his hairline had bled profusely, but now had almost stopped.

Rachel knelt beside Ellie, handing her a pair of scissors from her bag. "Cut his hair back a bit from the cut, and I'll clean the wound."

Ellie began trimming Daniel's hair away from the cut. "Does it hurt much, Daniel?" she asked guardedly, "I'm trying not to hurt you."

Sitting patiently as she attended to his head, Daniel responded, "No, I actually feel a bit better now that you're helping me."

Rachel finished cleaning out extraneous matter and reached for poultice to spread over the open area. She offered the jar to Ellie. "Maybe you'd rather do this, Ellie".

Her eyes wide with fear, Ellie said falteringly, "I—want to."

As she reached for the poultice, Ellie prayed, *"I can do everything through Him who gives me strength."*

How much of the poultice do I use?"

"Place enough to cover the cut completely, directly in the wound. Try not to disturb it too much; we don't want it to start bleeding again."

Using her finger, Ellie applied the poultice along the wound. A little blood began to trickle. "Oh, it's bleeding again!"

Meg laid the bandage strip on the wound and wrapped the bandage around Daniel's head. "That's not enough to worry about dear; the pressure from the bandage will stop it. You did an excellent job. I couldn't have done it any better."

Daniel's lips spread into a wide, beaming smile. He whispered, "Thank you . . . you're a very pretty nurse."

Meg and Rachel exchanged amused glances, while Ellie, red-faced, touched her finger to his nose and said, lightly, "Shhh."

John helped his son to his feet and into the wagon. Daniel eased into the place Ellie had made for him behind the seat. She and Meg would retake their places beside Rachel.

"It might get a little bouncy, Daniel. Just holler out if it gets too bad." Then to Ellie he said, "Ellie, maybe you can find a pillow or something to help cushion his head from the jarring and bouncing."

As gracefully as she could, Ellie climbed back behind the seat and positioned herself so Daniel's head would rest in her lap.

"That'll do, I reckon," John muttered. "Lottie, help me load Daniel's saddle and bridle onto the wagon. Daniel lost a good horse today, maybe we can buy us another when we reach River Oaks, Uncle George's plantation."

Rachel gave her husband a concerned look. "When we get there, you ask George if he knows of a surgeon nearby. Daniel's wound is a bit more than a scratch, and he may need more than my poultice."

John settled back in his saddle. "Is everybody ready to move? How about you Daniel?"

Daniel waved his arm. "I'm ready."

Heeling his horse's flanks, John said, "Let's go!"

They'd been riding for a while when John raised his hand and brought the wagon to a stop. He rode back to check on Daniel. Ellie was helping him to a sitting position.

"How are you feeling, son?" asked John.

"None the worse for wear, I guess," replied Daniel. "I've got a bit of headache, but I'll manage."

"Everyone wait here, while I ride up and scout what's ahead. Patrick believes Clinton has already landed some or all of his army, so we must be ready for whatever comes. While I'm gone, check your rifles and pistols, make sure they're loaded and primed."

John spun his horse around and set out up the road.

"Do as your father said," Rachel said, "Until we put a good many miles behind us, we must stay alert."

Satisfied his weapons were ready, Daniel said, "Can you use either of these, Ellie?"

Looking apologetic, she replied, "I know how they work, but I've never fired any kind of gun."

With no sign of displeasure, Daniel said, "There's no need for you to feel badly; we'll have time to teach you once we reach home. For now, hold one pistol for me and keep the shot pouch handy."

Reaching into his shot pouch, Daniel retrieved a paper cartridge. "Can you make a cartridge?"

Sheepishly, Ellie shook her head and replied quietly, "No."

He smiled and held her hand. "Tonight will be a good time to begin lessons on making a frontierswoman of you."

It wasn't long before John returned. He dismounted and took a cup of water from Lottie. "I could see a goodly number of redcoats ahead engaged in building a redoubt from the Ashley toward the Cooper River. They're not yet in musket range, so we shouldn't be fired upon, but we'll be in plain sight."

In a grim tone that matched his furrowed expression, John said, "We'll ride past them in a leisurely fashion and stop if we're hailed. Follow my lead if we're forced into an interrogation of any sort."

Patting his waistcoat pocket for his papers, he said, "Any questions?"

The women and Daniel all shook their heads, and John nodded and wheeled his horse around to set out at a leisurely canter.

They rode in silence until John stopped them atop a scant rise. In front of them lay open ground for as far as they could see. To their right was a sea of men digging and hauling dirt in wheelbarrows. Surrounding them were an equal number of soldiers, standing guard to protect the diggers from any attack from Charles Town.

"There they are." John said, matter-of-factly. "It won't take them long to build their siege works with that number of men, especially with no patriot army to shoot at them."

Twisting in his saddle, John scanned his family. "Remember, we're just on our way to stay with our relatives until they successfully free our city. Smiles go a long way."

They were nearly half way across the open plain when musket fire erupted from the redcoats. John saw horsemen riding hard toward them.

He started his horse in their direction and said, "We'll go a ways toward them and show them we're not afraid of them."

John stopped as the soldiers rode up and surrounded the wagon. Leading them was a young red coated British officer. He looked to be yet in his teens, but nonetheless, the bare sword in his hand augmented his youth to that of a grown man.

Sheathing his sword, the young lieutenant said briskly, "I am in the company of his majesty's loyal subjects, am I not?"

John, with an amiable tone, replied, "You are sir, and we're grateful his majesty, King George, has seen fit to send his army to free us from the fanatical rebels. Welcome to South Carolina, sir."

With just a touch of overconfidence to his manner, he extended his hand. "May I see your papers attesting to your loyalty to the crown?"

Ellie could feel the leering stares of the soldiers as she held Daniel close to her. She kept her eyes down and nearly closed, but one of the more brazen soldiers leaned from his horse and attempted to lift her face with his hand.

His voice rough, he said. "Turn this way, girlie. Let's see what a lovely American lass ye' might be."

Ellie froze, terrified. Then feeling his cold hand touch her chin, Ellie let out a scream.

Daniel leaped to his feet and snapped, "Watch your manners, soldier. The women here are ladies and not for the likes of you."

The thunderstruck soldier nearly fell from his horse, and the young officer looked up sharply from reading John's document. "Back away, lads and be quick about it. Form a column behind me."

Handing the paper back to John, he said, "My apologies, sir, to your family and to the young lady. Some in our ranks have vulgar and uncultured backgrounds. I would advise you keep your family away from Charles Town until the siege is past."

Nearly strangling on his impulse to shoot as many of the soldiers as he could, John replied, "Aye, sir, and my family thanks you for your quick action."

The lieutenant nodded and said, "Godspeed to you and your family. You may be on your way."

John watched the young officer turn his men and lead them back to the encroaching redoubt.

Rachel turned in her seat and asked, "Are you all right, Ellie, dear?"

Ellie was standing close to Daniel. "Yes, ma'am. I'm sorry I screamed, but I wasn't expecting one of them to actually lay a hand on me."

When they were out of earshot, Meg said, "John, you're so believable pretending to be a loyalist. And I believe the young officer was taken with you after reading your Cornwallis passport, and he was so respectful and courteous."

John's eyes were still trained on the soldiers, now some distance away. "Hmph, that courteous young officer would've had no qualms about running you or any of us through with his gleaming sword, if he'd felt the slightest threat from us. I don't want any of you to forget that—ever."

The sound of rumbling thunder from hundreds of big guns resumed behind them, and they all turned to watch.

Looking toward the Ashley River, John said, "Look, you can see the plumes of smoke from the batteries themselves." Solemnly, he muttered, "And when Clinton gets control of the Cooper River, it will be all over. General Lincoln will have lost the option to retreat; all that will be left is surrender."

Ellie stood behind the wagon bench and said, "I'm worried about Patrick and Amelia, maybe she should've come with us."

"I know you're worried, but the risk is everywhere now, Ellie," Rachel said, sounding more confident than she felt. "Patrick and Amelia have many friends in the city, they won't be alone. There's help if they need it."

⋯⋯⋯

"We're not far from *River Oaks*," John shouted over his shoulder. "We'll be able to see Uncle George's place just over yon rise."

John knew this land. As a boy, he'd played in these woods and fields around the Santee and Wateree Rivers. Now, the sandy plateaus and forests of pine and evergreens were no longer a playground.

John was anxious to reach River Oaks. He hadn't seen his Uncle's home in several years, and he was eager to see and touch the only place he had ever called home.

The road they travelled was called the Camden Road. It was a branch of the Great Wagon Road that began in Pennsylvania and ran southward through the colonies on its way to Georgia. John felt good they would soon come to their first stop. Uncle George, a widower, would be glad to see them.

Nothing could have prepared them for what they saw when they topped a slight rise in the road. Scorched, blackened ground lay before them—Uncle George's beloved River Oaks was gone. All that lay before them was cold ashes where the main house had stood for so many years. Nothing was left standing. Only ashes remained where the barns, outbuildings, and workers' cabins once were. Nearly five hundred acres in wheat had been torched.

John felt the cold hand of death touch his soul. He had grown up here. George was his mother's only brother. When John's father had been killed in the French and Indian War, this uncle and his wife were the ones who took John and his mother in. His mother was buried in the family cemetery.

"Tories," he said quietly. Turning to his family, he said, "Take hold of your weapons and be watchful."

Nudging the flanks of his horse, he started down the gentle slope toward the desolate ruins. Rachel paced the wagon a few yards behind him as they made their way along the barren drive.

They reached what had once been the elegant entrance to his boyhood home. The home he loved so much now lay ruined, burned to the ground. Just a few charred timbers stood here and there as silent sentries. Weeds grew through the ashes of the foundation.

John slowly stepped down from his mount. "Everybody stay put for now. Don't go wandering off, we don't know who or what may be lurking around. Keep your weapons in hand."

He was standing in what had been the winding circular drive. He stood in dazed silence and stared at the mound of ashes before him. Some of the brick edging of the garden poked through the ash. Toward the back, he was able to make out where the outside kitchen had stood.

It had been three years since John had seen his boyhood home, and he had been anxious to see it all again. He scanned the property, and it was all the same. River Oaks had been razed by the enemy. No building was left standing. Destruction and rubble were everywhere. George's cattle and horses were gone.

It was quiet; nothing moved but the wind. The fire had long since died, leaving the smell of burned wood and death. A gust of wind carried spindrifts of ash high into the air.

"This was my home," he mumbled to the wind. "Now, there's nothing."

John walked to the remains of the barn and found his uncle's anvil. The anvil was unscathed. He cleared ashes from the stone floor surrounding the forge and counted seven stones from the edge of the hearth. With the point of his knife, he loosened a stone and tossed it aside. Sheathing his knife, John reached into the cavity to remove a metal box. He hefted it, and its weight brought a smile of satisfaction to his face.

He stood for a moment with the box in his hands, then returned to the wagon. Handing the box to Lottie, he said, "I guess the cowardly assassins didn't know about this."

With his voice tight with emotion, John said, "Drive the wagon to the cemetery, and we'll leave."

He knew they shouldn't linger here out in the open, but he wanted to pay his respects to those who meant so much to him. Trudging over the scorched ground, he led his horse to where his mother, his aunt, other family members lay. The headstones looked stark and cold set on this high knoll, and the smell of ashes permeated the air. On the end by John's aunt was a fresh grave. John walked down and stood before it.

"It's probably Uncle George. Some friend, someone, came and laid him to rest," he said, his voice trembling.

Unable to hold them back, John ignored the tears that spilled down his face. He stood before his family with his head bowed and behind him Rachel whispered:

"*I have fought a good fight, I have finished my course, and I have kept the faith.*"

John took one last look at the desolation of his boyhood home before he said, "We need to keep moving. There's an inn just a few hours ahead where we can stay for the night—"

Rachel broke the pensiveness of the moment. "Can we stay a few days? Daniel needs some time—a day or two at the most—to recuperate."

Nodding, John replied, "We all could use some rest. The owner, Abraham Deskill, is a good friend and a true patriot. He calls his place the Eagle's Nest. If we set a good pace, we should make it before dark."

About a quarter mile from the inn, several burly men stepped out in the road to block their way. Their long rifles were aimed directly at the family.

"Hold up!" One of the men said, his voice raspy. "You there on the horse, step down and come closer—everybody else keep still with your hands in sight."

John dismounted carefully and walked toward the man doing the talking, taking care to keep his hands away from his pistol.

He stopped a few steps from the man, who had just begun to speak, when a younger man in the group cried out, "That's Mr. Hamilton and his family. They're with us, for sure!" Placing his rifle in the crook of his arm, the young man came up with his arm extended. John, at first, was puzzled. He was relieved this man knew him, but he didn't look familiar.

Suddenly, from the wagon, Daniel called out, "Is that you, Joshua?"

Still pumping John's hand, young Joshua said, "Yep, good friend, its ole' Josh." Turning to his friends, Joshua said, , "These people are long-standing patriots, I know them all, except the pretty lass holding on to Daniel."

Joshua paused to smile at Ellie with admiration. "Who's your friend, Daniel?"

Daniel forgot about his headache. "This is Ellie Turnwell of Charles Town—my betrothed."

Slapping his leg, Joshua said playfully, "Well, congratulations to the both of you, although I'm afraid Miss Ellie has got the short end of that bargain."

The men with Joshua had lowered their rifles and gathered near the wagon. "Can anyone tell us what happened at River Oaks?" John asked.

Joshua was the first to speak. "It was a Tory raiding party. We figure it was Rufus Sherman's men that did it, considering the bad feelings that have been going on between your uncle and Rufus for years." Joshua paused to clear his throat, "I suppose you saw the fresh grave?"

John nodded. "Uncle George?"

"Yes, the heathen who killed him just left him lying where he fell. Some of us here buried Mr. George." Lowering his voice, Joshua leaned in closer to John, as if he didn't want the women to hear. "He'd been scalped to make it look like Indians. It wasn't a pretty sight, I can tell you."

Solemnly, John said, tipping his hat, "Thank you men for your good deed, we're in your debt. We'll be staying at the Eagle's Nest."

CHAPTER TWENTY ONE

WAR COMES TO TRENTON

T hree days ride from the Eagle's Nest, John and his family turned down the graveled drive to their home. Caleb saw them and began running toward them. "Mercy! It's th' Lord's answer to my prayers! Y'all are all back!"

John leaned down to shake hands with his lifelong friend. "And it's good to be back, Caleb. Give us time to get the women settled and we'll talk. I want to know what's happened since we left."

An hour later, John found Caleb at the barn. "Caleb, what's the situation in Camden?"

Caleb rubbed his whiskered chin, his face downcast. "No good news, Mistah John." Shaking his head, he continued, "Nossir, it's all bad."

Placing his hand on his friend's shoulder, John looked at the man who had been a part of his life since before he could remember, "It does look that way, my friend, but we're not beaten just yet, not by a long shot. Reverend Thomas Fuller, nearly a hundred years ago, penned the words, 'the darkest hour of all is the hour before day.' I hold that proverb is meant for us today; that there's hope even in the worst of circumstances."

Caleb nodded. "Good words, Mistah John, mighty good. Mebbe that's where we are, that "darkest hour," because the redcoats have taken over Camden."

He lifted his gaze to John. "They've spread the word that General Clinton has taken Charles Town and captured all our army men."

Caleb watched for John's reaction. John returned his gaze, and said, "Charles Town was about to fall when we left, Caleb, so that's no surprise, and Camden has been a prime target for some time now. But the British will have their hands full holding both those places, mark my words."

⸺◦◦◦⸺ ⸺◦◦◦⸺ ⸺◦◦◦⸺

Nearly a month passed before John and Daniel rode off to meet up with General Horatio Gates. It was the first time for Daniel to go with his father on a foray where they were likely to confront the enemy. The women had settled into a routine of splitting the daily work, and Sarah volunteered to be first up in the morning to rekindle the kitchen hearth fire.

On most mornings, she would use this quiet time to write to Gideon. Sitting at the kitchen table, she would unfold her only letter from Gideon. Knowing he had held these pages in his hands, she lovingly pressed and smoothed the creases with the palm of her hand. She would re-read the pages she knew so well, trying to glean more of his thoughts from his words. Sarah cherished this time alone, this quiet, special time with Gideon.

My Cherished Husband,

It is early morning, and I've just rekindled the hearth fire. The kitchen is quiet for I'm the only one not still in bed and fast asleep, but I so want to write you a few lines. I announce to you this morning, with much joy, that I carry our child. I'm so happy and would be more so if you were sitting here with me now.

Aye, my heart aches for your arms to be around me, my husband. This war has stolen irreplaceable memories from us. We have missed the joy of my laying in your arms and telling you I carry our child. Instead, you will read this letter in some faraway place beyond my embrace, and will not hear the first cry of your babe.

I don't wish this letter to be melancholy, so I'll tell you that Daniel is in love with Ellie Turnwell, a young woman he met in Charles Town. Ellie is the daughter of your mother's best friend.

The circumstances surrounding their meeting are rather intricate for my short letter, but you should know that Daniel and Ellie seem well suited for each other. Already, I see a more serious side of your brother.

I haven't yet told your parents of your approaching fatherhood. I wanted to wait until I was certain of God's plan for us first. On the morrow, I plan to break the news.

'Tis time for the others to be up, so I will continue my thoughts to you tomorrow.

I remain your loving and devoted wife,

Sarah

Belle, the cook, soon had a breakfast of bacon, eggs, biscuits and butter underway. It was all Sarah could do to not to become ill from the odious smell of bacon frying. She was thankful that she was able to eat a bite of her biscuit and a nibble of the scrambled eggs.

Ellie pushed her barely eaten breakfast away and looked intently at the others sitting around the table. "Mama Rachel, do you think Daniel and Papa will be gone long?"

Shaking her head, Rachel answered, "My dear, John doesn't know the answer to that question himself. I'm afraid we'll just have to trust that God will protect our men and bring them home safely as quickly as possible."

Extending her hands, she said, "This would be a good time for prayer. Let's hold hands while we pray for the safety of our men."

At the table, hand in hand, the women bowed their heads, and Sarah prayed: "Father, we pray that you will look after Papa John and Gideon and Daniel wherever they may be. Protect them with your mighty shield and encourage them when they face the enemy. Reward their abiding faith in you and our Savior with your sustaining presence. Wherever their duty takes them, we pray you are there for them. These things I ask in the name of Jesus. Amen."

Sarah scarcely finished her prayer, when she suddenly felt faint, and her stomach felt as though it would revolt from the smell of fried bacon lingering in the air. Hoping it would pass, she pressed her napkin weakly to her mouth.

Ellie noticed the color drain from Sarah's face. "Sarah, what's the mat—"

Sarah leaped to her feet, holding her stomach and ran for the back door. Barely reaching the porch edge, she retched hard. It seemed the spasm came from her toes, and she vomited until her stomach would yield no more. Clinging to the post, she felt someone beside her. It was Rachel with a cold, wet cloth.

For a moment, neither spoke. The silence was deafening until Sarah said, "I carry Gideon's child."

"We've thought as much," said Rachel, with a smile. "We've noticed you seem to be on edge lately."

Sarah turned her head. "All of you know?" She felt herself blush, putting her hand to her throat. "But why haven't any of you said anything?"

"Oh, the girls wanted to; they're so happy for you," said Rachel, "but I told them to allow you the courtesy of announcing yourself that they are soon to be aunts."

"And you will have your first grandchild," Sarah said, suppressing a laugh.

Taking Sarah by the arm, she replied, "I've had time to think about that, and I'm pleased that I'm soon to be a grandmother—more than I could ever tell you. Let's go inside, and you can share your good news with the others."

—◦◦◦— —◦◦◦— —◦◦◦—

The sheets and clothes fluttered and popped in the afternoon breeze as Rachel bent to pick up the last damp sheet from the clothesbasket. With it pinned to the line, she absently tucked a stray lock of her auburn hair back under her bonnet and surveyed her day's work.

It was only mid-afternoon, and the week's washing was done. Usually, the sun was setting when she finished, but with Sarah and Ellie helping her, the work went faster, and Lottie was almost done with the week's bread making. Meg was making herself useful by spinning flax into linen thread, singing as she turned the wheel.

Rachel shielded her eyes to watch as Caleb, their top hand, rode through the peach orchard. Yesterday, he'd told her that enough peaches remained for another picking.

Caleb had been a slave all of his life until John inherited the sprawling farm. John had freed all of his grandfather's slaves and seen that mothers were reunited with their children and fathers and husbands were reunited with their families. A few of the freed families left, but some like Caleb and his wife, Belle, had remained with John.

Rachel never tired of this view where their rambling two-story home overlooked the acres upon acres of pasture and her beloved peach orchard. Behind the orchard, she could see the small herd of cattle feeding in the sweet-clover field.

John's father had acquired the property in 1720 and built the house for John's mother, and throughout his lifetime, the large estate was known as Trenton, his wife's maiden name. The elder Hamiltons had six children, of which only John survived to adulthood.

Rachel saw her daughter, Lottie, coming toward her from the house. "Ma, the bread is in the oven and should be ready in a few minutes."

Pointing to the hickory pole leaning on the clothes line, Rachel said, "Would you prop the line up with the pole, dear?"

Lottie set the pole under the sagging line. "Ellie and I want to go riding. We won't go far; I promise."

Rachel gazed at her daughter. Rachel remembered herself at that age and wondered what, in this troubled world, lay in store for Lottie. "You've got bread in the oven, and I'm sure Ellie isn't finished peeling peaches—maybe tomorrow."

Tilting her head, Lottie said, "Listen, mama . . . do you hear it?"

With the empty laundry basket on her hip, Rachel glanced toward her daughter. "Hear what, dear?"

Lottie replied, her head still tilted, "It sounds like drums."

"I hear it too," said Belle, coming along behind Lottie from the kitchen. The fear in Belle's eyes as she looked toward the road was obvious.

Rachel lifted her head and listened. The cadenced beat grew louder, and she felt a wave of nausea in the pit of her stomach.

With her clenched fist pressed against her stomach, she whispered, "Its Lord Rawdon's drummers."

Suddenly, a neighbor boy astride a Spanish pony appeared from a treeless rise beyond the road. He was riding headlong, straight for Rachel. The sound of the drums was getting louder, but Rachel kept her eyes on the boy. He wasn't bringing good news.

He cut his horse away from the drive and rode for the clothesline. For a moment, she thought he was going to ride the horse right through her drying laundry, but at the last second, he pulled the horse up short. He swung from the saddle and tossed the reins over the head of his pony.

"Miz Rachel!" he shouted, almost out of breath. "Lord Rawdon's—red-coated devils—are just down the road!"

Rachel felt as cold as ice. A month earlier, the British Battalion had left Camden in search of the American General Francis Marion, known as the 'Swamp Fox', and now they were returning.

Maybe they're retreating. Somehow, Marion must have beaten them, she thought

Lottie slipped past her on her way to the house. Dropping the basket, Rachel shouted, "Run, Belle! Get in the house!"

They reached the door just as Lottie came back out, armed with her rifle. Nearly colliding, Rachel grabbed her by the arm and pushed her back in the house.

When they were all safely inside, she slammed the door and locked it behind them. Visibly upset, Lottie's chest heaved as she tried to catch her breath. "Why—did we run, Ma? If Pa were here—he wouldn't run."

Rachel didn't respond right away. She looked at her daughter. At sixteen, nearing seventeen, she had grown up a lot just in this past year, but in most ways, she was still a girl yearning to be a woman. She reached to brush stray strands of wheat-colored hair from her daughter's forehead, but Lottie jerked her head away. Wide-eyed, Belle stood beside them, staring at Rachel waiting for some response to Lottie's question.

Exhaling loudly, Rachel said, "I'm not as sure as you, Lottie, what your father would do if he were here, but since he isn't, and you are not yet full-grown, I must do the thinking for all of us."

"But, Ma!" she moaned. "I wasn't gonna' shoot nobody. I just want'em to know we ain't one of'em!"

"'Tis no secret, Lottie, about this family's stand for freedom. We're known in every corner of Camden District as tried-and-true Whigs, but with a battalion of villainous redcoats scurrying past our door, 'tis not the time to remind them of it."

Belle's eyes brightened. "Maybe they're scurrying away from our army."

"Maybe," murmured Lottie as she peered through a window pane, "They're passing by now and seem to be in a bit of hurry."

Belle had moved in beside her at the window and was gaping over Lottie's shoulder.

"Shoo! Get away from that window, the both of you!" Rachel chided. "They'll be gone as quick as they came, and we've got work to do. Go fetch Ellie and Sarah from the back porch and lock the door."

Shaking her head, Lottie said, "It just ain't right, Ma, it just ain't."

Sighing, Rachel said, "Stop using the word ain't. Elder Hobbs would be shocked to hear you speak that way. He's told me you were his brightest pupil. Now, what isn't right, Lottie?"

"It ain't—isn't right that we should just stand by and submit to the insults and assaults from our so-called friends and neighbors. Sooner or later, those fiendish Tories will make a raid on us, Ma. It's coming, and you know it."

Belle had lingered at the window and breathlessly watched the dazzling British troopers' red coats, their dashing plumes, and shining helmets.

Suddenly, Belle shrieked, "Miz Rachel, they've turned down our drive! They're coming here—oh, Lord help us—please, Lord help us!"

"Hush Belle, stop that crying and help Lottie with the churning."

Rachel's heart nearly stopped when she saw the soldiers had turned off the main road and were coming down the one-half mile dirt lane to her house. From the window, she saw a mixture of redcoat regulars and some green-coated Tories. Leading the regiment was a smartly dressed British officer closely followed by three aides and a regimental color bearer.

"You girls go to your rooms and lock your doors, and Belle, you go to the kitchen and tend to the bread—wait for me there," Rachel said. "Lottie, hide our pistols and rifles, but leave John's musket and shotgun out." Rachel then hurried to the veranda.

The troops came to a stop across her front lawn with no regard for her flowers and shrubs. The British officer dismounted and adjusted his coat. He was dressed in what appeared to be his finest scarlet uniform and starched white shirt and breeches. He wore a smart black hat with gold trim along the edges. His powdered white wig was turned up in curls on the sides with a silk black bow holding everything in place at the back of his head.

Rachel stood as relaxed and composed as her trembling legs would allow. She was thankful that the men in her family were not home.

Her eyes followed the officer as he ascended the steps. Up close, he looked to be in his mid-forties, a man accustomed to authority, and his bearing reeked of British snobbery. His eyes studied her as if she was a common tavern wench.

Bowing deeply, the officer said in a brusque voice, "Madam, Colonel Francis Lord Rawdon at your service."

With her chin raised, Rachel tried to appear much calmer than she felt. In her finest English voice, Rachel replied coolly, "Lord Rawdon, I'm Rachel Hamilton. Your men have ruined my prize roses and trampled a hedge that I've taken great pains in nurturing to its present height."

With no apparent regard to her comment, Rawdon said, "Mrs. Hamilton . . . then I have the pleasure of speaking with the mistress of this house and plantation?"

"It belongs to my husband." Her eyes never left her trampled roses.

"Is he home?" Rawdon's eyes remained riveted on her. He was intrigued by her British accent and apparent no-nonsense demeanor.

Rachel turned and confronted him directly. "He is not."

He continued his interrogation. "Is your husband John Hamilton, the rebel?"

Stiffening at the slur 'rebel', Rachel replied emphatically, "John is a colonel in the army of his country, fighting against those who've invaded us."

"I fear, madam," said Rawdon, "we differ in opinion. A friend to his country will be the friend of the king, our master."

"Haven't you heard sir? That's why we're fighting. In our country only slaves acknowledge a master," Rachel replied with a tone of disrespect.

CHAPTER TWENTY TWO

THE BURNING

Rawdon's face reddened as he struggled to find words of rebuttal. Finding none, he turned his back to Rachel and addressed his aides, "Have the men pitch their tents in the orchard and pasture beyond, and set up pickets in all directions and on the roads."

Turning back to Rachel, he bowed crisply. "Madam Hamilton, my men and I require the temporary occupation of your property. And if it would not be too disagreeable to you, I will take up my quarters in your house."

Rachel recognized Rawdon was not asking for lodging; he was only informing her of his intentions to use her home as his billet, and she would have no say in the matter.

Looking him directly in the eye, Rachel said, "I have a room on the first floor reserved for unexpected guests that will be suitable. It's the third door on the right from the main hall."

His eyes narrowed slightly as his face hardened. "Where are the family's weapons, madam?"

"What my husband left for me is in the main hallway," she said, pointing to the door.

A slight motion with his hand signaled a sergeant to enter the house. Rachel felt her throat tighten as she waited for the soldier to return.

Kicking the door open with his dirt-covered boot, the sergeant came out with the shotgun and musket. "Found these, Colonel."

"Store them in one of the baggage wagons, sergeant," said Rawdon. His eyes darted to Rachel. "These two are the only weapons you have, madam?"

Rachel nodded. "Those are our hunting guns. We need them to provide meat for our family and protection against the Indians. What is your king's need of them?"

An unpleasant, forced smile spread across his face, but his eyes remained distant. "A mere precaution, madam, I'll have a receipt drawn up for you."

Settling in one of the veranda chairs, Rawdon grew quiet, watching his troop set up their tents. His eyes took in the terrain in every direction.

Moments passed before he looked around, and he seemed surprised to see her still there. "Tell me, madam, your English voice intrigues me. Do you have notable heritage?"

Maintaining her aloofness, Rachel responded, "Foremost and most notable, I am an American by birth. My father, however, was the Earl of Hayecrest, master of Fairview on the peninsula north of Charles Town."

He looked at her openly from her head to her shoes. "Your dress, is it imported?"

Rachel instinctively brought her hand to her throat as his gaze made its way over her. Ripples of anger swept through her as she fought the urge to slap him senseless.

Speaking with the accent of her British upbringing, she said, "If I may continue to answer your question of my peerage. My mother's father was the Duke of Grandshire." She continued to stare with undisguised contempt. "It's quite evident by your vulgar comments that you would have some difficulty proving your peerage."

Ignoring her taunting slight, he said, "At the risk of offending you further, madam, would you tell me if any part of Colonel Sumter's army is in the vicinity?"

There was a moment of silence while Rachel considered whether to continue conversing with her unwelcome guest. She decided this was an opportunity for her to do her part for the cause.

She replied icily, "As you probably already know, sir, the entire Piedmont from here to North Carolina is Whig territory. So, you shouldn't be surprised if Colonel Sumter came, at any moment, leading a charge of militia rangers to relieve you of the chair upon which you now sit."

Her eyes remained fixed on him. "Last week, the men led by General Francis Marion, the Swamp Fox as you British call him, billeted a few miles south of Camden. I'm not aware of his present whereabouts, but I'm told he has scouts seeking your camp. My husband and his men ride with the general in this pursuit."

Taking her answer literally, Rawdon rose quickly from his chair and took her by the arm. She felt his grip tighten as his deep brown eyes stared directly into her face.

"Madam, I've no doubt that you are being less than truthful, since I have my own scouts out for the purpose of locating and engaging these feckless rebels, and I feel you exaggerate about the proximity of Marion."

She swallowed to hold her nervousness in check and kept her eyes locked with his. "I'm not concerned with how you receive what I've said, and I wish you would remove your hand from my arm."

Rachel wanted to keep him guessing. It was apparent he was unaware that John and his men were with General Gates just a few miles north, or that she had no idea where any of the other patriot militias might be. She felt if he believed any part of her story, he might not linger, but move on. In any case, she wanted to, somehow, let John know about the great number of the enemy that were now encamped on their property before he and his men came riding straight into their arms.

Rachel had quickly realized the orchard encampment of the British was completely screened by the fences and hedgerow from the view of anyone approaching from the north. John and his men, if they should return, would be half-way down the drive before the encampment could be seen. She worried that her husband and his men would be captured if they came back now.

Rawdon slowly released his grip on her arm and retook his seat. Two of his aides joined him on the veranda. Rachel remained standing looking wistfully down the one-half mile lane that led to the main road.

Suddenly, one of the aides asked, "Excuse me Colonel, but isn't it true officers in our army will receive parcels of land such as this estate after America is conquered?"

"There's no doubt," replied the Colonel, "the officers of the king's army will receive large possessions of the conquered American provinces."

Rachel knew their conversation was meant to ridicule her, but she couldn't hold back. She had to speak.

"The two of you are somewhat presumptuous believing you'll conquer our country. The only land that will ever remain the property of any British officer will measure six feet by two feet."

Rawdon dismissed her comment with a wave of his hand. "I regret, for your sake, to say this, but your beautiful plantation will be the home of royalty once we finish with the last of you rebels."

Suddenly, several volleys of gunfire shattered the quiet afternoon. Rawdon and his aides stood quickly, staring in the direction from which the shooting came.

"Most likely the pickets in a skirmish with a local," one of Rawdon's aides said.

Frowning deeply, Rawdon shook his head in disagreement. "Nay, that was the sound of rifles and muskets. Order boots and saddles, and you, Captain, take your troop in the direction of the firing."

Rawdon remained on the veranda to oversee the results of his orders. Rachel watched him as he stood with his hands clasped behind his back. His eyes seemed to miss nothing among the orderly clamor of his troop getting in the saddle, ready to ride.

Meanwhile, the captain led his men dutifully toward the main road and disappeared from view.

<hr/>

Rawdon's face hardened, and he spun around to focus his eyes on Rachel. He couldn't make up his mind whether or not she was telling the truth, so he decided not to risk being overrun while still in camp. He shouted orders to form the troops and quickly mounted his own horse to lead his men in the direction of the shooting.

Meanwhile, scouts from John Hamilton's troop had already discovered the captain's party and were waiting off the main road in ambush. After a brief skirmish, the patriots killed over half of the captain's troop and were now close behind the retreating captain and the remnants of his men. It was a running fight with rifles, muskets, pistols, and swords gleaming in the afternoon sunlight.

John, with Daniel and his militia, stayed in hot pursuit of the captain's group, whose number had dwindled to only four. John and Daniel were completely unaware of the larger complement of enemy soldiers readying to ride toward them.

———————

The veranda door slammed startling Rachel. She turned to see Meg, with their daughters, running wide-eyed toward her. Ellie was the first to see John and Daniel make the turn from the main road onto the drive chasing the captain and his men.

"Look!" Ellie shouted, "Its Papa and Daniel! They're trapped!" She ran to the yard, not caring for her safety, yelling at the top of her voice. "Stop, stop! Go back . . . turn around!"

Many of the British soldiers turned and faced Ellie, their bayoneted muskets pointed straight at her. Meg ran to her and pulled her back to the porch.

Holding Ellie firmly by her arm, her mother said, "We can't do anything for them, child. They are in God's hands. We must stay here, together. Those men out there are ready to kill; man or woman, it's no difference to them."

As they looked on, unable to help either of their men, the women gasped when they saw John jerk back on the reins so roughly that his horse was brought to a sliding stop. He and Daniel had nearly collided with five hundred mounted Loyalists.

Without any signal from John, his men scattered in every direction. With a wave of his arm and a shout for Daniel to follow him, John wheeled his horse to the right toward the lane's split rail fence. Rawdon immediately sent men in pursuit.

John felt the rippling muscles of his gelding's powerful legs as they dug into the loam, throwing wedges of grassy dirt high behind them. Its mane flowing, John's mount ran flat-out as it came to the four-foot rails, and it easily cleared the top rail, landing without breaking the rhythm of its gait. John, crouching above the saddle, was almost thrown, but he managed to stay with the horse by holding a handful of mane. Across the pasture, another fence loomed ahead, and John readied himself for the jump. He felt the horse's gait shift as they neared the obstruction, as if it were measuring its approach. Then it cleared the fence with ease.

Daniel's mount leaped the first rail and then the other, as muskets pounded the air. Another volley sounded, and musket balls whizzed above their heads and pelted the surrounding trees.

John looked over his shoulder to see if Daniel had made it. Pure relief washed over him when he saw his son riding hard a half-length behind him. The creek ahead would be one more hurdle, and then it would be just a short run to the wooded bottomland and safety.

⚜ ⚜ ⚜

Fearing that a larger militia was waiting in the woods, Rawdon ordered the bugler to sound recall, and the lieutenant and his men held up at the creek. They could only watch as John and his son disappeared into the woods.

Rawdon rode back to the house where he met with the captain who had been ambushed on the road. He listened as the captain gave his report.

"Sir, I cannot tell you the number of rebels we encountered. We rode into a carefully prepared ambush. The enemy struck from behind trees, and more than a few were actually aloft in the trees. They offered very few targets. I lost fifteen men, three during the retreat."

Rawdon didn't utter a word for a few seconds, then he said, "Tend to your wounds, captain, and see to your men—what's left of them."

The lieutenant had been waiting to make his report and now stepped forward. Saluting his commander, he said, "Sir, we turned at the bugler's recall, but it's doubtful we would have caught them after they made the woods, anyway."

Rawdon nodded. "Thank you, Lieutenant. See that pickets are posted across the creek."

Rachel and the women had not moved from the end of the veranda where they had witnessed John and Daniel's narrow escape. Although, it had lasted only a few minutes, Rachel was still reeling from the vision of so many muskets firing at her men. With her hands covering her face, she began praying softly to herself, thanking God for shielding her men from harm.

Rawdon's voice interrupted her thoughts. He had ridden to where they were standing, and his dark eyes glared hotly at Ellie. "Step forward, girl. Let me have a closer look at you."

Ellie's face turned ashen. Meg placed her arm around her daughter's waist and together they stepped closer to the edge of the veranda.

"What's your name, girl?" he said.

Her eyes were fixed on the floor at her feet. "E-Ellie," she breathed.

Rawdon, in a fit of anger, spurred his horse forward, coming within a hairsbreadth of riding the horse onto the veranda. He yelled out a string of violent oaths and curses that filled the air. His agitated horse snorted and stomped, and tossed his head.

The women, thinking the horse would come up onto the veranda, had scurried back against the wall of the house.

He pointed to the edge of the veranda, just inches from his rattled horse. "Get back here, you rebel wench, and say your name clearly."

Meg stepped closer with her and whispered in her ear. "Don't be afraid of him, Ellie. Look him straight in the eye. He's the enemy, and he just tried to kill John and Daniel."

Still regarding him warily, Ellie lifted her eyes and returned his stare. "My name is Ellie Turnwell. You just tried to kill the man I'm to marry and his father."

"You played no small part in this skirmish." His eyes narrowed menacingly. "It's a hanging offense to give aid to the enemy on the field of battle . . . what is your age?"

Ellie's gaze focused on his eyes. "I'm eighteen."

Stepping between Ellie and Rawdon, Rachel shouted, "Stop it, stop it right now! You're frightening her. She made no difference in the outcome today. We could only stand by helpless and watch as your men fired their muskets at point blank range and not bring down two men—not even wound them, and then the poor horsemanship of your dragoons allowed them to escape."

Rachel felt heady and breathless, and her passion shocked her. Rawdon looked disconcerted by her outburst. Finally, he replied, "Madam, neither your gender nor your religion affords you protection from your show of obvious disrespect for his majesty's servant. I would suggest you guard your tongue, lest it lead to your undoing."

He dismounted and walked leisurely to the steps, and took his seat in the chair that he seemed to favor. Rachel quickly ushered the women into the house.

Rawdon stood quickly, his shoulders back with his hands clasped behind him. He was certain his reputation would suffer from the outcome of today's run-in with Rachel's husband. He knew it wouldn't be difficult to magnify the girl's actions. He might be troubled later with Mrs. Hamilton's testimony, but after the war, she could be silenced also.

"Hold on madam, I should like a word with you." Seeing he had her full attention, he said, "I want to make my position concerning Ms. Turnwell perfectly clear. Your passionate outburst didn't absolve her. War is a deadly business, and the girl injected herself onto the field of battle. She became a participant, can you understand that?"

Rachel felt she was in a horrible nightmare, caught in a spiraling storm. She was being swept away from everything she knew and held dear. She looked at this hideous man and knew for the first time in her life: she was capable of taking another human's life. Her emotions were running rampant. She wanted to kill him, but she knew that wouldn't save Ellie, so she would answer him.

"No!" she cried. "No sane person would understand your barbaric reasoning. Ellie thought her loved ones were about to die before her eyes. It had nothing to do with your contrived 'field of battle'.

Rawdon's face was unreadable. For a moment, Rachel thought he might understand the innocence of Ellie's actions.

Then she saw her words had been in vain. His face slowly took on a contemptuous expression that told her he remained unmoved by anything she had said.

His mouth pursed as if he was about to speak, but Rachel, tired of listening to him, injected, "Your face is a mirror of your barbarous heart, Colonel, and I know no other words to say which may alter that. Therefore, I must beg your leave now, and attend to my family. They're upset after watching their father and brother being fired upon so callously under the orders of a man who calls himself a gentleman."

⸎ ⸎ ⸎

Rawdon watched Rachel leave and enter her house. Her impassioned pleading left him exhausted. *Your family's treason shan't go unpunished, madam. You have my solemn word; you shall rue the day you chose to insult an officer of the crown.*

Rachel went inside, closing the door behind her. She leaned back against the door, resting her head against it for a few moments. *Why Lord . . . why must this disgusting man defile our home?*

She found Meg with the young women huddled around the kitchen table, whispering and clinging to each other.

By the look on Ellie's face, she was scared terribly. "What else did Rawdon say, Mama Rachel? Does he still intend to hang me?"

Rachel hugged her tightly and kissed her forehead, and with more enthusiasm than she felt, responded, "I shouldn't worry, Ellie. Rawdon's fear of the inescapable retribution that would fall upon him from Daniel and John tempers his intentions to harm you."

Rachel's words brought some color to Ellie's features and firmness to her voice. "I don't remember running toward the drive at all, and I'm not sorry for what I did, Mama Rachel. I'm sure I would do it again, especially if I thought it would help Daniel and Papa,"

Turning to her daughter, Rachel said, "Where did you hide our pistols?"

"In the study, behind the bookshelves, why?"

"While I watch for Rawdon, you take all four of them to your bedroom, and make certain each is primed." Rachel looked at the others. "Go with Lottie and she will show you how to hide them in your clothing."

Sarah was taken aback at the thought of the four of them carrying pistols. Although she was capable of firing and loading a gun, thanks to her father, it had never occurred to her that she might actually need to carry one hidden in her clothing.

"Mama Rachel," said Sarah, "are we to keep our pistol with us at all times?"

Rachel nodded. "Yes, Sarah. At first, it may seem cumbersome and awkward, but we'll get used to it soon enough. I could be wrong about Rawdon, but I don't want to take a chance and regret not being able to defend myself or one of you, if he attempts to harm any of us."

"Five pistols against five hundred muskets isn't much defense," Meg said, plainly.

"You're right, dear, but it's enough to kill Rawdon, and he will be my target."

⚊◦◉◦⚊ ⚊◦◉◦⚊ ⚊◦◉◦⚊

Rachel awoke to find the soldiers on her property were moving out. Rawdon, after spending the night in the guest room, was astride his horse overseeing the troops breaking camp. He'd received an urgent message to take his men to Camden at once; Cornwallis's scouts had located General Gates with a large contingent of men about ten miles north readying to march south.

Hearing the front door of the Hamilton home open and close behind him; he wheeled his horse around.

"Good morning madam. I trust you had a restful night," he said, bowing to the neck of his horse. "As you see, we shall be vacating your premises this morning. However, I've ordered a platoon to set fire to your home, your fields, and every out building as we leave."

Rachel took a step back, bumping against a chair. She'd heard his words, but couldn't believe he would actually do it. Everything was still; not a leaf or a blade of grass stirred. The morning sun beat down upon his broad shoulders. Rachel searched his face for some sign of compassion, but found nothing. It was like looking at a statue carved of stone.

Finally, she found her voice, and moved to the steps. "But why—why would you destroy our home? How will that help you win this war?" she pleaded.

He remained silent, his eyes locked on her.

He sat with his left hand on his hip and his right resting on the hilt of his sword. It was clear he would not be moved by her pleading, but she had to know why. "Please answer me. Why would you do such a barbaric thing?"

For another torturous minute, he stared through her and he said nothing. He was enjoying making her wait.

Then he took a deep breath and exhaled loudly. "Where is your haughtiness this morning, madam? Where is your sarcastic criticism? Am I not the same uncouth lout as yesterday?"

Rachel stood stock-still, too distressed to respond.

"You have only yourself to blame, dear lady. For your family's rebellion, I will exact merciless retribution in the name of our sovereign, King George III."

Slowly, Rachel understood what he was doing. It had rankled him yesterday to lose over a dozen men to an enemy he considered unworthy. Today, he would strike his enemy in a very painful way by destroying something very dear to his enemy's heart—his home. And the more she pleaded and anguished over losing her home, the more pleasure it would bring him.

Later, she would try to describe the feeling that came over her when she could only look on while the flames consumed her home. Something like peace settled in her heart as a passage from the bible came to her. In a matter of moments, she remembered the passage of scripture in Philippians 4:11. ". . . *for I have learned in whatever situation I am to be content.*"

CHAPTER TWENTY THREE

CAPTURED

Stepping back up to the veranda, Rachel looked out toward the orchard. Armed with axes, several Tories were chopping down the peach trees. Across the orchard, the fields were afire. Swallowing hard, she said a prayer for strength. Everything was happening so quickly, Loyalist soldiers, some of them she recognized, were now entering her house and running out with armloads of her family's cherished possessions—things that had taken their family years to accumulate. She must hold herself together.

She steeled herself for what she was about to say. Rawdon had turned his back to her and focused his attention to his troop.

Raising her voice, Rachel said, "Colonel Rawdon, may I have a word with you?"

Turning his horse around to face her, his dark eyes were full of hostility as he glared at her. "What is it you wish to say, madam?"

She was surprised how calm she felt. Her stomach was quiet, and her heart wasn't racing away. He seemed to be impatient for her to say her piece, and that pleased her.

"The day is yours, Colonel. You may destroy everything here that my family has built, but we shall rebuild upon the ashes. The time is coming when there will be no trace of your footprints on our land, and we will still be free. Then your day of reckoning will come, and I hope I'm there to witness it."

"You rebels are a belligerent and contentious lot," Rawdon said. A smirk etched on his face. "I've reserved the honor of setting fire to your house for your neighbor, Rufus Sherman. He requested the opportunity, in fact, he seems anxious to set this fine home ablaze." Touching his finger to his helmet, Rawdon spun his horse around and rode away without looking back.

Hearing the name of the man who had twice tried to kill her husband sent chills down her spine. She had no idea Rufus was part of Rawdon's Tories.

"Good morning, my dear Rachel, I had no idea an opportunity like this would ever come my way."

The gruff voice came from behind her, but she recognized that voice! An icy wind blew through her heart, and she spun around to find Rufus standing close behind her. The pungent smell of sour sweat and filth that assaulted her nostrils was almost more than she could bear.

Rufus was a very big, broad Dutchman well over six feet tall. He had large hands and graying hair, partly bald in back. During the French and Indian War, stories abounded of him fighting three or four men at a time. Now, men seldom found it necessary to argue with Rufus.

"It's a pity that John and your son escaped by the skin of their teeth yesterday," Rufus said, resting his massive hands on his hips, "Had I, or any of my sons, been on the line, I have no doubt but that you'd be planning their funerals today."

He stood there with a malicious grin and wiped tobacco spittle from the corners of his mouth with his thumb. "I do believe a pretty woman as yourself would dress out fine in mourning clothes—yessir; I believe you would, indeed."

Rachel's eyes narrowed. "You pathetic excuse for a man! You dare to show your face when you know my husband is nowhere near. You and those like you are nothing more than fainthearted pretenders."

Before she could react, Rufus grabbed her by the hair and slapped her hard with the back of his hand. Her head exploded in a flash of light and pain. The blow sent her sprawling across the veranda floor into a table, knocking it over.

His dark eyes burned with hatred as he glared at her lying on the floor at his feet. "Surely, woman, you're aware it's only a short while until Lord Cornwallis will have this entire country under martial law!"

She laid nearly unconscious, arms and legs askew. Her senses slowly came into focus, and there was a strange taste in her mouth. She realized it was blood. Rachel willed herself to stand upright; her legs trembled from the strain. She touched her mouth, and her fingers came away, wet, warm and red with blood.

Behind them, the door slammed. It was Sarah and Lottie, and they each had a pistol aimed at Rufus's chest.

"Step away from my mother-in-law, or I'll shoot you, Uncle!" cried Sarah in a voice breaking with agitation.

Two British regulars, one a sergeant, had been standing by to assist Rufus in torching the house. The sergeant leaped to the veranda and addressed the two young women. "I'll be giving you lasses a pass this time, but if you don't put your weapons aside *now*, I'll have a squad of his majesty's finest run you through and give them the sport of the other women here. Now make up your mind, you nits, and be quick about it."

Sarah and Lottie stepped back. They laid their pistols on a nearby table and lowered their heads.

Rachel's face was puffy and reddened down one side, and she could only see out of one eye. The other was swollen shut. She glared at Rufus with unrestrained hatred and said, "I don't wish to discuss the eventual conclusion of this war with a man who beats women. I will, however, remind you that your king is alone in a world war, and your pledged allegiance to him will carry you to your own destruction. When the war ends, you and your kind will be a long way from home."

The soldier stood there a moment, his hard eyes staring at Rachel. Then he shouted to some men herding the Hamilton's few head of cattle, "Let's move, and get busy! We need to be away from here before the hour is up."

As if he was just now aware of Rachel, the soldier said, his voice barren of any compassion, "My men and I will be availing ourselves of your stores and the victuals you've got on the stove, m'lady. We're herding your cows to the road. His majesty's troops are a hungry lot. We haven't had beef in over a month."

He watched his men drive the cattle and said to Rachel, "We'll be leaving you the wagon and mule. You have less than an hour to load up what belongings you have left before we set fire to the house."

Stunned, the women stood there for a moment. Then Lottie swept up her pistol and headed toward the barn. "I'll get the wagon, ma!"

The soldier shouted, "Halt, girl! Ye'll be having no need of that pistol. Th' men of the 33rd Foot don't care that you're female. You'll be dead ere you get to your barn. Now lay it back on the table and fetch the wagon for your ma."

Then he shouted to his men, "Watch for the young rebel lass. She's coming out to fetch their wagon. Leave her be!"

Lottie left quickly, and Rachel and Sarah frantically began gathering clothes and possessions.

Rachel's eyes darted to the sergeant. "Please get off my porch and take your confederate with you. My children and I must hurry, and you're in the way."

Rufus clenched his fists and took a step toward her, but the sergeant grabbed his arm and spun him around.

Snarling his words, the sergeant said, "Let her go. We can't fall behind here. We don't know just where the rebels are right now. Besides, I didn't come over here to fight women and children."

Without waiting for them to leave, the women busied themselves in collecting the few possessions left for the wagon.

Ellie and Sarah struggled to get their clothes gathered on blankets and down the stairs. The time was passing quickly, and they kept at their work in dazed silence. Rachel and Lottie were struggling with a trunk of clothes when they saw some men with torches heading for the barn.

"Hurry, girls," Rachel said sharply. "Look around for things we've overlooked. Lottie, fetch the box from the hearth. Those men will be coming to the house next."

Lottie retrieved the metal box from beneath the brick hearth. "Here it is, Ma. I'll push it underneath the mattresses."

Giving her a quick hug, Rachel said, "Don't let any of the men outside see you."

The barn was now engulfed in crackling flames. Lottie could feel the heat from the raging inferno. She saw men with torches going toward the house. She wanted to take her pistol and fight them off, but she knew she couldn't stop them.

I'll remember this day, and I'll remember Rufus Sherman, too. There was just too many for one girl to fight.

Running back to the house, Lottie threw the door open in a frenzy and ran inside shouting, "That's it, we have to leave! They're coming with the torches!"

Rachel seemed not to hear her. She was bundling her skillets and pots in a quilt. Lottie ran to her, jerked the quilt from her, and began dragging it to the door. Ellie took one end of the quilt, and together, they were able to get in the wagon.

Outside, Lottie said, panting for breath, "Ellie, find your mother and then get in the wagon with Sarah and stay there. I'm going back for Ma, and then we have to get away from the house. It's already burning."

Just then, Rufus and two soldiers with torches came around to set fire to the rear of the house.

Waving her arms, Lottie shouted, "Wait! My ma is still in the house. Give me time to get her out!"

They shrugged and shook their heads. Rufus said gruffly, "You've had your time, girl. We've tarried here as long as we dare."

"Take the wagon up the drive and wait, Ellie!" Lottie cried out loudly. "I'm going in to get Ma!"

Smoke was beginning to fill the house. Tongues of flames licked at the hallway walls. Intense heat made it difficult to breathe. Lottie's eyes darted around in search of her mother. When Lottie found her, she was huddled in her sewing room grasping her loom.

Lottie ran to her. Bending, she struggled to lift Rachel to her feet. "Ma, everything's burning, we've got to leave now."

Rachel coughed fitfully and nodded her head. Together, they made their way out the back and to the drive where Ellie and Sarah were waiting with the wagon. Looking back, the four of them watched the flames leaping from the roof. The main house was now ablaze; the flames roared high into the air—a falling roof timber sent a burst of sparks wildly into the blowing wind.

Clinging to each other for support, the two women were able to make their way to the wagon. In a muted voice, Lottie said, "Let's climb up and get away from here, Ma. There's nothing left for us here."

Rachel leaned against a wheel for support. She couldn't pull her eyes away from the inferno. Shaking her head, she whispered, "Ten years of sweat and back-breaking effort is going up in smoke, and for what purpose? Do Rufus and his ilk really believe victory will come to them from this?"

Beyond the house, the barn had nearly burned itself to a mound of ashes. In soulful silence, Rachel and the girls watched as the roof of the house collapsed into the smoke and flames.

They watched until only scattered fires remained. The chimneys stood like a sentinel among the ashes and remnants of furniture that signaled where the rooms had been. Sighing heavily, Rachel climbed into the wagon.

CHAPTER TWENTY FOUR

THE PRISONER

Rachel finished her prayer and took a deep breath. "Girls, unless one of you can think of something else, we're going to make our temporary home in the rooms over John's shop right in the middle of town."

"But Ma, Cornwallis is encamped all around Camden, and Rawdon left to join him," exclaimed Lottie.

Ellie gasped suddenly, her eyes widening in shock, and her hands reflexively covered her mouth. "And I don't feel safe anywhere near Rawdon," she said, a slight tremor in her voice.

Rachel covered Ellie's hand with hers. "For some reason, dear, Rawdon decided to take out his frustration by burning us out. He forgot about you the moment he left Trenton in ashes. We'll all stay out of sight until John can find us a place to join him."

Facing the others, she said, "Besides, we won't be seeing those men. If they lose the battle that General Gates is set to bring them, they'll be scurrying back to Charles Town and fast. Even if they win, they'll be on the move to North Carolina and Virginia soon enough."

It was almost noon when Lottie drove the wagon into town. Broad Street was busy, but few people took notice of their wagon. British redcoats seemed to be everywhere, casually strolling from store to store, as if they were in England itself.

Warily, the women kept their faces turned away from any curious eyes. John's leatherworks business was another block away, but Rachel couldn't help looking as they passed the familiar stores and shops. She felt some comfort from seeing Mr. Kendall in front of his print shop tacking up his latest edition of the news. The aroma coming from the bakery and coffee shop roused their appetites as they drove by.

"We're almost here, girls. Lottie will see you to our new home while I'm at the bakery buying some fresh bread and teacakes."

Rachel didn't meet anyone she knew on her way to the bakery. On entering the shop, she was caught off balance by the crowded tables. She was surprised to see it was still one of the most popular places in town. The customers all seemed unaffected by the war. Just a few miles north, her world was burned to the ground, and these people went on as if there was no fighting at all. The sight of so many British soldiers was disquieting even though they had not taken any special notice of her when she came in. While at the counter, Rachel couldn't help overhearing conversations about the upcoming preparations to move out north toward Charlotte in hopes of meeting General Gates and his army.

When Rachel had returned from the bakery, she found Meg and the girls waiting for her in the rooms over the leatherworks. "Ladies, since we may be here for awhile, we must get busy cleaning these rooms. Shortly, I'll call on Mr. Kendall and place an advertisement for some pieces of furniture, and I want to speak to the men downstairs in the shop, so they'll know we'll be staying here until John can rebuild."

Lottie sat on the floor, broke off a chunk of warm bread, and took a large bite. "Maybe we can find someone close by who sells butter and eggs," she said, chewing.

The women sat in a circle and ate the bread in silence until Rachel stood and said, "Let's finish up, girls and start with our cleaning. I'm going downstairs to the shop and borrow some buckets to carry our water, and ask one of them to bring up some firewood for the stove."

Lottie stood and looked around at the bare walls. "I had no idea we had these rooms, it's almost a small house."

"When your father and I first came here, the town was called Pine Tree Hill. There were only one or two businesses already established when John started building this shop." Then she stopped and whispered, "These four rooms were our first home; Gideon was born in this room."

Tears spilled down Sarah's face as the women stood pensively for the next few moments. Breaking the spell, Rachel said, "Let's go, girls. We're wasting time with all of this sentimental conversation. There's a mountain of work to do before we sleep."

⊷⊷⊷ ⊷⊷⊷ ⊷⊷⊷

John and Daniel rode their horses to near exhaustion before they stopped deep in the swampy woods on the edge of their farm. By the next day, they had rejoined their militia and now headed to meet up with General Gates.

Daniel could see his father was worried about the British encamped at their farm. "Pa, maybe we ought to go back. Gates isn't likely to need us anyway. He wouldn't be marching south unless he figured he outnumbered Cornwallis at least two to one."

Twisting in the saddle, John said, "I've given that a lot of thought since yesterday, Daniel—a lot of thought. I suspect that was Lord Rawdon's Legion we run into, but I doubt they're still there. Reports from our scouts are telling us Cornwallis is preparing to leave Camden, and he'll want Rawdon with him."

Straightening himself in the saddle, John continued, "I caught a glimpse of your mother on the veranda as we started our run for cover. She looked regal—very dignified. I doubt Rawdon bested her in any conversation they've had. No matter how difficult it gets, your mother is always determined to have the last word."

It was late afternoon when John and his men reached the settlement of Claremont. General Gates had bivouacked his army and made final preparation to attack Cornwallis before dawn. John held his men just outside the camp and rode toward a tent with a guard posted at the entrance. He figured the only tent needing security would be the command headquarters, and that's where he would most likely find General Gates.

John pulled his horse up at the front of the tent and dismounted. Nearing the guard, he said, "Colonel John Hamilton reporting for duty as ordered by General Gates. Would you tell the General I'm here with two hundred-fifty able-bodied men ready to ride?"

The guard saluted and disappeared into the tent. Shortly, the general came out. Although John had never met the general, he wasn't surprised at the man's appearance. Except for the color of his uniform, Gates would pass for an imperious British officer. His uniform was crisp, pressed, and his boots highly polished. He wore an expensive looking powdered wig placed, with some care, over his own hair.

Coupled with the stories he'd heard and dismissed as gossip, John tried to look past the out-of-place image of the parade general that stood before him.

Despite his haughty appearance, Gates extended his hand and invited John into the tent. "Come in, John, and we'll talk."

Motioning for John to take a chair at the small table serving as a desk, Gates sat across from him. "I'm afraid you and your men rode for naught, Colonel. I have presently under my command nearly four thousand men who are ready to send Cornwallis back to Charles Town."

John listened intently as his commander laid out his battle plan. It was a favorite of every British General; nothing Cornwallis had not already faced many times. John wanted to make some suggestions, but he realized the general wasn't asking for advice and was known to be easily offended at any criticisms of his tactics.

Finally, Gates ended his soliloquy. "I'm ready for anything from Cornwallis, and I've no doubt I shall be victorious tomorrow. Now I'll give you new orders, Colonel. We've received word that Cornwallis has significant storage of powder and other supplies at a plantation near Spears Creek. I would like for you and your men to relieve the British of their burden and forward it to me."

General Gates stood, and John did likewise. It was evident the pompous man needed nothing from him, not his complement of fighting men and certainly not his tactical advice. John saluted and left the tent.

Back where his men had been waiting, John said, "Gather round men, we've been given new orders."

The men formed a tight group and sat or kneeled in a semi-circle and waited to hear what lay ahead. John cleared his throat. "Men, the general feels the army he already has is enough to beat Cornwallis tomorrow without our help. So we've been ordered to attack a supply outpost near Spears Creek."

An instant murmuring rippled through the men. A man near the front raised his hand. John recognized him to ask his question.

"Begging the general's pardon and yours, too, Colonel, but since this war started, we've never had too many fighting men. Does the general know Cornwallis will have Colonel Banastre Tarleton and his merciless dragoons at his side?"

John swallowed to keep his feelings hidden. "The general didn't ask for my advice. He just gave me orders to overtake the supply station on Spears Creek and come away with what powder is there. You men rest up, and we'll ride in about four hours."

John's men pulled out several hours before daylight and rode through the night to arrive just before dawn at the Tory plantation. The creek was between them and the plantation house. These men knew their work and few words would pass between them and John during the task ahead.

Turning to his son, John whispered, "Daniel, pick a man to go with you and take a look. The rest of you men stand easy, if we're lucky, we'll catch'em just as they're waking up."

The large farmhouse sat high on a hill overlooking Spears Creek. The British were barracked inside the sprawling home, and no sentries were posted anywhere. About one hundred yards from the house, John sent his long rifle sharpshooters high in the trees to sight in on the main door.

After Daniel returned, John split his men into three units and attacked from two sides, holding about eighty mounted soldiers in reserve. The British were just waking, and the suddenness of the attack threw them into chaos. Failing twice to mount a counterattack, the British commander attempted to rally his force to meet the attacking patriots, but he was shot from his horse almost immediately. Any hopes of a counterattack died with the Loyalist commander. The redcoats fought on without their leader, but were soon overrun. Those who lived to run away were chased until they were captured or killed. The fight carried on for a little more than an hour before it ended with a patriot victory.

From a stand of trees some distance away from the fray, a figure raised his rifle and braced it against a tree. He took deliberate aim at John's horse and fired. Flame erupted from the octagonal barrel with an ear-splitting "boom" as grayish smoke billowed, obscuring the shooter. John heard the impact of the bullet as it slammed into his horse—the gelding stumbled and fell, throwing John headlong onto the dew-laden weeds. Before he could stand, he was recognized by Tories around him, and in the confusion of battle, John was captured.

Tory soldiers bound him hand and foot and flung him in one of their baggage wagons as if he were a sack of grain. A driver jumped up to the bench and cracked his whip. The team lurched forward, and the wagon was soon hurtling toward the Santee River. The Tories had lost the gunpowder, but had captured one of the most wanted rebel militiamen.

Every bone jarring turn of the wheels carried spasms of pain throughout his body, but he kept trying to keep his mind focused on what was around him. The landscape began to reflect the soft even light of the dawning sun.

The horses were blowing hard with the strain of holding their pace, and the harness trace chains rattled from the jostling as the wagon creaked and the miles rolled by.

A rough hand jostled him. "We'll be taking a short break here, Colonel. You just lay there all quiet-like and we'll be movin' along in a little while."

John relaxed as best he could, but his mind was too burdened for him to sleep. *By now Daniel and the boys know I've been captured . . . sure hope Daniel uses his head when he comes.*

Their nooning stop was short and the wagon was soon speeding over the dusty road again, and the sleep that had not come finally shuttered the noise and jarring from his consciousness.

John was dragged from sleep by the sound of the driver shouting, "Whoa!" The wagon rumbled and rattled to a jolting stop. John managed to brace himself to a sitting position and could see the men were stopping for the night. It took little time for them to build a small fire, and picket their horses for the night.

Suddenly, rough hands took hold of him and pulled him from the wagon. John landed on his stomach, knocking the air from his lungs. He lay there silently gasping, no air passing in or out of his starved lungs. Pain shot through his arms as he was grabbed by his wrist manacles and dragged across the damp ground to the side of the wagon. The soldier quickly secured his wrist shackles to a wheel spoke. John's lungs expanded as he gulped in air, but his head was spinning, and his chest ached.

The irons forced John to sit with his left shoulder against the wheel. The heavy iron chains clinked against the shackles when he nudged closer to the spokes so he could rest his arms on the axle hub. His thoughts rambled and wandered while he stared into the starry sky.

A shiver rippled through him, and he drew his legs up to his chest to ward off the night air. He was mesmerized by the crackling campfire. The light from the flames danced across the faces of the soldiers. John watched the fire burn down to glowing embers, and the soldiers settled into sleep. He shifted his position, and stabbing pain ran through his right arm. He leaned closer to his outstretched arms and dropped his chin to his chest.

Merciful sleep soon overtook his racing thoughts, and he drifted in and out of a restless slumber throughout the rest of the night. It seemed he'd just closed his eyes when he awoke with a start to find the red-coated sergeant standing over him. Dawn was just breaking over the eastern horizon in muted rosy shades.

The rattling of the chains as the sergeant loosed him from the wheel cleared the cobwebs from his head, and it all came back rushing into his mind. He was still a prisoner despite the erratic dreams of home and the warmth of his own bed beside Rachel.

"Stand up, you worm," said the sergeant, taking hold of his collar, "I'll not be carrying you to the wagon while you have two good legs of your own!"

John stood awkwardly on his wobbly legs and tried to walk toward the rear of the wagon. After a step or two, his legs gave way, and he fell in a heap beside the sergeant.

Suddenly, he felt a sudden explosion of pain in his ribs and he gasped. John doubled up. The sergeant kicked him again, and John curled up tighter, bringing his knees up close to his chest. Agonizing pain burned his eyes and blurred his vision. In the recesses of his mind, he knew he had to stand, or the sergeant would kick him again.

Reaching deep within his heart, John willed himself to stand. With his feet under him, he held onto the side of the wagon and limped slowly around to the back. Stretching his arms to pull himself into the wagon brought searing pain in his rib cage that caused him to gasp aloud.

Gritting his teeth, John pushed past the pain and crawled onto the wagon bed. His breath came in ragged pants while he lay there and listened to the mocking laughter of the sergeant and his cohorts.

CHAPTER TWENTY FIVE

THE PLAN

A myriad of thoughts sped through John's mind, but in spite of his pain and the Tories' taunting insults, his head began to clear. He lay still while he felt his anger rise in his heart.

I know I can find a way through this, if I just keep my wits about me, he thought.

John looked down at his hunting shirt. In his mind's eye, he could see the flax stalks that he and Daniel had cut become homespun linen under Rachel's skilled hands, and how she had made this shirt for him on his last birthday.

The wagon lurched forward and began clattering noisily toward its destination. John sat up and said, "Driver, where are you taking me?"

For a moment or two, the driver seemed not to hear him. Finally, he shouted over his shoulder, "You're on your way to the jail at Fort Ninety Six, that is, if the hangman doesn't get you first. We haven't had a hanging in a while, so maybe the colonel will have you dance for us." He threw his head back and gave a booming laugh that echoed through the trees.

'*Hangman.*' Cold chills ran through his heart when he heard those words. He had to find a way to escape before his captors arrived in the town that was a hotbed of Tory sympathizers.

Pulling on the chains that bound him, the reality of his predicament settled over him like a dark cloud. *Who am I trying to kid? I can't escape these chains. My only hope is that Daniel and the boys can catch up with me before we reach Ninety Six.*

The wagon rumbled and bounced on down the road, and John soon fell into a fitful, nightmarish sleep. He was awakened when the wagon came to a jarring stop.

He heard the driver cry out, "'Tis four of us with a rebel prisoner. It's John Hamilton, himself. Open the gate!"

John heard the loud squeaking of the huge hinges as the front gate swung open. In a moment, the wagon rolled inside the formidable walls of Fort Ninety Six. By the time the wagon stopped, a crowd had gathered around the wagon. The name John Hamilton had brought everyone within earshot close to see the imposing rebel leader.

With no warning, the burly sergeant, who had roughed him up earlier, grabbed him by his collar and dragged him from the wagon, flinging him to the ground. The growing crowd jeered and laughed.

A woman ran up and spat on him. "I curse you John Hamilton; you killed my only son. I pray that my husband will be your hangman."

Others, who had kept their distance, began to follow the woman's lead. Some shouted oaths and curses in his face, a number of the women spat until spittle ran down his face to drip on his shirt, and a few, taking advantage of his iron shackles, hit him with their fists. One wizened old man, evidently blind, was led close to John.

He reached to touch John's head, and swiftly brought his cane down across John's brow. The blow knocked John unconscious, and he slumped over in a heap while the old man was led away through the cheering mob.

<hr />

John woke up with a throbbing headache. Opening his eyes, he stared into the black darkness. An incredibly foul odor permeated the air almost causing him to retch. His mind was clearing, and he recalled the crowd and their insults. Turning a bit so he could sit up, the heavy iron shackles rattled and clinked.

A hoarse voice spoke from somewhere in the darkness. "It's about time you come awake, friend. Ben and me was beginning to think they killed you. Are you really John Hamilton?"

John felt disoriented from the blackness of the room, but he answered, "Yes, I'm John. Do I know you men?"

"Yessir, we're Eb Sanderson and Ben Nettles from around Sparrow Swamp. We rode with Captain Smothers. We were ambushed crossing the Broad—lost a lot of us that day, including the captain. About fifty of us were brought here."

John remembered hearing of the fight. "You men have been here since that time?"

Eb answered, "Yessir. That was '78. What year is this?"

Hesitating, John said, "Eb, it's August 1780."

Neither of the men said anything for a few moments. John heard one of the men sigh heavily.

Ben finally spoke, "I felt we'd been in here a year or better, but there's been no way we could know for sure. We don't hear anything about the outside."

The men fell into a prolong silence, John felt his stomach settling, and his eyes were adjusting to the heavy darkness enough that he could make out vague shapes that he took for his fellow prisoners.

"Colonel," Eb said, his voice hoarse but steady, "How does the war go?"

John could hear the quiet desperation in his voice, and pondered how to answer such a question.

A scraping sound broke the silence, and John said, "Are there others with us?"

Eb answered, "Yessir, there's about twelve of us now, give or take. We started off with thirty-one in this one room, but for some time, we've been dying off at about one a week."

John cleared his throat, and said, "You asked me how goes the war, and I can tell you we've lost some big battles recently and we'll likely lose more in the next few months. But I want to make sure you men know there's plenty of fighting patriots in South Carolina and we're taking it to them every day."

The room fell quiet again. Then came an unfamiliar raspy voice. "You ain't just speechifying are you Colonel? You can say it plain 'cause there ain't a man here that's given up."

A murmur of agreement rumbled the walls of the room. John could almost feel the driving determination of these men who had endured horrible conditions and were now facing near certain death. Their hearts beat with the same fervor that caused them to leave everything behind and go to war against their monarch.

John sat a little straighter. "Men, since May of this year, we've lost our entire southern army. The British now occupy Charles Town, Savannah, Augusta, and probably Camden, but as bad as that is, we are gathering our forces to fight back. We have some able men leading us now, men like General Francis Marion and Colonel Sumter."

Eb asked, "How did you come to be captured, Colonel?"

John felt his leg had gone to sleep and shifted to relieve the pressure. "My recollection is a bit fuzzy, Eb, but I do remember my horse being mortally wounded and pitching me forward. I no sooner had time to stand when hands took hold of me and threw me in a wagon and here I am. We had just engaged a contingent of Tories guarding a store of gunpowder, so I don't know how that ended."

A week passed, and still the men never tired of listening to John talk of life outside their putrid and noxious world. John found, to his amazement, that no matter how broken-down their lives had become, there remained in these men a strong, burning desire for the liberty of their cause. He could hear it in their voices and conversations. If anything, their passion was now even stronger, more determined than it had been when they'd first gone to fight. Now he knew the British would never win this war.

Morning came and John was roused from his restless night of on again-off again sleep by someone jerking on his shackled legs.

"Wake up, you rebel scum, you're not a colonel any longer," a burly guard snarled. "Stand easy while I remove these chains from your legs. You have a visitor."

John's legs were a little wobbly, but he managed to stand while the guard removed the shackles. He felt free without the weight of the shackles, even though his arms were still bound by iron manacles.

The guard stepped aside and a woman entered the dark room. Stepping outside quickly, the guard slammed the heavy door shut, locking her inside. The hefty stench of a necessary made her want to gag, but with all her might, she held it back.

"Colonel Hamilton?" she said distinctly, "My name is Martha, and I'm the sister of Nathaniel Gibson. He rides with you."

John could see the outline of a tiny frame, and the delicate scent of lavender wafted in his direction cutting the cell's foul stench. "Hello Martha, I'm John Hamilton. To what do I owe the extreme pleasure of your visit?"

Lowering her voice to a bare whisper, Martha replied, "My family and I live here among these heathens, and I've come to tell you that Daniel and Nate are set to break you and the others free tomorrow night around midnight."

A low, sustained murmur went through the group. John whispered over his shoulder, "Hold it down, men. We're not out, yet." He turned back to the girl. "Miss Martha, we appreciate you taking such a risk to bring us this good news."

Her eyes had adjusted to the darkness and she held out a bundle to John. "I brought some bread and smoked venison for you and the men. I had to bribe the guard with a loaf and meat to get in to see you, but it's a small price to pay for setting you men free."

Unseen men delivered their thanks to Martha from the darkness. Tears spilled down her face. "Colonel, my brother asked me to tell you the raid was successful and they will be using the redcoat's own powder when they come tomorrow."

"That's good to know, Martha. I'd been wondering how we fared in that skirmish. Did your brother say anything about any of our men getting wounded or killed?"

Responding quickly, she said, "Two were wounded, sir, and one man, who Nate didn't name, was killed."

A moment passed and John said, "It might be time for your family to leave, especially after tomorrow's attack so soon after your visit today."

"Thank you for the advice, Colonel. I'm leaving with my children tomorrow morning, heading for Sycamore Shoals, and my husband will leave in the confusion with all of you tomorrow night. My husband plans to meet us at the shoals and, from there, take us to Fort Watauga across the Blue Ridge."

Without warning, the door opened and a shaft of light thrust its way into the room and the guard stood in the open doorway. "All right, lady, time's up."

Martha quickly said a prayer for the men and retreated into the hallway. The door slammed shut, and the prisoners heard the sound of a big key turning the lock.

John and the men devoured their meal quickly, and the talk turned to tomorrow's chance for freedom. John could hear the exhilaration felt by the men in their voices; each man had something to say. Some choked on their emotions and couldn't finish expressing their thoughts, but to a man, they wanted to finish the fight.

Realizing the guard hadn't replaced the shackles on his legs. "Men, I know each of you will be returning to your homes and loved ones. I suggest to each of you to stay home and give yourselves time to heal and recover before you rejoin the fight."

John sensed the anticipation within the men. "The next few months will be intense and demanding on us, because we'll be taking the fight to the likes of Cornwallis, Rawdon, and Tarleton. There'll be much riding and little sleep as we hound them into submission, so get yourselves in good condition before you come back. I assure you there'll be enough fighting to go around for the next few months."

Hours passed slowly until the day ended, and the next morning the men in the cell awakened to their usual morning ritual. The guard banged on the door and then slid bowls of bug-infested gruel through a small door.

After the men had eaten, the heavy cell door swung open and the guard said, gruffly, "Let's go, Hamilton. It seems Colonel Cruger wants to see you. I'll be having my eyes on you the whole time, so any move from you that I don't like will bring swift retribution upon your head. Do we understand each other?"

John answered with a nod of his head.

Outside, he breathed deeply. The afternoon fresh air filled his lungs. The cloudless sky never looked so blue, and the towering pines gently swayed in the soft breeze.

A jarring pain in his ribs brought him out of his reverie. "Move, you sorry rebel, no more stopping unless I tell you," yelled the guard.

After about one hundred yards, they came to a nondescript wooden building. The guard shoved John aside and knocked briskly on the door.

"Enter," someone called from inside.

The guard elbowed John through the open door and followed him in. John felt his heart almost stop when he saw Wesley Morton sitting near Cruger's desk.

Morton! So this is where he's been hiding! John managed a tight grin. "How's your leg, Wesley? Horse bites can be worrisome, but I see you've managed well since you escaped from Mackenzie's place.

A cynical smile crept across Morton's lips. "Well, if it ain't the Colonel himself, I had no idea we would ever meet again. You can't know how much pleasure this brings to me for you to stop by. Just so you know, I now limp because of you—I'll be settling that score while you're here."

John looked past Morton, determined to shut out his taunting. He allowed his mind to take him down the trails and paths to his beloved Trenton farm. He was standing on the farmhouse veranda where he could see the acres and acres of pasture, his cattle feeding on the clover rich grass, and his sweet, sweet Rachel, laughing and running toward him.

Suddenly, a gravelly voice brought him back to the reality of where he was. It was Colonel Cruger, an American Tory from New York, now the commandant of the settlement of Ninety Six.

"Colonel Hamilton, please accept my apology for delaying my welcome to you, but my duties kept me away. I understand you've been lodging in our jail for the past fortnight."

John had carried the malodorous stench of his cell on his clothes and in his matted hair, and Cruger opened a window behind his desk for some fresh air. "I'm sure you can appreciate the importance of your capture. I won't embarrass you with the particulars of your notoriety, but you should know your being detained will be exploited to the fullest to discourage your fellow rebels."

John looked at Cruger. "If your plan is to use me to demoralize the brave men and women who're fighting for their God-given freedoms, then I tell you now, you've set yourself a goal you'll never reach."

Cruger's face hardened as John watched his eyes narrow to mean, black slits. "I'm not surprised at your reaction, Colonel. Wesley told me to be prepared for your stubbornness. But I will tell you now: if you refuse to cooperate I shall send a contingent of men to kidnap your wife and other women of your family and deliver them to me—after my men are done with them, of course." Straightening to his full height, Cruger stated with chilling coldness, "Then, as they are forced to watch, I'll have you hanged by your neck until you tire of dancing and leave you there until your bones are bleached white."

John swallowed with difficulty, but remained outwardly calm. He studied his feet as if he was deep in thought. He figured that by playing along, he could buy himself some time—he needed to stall until Daniel and his men got here tonight.

Leaning against his desk, Cruger said, "Colonel, I can't deny that you've been one of the toughest and most effective rebel militia leaders in the colony. But the time has come for men like you to accept that yours is a cause for which defeat is inevitable."

Stepping back toward the open window, Cruger pressed the issue. "Already, there've been many men of your standing and prestige who've accepted the king's generous offer of parole and gone on to regain their lives as loyal subjects of his majesty."

***

John had paid little attention to the Colonel as he made his pitch to convert him, at least until he made his barbarous threat to harm Rachel and their girls.

Through the window, John could see soft white clouds drifting across the pale blue sky. A peaceful scene, but a storm was building in his heart and the coldness of death crept over him as he surveyed the pompous, grinning Colonel Cruger. Fighting the urge to strike out at the devilish creatures around him, he struggled for control of his emotions.

Exhaling a long, deep breath, John's eyes covered both men. John knew he had to play this right. Any misstep and the

Colonel would likely carry out his threat—and without delay. John's face bore the look of a man who had run out of choices, and he forced a tone of submission in his voice. "Colonel, if I yield to your demands, what assurance do I have that you will not bother my family?"

Cruger stood back from his desk, his eyes alight with excitement. "Ah, Wesley, you see how quickly these rebels capitulate? Here is your stalwart John Hamilton, the hero of the traitorous Americans groveling at my feet."

Cruger adjusted his coat, his expression one of gloating, while he held his answer to John's question. After this pause, he came around his desk to stand before John. He held a perfumed handkerchief to his nose to allay the stench.

"I've decided to allow you the night to accept my generous offer of parole. You must be prepared to give me your answer on the morrow. If you accept and sign the document attesting your unfettered loyalty to our king, then you have my word that no harm will come to your family."

Cruger motioned for the guard to take John back to the jail.

<hr />

"Have any of you men seen my Pa?" asked Daniel. He cast a worried look around as the men gathered round him, some on horseback, others afoot, having lost their mounts during the skirmish.

The dispirited faces of the men gave Daniel his answer. In the intense moments of battle, these men had fought for their own survival, and no one remembered seeing what might have been the final moments of their leader.

Dismounting, Daniel gave what the men took as an order. "Spread out and cover the area, look for wounded, anything that might tell us what happened to Pa—I mean, to the Colonel."

The men began their search for John. It was a sobering task to walk among the lifeless fallen who, earlier in the day, were living men.

Daniel was almost ready to admit defeat in finding any trace of his father when he heard a voice calling from across the field. "I found his horse! Over here, Daniel!"

A coldness settled in his heart as Daniel ran to the see if it was, indeed, his father's horse. Kneeling beside the fallen animal, he ran his hands over the saddle that he knew so well. Daniel wanted to run away somewhere—anywhere and never stop running, but he knew his father might still be alive, and he needed to keep his wits about him if he was to help him.

Sucking in a lot of air, Daniel said, "Look around good, men. He could've been thrown when his horse went down."

Suddenly, a low moaning came from the underbrush nearby. The men scrambled toward the sound. Daniel felt his heart leap, hoping it was his father still alive.

Now the wounded man held his arm high. A body lay across his chest. The dead soldier was pulled off the one who had moaned, and Daniel looked closely into the man's face.

Crestfallen, Daniel sat back on his heels. "It's Jeremiah."

At the sound of his name, the wounded man's eyelids fluttered. "Daniel . . . that you?"

Leaning closer, Daniel answered, "It's me, Jeremiah. Where're you hurt?"

Jeremiah's eyes had closed, his breathing came in gasps. Daniel knew his friend was dying.

Then he roused and opened his eyes again. "Th—the Tory pig-stuck me, Daniel," he whispered hoarsely, "It was early in the fight . . ."

Jeremiah sighed heavily and fell silent. Daniel sat back and said, "Don't try to talk, friend. Just rest easy."

Suddenly, Jeremiah's hand went to Daniel's shirt, and with strength that surprised Daniel, he pulled him close. "I'm dying, Daniel, and . . . I must tell you about the Colonel."

Daniel felt his heart as it pounded in his chest. "What happened, Jeremiah? What happened to my pa?"

Jeremiah's soulful eyes searched the faces of the men gathered around him and came back to rest on Daniel. "They took the Colonel . . . to Ninety Six."

Daniel quickly came to his feet and looked around the group. "Two of you stay with Jeremiah and the rest get ready to ride. We'll take the Tory gunpowder and artillery pieces with us. Let's go, we must catch them before they reach the fort."

The men hurried to their horses without any hesitation. To them, it seemed natural that Daniel would assume command until John could be rescued.

Daniel rode like the wind, setting a fast pace for the men to follow, and the men, all with good horses, stayed with him, knowing it would take a miracle for them to catch up with the Tories.

Toward noon, Daniel heard one of the men call out, "Hold up, Daniel. Our horses can't keep this pace."

Daniel looked back and saw men dropping back; only a few were able to stay with him. Lowering his head, Daniel pulled back on the reins. He knew the horses were exhausted, but he wanted to keep going, even if his horse collapsed; if he were left afoot, he'd run until he caught the men who held his father.

After taking care of their horses, the men built small fires for coffee. Daniel stood in the midst of the camp and said, "I wasn't thinking straight, men. If we'd caught up with'em, some of us would've been wounded or killed for sure."

He hesitated and took a deep breath. "We didn't catch'em . . . the fort's less than five miles ahead, so they already have pa in the jail."

Daniel scanned the faces of his men. "We've got to come up with some kind of plan if we expect to rescue Pa. Does anyone know the layout of Ninety Six? Where's the jail located?"

One of the men replied, "The jail is in the middle of the town and the Tories have put up a ten foot stockade around the town."

Daniel placed his empty coffee cup between his feet. "How far would you say the jail is from the stockade wall?"

The man frowned as he scratched his scrubby beard. "I reckon the town is about two, maybe three hundred yards across, so it'd be half that to the wall."

With his finger, Daniel drew in the dirt and began to think through a way to break his father out of the Ninety Six jail. Some of the men, taking advantage of the quiet, stretched out for a nap.

A man settled down beside Daniel. "Daniel, I'm Nathaniel Gibson, Nate for short. I'm from Benton's Shoals about ten miles north of Ninety Six. I have kin that live inside the stockade; it's my sister, her husband, and their passel of kids. I'm known there and can come and go easy."

Daniel looked up quickly, his eyebrows raised. "Your folks, are they Tories or Patriots?"

A subtle smile spread across Nate's face as he leaned closer to Daniel. "They pretend to be loyal Tories, but no hearts beat stronger for freedom than does my sister's and her husband's. They'll help us free John, for sure."

Daniel and Nate talked for a while longer while the others stretched out on the grassy ground. Very quickly, they were the only two who remained awake. An idea began to grow in Daniel's mind until he felt he had a plan that would free his father. But to make it work he would need someone proven who could make small bombs and dependable timed fuses. The man he wanted was his brother, Gideon, but there was little chance of locating him since Gideon was somewhere in the backcountry of North Carolina.

CHAPTER TWENTY SIX

ON THE RUN

Daniel stood and shook hands with Nate. "I believe we've come up with something that'll work, Nate. Now let's rouse these men and let'em in on it."

Waiting until the men settled down, Daniel said, "Men, I rode today like a man possessed. I had only one thought, and that was to rescue my pa. I appreciate your loyalty to my father, but we would've lost some good men if we'd stormed the fort's gates today."

Daniel felt his emotions knotting in his throat, so he swallowed hard. It wouldn't do, he knew, for him to choke up in front of this group of seasoned veterans.

"Listen close, men. Nate has given us a way to rescue Pa. It'll take a fortnight or so to put this together, but in the meantime, Nate has family living inside the stockade. His sister will be visiting Pa. She'll be able to take him food and let him know we're coming."

The militia would play a diversionary role in order to give Nate and Daniel, who would be inside, time to reach John and bring him and the others out.

The troop of men didn't linger after Daniel's briefing. Most could only afford to be away from home a short time since they were the sole providers for their families. All said they would return when called to do their part to rescue John.

Daniel turned east to head for home. It was a trip he dreaded, but one that he knew he must make. He had to tell his mother that her husband was a prisoner of the Tories.

Daniel reached the Camden Road that would take him within a mile of his home. He decided to make his way through the bottomland woods just in case Lord Rawdon and his Legion were still encamped at his family's home. It had been just a week since he and his father had escaped Rawdon's Tories by outrunning them through this wooded area.

He was eager to get home, to see Ellie again, to hear her voice, and to see and touch all the things of home that he'd taken for granted.

Just a short while, and he'd be there, over the next rise he'd see the back of their house. Maybe Ellie would be out back, and they would meet first. There was a burned smell hanging in the air, and some of the trees bordering the back of their property had signs of being near intense heat.

His horse made the last steps to the top of the rise, and he couldn't believe his eyes. There was nothing standing—nothing. Every building had been burned to the ground; only a few timbers lay scattered here and there as testimony that buildings had once been here.

Warily, he guided his horse around the ashes until he was at the remains of the main house. Behind him, the fields had been torched, and his mother's beloved orchard lay beneath ashes. He could see none of their animals; he supposed the British had taken the cattle for the meat.

Far down the drive, he saw Caleb riding toward him. Daniel rode to meet him. "Caleb, can you tell me if my mother . . ." He choked on the words and couldn't finish.

Caleb eased his horse beside him and reached to touch his arm. Nodding his head, Caleb said, "Mr. Daniel, all the ladies is safe and staying in town over the shop, but it's not safe for you to be seen in town, 'cause it's full of Tories and redcoats. Colonel Rawdon is living in Mr. Sam Garrison's nice house."

"Caleb, where's your Belle, and the others?"

Hanging his head, it was evident Caleb was struggling to hold himself together. "Me and Belle was the only ones to not get caught. We hid in the swampy woods out back, but the others was all rounded up and took to be sold in the West Indies."

For a moment, Daniel was stunned. "But all of you are free. Didn't they show the Tories their papers?"

Shaking his head, Caleb replied, "Their papers was torn up and burned. Papers just ain't enough Mr. Daniel . . ." Shaking his head, he said, ". . . just ain't enough."

Daniel looked at the man who'd been part of his life for as long as he could remember. "Thank you for letting me know about my family. I'll be going now, but don't worry about me. I'll find a way to see my ma and Ellie." He extended his hand, and they shook. "Caleb, where are you and Belle staying? Do you need anything?"

Caleb's soft smile broke into a chuckle. "We're all right. I've got your papa's boat, and we're eating fish. We're staying in somebody's old log cabin, down by the mill creek. Don't look like nobody's lived there in awhile."

Nodding his head, Daniel said, "I know the place, Gideon and I camped there when we were boys."

Daniel untied his rifle and shoved it toward Caleb. "Here, take my rifle, so you can provide meat for your family."

Pushing back, Caleb refused the offer. "No, I can't take it, Mr. Daniel. You're a hunted man, and it may save your life—nossir, I can't take your rifle."

Refusing to take the rifle back, Daniel said, "I'll be able to find another, Caleb." Daniel pointed to his pistols tied to the pommel, "Besides, I'll still have these. Now take this for your family's sake."

Reluctantly reaching for the rifle, Caleb looked straight into Daniel's eyes, his voice tinged with deep emotion, "You're a fine man, Mr. Daniel and the son of a fine man. I'm taking your rifle for my family."

With his hand on Daniel's shoulder, Caleb said, "Don't be worrying about the farm none. When the time comes, we'll rebuild everything, so it'll be just like it was."

Daniel, choked with emotion, could only nod his head. The men shook hands and parted, promising to meet again.

<hr />

Twilight was giving way to a moonless night when Daniel climbed down from a tall pine where he had roosted since mid-afternoon and, with his spyglass, watched the activity near his family's leatherworks business.

At first look, he saw nothing out of the ordinary. Business seemed brisk and usual along the stores and shops of Camden. He was tired of squinting his left eye and staring with his right, but he knew Rawdon would have a sentry posted to watch the shop, and he knew he would keep looking until he found where Daniel was hiding. The sun was fading for the day when he saw what he'd been looking for. Across the street, he found his man.

Just a few minutes earlier, Daniel had observed a man dressed in Tory green and armed with a musket go into Rufus Sherman's Mercantile Store, and moments later a different man, also in Tory green and armed, left. Daniel knew he had witnessed the changing of the guard, but how was he going to slip by this sentry and see Ellie.

Daniel knew the British were expecting him to contact Ellie and his family. Rawdon wanted to be the one who captured John's youngest son, so Daniel would have to find some way to get past the sentry without being seen, but that wasn't going to be so easy.

Daniel sat on the ground and leaned back on the pine. Rawdon had laid the perfect trap, with the perfect bait, and Daniel stared into the fading light as a chill of resentment and bitterness crept into his heart.

Finally, Daniel sat up, and then he stood and began to pace— he'd found a way to get in. It would be a bit risky, but unless he thought of something else, it was going to have to do.

First, he would need the help of the men working in his father's shop, but that was a minor thing, and he would take care of that tonight. Before noon tomorrow, he'd be holding Ellie in his arms.

⸺•◦◉◦•⸺ ⸺•◦◉◦•⸺ ⸺•◦◉◦•⸺

The sun rose with its usual splendor and by mid-morning the streets of Camden were alive with business activity. No one paid any special attention to a wagon loaded with tanned deerskins coming down Broad Street driven by a dull and featureless man. The wagon stopped near the front door of the shop, and the driver quickly hopped down and hurried inside.

Inside the shop, Daniel stopped long enough to speak with the employees about the load of leather outside, and then he hurried upstairs. He paused a moment before he knocked. Taking a deep breath, he tapped on the door.

He heard soft footsteps, the door opened, and there stood his sister, Lottie. She stared at him, standing there before her, dirty, disheveled, and in need of a bath, his hair uncombed and in tangles. It took a minute for her to recognize him.

A scream nearly erupted from her throat, but she caught herself in time. "Daniel! Is it you? Yes, it's you!" She pulled him inside and hugged him with all her strength.

"Easy there sis, you'll break one of my ribs," he said half-seriously.

Footsteps came from the other room, and there before his eyes was his wide-eyed Ellie. He took a step toward her, and she looked as though she might run.

He stopped and held out his arms. "It's me, sweetheart. It's Daniel. I know I look a sight, and I need a bath, but I'm your Daniel."

Ellie ran to him with outstretched arms and clung to him. "Oh, Daniel, I thought I had lost you when General Gates was defeated. Not seeing you among the prisoners who were paraded through town, I thought you'd been in the thick of the battle and were wounded or killed."

The fragrance of her came powerfully to him. "We weren't in the fight with Cornwallis. Gates told Pa we weren't needed, and he sent us to ambush a Tory supply depot on Spears Creek."

Daniel looked over Ellie's head and saw his mother standing at a door. Her face was strained, and she looked as though she would faint.

He ran his fingers through his unruly mop of dark hair. With Ellie under his arm, he walked to his mother.

He tried to smile, but couldn't. "Hello, Ma."

Her voice strained with foreboding, Rachel asked, "Where's your father?"

Daniel had already decided to tell his mother quickly, in a matter-of-fact manner, about his father. Without hesitating, he answered, "Pa's a prisoner in the Ninety Six jail. They took him yesterday morning."

Rachel's eyes rolled back, she swayed and fell against the door opening as she slumped to the floor. Daniel rushed to her and eased her falling.

"Quick, Sarah, get a chair for Ma."

Not knowing what else to do, Daniel patted his mother's hand. "Wake up, Ma. The men are riding with me to snatch Pa out of that jail. He's going to be all right. Please wake up!"

Rachel's eyes fluttered open, and she looked around. Her cheeks, which had whitened a few moments ago, were now regaining some color. It was plain to see she was embarrassed.

Her eyes locked on Daniel. "Help me up, and tell me what happened, son—all of it, don't leave anything out. I'm sorry I did such a foolish and weak thing. I suppose I haven't been getting enough rest lately."

"We weren't in the main fight with Cornwallis. Gates sent us to attack a Tory farm up on Spears Creek for the supplies stored there." Daniel began as he knelt beside his mother and held her hand.

"Pa's horse was shot from under him, and before he could stand, he was taken prisoner and carried off to Ninety Six. Jeremiah was killed trying to rescue Pa. This all happened in the first few minutes of the fight. I didn't know Pa was missing until the fight was over, and by that time, the Tories had too much of a head start on us."

Lines of determination hardened on Daniel's face. "Ma, I've put together a plan to rescue Pa. I can't stay here long, ere they decide to . . ."

"You can't delay, son, they're sure to make a spectacle of your father in hopes of breaking all our spirits." Rachel had risen to her feet, and her words were measured and calm. "I want to be a part of your plan. I'd be able to get into the settlement with a wagon of leather goods. No one would pay any attention to a poor woman peddler and her leather wares."

Shaking his head, Daniel responded, "I don't know, Ma. It's going to be risky and our family can't lose you. We just can't."

Lottie, who had been standing behind Rachel's chair, spoke up. "Brother, how do you plan to get Pa out of the settlement once you have him free?"

He leaned back against the wall. His shoulders sagged and his sleep-deprived eyes were barely open. "Nate and I will enter the settlement at night on the pretense of taking safety within the stockade walls on our way to Camden. We'll park the wagon where we can get to the jail quickly when the racket starts around midnight. Then we'll make our move to free Pa and any other prisoners who're able."

Touching Ellie's face he said, "Once we're outside of the jail, we'll move along the wall by the main gate. Our men outside will set some fused bombs to blow the gate doors away. Using the wagon, we'll make a run for the outside using the dust and smoke for cover, and then sharpshooters will cover our run for the woods if any Tories come after us."

Rachel had listened intently. "Of course that sounds risky to me, and how do you know John will be able to run? He may've been injured when his horse was killed, or the Tories may have hurt him since they've had him."

"I'm set to carry Pa if he's not able to walk. We'll get a report from Nate Gibson's sister, so we'll know what kind of shape Pa is in before we make our move. We'll be as ready as we can be to get Pa out safely."

"How can Nate's sister know anything about John?" asked Rachel.

"We hope she's been allowed to visit the prisoners." Daniel answered, "They pretend to be solid Tories, but they've been risking their lives for the past year and a half to get information out to Colonel Sumter and his men."

Her face drawn with anxiety, Sarah eased beside Daniel. She laid her hand on his shoulder and led him into an adjoining room. "Do you hear any news of Gideon?"

Sighing heavily, Daniel grinned for the first time since entering the apartment. "Gideon was alive and well as of last week, sister. He's on the move leading a group of men, including Vivian's husband. His group is making plenty of trouble for Tories up north of Charlotte. I heard Rufus was badly wounded and had a leg amputated. If that's true, then he's likely out of the war for good."

Sarah fell against him and hugged him tightly, and his arms went around her shoulders as she sobbed quietly. He heard a shuffle of feet and felt arms around him as the other women gathered round and wept with joy and praise for the news of Gideon.

Rachel tugged her son's sleeve. "Are you hungry, Daniel? We had just sat down to eat when you knocked."

He nodded, and his eyes caught Ellie's blue eyes as she gazed at him.

"You can sample the apple cobbler," Ellie told him. "I made it, but it's your mother's recipe."

Daniel sat down at the table. "I've never just *sampled* a pie before. Ma always baked two when Gideon and I were boys—one for each of us."

The women nibbled at the food on their plates and sat in awe as Daniel told them what it was like the day he and his father had run upon Rawdon's Legion at their farm, narrowly escaping almost certain death.

"It all seems like a dream now—a very bad dream, but I remember seeing all of you huddled together as we rode for the fences."

Ellie reached for his hand. "You didn't see me? I ran out toward the wagon drive, yelling and screaming for you to turn around."

Daniel looked at her, stunned. "You were out near the drive? You could have been shot by one of the soldiers or hit by a stray musket ball."

"I didn't stop to think of those things, I just knew you were riding straight into those redcoats, and I only wanted to save you, somehow."

Rachel injected. "Rawdon threatened to hang her after his men allowed you and your father to escape. I'm not sure how serious he was, but it scared all of us, nonetheless."

Pulling Ellie close, Daniel said tenderly, "I suppose this makes you my hero . . . my fairest angel hero."

CHAPTER TWENTY SEVEN

THE RESCUE

Without warning, their conversation was interrupted by explosive banging on the door. Daniel sprung to his feet. "Is there a way out the back, Ma?"

"There's a window at the end of the hall, but you'll have to jump," Rachel said.

Ellie followed him to the window where he paused only briefly and kissed her softly. "I'm depending on you to see that my mother doesn't put herself in harm's way by coming to the fort. Believe me, when I tell you I'm going to rescue Pa."

Bam! Bam! Bam! "Mrs. Hamilton, if you don't open the door, we'll be forced to knock it down, we're here on Lord Rawdon's orders," a man bellowed.

Rachel watched as Daniel slipped out the open window. He dropped to the alley, and Ellie watched him get to his feet and run in the direction of the river. She turned and signaled Rachel that he was gone.

"Close the window," Rachel whispered as she turned to the front door. "For what purpose are you pounding on my door?" she snapped.

"Open the door!" the voice yelled. "I won't ask again!"

Her heart pounded with nervous tension. Rachel gave one last look at the window at the end of the hall. "All right, I'm opening the door." With a nod to the women behind her, she pulled back the bar and opened the door.

Four men surged through the entrance, shoving Rachel and the other women against the wall. They filled the narrow hall, pushing the women aside into an adjoining room. Without giving any orders, the sergeant and his men began searching every room. It didn't take long for the strong odor of black powder, sweat, rum, and the general smells of masculinity to permeate the rooms.

A swarthy sergeant lumbered into the room. Directing his questions to Rachel, he snarled, "Where is he, woman? Or did he jump from the back window?"

Rachel stared at him blankly.

The sergeant took two quick strides and grabbed her by her arms. Jerking her to her feet, he shook her violently. "Out with it, you rebel wench. We know it was your son, Daniel, who brought the wagon of leather. There's no one but your employees downstairs, and no sign of the wagon driver, so tell me where he went."

Rachel felt she was in the midst of an earthquake. She couldn't stop trembling, and her head throbbed. Hiding her fear of this viciously tempered man, Rachel said with determined precision, "How dare you come into my home and threaten me and frighten my daughters."

Coming in unseen, an officer came to stand beside the sergeant. "Hold up, sergeant. There's no need to terrify these ladies. We can't expect a mother to yield up her son for the hangman."

The sergeant's temper began to subside, and he relaxed his hold on Rachel. She pulled herself away and stepped back away from both men.

Rachel regarded the young officer. He carried himself with the bearing and presence she'd seen in only a few officers in the military, on either side. It was evident he was an educated man, and there was something vaguely familiar about him. *I'm sure I know this man . . . who is he?*

Suddenly, Ellie said, in a tentative voice. "Andrew, is that you?"

A noncommittal smile crept across his face as he stepped toward the couch. He held out his hand to her. "At your service, m'lady."

She stood and extended her hand, and he bowed crisply, pressed his lips to her hand with a lingering kiss. An awkward silence ensued until Andrew turned to the soldiers.

"You may wait for me downstairs. I've sent some men to apprehend Daniel. They should be back with him directly. Fetch me at once, when he's brought back."

A cold shiver went through Ellie at the mention of Daniel's name. "What will you do, Andrew, if you find Daniel?"

Andrew did not respond.

Ellie's eyes darted toward Rachel, who had remained silent since Andrew's arrival. Rachel's face revealed nothing of what she might be thinking. Ellie retook her seat on the couch, deciding to follow her mother-in-law's example. The women sat huddled, waiting for Andrew to leave.

For several moments, all of them silently marked the ticking of the hall clock. At last, Andrew's voice broke the stillness, startling the women.

"Ellie, would you come downstairs with me for a moment of private conversation?"

Her lips pressed together in a tight grimace; she shook her head no.

Andrew heaved an audible sigh and turned to leave, but Ellie's soft voice broke the silence. "Wait. You cannot expect me, as Daniel's betrothed, to be alone with you, Andrew. Moreover, what could you possibly think I would want to hear from you?"

He studied her face for a moment and with a look of smugness, he replied, "Very well, I suppose his mother would be interested to know what awaits her son." Flexing his riding crop in both hands, Andrew said, "When Daniel is brought to me, I shall have the honor of hanging him from the public square, and please don't ask me for clemency for your man. This is by direct order from Lord Rawdon and cannot be changed."

The color drained from Ellie's face. As frightened as she was for Daniel, she wouldn't allow herself to show any fear that Andrew could see. "Daniel needs no plea from me, especially if you've sent the likes of the men who just left; they'll not catch him."

Andrew tapped his knee-high boot with his riding crop. A malignant smile spread across his face, "I agree, dear Ellie. That's why I've sent local men to bring your Daniel back to me. The men tracking Daniel are the sons of a Colonel Rufus Sherman, who has suffered the loss of a leg from a skirmish with Daniel's older brother. The colonel assures me his sons know the countryside as well or better than Daniel."

Andrew remained as he was for a moment. "I must, regretfully, take my leave, ladies. I'm dining with Lord Rawdon tonight. Nothing would please me more than to report to him that Daniel is in my custody." Bowing expertly, he said, "Until we meet again."

Following Andrew to the door, Rachel locked the door and replaced the heavy wooden bar. She returned to the room where the other women still sat on the couch, and took her seat beside Ellie.

Taking Ellie's hand, Rachel said, "Don't fret too much for Daniel. I don't remember my boys ever being bested by those Sherman brothers."

⸻ ⸻ ⸻

Daniel leaned against a towering red oak. His body was shaking from exhaustion. Gasping for air, he knew he was in a ticklish situation, but he didn't regret it. The chance to hold Ellie in his arms was worth the risk, and giving his mother hope that his father would be set free was something he would definitely do again.

Now, he had to put some distance between him and the men he knew that would be coming after him. He was in a truly bleak situation, but he was a fast runner and was confident he would be able to stretch his lead. There was no guessing what was in store for him if he was caught—a prompt date with the hangman, most likely, and that sent a cold chill down his spine. What he did know was that he was running for his life.

He started out again and soon came to the road to Fort Charlotte and without hesitation headed in that direction, running in the woods alongside the road. After he'd run for a while, he stopped to listen, and faintly, just barely, he thought he heard the sound of pursuit. He stood still and listened carefully. Someone was following him, and he was good if he had gotten this close. Daniel crouched low and listened again. Something behind him cracked—maybe a limb. There were two after him.

Maybe, he thought, looking back from where he came, he could backtrack and get behind them. He considered this a moment, then decided he would stay put and make them come to him. Where he stood was as good a place as he was likely to find. This area, thick with trees and underbrush, would provide him some protection if it came to shooting.

Daniel pulled his pistols and checked the load in each. Then, cautiously, he moved through the trees for a better spot to defend himself. Keeping his eyes peeled, he knelt behind a gigantic red oak.

Suddenly, some twenty yards away, a man jumped up ahead of him, and at the same time, he heard the crack of a long barreled rifle from somewhere behind him. One of them had managed to get ahead of him. *They're good, must be local Tories.*

Flinching, he heard the singing round ball spin past his head and slam into a tree. The man ahead was taking aim with his rifle, and Daniel knew he was about to squeeze the trigger.

Daniel leaped into a sprint at a right angle to the man about to shoot him. It would be hard to hit a man running full speed through the woods with so many trees, but the man took his shot and Daniel heard the familiar thud of a round ball slamming into a tree trunk.

Armed with his two pistols, Daniel turned and started running as fast as he could toward the shooter. As he drew closer, he saw his attacker was Eb Sherman, and Eb was coolly reloading his long rifle. He'd already dribbled a bit of powder in the flash pan and covered it with the frizzen, and was now ramming the remaining powder, paper, and ball into the barrel.

Daniel let out a blood-curdling war cry of the Cherokee Indians and was almost within range to fire his pistol. A few more yards and he would have him, but he could see Eb ram the ball home. All the while, Eb was listening to the noise of Daniel running toward him. As he pulled the ramrod from the barrel, he looked up to see how close Daniel was from him. Eb, seeing Daniel bearing down upon him, dropped the ramrod at his feet instead of replacing it in its storage pipe.

It was now or never, Eb was about to take aim and fire, and Daniel needed to move only a step or two farther to take his shot, but he saw he wasn't going to get it. Eb had now cocked his hammer and swung his rifle up in one smooth, fluid move. Daniel was looking at the business end of a Pennsylvania long-rifle. He threw himself to the ground just as he heard the shot. As though the moment was frozen in time, Eb looked wide-eyed at Daniel lying prone with his pistol aimed at his chest.

Squeezing the trigger was an instinctive move for Daniel. Facing him was a man who had taken two shots at him with the intention of killing him. The pistol fired, sending a round ball slamming into Eb's chest. A small cloud of dust flew when the ball struck Eb's shirt.

Before he could take another breath, Daniel heard the crashing sound of someone running toward him. It had to be Eb's twin brother, Eli. Swapping hands with his pistols, Daniel remained as he was. In a few moments, he could see Eli approach his brother.

Wild-eyed, Eli cried out when he saw his brother's lifeless body. Like a cat, he wheeled around, but it was too late. He saw Daniel at the same time Daniel's pistol fired, sending a round ball into his forehead. Eli fell on his back beside his brother.

Daniel sat for a moment and unconsciously reloaded his pistols. With the two brothers lying just a few feet away, a portion of scripture came to his mind. *For it is written: He will give His angels orders concerning you, to protect you,*

"No doubt about it," he muttered, "I've kept God's angel busy today . . . Thank you, Lord."

He listened to the woods for a few minutes, hoping the two men had been alone. When he was sure they had been the only ones tracking him, he took their rifles with the powder horns and shooter's bags, and set out to meet up with Nate.

⁕⁕⁕⁕⁕⁕⁕⁕⁕

Some days later, Daniel and Nate were hard at work making grenade bombs with timed fuses. Neither man had actually done this work before. Their only experience was helping other men put these lethal explosives together.

Wiping sweat from his forehead, Nate said, "Maybe we ought to test one or two of these before we get too far along. What do you think?"

Sitting back on his haunches, Daniel answered, "That's probably the first sensible thing either of us has said this morning. The fuses are our biggest worry. My brother Gideon can make'em blindfolded, and I've watched him many times, but I'm not so sure these will be as dependable as his."

Nate watched his friend finishing a length of fuse. "Let's test that one you have in your hands."

By cutting varying lengths of the fuse material, the men began their tests. After most of the morning passed, they were satisfied with the results. By the end of the day, the gunpowder wagon was filled with enough fused bombs to create a diversion that would allow Daniel and Nate to free John.

Daniel looked at the loaded wagon. "I think we have enough to do the job. I want these to sound as if there's a regiment attacking the fort. If our guys can keep Cruger and his officers occupied on the east side of the settlement just long enough for us to get Pa out of the jail, they'll have done their job."

At daybreak, Daniel and Nate set out to rendezvous with their militia. They tied their mounts to the back of the wagon and rode together in the wagon. For several miles, neither man said much, both preferring the solitude of their own thoughts. They stayed off the main road to Ninety Six, travelling by way of wooded Indian trails. It was slow going, but they were less likely to be discovered by one of the many bands of Tory militias now roaming the countryside.

The sun was on its downward arc when Daniel and Nate were met by a picket from their troop. "I heard your wagon some time ago," said the grinning rider, a young boy with freckles covering his face. "Sounded like a wagon train."

Daniel returned his grin and reached behind to hold up one of the grenades. "We'll soon be making even more racket."

Once in camp, Daniel wasted no time in rehearsing the details of tomorrow night's action. His plan to distract the Tories long enough to free John was met with general agreement among the men. Nate's sister had come to give them John's location inside the jail. She had left the settlement on the pretense of picking blueberries. While she talked, two of the men left to pick the berries for her to take back.

Nate's sister sat before the group and spoke to Daniel. "Your father's on the second floor of the jail, and there are three Tories guarding each floor. One man is at the entrance and two guard the stairs. Each is armed with one pistol and a cavalryman's sabre. Mr. John seems fit enough to run; he didn't mention any wounds," she said, evenly. "I've visited him today with a good plate of food and was able to tell him he would be rescued tomorrow night. I could tell he was very pleased."

Daniel thanked her for the risk she and her family were taking. "It's people like you and your husband that keep our cause alive. I told my mother about your part in this, and she sends her heartfelt thanks."

Her face flushed with embarrassment, and her eyes fell to her hands, neatly folded in her lap.

CHAPTER TWENTY EIGHT

PRISON BREAK

The next day had passed and it was now approaching dusk when the militia moved in place. Daniel placed four of the confiscated British artillery pieces about six hundred yards to the rear of the extended line of sharpshooters. He figured a combination of solid shot and exploding bombs would create enough confusion and pandemonium to divert attention away from the settlement's jail.

On a hill overlooking the settlement, the Tories had garrisoned five hundred men in a star-shaped fort, while, about two hundred yards away, lay the settlement of fifteen houses, and several businesses including a two-story brick jail and a courthouse.

Daniel and Nate approached the main gate in their wagon. Secreted under the driver's bench was a wooden case loaded with their fused bombs.

Nate could feel beads of sweat trickling down the back of his neck. "Can you run fast, Daniel?"

"Like a rabbit, when I'm scared," answered Daniel

"Are you scared now?"

"Yep, ain't you?"

Wiping his brow with his sleeve, Nate replied, "I've been scared since we rode up here in this wagon loaded with our homemade bombs."

"I can understand that," Daniel said.

"Whoa," called Nate, bringing the wagon to a stop.

A sentry came around the wagon to the driver's side. "What's your business here, this late in the day?"

Nate, with a disarming grin, looked down at the sentry. "We were on our way to Camden when night caught us. We thought we might camp inside the town's walls till morning."

The sentry's eyes narrowed. "You're traveling light. Where're you fr—"

Suddenly, the cannons' thundering roar shattered the serene and peaceful evening. The startled sentry shouted, "Get inside! Get your wagon inside so I can close the gate!"

People began running in all directions, the screams of the wounded blended with cries of hysteria. Daniel and Nate rushed the door of the jail. Turning the knob, they found the door barred. Quickly, Daniel placed a fused grenade against the door and ran. Before the smoke cleared, the two men pushed the door open and rushed inside.

They found one man dead, sprawled near the door. Another was sitting upright against a wall, stunned by the blast. A third man was attempting to crawl up the stairs, bleeding profusely from his face.

Daniel ran to him and pulled him roughly away from the stairs. Putting his pistol in the man's chest, Daniel said coldly, "Lay still if you want to live."

Nate quickly rounded up the men's weapons and threw them out the door. From the foot of the stairs, he shouted, "Come down *NOW* with your hands on your heads, and you won't be harmed. You have until the count of three."

Even before Nate had begun to count, three militiamen scurried down the stairs, their hands clasped atop their heads. The sight of their stricken comrades quickly subdued the three Tories.

His palm extended, Daniel snapped, "Which one of you has the key to the Colonel's cell?"

The guards glanced at each other but didn't respond. Daniel slammed the guard nearest him against the wall and jammed his pistol into his stomach.

"I'm not repeating the question, if I don't get the key this instant, I'm going to kill all of you."

"I have it!" cried the guard sitting against the wall. He flung it across the floor, and Daniel urgently took it in his hands. Then he took the stairs two at a time and within moments had his father free.

Knowing that time was running out, Daniel said, giving John one of his pistols, "No time to talk now, Pa. Stay with me; we've got a wagon just outside."

Haggard-looking men began gathering behind John, and he grabbed his son by his arm. "Wait Daniel, there are other men here. We can't leave them behind."

Daniel spun around. "You men who are strong enough, carry those who need help. We've got to hurry."

Downstairs, Nate had the guards lying face down, with their legs shackled. Daniel paused at the door turned to his father and said, "Let's go, Pa."

Canisters of grape shot from the cannons still rained down randomly, and people had taken shelter inside their homes or other buildings. Nate lowered the rear gate of the wagon and helped the men get in while Daniel stood vigil over the village common.

Nate nervously watched the men coming from the jail. Many were being carried. He watched as John helped a man onto the wagon and run back for another. There seemed to be an endless line of men struggling to reach the wagon.

Finally, the last man was on, but there were already too many men in the wagon, so many the rear gate couldn't be raised. Nate whispered, "We need to be moving, before the shelling stops, Daniel. The main gate should've blown by now."

The moon broke through the clouds, its pale light awash over the common. Musket fire erupted from a rampart near the gate. Daniel heard someone moan from the wagon.

Daniel passed his father his tinderbox. "Grenades are in the box under the bench. Toss a few at the rampart as we go by— the fuses burn for less than a minute. We're going to make a run for it; we can't wait any longer for the gates."

John passed grenades to the able-bodied men near him as Nate turned the wagon around to make the one hundred yard run for the gate. Suddenly an explosion ripped the gate from its hinges sending splinters of wood in all directions. Nate was hit by a piece of lumber that rendered him unconscious. John quickly took his place in the driver's seat and snapped the reins. "Giddyup! Everybody hang on!" cried John. The horses lurched forward, jerking the wagon toward the gate. A dozen men who'd spent the day without any hope of ever being free again, were now huddled tightly in the bed of the wagon. They clung to each other and to the sides as John drove at breakneck speed across the common toward the gaping hole where the barred gate had once stood. This ride would be remembered among these men and passed down to their families for generations as the ride of their lives.

John drove through the dust and smoke, and several men threw their grenades as the wagon passed the rampart, scattering the Tories, some retreating without their muskets. The wagon didn't slow as it passed through the gap in the wall, leaving its own cloud of dust behind.

"Head for Beaver Swamp, Pa, we've set up camp on Coon Island," shouted Daniel. "Did we leave anyone?"

John drew himself straight; his spine stiffened, "No son, we brought them all out."

Three days later, Rachel and the girls had just sat down for tea when brisk knocks at the door quieted the women's conversation. Startled, Rachel looked toward the door, a sense of uneasiness gripped her chest.

Sarah took her mother-in-law's hand. "I'll see who it is."

Coming to her feet, Rachel smoothed her skirt and tucked a stray tendril of her auburn hair under her bonnet. "Thank you Sarah, but I should be the one to see who's calling this late in the day."

Before Rachel could reach the door, the knocks repeated, this time a bit louder. "I'm coming," she called out. She could hear the muted footsteps of the other women behind her.

Rachel opened the door to find a tall young man standing awkwardly before her with his hat clasped in his hands. "Mrs. Rachel, I come from your husband, John, to tell you he's safe and sound in our camp at Beaver Swamp."

Rachel pulled the courier inside and quickly brought him to the table. His face reddened as the women introduced themselves. At another time, they would have found his timidity amusing, but this evening, they were all anxious to hear news of John and Daniel.

"We have some venison stew with potatoes and cabbage," said Lottie, pouring him a cup of tea. "Would you care for some?"

The young man's eyes lit up. "Yes ma'am that would be mighty nice of you. I missed supper to deliver the Colonel's message."

Rachel injected, "Is there more from my husband? Will we be able to come to him?"

Ellie placed the bowl of stew before the young man, and he ate hungrily.

The women's eyes discreetly followed his movements. It was evident that he'd missed more than today's supper.

He scraped the last of the stew from the bowl, and, wiping his mouth on his sleeve, he looked up and suppressed a belch. "Ma'am—ladies that was the best stew I've had in a long time. Reminds me of my ma's cooking."

Rachel watched him anxiously. "What more can you tell us? Does my husband want us to come to him? Surely, he sent some word for us."

Nodding his head, the young man replied, "Yes ma'am, there's more. The colonel wants you and the other ladies to pack up what you need for travel. He's getting a wagon outfitted to carry y'all to your flour mill on Sandy Creek. The colonel said you should be ready to leave Friday next."

Lottie's eyes widened with excitement at the words 'Sandy Creek'. She rose quickly and took the young man's empty bowl.

"I'll get you another helping," she said, "What else did Papa say?"

Rachel went to her daughter and took the bowl. "Take your seat at the table, Lottie, and we'll hear the remainder of what he has to say."

Paying no attention to her mother's mild rebuke, Lottie sashayed back to her seat, and the young courier continued as though there'd been no interruption. "I got the impression from the Colonel's words that the Sandy Creek Mill area had some family meaning, but I could be wrong."

He glanced at Lottie, whose eyes weren't focused on anything around her; she seemed to be lost in some reverie. "The Colonel wants to meet you all on the north side of the swamp," the man said. "You'll be taken there by one of the men downstairs in a wagon loaded with various leatherworks that's bound for the Charles Town market, but of course, it'll be delayed until we have all of you safely with the Colonel and his men."

Rachel came to her feet and untied her apron. "Young man, when you return to my husband, please tell him we are well and shall be ready to leave Friday next."

The young courier nodded as he finished his meal. "There's a Tory across the street watching your shop, so I'll be stopping downstairs to pick up a new cartridge belt and box. Maybe, I'll pass for a customer."

Rachel listened as his footsteps on the stairs grew fainter. She locked the door and met Lottie on the way back to the kitchen. "Did the young man leave any stew for us?"

Ellie was ladling the bowls when they took their seats at the table. Rachel found she was unable to speak. She shut her eyes briefly and thought of John's strong arms around her. Turning away for a moment, she knew she must force back this whirlwind of emotions so she could deal with the present.

Sitting beside her mother, Lottie said expectantly, "Mama is the mill still running? I remember we stayed there for a while when I was younger."

Feeling her emotions settling, Rachel lifted her spoon, delicately sampled her stew, and set her spoon aside. "Before the war, that particular mill produced some of the finest flour anywhere in the backcountry. The flour and the cornmeal, too, from the Sandy Creek Mill, established the Hamilton name as first among the colonies millers. People traveled great distances for that mill's flour and meal."

Wiping her hands on her apron, Rachel turned away from the hearth. "But to answer your question, dear, the mill's been idle since Tory renegades raided it and killed our miller, Noah Walters."

Turning to Lottie, Rachel said, "We lived there for a short time before moving to Camden. At Sandy Creek, the Alcotts were our closest neighbors and became our dearest friends."

Her elbows propped on the table, Lottie nodded, "I remember a sawmill that was very noisy."

"Yes," Rachel said, "And we were two miles from it, too. But it's a nice settlement, maybe thirty families that live close by. The Alcotts own a nice inn with a tavern and separate room for dining about a mile from the creek."

Sarah leaned closer to Lottie. "Have you received any word from Robert?" she asked gingerly.

Shaking her head, Lottie couldn't hide the disappointment she felt. Instantly, Sarah regretted asking her sister-in-law about her beau. Lottie had become her best friend, next to Ellie, and she couldn't bear to see Lottie hurting this way.

"It was so callous of me to ask such a question," Sarah said, "Can you ever forgive me?" She grasped Lottie's hand. "Only one of Gideon's letters has reached me."

Forcing a scant smile, Lottie replied, "Of course, I forgive you, Sarah. I suppose it's silly for me to behave this way after more than two years. There are so many things to prevent Robert from writing a letter and then finding some way to post it."

———

The day arrived when the women would be taken and reunited with John and Daniel near Beaver Swamp. John had devised a plan of building a false bed in one of the wagons used to transport leather goods to market. The women would be hidden under the false bed, and the leather merchandise would be loaded above the bed. The wagon would be loaded and then leave following the usual schedule to avoid unnecessary attention from the guard posted across the street.

The women sat quietly waiting to be called downstairs. "How do you feel, Sarah?" asked Rachel, her voice filled with tension.

Sarah reached and gripped Rachel's hand. "I'm fine Mama Rachel; I'm looking forward to seeing Papa and Daniel again. This will be a story for me to pass on to the babe I carry."

After some time had passed, the women's thoughts drifted inwardly, and the room quieted. Sharp knocks at the door broke the silence. The women's chairs scraped the floor as they pushed back hurriedly. Rachel was the first to reach the door.

Hesitantly, she cracked open the door. Seeing the man who was to be their driver, she pulled the door all the way open.

The man, his hat clenched in his calloused hands, said, "Ma'am, are you and the ladies ready?"

Rachel, responded quickly, "Yes we are. What should we do next?"

He said brusquely, "Follow me and no more talking. For some reason, there're two guards across the street today. Don't know what that's about, but once you ladies are in the wagon, you can't make any noise. No coughing, sneezing, or moving about until I say it's safe."

The man then turned and motioned for them to follow him, but Rachel touched his arm. "Can you wait just for a moment of prayer?"

He nodded and stared at his feet. Rachel began: "Almighty God, we commit ourselves to your perfect care on the journey that awaits us. Bless this young man as he risks his life today, and I pray for your hedge of protection to be about each us, and may your angels accompany us in all our ways. These things I ask in the name of Jesus. Amen."

CHAPTER TWENTY NINE

REUNION

The women were taken to the wagon one at a time, hidden behind the large bundles of leather goods the loaders carried. Across the street, the two guards took only a casual interest as the wagon was slowly loaded.

Finally, the driver took his place on the bench and released the brake with his foot. Suddenly, the Loyalist guards came to life, and one of them shouted, "Hold up, driver, I'll be riding with you."

Setting the brake hard, the driver waited, uneasily, for the Tory to climb up beside him. The Tory told the driver to turn the wagon around and head south.

"Where're we headed?" asked the driver. "I've got a seafaring captain bound for London waiting in Charles Town for this wagon load."

"Do you now? And your cargo is leather goods made in Hamilton's shop?" he said with a caustic smile. "We're going to pay Lord Rawdon a visit. He believes the escaped rebel John Hamilton may try to spirit away his women."

The driver looked straight ahead, his mind racing. *He knows the women are under the cargo. I have to think of something before we get to—*

"Don't try anything," the Tory said, with a malignant smile that spread across his swarthy, sunburned face. "I see it in your face; the colonel wants to see you dance for him—from the end of the hangman's noose—now slowly ease your musket to me."

The man's words sent a sickening chill through the driver's heart. Death awaited him only ten miles away. Sorrow sapped his strength, and his shoulders sagged as his hands trembled holding loosely to the reins.

Suddenly, a beefy hand pounded his back, jarring him from his self-pity. "Come now, my good man," roared the Tory, mockingly, "You chose your path; now face it like the man you are. 'Tis a fine day to die for what you believe to be right." Punching the driver's arm with his fist, the Loyalist threw back his head and roared with laughter.

Startled, the driver, with tired, bloodshot eyes stared at the Tory soldier. Memories flashed through his mind of past battles and skirmishes with men just like the man he now faced. Many times, countless times, he'd been bested only to reach down within himself and muster whatever it took to save himself or the men with him.

The driver straightened his back, extended his shoulders, and breathed deeply. The fresh countryside air filled his lungs. There was no fear left in him now; he knew what he must do and was ready to do it.

The wagon creaked and lurched as the wheels rolled their way toward Lord Rawdon's camp.

After some distance, a female voice abruptly shouted, "Stop! Stop this wagon right now. We must get out. Sarah is delivering her baby!"

The driver pulled back on the reins, stopping the wagon, and the Tory soldier grabbed him by his collar and yelled, "Get this wagon moving, *now*! We're not stopping for the birth of another rebel."

Ignoring the soldier's order, the driver set the brake and jumped to the ground. He quickly ran around the wagon and dropped the rear gate. Rachel's face was the first to appear. Squinting her eyes from the change of light, she held her finger to her lips and climbed out.

Standing beside the driver with a hand hidden under her apron, Rachel frantically shouted to the Tory soldier, "Get down and start a fire—hurry! We must have hot water! Sarah is about to deliver her child!"

Sarah let out an anguished cry of pain; the soldier's eyes widened, and his mouth went slack. Then, as the fog lifted from his senses, he sighed and climbed slowly down from the bench. When he reached the back of the wagon, Rachel was waiting for him with her pistol pointed at his head.

The Tory stopped in his tracks, and his face hardened. "What's the pistol for, woman?"

His eyes narrowed, and he glanced toward the driver. A seasoned and hard-bitten veteran, he weighed his chances of making a lunge for Rachel and disarming her before she could fire her pistol.

His thoughts were interrupted when the driver pulled his hunting knife and stepped forward. The driver feigned a smile and in a mocking tone said, "It seems you're contemplating something drastic, sergeant. Let me help you make up your mind. I give you your words, 'Come now, my good man. You chose your path; now face it like the man you are. 'Tis a fine day to die for what you believe to be right.'"

Rachel kept her stance; the pistol in her hand was steady. The hulking guard tried to stare her down, but finally averted his eyes. She spoke with icy crispness, "Before you try anything rash, I want you to understand that I have no compunction to putting a ball into your miserable brain, should you try anything foolish."

She looked at the man more closely, "I remember you. Weren't you with Rufus Sherman when my home was set afire?"

Stone-faced, the Tory kept his eyes on the ground and didn't respond. Rachel felt her chest tighten as an angry heat rose from her neck. "Look at me! If it was right, on that day, to destroy everything my family held dear, down to the last blade of grass, then you should still be proud of your part. Now look at me and give me your answer."

He lifted his face until he glared down his nose at Rachel. Defiant arrogance was etched across his weathered face. "Aye, I'm your man, madam. I was there with my torch, and my only regret is that Lord Rawdon didn't see fit to hang the lot of you."

During this time, the other women had climbed out of their hiding place and now brandished their pistols at the guard.

"What are we to do with him?" asked Meg looking at the driver.

Shrugging his shoulders, the driver said, "I think we should take him with us and let the colonel decide. This one has bragged that he was one of Rufus's men who torched the colonel's home and crops. Maybe we'll witness one of the king's own meet the end of the hangman's noose."

"We'd better get started, then. It's a ways yet to Beaver Swamp," said Rachel, her eyes riveted on the guard.

They bound and gagged the guard, and then stuffed him under the false bottom of the wagon bed with enough merchandise to allow the women to ride behind the bench. Then the driver set out for the north edge of Beaver Swamp.

It wasn't long before the sound of hooves reached their ears. Several riders swept out of the trees some distance ahead of them and were blocking the road. Rachel looked hard towards the riders. "Only one wears a red coat. The others are in militia green. Hold up driver."

The driver stopped the wagon and set the foot brake. He reached for his musket, but Rachel said, sharply, "Wait, let's not show them we have weapons yet. There are five of them, and we only have two muskets. We must wait until we're closer and then surprise them if we're to get out of this."

Without turning her head, she breathed, "Girls, take hold of your pistols and cock the hammers. Hold tight to them and keep them out of sight, and make up your mind now on who these men are. They're set on hanging the men of our family and likely the women, too."

The riders approached. "Here they come, everyone all right back there? Wait until I shout 'now'."

Each woman whispered yes.

The Tory militia had cut the distance in half when Rachel's eyes widened in shock. "The redcoat is Andrew!"

Ellie let out an audible gasp.

The driver, in a steely whisper said, "Not to worry, Miss Ellie. I'll take care of the officer for you."

The militia riders drew up a few feet in front of the wagon. Andrew swept his arm in a circle, and the Tories encircled the wagon. There was a determined expression of coldness about his face and a menacing chill in his eyes. His sullen stare lingered an instant on each face. Ellie returned his threatening glare, and he saw no gentleness in her expression.

His voice clipped and stern, Andrew said, "What have you done with Sergeant O'Bannon?"

No one answered.

"Very well, your silence speaks for itself." He motioned to the man at the rear of the wagon. "Tie these women securely, and we'll take them to Lord Rawdon."

Rachel's eyes had been busy. She saw the soldiers had relaxed when they saw the wagon held only one man; women posed no threat to these men. Andrew, himself, directed his attention mainly to the driver. Two of the soldiers dismounted and took leather strips from their saddlebags, while the remaining two casually sat astride their mounts, loosely resting their muskets across their saddles.

Rachel leapt to her feet and cried, "Now!"

The women would say later; it was like a nightmarish dream. Andrew's men were caught completely by surprise by the sight of four women standing, almost in unison, with their weapons, firing point-blank at the horror-struck soldiers.

Andrew's horse reared up from the commotion just as he unsheathed his sword, and by the time Andrew brought the animal under control, he saw the driver had a musket aimed at his chest. Andrew brought his heavy sword down across the barrel of the musket just as it fired. His sword broke at the hilt, and Andrew turned his horse, spurring him back in the direction of Rawdon's camp.

Rachel, in the meantime, had taken the other musket and now sighted down the barrel toward the fleeing Andrew, but his horse had already sped him away to safety.

Rachel sighed and reluctantly lowered the musket. "No need to waste a shot," she muttered.

Dejected, the driver, said, "I was too slow . . . just too slow, but I nicked him, just above his elbow."

———————

Knowing he was safely out of musket range, Andrew drew his mount up short and spun the horse around. His mind was reeling and staggering with confusion. He was still stunned by what had just taken place, and unable to grasp that the women had been armed, especially Ellie. Blood dripped from the fingers of his right hand, and a searing pain throbbed just above his elbow. He watched as the women rounded up his men's weapons and horses. He slapped the reins, dug his heels in the flanks of his horse, and spurred it through the woods.

———————

By the middle of the afternoon, the creaking and clattering wagon rolled into John's camp. Ellie jumped from the slowing wagon and ran to Daniel with outstretched arms.

She clung to him, sobbing. "Oh, Daniel," she groaned. "I can't bear it any longer with you traipsing off here and yon and not knowing if you're hurt or worse . . ."

Rachel was climbing down when John reached her. He took her in his strong arms and spun her around until she was breathless. He lowered her until her feet touched the ground and then kissed her tenderly. They clung together and gazed into the other's eyes amid the clamoring voices around them.

He caressed her face and whispered, "I thank God every day for bringing you into my life, Rachel. God has blessed me far, far beyond anything I deserve."

Clearing his throat, the driver of the wagon said, "Pardon my interruption, Colonel, but we were set upon by a small detachment from Lord Rawdon's army. Thanks to the ladies, we left all but their officer dead on the road. I expect he wasted no time in getting back to his camp."

John's arm lingered around Rachel's waist and his eyes gazed around to the women. "I've always admitted my wife and daughter were as good or better at hitting what they aimed at than myself. It's good to hear my sons will have straight shooting wives as well."

He motioned to Daniel. "Son, send a couple of men to backtrack and pick up Andrew's trail to Rawdon's camp. Tell'em to watch things and if it looks like Rawdon decides to come this way, then get back here quick. That should give us time to get ready."

The small settlement of Sandy Creek boasted a population of thirty families. Along its only street were a courthouse and jail, a tavern and inn, a general mercantile store, and a church. Hamilton's Mill was a few miles from town on the east bank of the creek.

The three-story mill, built into the steep bank of the mill creek, had stood idle since the summer of 1776 when the man John had hired to run it was killed during a hit and run raid by renegade Loyalists. His widow went to live in Savannah, Georgia with her people.

The next few days, the Hamilton women spent their time washing, scrubbing, sewing curtains, and mopping, putting the house in livable shape. John and Daniel were kept busy hewing timber and sawing lumber to make the tables, chairs, and beds for their new home. By the end of the week, the family moved in.

Supper was the first meal in their new home. Holding hands for John's blessing of the meal, each member of the family silently added their own heartfelt words of thanksgiving.

After the meal, Rachel joined John on the stone porch. "This is a good place John, but we're really not any safer here than we were at Trenton, are we?"

Sipping his coffee, John gazed toward the west at the misty Blue Ridge Mountains. "I'm afraid not, sweetheart. And to make matters worse, Cornwallis has a new dog in the hunt, a Major Patrick Ferguson."

John rose to stand at the edge of the porch. "He's been recruiting Tories from Ninety Six to the eastern slopes of the Misty Mountains. Reports have come to me he's already established a sizable camp up in Gilbert Town."

An audible sigh escaped Rachel's lips as she stepped to his side. "What's to become of us, John? So many of your men have given up and gone back to their homes. It all looks so hopeless."

He turned to her and gripped her shoulders with his strong hands. "I can't argue that, Rachel. Cornwallis, in his mind at least, has Georgia and the Carolinas safely in his pocket. Since Charles Town fell, many of our people have fallen by the way, and with Camden now in the hands of the British, even more have abandoned hope we can save our country.

"But, I must tell you, I haven't given up," he said, "Daniel hasn't given up and I know Gideon is out there somewhere pestering redcoats and Tories."

Rachel turned her back to him and leaned against his chest. "Oh John, forgive me for whining and sounding so melancholy. I'm so proud of you and our sons for your unflinching strength."

"I'm not any stronger than any other man, Rachel, but I refuse to let my emotions get in the way of my God-given common sense," he said evenly. "The obvious outcome is right there in front of our eyes."

She turned back to face him. "What are you talking about? What's obvious?"

His mouth turned showing his familiar lopsided grin. "It's right there on any map of our colonies. The British are strung out from Savannah to Charlotte and have plans to extend themselves all the way to New York. They cannot defend and keep the territory they claim to own."

Rachel could see the enthusiasm in her husband's face and hear it in his voice. She said, "I hope you're right, husband, but we need to win some battles to encourage everyone."

She broke free from his embrace and paused at the door. "Before we go in, I want to tell you about Lottie. She's planning to spend the day with the Alcotts tomorrow. I'm going with her, but I'll not be staying long. I want to get reacquainted with Hannah and make certain it will be all right for Lottie to stay for the day's visit."

"It's about Robert?"

"Yes. Now when you speak to your daughter, do it lovingly," Rachel said, "She was smitten with Robert, and she loves him still from afar."

"I know." John put his arm around her, and they went back into the house.

A LOVE LOST

The horseback ride to the village of Sandy Creek gave Lottie a rare chance to have her mother all to herself. She was now seventeen, but she had the essential nature of a much older young woman.

"Mama, I'm glad you're with me this morning," Lottie said. "My mind is racing like a runaway horse, and my heart is pounding in my ears."

Rachel reached from her horse, touching Lottie's arm soothingly.

"Mother, what do I say to Robert's parents? They don't know me, and I don't know them."

"Just be yourself, dear. You have many friends, and they all love you, just for yourself. Robert's parents will warm to you, especially if he's written to them about you."

Lottie sighed and pulled back on the reins. "But what do I say ... what is there to talk about?"

Stopping her horse, Rachel twisted in the saddle to face her daughter. "Now, I want you to calm down and listen to me for a moment. Take a deep breath and let it out ... good ... now listen to what I'm about to tell you."

Lottie did as her mother said, and Rachel said, "If you'll remember why you're making this call on the Alcotts, the conversation will take care of itself. I've already told you to be yourself, and you'll be fine. Robert's parents will be excited to see you, and will love you for making this effort to ask about their son."

Lottie nodded.

"Was I helpful, at all, dear?" Rachel asked, hopefully.

"Yes Mama, you always know just what to say. Thank you from the bottom of my heart."

<hr/>

The Alcotts were the owners of Sandy Creek's only inn and tavern. Their home was a short distance behind the two-story business. Rachel and Lottie decided to stop at the house first.

Lottie lifted the heavy brass door knocker and let it fall. After a moment without anyone answering the door, Lottie looked at her mother. Rachel tilted her head toward the door and as Lottie reached for the knocker, the door was pulled open.

Before them, stood a diminutive woman dressed in a simple gray dress with a full white apron. Atop her head, she wore an everyday linen mobcap. Stray strands of gray hair had escaped from under her cap, now curled with dampness. Tiny droplets of sweat lay across her forehead at her hairline. It was evident she was busily at work and wasn't expecting visitors.

Looking at her callers, the woman said in a soft, friendly voice, "Please excuse my appearance, ladies, but I'm doing a bit of housecleaning." Pausing, she said, her hand clutching her throat, "Rachel Hamilton is that really you?"

Laughing, Rachel said, "I'm afraid so, Hannah. I'm surprised you recognized me after all these years."

"It's because you haven't aged a day, girl. How do you do it?" Hannah paused and looked at Lottie. "And who is this fair maiden? Don't tell me she's your daughter!"

Lottie felt her face reddening, as she became the focus of attention. She answered, "Yes, ma'am, I'm Charlotte, but I'm called Lottie by everyone who knows me. Are you Robert's mother?"

There was a subtle twitch in Hannah's smile, but she recovered quickly. Her voice took on a softer tone. "Yes dear and might you be the Lottie in Robert's letters? We never connected you with Rachel's children," Stepping back and opening the door wider, Hannah said, "Please come in, and we'll have tea."

Rachel felt a sudden chill grip her chest and looked at her daughter to see if she caught the change in Hannah at the mention of her son. *Maybe I imagined something that wasn't there; maybe I'm a little edgy myself for Lottie,* Rachel thought.

Hannah returned with a small bundle of letters and sat in a wingback chair next to Lottie. The letters, soiled and creased, were bound with a blue ribbon. Holding them in her lap, Hannah said, "Lottie, I must tell you Robert was killed in the battle of Savannah, Georgia. He was brought home by his best friend, James Campbell, and lies now in our family cemetery next to his two sisters who died in a barn fire."

Lottie's face had turned ashen. Her hands, which lay folded in her lap, trembled noticeably, and a look of horror and pain filled her eyes. The room seemed to be spinning, and she couldn't draw enough air to breathe. Everything seemed to blur, and before anyone realized what was happening, she slumped from the chair and lay in a crumpled heap on the floor.

Rachel jumped from her chair and knelt by her side, gently patting her cheek. Hannah left and returned quickly with small glass of cider. Rachel raised Lottie's head and spilled a few drops into her mouth. The girl coughed and gagged as the cider trickled down her throat. Rachel continued to hold her as she began to regain consciousness.

Lottie's eyes fluttered open, and she saw her mother's dispirited face full of worry and concern. "Did I faint, Mama?"

Afraid she couldn't stop the tears if she spoke, Rachel could only nod.

Hannah, looking over Rachel's shoulder, said, "I'm sorry for you child . . . and I'm sorry for Robert, and I must tell you that my anguish of that afternoon when James brought him home is freshened today. Although, it was two years ago, this December, I remember it as though it were yesterday."

"Would you help me up, Mama? I'm sorry I frightened you so," Lottie said, smiling weakly.

Settled in the chair, Lottie took another small sip of the cider. She dropped her eyes and fell silent. The only sound in the room was the ticking of the mantle clock across the room.

Finally, ignoring the tears that slid down her face, Lottie took in a deep breath and said, her voice hollow and low, "Please take me to him, Hannah."

The three women made their way across a back meadow toward a grove of gnarled and beautiful old walnut trees. Still some distance away, Lottie was taken by the serenity and beauty of the trees. Nearing the neatly arranged headstones, Lottie went to the newest. Someone had planted colorful flowers in a small bed at the foot of his grave.

Rachel worried about her daughter. Outwardly, she seemed so controlled and steady, but Rachel knew Lottie's heart was crushed.

After a short while, Hannah stood next to Lottie. "Let's go inside, dear. James brought all of Robert's things back with him and you can read his letters—he wrote of you in every one."

Lottie nodded and said, "I would like to see his room if you would allow it."

"Yes, we'll do that first, if you want to, and then we'll go back to the parlor for his letters," Hannah said, a smile spread across her tanned face.

On their way back to the house, Lottie took her mother's hand and squeezed it tightly. Leaning toward Rachel, she kissed her lightly on the cheek and whispered, "I'm glad you're here with me today, Mama."

Back at the house, Hannah opened the door to Robert's room and stepped aside to allow Lottie to enter first. Lottie stepped hesitantly into the room. On the ledge of the curtained window, there was a vase of fresh flowers. The room was sparsely furnished with only a single bed, mirrored dresser, and table with a wash basin and pitcher. A chest with four drawers was against the far wall.

Hannah went over to the window and moved the vase aside. She turned and motioned for Lottie to join her. With one arm around Lottie's waist, she ran a hand across the ledge. "Do you see these notches? Each one represents a pirate or other villain Robert killed. He did this with a hunting knife his father gave him for his eighth birthday."

Lottie's trembling lips stretched into a smile. "He did this when he was eight?"

"And I'm ashamed to say, I spanked him for it," answered Hannah, shakily.

Lottie turned to Hannah. "You spanked him, Hannah? Had he disobeyed you in some way?"

Hannah dropped her head and stared at the ledge for a moment. She passed the tip of one finger along the path of notches. Sighing heavily, she said, "No—Robert hadn't disobeyed me—in all the years we had him, he was a good son. He always obeyed Joseph and me."

Turning away from the window, she dabbed her eyes with a handkerchief from her apron pocket. Exhaling audibly, she added, "Robert's father and I had an argument over the knife. I thought Robert was too young to have his own knife. For days, I carried resentment in my heart, and one morning I came in to wake Robert and saw the notches on the window ledge. I lost my temper and spanked poor Robert when what I really wanted was to spank his father."

⸻ ⸻ ⸻

In the parlor, Lottie carefully untied the ribbon and saw that there were three letters. She began reading with the oldest. It was dated December 12, 1777, just a few months after he had stopped by to see her on his way to Williamsburg. In it, he told his mother about a beautiful young woman named Lottie Hamilton and how much in love they were. Nearly half of the letter was about his newly found love.

Tears flowed freely down her face as she read and reread his words. Lottie was vaguely aware that Hannah and her mother had left her alone to read the letters. She read them all slowly.

Reading them chronologically, Lottie soon came to the one in which he told his mother about the promise he'd made to

Lottie's father. Her eyes widened as they passed over his words until she reached the end, when she clasped the letter to her bosom and cried.

Now she knew why she had never received a letter from him. It was because of a promise he'd made to her father. Robert had given his word he wouldn't contact her until after the war.

When her tears stopped falling, Lottie neatly folded the letters, tied them together with the ribbon, and made her way to the kitchen where Hannah and her mother were waiting.

"Are you all right, dear?" asked Rachel. "It's time we should be leaving."

Lottie sighed heavily. She knew her mother was sympathetic and wanted to help her, but Lottie couldn't think of leaving just yet. She wanted to spend some time with Robert's mother and go back to his room one more time.

Managing a fragile smile, Lottie replied, "No I'm not all right, Mama. Right now, I feel hollow inside and my heart's breaking, but you should go on and see about Papa and everyone. I want to stay with Hannah for a while."

Lottie looked at Hannah for her permission, and Hannah said quickly, "Certainly child, you can stay as long as you like. I want Joseph, Robert's father, to meet you before you return home."

Tears spilled down Rachel's face as she looked at her daughter. "I can't leave you in such a state, dear. I'll stay a little longer, and we'll see how things are. Will that be all right?"

With a slight nod of her head, Lottie said, "I suppose."

The morning passed with Lottie and Rachel helping Hannah prepare dinner for her husband. Hannah's recollections of Robert were a meandering look back on his life. Some were heartfelt and brought tears, but some of his escapades in growing up were humorous enough to bring laughter.

Rachel watched her daughter as she alternately shed tears and laughed. *I'm glad we stayed. This is good for Lottie; she'll be able to remember this day with his parents for the rest of her life.*

Meeting Robert's father was like seeing a slightly heavier and older Robert. Even his voice was disconcerting to Lottie. It was Robert's voice. Lottie barely spoke during the time he was there.

After Joseph returned to tend the tavern, Lottie said, "Miss Hannah, may I have a few moments alone in Robert's room? It'll soon be time for us to leave, and it would mean so much to me to have that quiet time."

Hannah's eyes teared up. "Yes, Lottie, I think it would be a good thing, and your mother and I will finish cleaning the kitchen."

As Lottie left to go upstairs, Hannah took a deep breath and whispered, "I think Lottie will always remember Robert as her first love."

"Yes," Rachel agreed. "I'm sure of that, myself."

An hour had passed when Lottie came down from Robert's room. She found her mother and Hannah having coffee on the back porch.

Lottie extended her hand and touched Hannah's shoulder. "Miss Hannah, it's time for us to leave. I want to thank you for sharing Robert with me today. You must know I truly loved Robert, and I believe he loved me. Before he left for the army, he asked me to marry him, and I said yes."

Her throat tightened, but she clenched her teeth and willed it to stop. "I want you to know that I will never forget him."

Hannah stood and moved to Lottie's side. "It is I who should thank you, Lottie, for spending the day with me. You'll never know how you've lifted my heart today."

Taking Rachel and Lottie by the hand, Hannah said, "Lottie, I want you to get on with your life, for God has a husband for you. Will you do that?"

Lottie hugged Hannah tightly and, with her voice trembling said, "Yes ma'am, I will do that . . . goodbye."

Retrieving their horses, Rachel and Lottie rode to the cemetery. Rachel stopped her horse some distance back, and Lottie went on alone. Dismounting, Lottie knelt by Robert's grave and prayed silently for a time before she stood and remounted her horse to head for home.

The sun was sinking when they reached the ancient Cherokee Indian trail that would take them home. The trees cast long shadows that stretched across a trail that was barely wide enough for one horse. Although there'd been no Indian trouble in this area for a number of years, Rachel's nerves would be on edge until they could see the lights from the mill.

Lottie had been quiet for most of the ride home. Now, Rachel broke the silence. "It'll be dark when we get home, and your Papa is going to be fussy."

Twisting in the saddle, Lottie said over her shoulder. "He'll be all right when we tell him about Robert. Papa told me he liked Robert."

They rode steadily along, neither talking, until the last streaks of sunshine faded and night covered the trail.

"Give your horse its head, Lottie, and he'll take us home. He can see much better than you or me."

After nearly another hour had passed, Rachel was beginning to think they might be on the wrong trail, when Lottie cried out, "I see the lights, Ma, straight ahead. We made it!"

John was on the porch looking anxiously toward the direction of the trail when he heard them. As they rode up to the house, he walked out to meet them.

"You two will give me gray hairs yet," John said, helping first Rachel and then Lottie dismount.

Noticing her husband's horse saddled and ready to ride, she laughed. "Were you about to come to our rescue, sweetheart?"

"Well, uh, I—"

Before he could respond to Rachel's kidding, Lottie threw herself into her father's arms and burst into tears. He caught her and looked toward Rachel, a questioning expression on his face.

The hurt he saw in Rachel's eyes only confused him more. He pulled Lottie's arms from around his neck and held her at arm's length. "What is it, princess, that has you so upset? Is it about Robert?"

Still sobbing, Lottie could only nod her head. John pulled her back close to him and held her until she was able to tell him what terrible thing had happened today.

Daniel came out and put the horses away, and Rachel went inside. John and his daughter remained there under God's canopy of stars.

Lottie's sobs soon ebbed away. Her head rested against her father's chest. "Papa?" she whispered.

John looked into her eyes. "I'm here, sweetheart. Are you able to tell me about today?"

"Yes Papa," she looked at her father with soulful eyes. "Robert is dead. He was killed almost two years ago at Savannah."

———————

The conversation at supper was subdued. The news of Robert's death was a shock to everyone. Lottie, who generally carried on a teasing banter with Daniel and kept a chatty exchange going, barely lifted her head and just pushed her food around her plate with her fork.

Rachel cast nervous glances toward her husband, and tried to cajole Lottie into a better mood. She raised her eyebrows at Daniel in hopes of coaxing him into one of his playful exchanges with his sister, but he shook his head discreetly.

That night Lottie went to bed early and was asleep when Ellie and Sarah came in to sleep. Rachel looked in before going to her room.

Sarah whispered, "She'll be all right, Ma. We'll be here if she needs us."

Rachel kissed each of them goodnight as she left. Entering her room, she saw an anxious look in John's eyes. "Did you check on her?"

"Yes, she was fast asleep, and the girls said they would watch her," she replied with some strain in her voice.

He finished undressing and climbed into bed. "I believe she had deeper feelings for Robert than we thought."

Rachel slipped under the covers. "Yes," she replied. "Another man will fill that void in her heart, someday, but she will never forget Robert . . . he was her first love."

Snuffing the candle, John lay back and waited for sleep, and Rachel rested her head on his shoulder and closed her eyes. It had been a long day.

CHAPTER THIRTY ONE

KING'S MOUNTAIN

A storm threatened the next morning with dark, ominous clouds lingering overhead as the family gathered for breakfast. The sound of approaching horses caught John's attention. He looked at Daniel, whose raised eyebrows showed he'd heard them, too. Both men got up and went to the door.

Daniel said, over his shoulder, "It's Silas Littlefield and his son."

When the two men reached the house, John opened the front door. "Good morning Silas, you and your son step down and have some breakfast."

Rubbing his horse's withers, Silas said, "I'm beholden to you, John, but me 'n my boy have a sight of riding to do this day if we're to get everybody told about this British Major Ferguson that's holed up near Gilbert Town. That's about two days ride due north of us."

"Is this the man who's been recruiting Loyalists up around Tryon County in North Carolina?" asked John.

Nodding his head, Silas answered, "Yep, one and the same, and he's right cocky. I heard he's issued a challenge to the

Overmountain men of Watauga to put down their guns or he'll cross over the Blue Ridge and kill'em all and burn'em out."

"Colonel Isaac Shelby's commanding the Overmountain men, and last I heard he had about six-hundred men, and John Sevier has more than two-hundred long hunters with him. Reckon Ferguson knows that?"

"Don't know the answer to that, John, but I do know Ferguson has stirred'em up, and that's what I'm here about. They're not going to wait for Ferguson to cross the Misty Mountains, they'll be coming across pretty soon to track him down and make him eat those words."

"They're looking for men to join them?" John said.

"You guessed it. Shelby has put out a call for their men to meet at Sycamore Shoals. I was told they'd be coming over the mountain just as soon as they got their men together. If you, Daniel, and as many of your men as you can round up, want to help the Overmountain bunch, then be at Ramseur's Mill by Wednesday, next."

John rubbed the stubble on his chin. "That's cutting it close, Silas, for me to have time to round up many of the men who've ridden with me, but you can definitely count on me and Daniel."

With a thundering clap, several fingers of lightning arced across the northern sky. A storm looked inevitable. Silas jerked back on the reins. "We'd better get along before the storm hits. See you at Ramseur's Mill, John."

His eyes scanning the dark sky, John extended his hand to Daniel's shoulder. "Let's go, son, we've got a bit of packing to do before we can leave. I'll stop by the dining room and tell your Ma and the others."

Just as John rejoined the women at the breakfast table, another sizzling, crackling bolt of lightning lit up the room, followed quickly by a thunderous clap of thunder. Storm clouds had been brewing since yesterday, and now rain was coming down in sheets, driven by the cool September wind.

Rachel poured John another cup of coffee and waited for him to say what the men's visit was about. She knew he would get to it in a moment, and there was no need for her try and hurry him.

John took a swallow of his coffee. "Daniel and I will be leaving as soon as we get our things together. We're to join Shelby and Sevier from across the Blue Ridge at Ramseur's Mill and help chase down the Loyalists riding with a Major Ferguson."

"Where's Daniel, now, Papa?" asked a serious-faced Ellie.

"He's out rounding up our horses. He should be back shortly to get his things together." John answered.

Sarah pushed back from the table and took an empty chair next to John. "Papa, will you ask about Gideon when you meet up with the others? I received another letter from him last month, but at the time he wrote it, he hadn't received any of mine."

John reached out and touched Sarah on her cheek. "I'll do just that, daughter; now put a smile on your pretty face for me."

Sarah giggled and smiled widely for her father-in-law. "Thank you, Papa; it's easy to smile for you."

Everyone gathered on the porch, as John and Daniel prepared to mount their horses. Rachel stood close to her husband of twenty-one years, and Ellie held on to Daniel as though she could keep him with her. Standing a few steps back was Meg, Sarah, and Lottie.

John opened his arms for Rachel. "Goodbye for now, my love. I'll be back before you know it."

Rachel nestled close and wrapped her arms tightly around him, and their lips touched for a lingering kiss.

Pulling back, Rachel whispered, "Don't forget to say goodbye to Lottie and Sarah."

John opened his arms, as he looked past Daniel and Ellie. "Come, daughters, it's time for Daniel and me to leave."

Lottie and Sarah, with tears streaming down their faces, eagerly ran to him and fell into his open arms. Kissing each on her forehead, he said, "Now, I've saved my most special goodbye for each of you." Lifting their chins, his eyes searched their faces. In a voice that was clearly from his heart, he said, "I want you both to wake up each day with a smile in your heart and on your face . . . will you do that for me?"

Her chin quivering, Sarah spoke first. "Yes Papa, and please hurry home."

Lottie dabbed the tears from her eyes and kissed him on the cheek. "I'll smile every day for you, Papa."

After their hugs and kisses, John cleared his throat and said, "We'll have to go now, there's a good bit of riding for us to get the call out to our men before we head for Ramseur's Mill."

"The both of you take care and come home safely," said a teary-eyed Rachel.

John nodded, "We'll be home before you know it."

By the time John and Daniel were on their way, the storm had passed, leaving the ground muddy and slippery. When they arrived at Ramseur's Mill, fifty men were riding with them.

Waiting for them were Colonel Isaac Shelby and a group of six militia leaders from settlements throughout the Piedmont. Together, these men commanded an army of over one thousand seasoned fighting men.

Daniel and his father's men dropped off at the encampment to acquaint themselves with the men they would soon be fighting with, and John headed for the live oak where Shelby was conducting a meeting with the leaders.

Waving as John drew near, Shelby, in his booming voice, said, "Men, I see John Hamilton has come to join us. John, how many men are with you?"

John nodded his head to the group and said, "About fifty is all I could round up and get here before y'all left, but we're ready to fight."

"Well, take a seat, John. I imagine you know most of the men here, especially one of them."

John had only given the group a cursory glance as he rode up, but the tall, bearded man now standing could only be one man . . . Gideon!

Gideon made his way quickly through the crowd and unabashedly grabbed his father in a crushing bear hug. Pushing Gideon back to arms length, John looked at his son from head to toe.

"Well, you look fit, son."

Feeling his eyes watering, John looked toward Shelby. "Isaac, speaking for myself and my men, we stand ready to serve whenever and wherever you and the others see fit. Now, if you men will excuse us, my son and I need a bit of family time. We'll be over at the encampment with his brother."

⊰⊶✖⊷⊱ ⊰⊶✖⊷⊱ ⊰⊶✖⊷⊱

Daniel saw his father walking toward him, but from a distance didn't recognize the man with him. He watched curiously until he noticed their stride was the same and their build was similar. Then, he knew it was his brother. Daniel raced the remaining distance and nearly knocked the wind out of Gideon.

Daniel took him by the arm and said, "Brother, you look a sight with that beard, but it's such a welcome sight. I never thought I'd miss you like I have. Come, let's talk over some coffee."

Sitting near a campfire, the father and his sons talked and reminisced. Gideon's eyebrows arched and he asked, "How is Sarah, Pa? Do you have a word from her?"

Feeling the euphoria from sitting between his grown sons, John swallowed the tightness in his throat. "Sarah pines for you every day, and she's healthy and robust. She's the first to arise every morning and one of the last to retire for the night. I suspect staying busy helps her loneliness."

A smile creased Gideon's face. "I need to see her, Pa, and right after this—"

Daniel jumped to his feet. "Nope, there's no 'right after this', you're fixing to get cleaned up and scrape that beard off. Then, me 'n Pa are going to send you off to our old mill at Sandy Creek. That's where you'll find Sarah, and that's where you need to be . . . how about it, Pa?"

John got to his feet. "I'd already thought of that, myself. Now, get started and you can be there by breakfast."

Daniel pulled his brother to his feet. "C'mon, I've got soap, a razor, and a change of clothes that should fit you close enough."

Gideon was soon on his way home, and John headed back to find Shelby. The meeting had concluded, and John caught up with him at his camp.

Extending his hand, John said, "How did the meeting go, Isaac?"

Offering his friend a place beside him at the fire, Shelby said, "Could've been better, but it could've been worse, too, I reckon."

"How's that?" asked John.

Pitching the remains of his coffee near the fire, Shelby responded, "Well, we couldn't elect any one of the men to lead us, so all seven of us will take part in leading us to victory."

He chuckled and looked at John. "Think that's going to work?"

John shrugged his shoulders. "This army doesn't need a General as I see it, Isaac. What we do best is hit what we aim at, and we can do that without offering the enemy much of a target. I believe men like us will decide how this war ends; I really do."

"It's come down to a civil war, John. When we catch up with Ferguson, he'll be the only British combatant on the field. His army is made up, as is ours, of men born in this country. Whether that's a good thing or not, will be decided by those who come after us, but in a few days, Americans will be fighting Americans."

"Where is Ferguson bivouacked now?" asked John.

Shelby packed his long-stemmed briar and lit it with a sliver of wood from the fire. "Me 'n Charles McDowell left him in Gilbert Town a few months back. We were riding hard to get back over the Misty Mountains to protect our crops. Our scouts found him heading south toward a spur of the Blue Ridge at a place called King's Mountain."

He gazed at the fire through the cloud of aromatic smoke. "Our scout got close enough to nab one of Ferguson's men and haul him back. After a bit of convincing, the man told us Ferguson knows we're after him, and that he's planning to set up his defense on top of King's Mountain."

"He could do worse, I reckon, but if we can isolate him from Cornwallis, we've got enough men to surround him," John said, "and if nothing else starve him out. Are we going to King's Mountain?"

Nodding his head, Shelby said, "We'll be pulling out at first light. We have scouts following him." Tapping his pipe bowl on the palm of his hand, he went on, "Why don't you ride with me, John. Your men know most of mine and will make a good fit."

John put his hands on his knees and pushed himself to his feet. "Sounds good to me, Isaac, we've just teamed up with Gideon's men. I sent him home to see his wife. She hasn't seen him since he was captured at Monck's Corner."

⬥⬥⬥⬥

September had turned to October. The weather was changing, and the nights were turning cold and wet when the militiamen headed south toward King's Mountain. Although the ranks had swollen to more than eighteen hundred men, it couldn't be called an army in the strictest sense of the word. All the men were volunteers; none were paid. Each expected to serve for only a few weeks before returning to his home to tend to his chores, his farming, and personal matters. The men were all skilled hunters, woodsmen, and feared as fighters, but they lacked the discipline of a military unit. Without a structured chain of command, the patriots depended on their Indian-style tactics to challenge the best army in the world, and the British military generally dismissed any threat from the American volunteer militia.

After an all-night ride through a cold, rainy October darkness, these Patriot militiamen surrounded their Loyalist prey atop a promontory rising some seventy feet above the surrounding countryside.

The sound of their approach muted by the rain-softened ground, they neared the mountain undetected. They had already encircled the mountain by the time Ferguson's sentries spied them.

The Patriots moved up in an area of trees and rocks, darting from cover to cover. They were soon spotted by the Loyalists above, whose shots were mostly passing overhead.

John called out to the men nearest him. "Stay low, men. For awhile at least, they'll be shooting high, but they're sure to correct their aim pretty quick."

The Patriots held their fire until they were half way up the side of the mountain. Then they heard Colonel Shelby cry out, "Pick your shots, men! Don't waste a shot."

⚫⚫⚫ ⚫⚫⚫ ⚫⚫⚫

Major Ferguson was a brave and ferocious adversary, and was only slightly outnumbered. If this fight had occurred on an open field of battle, he might have given the Patriots more of a fight, but here on this barren mountaintop, he was at a great disadvantage. He couldn't see the enemy; they hid behind rocks, trees, and embankments.

By the Patriots third assault up the face of the mountain, their deadly shots had taken their toll of the ranks of the Loyalists, and they were able to take the crest of the mountain. By this time, some in the Loyalist's ranks tried to surrender, but Ferguson, atop his white stallion, would ride to the man and cut down his white flag with his sword.

After the Patriots gained the flat terrain of the mountaintop, Major Ferguson made an easy target for them. He was the only man astride a horse, and he was trying to be everywhere at once, shouting encouragement to his shrinking army. Then, from an unknown Patriot, came the shot that ended the battle. Ferguson was mortally wounded and was knocked from his saddle.

The Patriot's decisive victory and the death of Major Ferguson spread throughout the colonies and became a pivotal moment in the struggle for American Independence. The battle had lasted a little over an hour and not a single man of Ferguson's force escaped. The patriots had killed or captured every British soldier in the battle, forcing General Cornwallis to retreat from Charlotte, North Carolina and northward to his destiny at Yorktown.

CHAPTER THIRTY TWO

HOME AT LAST

Gideon had ridden all night, but when the sun was coming up over his left shoulder, he knew it was worth it. In the distance, he could see a grassy clearing gently sloping down to the creek bank.

He eased his horse down to the creek, stepping down while his horse drank from the flowing waters. Gideon looked first upstream and then downstream. A faint smile creased his face. He recognized this crossing. Years earlier, he and Daniel had come from the mill with a load of flour and meal for their father's store in Camden and forded the narrow creek here. He closed his eyes; Sarah was just minutes away.

Turning his horse around, he swung into the saddle and set out for home.

Gideon approached a familiar ridge. The mill was just on the other side. Topping the ridge, he pulled back the reins. There below was home, and he could see a thin tendril of smoke rising lazily from the chimney. He dug his heels into the flanks of his horse and she lurched forward.

Gideon saw Sarah at the door just before he reined his horse back from a gallop. He left the saddle before Shadow had completely stopped and ran to her as fast as his legs would carry him.

Just as he reached her, a sob caught in her throat, and she choked it back. Tears ran down her face, and she buried her face against his chest.

After a moment, he held her and gazed into her sky blue eyes, and brought his hand to rest on the upper swell of her belly.

"My Gideon . . ." Sarah whispered before he kissed her.

They held each other, vaguely aware of voices around them, but their eyes were locked and the world was far, far away. Gideon felt his heart beating very rapidly and pounding loudly as a drum in his chest.

Finally, Rachel said, "Let's get out of the doorway, or we'll freeze."

Chilled from his ride, Gideon went to the warm hearth, and Sarah stood next to him.

"I know you're hungry, Gideon," Sarah said, her face aglow. "We were just about to have breakfast. I'll pour you some coffee while we wait on the biscuits."

Rachel tugged on his arm. "Come and sit with us while you drink your coffee. Your father and Daniel are out chasing Patrick Ferguson."

Chuckling, Gideon said, "That's why I'm here, Ma. I just came from the rendezvous where Pa and Daniel are. Pa insisted I come home. I feel guilty about doing that, but my men went along with the idea. Seems like I was the only one of our Monck's Corner group that hadn't yet been home."

Sarah brought the biscuits to the table and Lottie and Ellie set the set the ham and eggs near Gideon. He was about to stab a biscuit with his fork, when he felt his mother take his hand. He bowed his head and said his own prayer while his mother prayed the meal's blessing.

Then Gideon busied himself with the meal, basking in the attention he was receiving from the women of his family.

After cleaning his plate, Gideon spied two biscuits were left. With his knife, he smeared them with honey and washed them down with his coffee. He suppressed a burp and saw that the women were all smiling.

Feeling the warmth rising from his neck, he said sheepishly, "It's been awhile since I've had real food."

Pouring her son another cup of coffee, Rachel said, winking at Sarah, "You'll have to remember, Sarah, your husband eats like two men." Then she turned to Ellie, "And Daniel is just like him."

Laughing, Sarah said, "I learned that in the short time we had before Monck's Corner."

After breakfast, Gideon told how he and his men had been harassing the Loyalist militias as far north as the upper reaches of North Carolina. Most recently, they had joined with Francis Marion, the 'Swamp Fox' to successfully slow Cornwallis's northern march to Virginia.

The women began cleaning up the kitchen, and Gideon stretched and yawned. Sarah pushed him toward the door. "Go to bed, you've been awake all night. I'll wake you this afternoon."

Kissing her softly, he said, "That's a good idea." Touching his mother on her arm, he asked, "Ma, why is the family here at the old mill?"

Wiping her hands on her apron, Rachel's face took on a solemn expression. "Trenton is gone—not a building left standing."

Gideon stared at his mother in stunned disbelief. "But why? Was it Cornwallis during the Camden skirmish?"

Sitting down at the table, Rachel closed her eyes, reliving the horror of that afternoon.

Leaning across the table, Gideon said, "Are you all right, Ma? We can talk about it some other time, if you'd rather."

Rachel's eyes gradually opened. "I'm fine, son. Sometimes, the memory of that day is so vivid that I can still hear the roar of the flames and see the plumes of smoke blotting out the sun."

She touched his arm and said, "Nay, it wasn't Cornwallis, although he's guilty of torching the homes of others. It was Lord Rawdon's barbaric work, carried out by that monster, Rufus Sherman."

Lottie leaned forward on her elbows. "And that's not all Rufus did, Gideon. He hit Ma so hard, she fell across the veranda floor, and her eye was swelled almost shut."

Gideon leapt to his feet, knocking his chair over and said angrily, "What does Pa say about this?"

"He doesn't know," Lottie injected.

Rachel shook her head. "Your father has too much on his mind already."

He looked at his mother, his face flushed with outrage. "You need to tell Pa. Sherman tried twice to kill him. Sherman destroyed our home and laid hands on you. This isn't about the war. The man's a murderous savage, nothing more than a wild animal."

Sighing heavily, Rachel said, "I suppose you're right, son."

"I know I'm right about the Sherman family, at least the men, anyway. A day of reckoning is coming soon for Rufus and his sons.

Ellie, wiping her hands on her apron, joined the conversation. "That day has already passed for Eb and Eli, the Sherman twins. They tracked Daniel in an effort to kill him, but failed."

Touching Gideon's shoulder, she said, "Daniel was almost caught when he came to the shop in Canton to tell us about your father being captured. Daniel barely got out the back window before the Tories burst in the front door. Eb and Eli were sent after him, but God's angel protected your brother. The twins haven't been seen nor heard from since that day."

The conversation lulled and Gideon exhaled an audible sigh. "Then there's only Rufus left. I wonder if he knows the consequences of his sins."

Lottie interjected, "If Pa was here, he'd quote a verse or two from the Bible. I can't do that as well as he can, but I do remember a verse in the Old Testament. The part that I recall is, 'For they sow the wind, and they shall reap the whirlwind.' I know there's more, but that fits the life Rufus Sherman chose for himself and his sons."

A cold snap in October of 1780 had gripped the Piedmont from Virginia to South Carolina. A rider came through with the news that the Overmountain men, with help from militia from the Carolinas, had defeated the Loyalists at a place called King's Mountain. Rachel fed the rider and gave him hot coffee before sending him on to tell the news.

Light flurries of snow had fallen most of the day when Gideon came upon Rachel and Ellie in the barn sitting at their looms. Walking around to face his mother, he said, "Ma, should you and Ellie be out here with no heat? It's beginning to snow outside."

Chuckling, she responded, "We're about finished, dear, and this is the last we'll do until spring. Did you come out here to see about us?"

Grinning, he said, "Well, actually I came to ask you a question about the mill. Does Pa have any plans to open the mill again?"

Rachel pulled the beater bar toward her and looked up. "He hasn't spoken to me about the mill at all, son, but then his militia duties leave little time for business matters these days. Why do you ask?"

"Nothing really, I may talk to him about buying it when he gets back."

⚫ ⚫ ⚫

Gideon spent the next few days looking around the mill, mostly taking inventory of what needed to be done to get the business up and running again. At first, Sarah was put off by the darkness and accumulated dust, but the more time she spent with Gideon, listening to him pointing out the different parts of the mill, the more she became ready help Gideon reopen it.

Climbing from behind the millstones, Gideon found his wife standing on a stool cleaning a window.

"Should you be up so high, darling? You might fall and—"

Wiping her nose with her sleeve, Sarah laughed and said, "Since you've been home, husband, you've worried about every step I take. Remember I have no brothers, and I helped my Papa with his chores every day, so I'm used to using ladders and foot stools to reach my work."

The sound of pounding hooves interrupted their conversation. Gideon reached for his rifle and Sarah pulled the pistol that she carried hidden under her apron. Sarah stepped on the stool and looked out the now-cleaned window.

"Oh it's Papa John and Daniel. Hurry, let's go meet them!"

Running outside, they met the men as they rode up. Ellie came from inside the house followed by Rachel and Lottie.

"What a welcome sight!" exclaimed John as he dismounted.

Rachel ran to his arms, and Ellie was waiting for Daniel to get down, while Gideon stood back with his arms around Lottie and Sarah. Overhead a flock of ducks flew noisily on their way south.

Lottie ran to the porch and called back, "Let's all go inside, where it's warm. We can listen to Papa and Daniel tell us about the skirmish at King's Mountain."

Gideon took their horses to the barn. "I won't be long, so don't start until I get back, Pa."

When Gideon returned, the family gathered around the dining table to hear the news that was fast spreading throughout the colonies.

John blew quietly on his steaming cup of chocolate. "For the past seven months, the British have won battle after battle, and in doing so, they've nearly destroyed our people's resolve to free our country."

His heart was overflowing with excitement, and he couldn't sit any longer. He stood and his voice was firm and steady. "But on Saturday afternoon, the seventh day of this month, we met the notorious braggart Major Patrick Ferguson, who was commanding over one thousand Loyalists. We came face to face that day and after little more than an hour had passed, Patrick Ferguson lay dead in a field beside his fallen comrades."

Searching her husband's face, Rachel said, "But John, what are we to make of this one victory after all that's happened after Charles Town and Camden?"

Swallowing the last of his chocolate, John answered, "I can't tell you what this victory means as far as ending the war, but I can say the British can't afford many more losses like King's Mountain. Cornwallis just lost a third of his army and is without any protection on his western flank."

Gideon leaned forward on his elbows. "Cornwallis is running out of options, Pa. He can't leave the Carolinas now, and his top commander, Banastre Tarleton, keeps losing men to Colonel Francis Marion. I'll wager Cornwallis will soon retreat back to Charles Town."

<hr />

Gideon and Sarah spent the rest of October cleaning and repairing the mill. John deeded the mill property to Gideon for one percent of the first year's profit.

Sarah came down from the third floor storage room to find Gideon. He was cleaning one of the millstones and looked up when she peeked in the door.

"Let's stop for dinner, husband," said Sarah, wiping the small beads of perspiration from under her nose.

A grin spread across his face as he looked at her standing in the doorway. "Just as you are now, my love, you're the loveliest creature under heaven." Touching her protruding belly, he whispered, "How's our son?"

Grinning, Sarah replied, "We're both doing fine, and the way this baby moves around and kicks, you may have your wish about having a son."

Gideon pulled her close. "I really have no preference whether we have a son or daughter as long as either looks like their mother and has her eyes. When I say 'our son', I'm kidding you."

Sitting down for the dinner meal, Meg gave the blessing, and around the table, hands were joined and heads were bowed.

John asked how the mill was shaping up. "Do you figure you'll be ready for the wheat harvest, son?"

Shrugging his shoulders, Gideon replied, "I'd like to have a millstone dresser to dress out the furrows on the stones when they need it. I met a man from Williamsburg, but he may not be willing to come this far, since it's still not safe for one man to travel alone."

Gideon reached for Sarah's hand. "We've named the business The River Road Mill, since the Hamilton name seems to stir up trouble among the enemy. I'm going to the Alcott's and post a notice for a millwright and dresser, and I may sneak into Canton and advertise in Mr. Kendall's paper."

"Speaking of names," Sarah injected, "Gideon and I've decided if our baby is a boy, we'll name him 'Phillip Gideon' and call him 'Phillip'."

Gideon interrupted, "And if we have a girl, her name will be Sarah Elizabeth, and she'll be called either Elizabeth or Beth."

After dinner, Lottie went back to the mill with Gideon and Sarah. Shivering without her cape as they walked down the steps toward the creek, Lottie said, "I can't stay outside, it's too cold without my cape. But before I go back in, I want to ask you if I can go with you when you go to the Alcott's."

Putting his arm around his sister, Gideon stopped walking and kissed her forehead. "We'll be glad to have your company dear sister, especially Sarah. Pa and Daniel will be with us; we're to rendezvous with Colonel Pickens. I expect we'll go early tomorrow, since Sarah's time is drawing ever closer."

Watching his sister go back to the house, Gideon said, "I wish there was something I could do for Lottie. She seems to have lost interest in life."

Taking him by the arm, Sarah reminded him. "It's only been three months since she learned of Robert's death. We all need to surround her with love until God sends a young man her way."

CHAPTER THIRTY THREE

COWPENS

December came in with bitterly cold days, and Sarah waddled about helping with the household chores, as she was able. One morning as they were busily sewing shirts for the men, Rachel remarked, "How are you feeling, today? You look as if you're uncomfortable."

Stretching her legs in front of her, Sarah shifted in her chair and with a grunt said, "This baby kicks and won't be still."

"Your time's close now; it won't be long."

"Mmmm, I'm ready now for Gideon to become a father."

Daniel came up from the cellar and went over by the fireplace to warm his hands. "Ma, the cellar is chock-full of treasures. I believe your garden this year was your best ever."

Rachel's face beamed as she looked up from her sewing work. "I believe you're right, son. God has blessed us with abundance this year. Did you notice the jams and jellies we have? Your Ellie and Sarah put up each one of those jars."

<hr />

Looking up from her stitching, Ellie cast a side-look at him. Their eyes met and lingered. *How different my life has become since I met Daniel . . . even more, I'm a different person. Never, in two lifetimes, would I've thought I would be anyplace other than Charles Town with servants attending my every need.*

She looked down at her slender hands of which she'd always been so proud. They were no longer soft and white, pampered with lotions and creams, but were the hands of a woman who had learned to cook meals, take care of their animals, and even tend to the kitchen gardens. One of her proudest accomplishments was learning the intricacies of spinning flax into linen.

She knew her hands would likely never be those of a woman of leisure again, but it didn't matter, none at all . . . because Daniel would tenderly caress her fingers with his kisses and tell her that her hands were beautiful.

———————

The next day, John and his sons rode up to Alcott's Inn to meet with a group of militiamen being briefed by Colonel Andrew Pickens about the state of affairs after the Battle of King's Mountain. Sarah and Lottie followed in the family's wagon.

The inn's meeting room was packed when Pickens arrived. He knew these men, and they knew the tall, wiry Scot-Irishman as a fearless and ardent Patriot fighter.

Standing on a chair, he knew by the focus of their eyes that he had every man's attention.

"Men, General Daniel Morgan has been ordered southwest of the Catawba River to cut supply lines and hamper British operations in the backcountry. Morgan has his army encamped at Grindal's Shoals on the Pacolet River. Word has reached us that Cornwallis has sent the young devil, Lieutenant Colonel Banastre Tarleton to turn back Morgan."

A growling murmur spread around the room as the men recounted their encounters with the notorious Tarleton.

Knocking the dead ashes from his pipe into the palm of this hand, Pickens said, "Just this morning, we learned Tarleton crossed the flooded Pacolet and is now pursuing Morgan. I can't tell you where Morgan is this morning, but I can tell you he's not running scared. Morgan is headed to Cowpens Crossroads about thirty miles south of King's Mountain, and there he'll stop to wait for Tarleton to catch up. It's going to be a bit touchy around the Pacolet River for the next few days, but Morgan's more than a match for Tarleton. I want you men to spread the word and meet me at the bend of the Broad River, south of Cowpens as soon as you can."

John and his family left early, and ate their cold meal on the trail home. John went over the information from Pickens. "From what I can figure, Andy and Morgan are planning to trap Tarleton at the Cowpens. They're depending on Tarleton's headstrong tactics. He rarely protects his flanks and uses his light infantry and dragoons to overwhelm the enemy by crushing them head-on."

Gideon asked, "What does Morgan have to counter that? I can tell you, Pa, I've met Tarleton twice and had to retreat to save my men on both occasions. He's a powerful enemy."

Nodding, John replied, "Andy only mentioned the general outline of what Morgan has in mind, but it sounds like it will work."

Gideon slowed Shadow to a walk and twisted in the saddle to look at John directly.

John paced his horse alongside Shadow. "Andy will have his sharpshooters formed to meet Tarleton's dragoons first. We'll be with them. We're to fire, aiming for officers and sergeants, and fall back behind the second line which will be our full militia. The full militia will fire two volleys and we'll all retreat to the third line made up of veteran Continentals. On our right flank will be Colonel William Washington's Cavalry to counter any charge by their dragoons."

Daniel interrupted, "We're going to have a fracas for sure. Tarleton fights like a madman, just when you expect he's beaten, he'll rally and come at you like a battering ram."

Rubbing his stubbly chin, John said, "We'll give him the fight of his life, son—our backs will be against the Broad River. If we gain the victory, it will be the beginning of the end for Cornwallis and the British in the southern colonies."

It was nearing dark when the family arrived home. Daniel and Gideon put their horses away.

During supper, John told the family that General Morgan had sent out a call to arms for the South Carolina Militia. He went on to tell them what he knew of Morgan's plan to trap and defeat Banastre Tarleton.

Rachel's heart nearly stopped at the mention of the man so feared by every patriot in the southern colonies. "What do you think of the plan, John? Everyone is afraid of Tarleton. There's been nothing but blood and slaughter wherever he's fought, and women and children aren't safe when he comes calling."

His eyes took in all around the table. "Not everyone is afraid of him. He's cold and ruthless, that's for certain, and his tactics have served him well when he was unknown to us. But we've learned since the early days, and his tactics are sure to fail him at Crossroads."

John backed away from the table. "Much depends on our militia. If we stand and deliver our two volleys and fall back, Tarleton will rush his men into Morgan's trap. Then we'll have him."

Gideon reached for another helping of peas. "If we win this one like we won King's Mountain, the British will have to abandon their plans of conquering the south."

Arriving the day before the battle, John and three hundred-fifty sharpshooters were spread out, joining in the first line with two other militia companies. John noted the militia line stretched some distance.

He leaned back to rest on his haunches. "Looks to be near a thousand of us farm boys to greet Tarleton come morning."

Gideon nodded, his eyes scanning up and down the line. "There'll be no ambush here—we'll not be hiding behind trees and bushes. No sir! We'll meet their finest on this road and prove our mettle. If we hold the line for two volleys, we'll slow'em down . . . maybe even stop'em."

Gideon saw the corners of his father's mouth barely tip upward. John understood the general feeling among the disciplined and well trained Continentals. It was their feeling that militias in general were undependable in battle. Although, militias from New Hampshire to Georgia had proven records as valiant patriots, too many of the farmer-patriots couldn't be counted on to make a stand against the blood-curdling sight of a British infantry charge—especially when the redcoats had bayonets affixed to their muskets.

These farmers turned soldiers were armed with weapons they used nearly every day. Attached to their waists were large hunting knives, some even carried tomahawks, but it was their long, slim American rifles that set them apart and made them legendary marksmen. These rifles, original masterpieces of the gunsmiths of Pennsylvania, were deadly accurate at 200 yards and could be effective at even longer ranges.

Scouts came in to report Tarleton's troops were just down the road forming up for the attack. The air was clear and bitterly cold as the Patriot skirmishers waited.

Finally, Tarleton ordered his infantry to attack. Tension had been building up and down the patriot line. Men shivered, the tips of their fingers numbed while their breaths floated on the frigid air in clouds of vapor. Idle chatter stopped; an unnatural quietness had come to Cowpens Crossroads.

Then it happened. A bugle sounded 'charge' and brave men flinched as their pulses quickened. The perfectly disciplined redcoats began moving briskly toward the unranked patriot line.

John and his men, all veterans of many skirmishes, watched and waited. On the Britishers came, their cadenced boots beating the solid dirt road as if it were a drum. The patriots stood firm. To a man, this was a familiar sight. They'd heard this music on other fields of battle; times when their feet betrayed them and they ran.

But, today was a new day. The victory at King's Mountain had shown them their formidable enemy could be beaten, and this is what they intended to do this morning.

When the command to fire finally came, the militia men shot with deadly accuracy. The British line stopped cold as one redcoat after another dropped under the feet of his comrades. The acrid gun smoke hung in the cold morning air, by the time a wind coming from the river cleared the scene, the redcoats had regrouped and were advancing forward.

The second patriot volley thundered and again the sound of dying men and screams from the wounded broke the air. British and American regulars alike were startled to see the grit displayed by the patriot line.

By the time the militias were in their orderly retreat, the American regulars could see the battle turning in their favor. The redcoats had stalled and were in disarray, many of their officers and sergeants lay scattered along the road either dead or wounded.

In the noise and confusion of the battle, an order by the commander of the Continentals was mistakenly heard as a call to retreat. Seeing the veteran Continentals retreating, other companies did the same.

Morgan quickly saw what was happening and called out. "Commander Howard, why're you retreating—are you beaten?"

Howard shook his head and pointed to the orderly retreat of his men. "Nay, General, 'tis a tactical move."

Morgan spun his horse around and shouted to the retreating regulars, "Face about men—stand where you are and await my order to fire."

Keeping in ranks, the Continentals and other companies came around and aimed their rifles. Morgan shouted the order to fire, and a volley was unleashed at the charging British infantry. Morgan's quick action and the Patriot's deadly accuracy stopped the British charge, turned the tide of battle. Pickens's militia, aided by the cavalry, came back to now completely surround the enemy. The British infantry began surrendering and laid down their arms.

The Americans controlled the battle, but General Tarleton, sensing defeat, managed to escape with his aides, and as a mark of his character, Tarleton left his dead and wounded where they had fallen.

The Battle of Cowpens, together with the King's Mountain, had a devastating effect on British morale, and caused Lord Cornwallis to pull troops from South Carolina and move them farther north, leading to Yorktown and eventually the end of the Revolutionary war.

CHAPTER THIRTY FOUR

A NEW HAMILTON

John and his sons rode up to the hitching rail and dismounted. Ellie came out with a serious expression on her face. "Sarah's time is here, she's abed now, and Lottie's gone to fetch the mid-wife. We're looking for them to arrive at any time."

Inside, Rachel was folding cloths and Meg was heating water. As Gideon passed the kitchen door, his mother stopped him. "There you are, son. Sarah's in your room."

"Has the baby come?" he asked, his voice thin and fragile.

A comforting smile spread across Rachel's face. "No, it's a bit too soon, and it may or may not be Sarah's time. First babies are unpredictable, but she's been in a bit of pain most of the morning, so I put her to bed and sent your sister for Mrs. Alcott. She'll arrive prepared to stay, if the baby doesn't come today."

"Can I see her?"

"Yes, but if she's asleep, don't wake her. She'll not be getting much rest until after she delivers."

Gideon opened the door slowly until he could see Sarah lying on the bed. For a moment, he thought she might be asleep, but her head turned toward the door. When she spied Gideon, a smile creased her face.

"You're back," she said, her voice subdued. She looked him over, from his head to his boots. "Are you whole?"

Opening the door fully, he came to her side. "Not a scratch. We barely got there in time to take part."

He knelt down beside the bed and took her hand. "How are you? What can I do?"

Gripping his hand tightly, she said, "There's nothing for you to do, husband. In fact, I want you to go out to the mill and wait. Mama Rachel or one of the others will come for you when our babe arrives."

He nodded and leaned over to kiss her softly. "Have you had much pain?"

She nodded her head slowly. It's hurts more than I can tell you, but it doesn't last long. I'm thankful it comes and goes."

Gideon pressed her hand to his lips, and then said, "I'll go now."

She held to his hand and said, "Wait, Gideon, I want to say something before you go."

He stopped and turned back to her. Her eyes brimmed with tears. "If anything should happen to me—"

"Stop—don't talk like that. You're a strong and healthy young woman, and you're going to have our child and do just fine, so just stop talking about something happening to you."

Sarah opened her mouth to speak, and he placed his hand over it. "No, don't say anything else, you just do what Mrs. Alcott or Ma says and have them call me the moment my daughter or son is here."

Sarah's eyes followed him as he left, and moments later, another spasm of pain spread from her lower back and ran through her belly. She was certain every muscle inside her was twisting and pulling. It was the most unbearable pain she had ever experienced, each time building to an intense peak before slowly subsiding.

Just then, Rachel came in with the cloths, and following her was Meg, carrying hot water.

Rachel came to Sarah's side and felt her forehead. "Meg, take one of the smaller cloths and bath Sarah's face." Then she said, "Sarah, I want to check you and see where we are."

Moments later, Rachel said, "My first grandchild is ready. Sarah, I believe you're going to deliver before Lottie gets back with Hannah."

John and Daniel followed Gideon out to the mill, and another half hour passed before Lottie was back with Hannah.

Hannah came into the room and went straight to Sarah. Sarah's trembling hand found Hannah's, squeezing it tightly. "I've never experienced such pain as this, Hannah, could something be wrong?"

Rachel brought a chair for Hannah. Leaning close to Sarah from the chair, Hannah said, "Nay child, 'tis all part of bringing life into this world. Now, you lie still for me." Hannah lifted Sarah's gown and in a few moments, she nodded and smiled at the other women in the room.

"You and the baby are doing just fine, dear." Motioning toward Rachel and Meg, she said, "Now, if you will help me transfer Sarah to the birthing chair, it'll not be much longer before we'll be welcoming another Hamilton to the family."

<hr />

The tone was subdued in the mill as Gideon waited with his father and brother. Daniel had posted himself at a window that faced the house, ready to announce the approach of any of the women.

About four o'clock, Daniel was dozing at his post, and John and Gideon were outside inspecting the dam, when Ellie and Lottie burst through the milling door with the news.

Lottie was the first to announce loudly, "It's a boy! I'm an aunt . . . where's Gideon?"

Gideon heard his sister's voice and ran to the house. Reaching the bedroom, he was met by his mother standing in the doorway holding a bundle wrapped in a soft blanket.

Turning back a corner of the blanket, she said, "This is your son. You should introduce yourself, so he will know his father's voice."

Gideon, his eyes widened with wonder, gazed at the tiny baby asleep in his grandmother's arms. "He's a bit red, don't you think, Ma?" he said, glancing at Rachel.

"That's the color of healthy babies. Would you like to hold him? I'd like to help Hannah with Sarah."

Taken aback, Gideon craned his neck to look past his mother. "Is something wrong with Sarah?"

Smiling, she passed the baby to his father and assured him, "Everything's fine. Take your son and show him to the family, but keep him wrapped up, and don't take him outside."

Suddenly, he was left alone in the hallway with his son. Tenderly, Gideon kissed the baby's forehead. "Hello Phillip Gideon, I'm your father."

Gideon brought his calloused hand to touch Phillip's face, and immediately, Phillip clasped his tiny fingers around his father's finger. Marveling at his son's movement, Gideon moved his hand back as if to pull away, but Phillip held tight to his father's finger. Smiling widely at his son, Gideon looked up to see Ellie coming.

"Ellie, I'd like you to meet your first nephew, Phillip Gideon Hamilton," he said proudly.

Glancing at Gideon, Ellie responded enthusiastically, "Ooh, I like that name. Phillip Gideon sounds so American."

Beaming, Gideon, his eyes locked on his son, said, "Sarah says we'll call him Phillip, so he'll not be confused with his father."

"Can Phillip's Aunt Ellie hold him?" she asked, reaching to take Phillip from his father.

"Certainly. Let's take him to the kitchen so he can meet the rest of his family," Gideon said.

Rachel had changed the bed linens and laid out a clean nightgown. After Hannah finished her ministrations, Rachel soon had her daughter-in-law into her nightgown and tucked in bed.

Standing by the side of the bed, Rachel said, "Now, Sarah, close your eyes and rest."

Taking Rachel's hand, Sarah asked, "Who has Phillip Gideon, Mama Rachel?"

Chuckling, Rachel replied, "His father has him, introducing him to his family."

Sarah sighed and felt herself relax for the first time all day. "Have Gideon bring his son to me. I would like for you to offer a prayer of thanks for Phillip."

Kissing Sarah's hand, Rachel nodded and left to fetch Gideon and Phillip.

After Rachel prayed, she went to the bedroom door. "We're a little off schedule, so I'll leave now and see if we can get supper going. John is likely hungry, and I know Daniel is starving, but I'll bring your plates here."

Sarah held her baby close and pulled back the folds of his blanket. Glancing at Gideon, she said tenderly, "He's such a small thing, but your mother says that's normal and that he's fine."

"Once he's able to eat your cooking, he'll be all right. He's a handsome young man, don't you think?"

Laughing, Sarah said, "That's normal too, his father's a handsome young man!"

＊＊＊

The first days of May brought the blooms and bright colors of spring. Several grain farmers had come by to contract with Gideon to buy their wheat from him. In the evenings, Rachel was spending time with Sarah, teaching her how to keep the mill's accounts.

John sat on the porch, his senses lulled by the stillness of the afternoon. A lone hickory tree, in full leaf, stood nearby. Unwanted dark flashes of violence rushed through his memory. A vivid memory picture floated past his eyes. It had been a day much like this one, when he rode up to find his miller dead, a man he'd known since he was a boy, hanging by his neck from a limb of the hickory tree.

With deliberate steps, John headed for the barn. He knew what he must do; the tree had to come down. Wood chips flew into the air as the axe came down again and again on the hickory.

Rachel came to the porch with little Phillip on her hip. Shading her eyes with her free hand, she looked on silently, watching the top limbs tremble with each blow of the axe. John's chest heaved, but he wouldn't stop to rest. It was as if he couldn't rest while the tree stood.

Then he struck the final blow, and the tree shuddered for a moment. John dropped his axe and pushed against the mighty trunk, and the tree fell with a resounding thud. He stretched and flexed his shoulders and stared at the huge tree lying before him; his inner storm was abated.

He heard the babbling sounds of his grandson behind him. "You've got to be quiet, if you're going to sneak up on anyone, Phillip." Grinning, he glanced at Rachel, "He gets that from you, Rachel. Talking runs in your family."

"Now, grandpa, be nice. He's just telling you that he loves you."

Rachel looked past her husband in awe at the gigantic tree that now lay in a heap of crushed and split limbs.

"Was this the tree?" she asked, in a low voice.

John nodded. "Aye, 'twas the thought of it standing another day that brought me to fell it."

Phillip leaned toward his grandpa and John took him. "How does it feel to be a grandma? I never thought I'd be married to an old woman."

"Mind your tongue, Grandpa Hamilton! It's you who'll likely need a walking cane ere long."

"I must beg your forgiveness, my lovely wife; you're the most ravishing creature my eyes have ever seen."

"Oh my, Phillip, listen to your grandpa, he goes from one extreme to the other without batting an eye." She took the baby from John. "Let's go inside, darling, and find your mother," she cooed at Phillip. "Grandma has to start supper."

John watched her walk away. Over her shoulder, Rachel said, "I know you're watching me, grandpa!"

Shaking his head, he gave a little laugh. "Aye, that I am," John murmured. "A most ravishing creature."

A rider came into view as he topped the ridge that ran west from the creek. Still some distance away, John watched him approach the house. When John stepped away from the tree line, the rider casually reined over in the direction of John. As he drew closer, the man looked a bit familiar, though John couldn't place him.

Pulling his horse up a few feet from John, the man climbed down and thrust his hand toward him. "Hello, friend, my name is Stephen Walters. Would you be Gideon Hamilton?"

"Nay, Mr. Walters, Gideon is my oldest son. I'm John Hamilton." Doffing his hat, the tall, broad shouldered stranger ran his fingers through his russet brown hair and slapped his hat against his leg.

John was about to lead him to the house to find Gideon, when the man's surname struck a chord in John's memory. He stopped Stephen and said, "Walters! Are you kin to the Noah Walters who milled the flour here?"

Stephen flashed a wide grin. "Yessir, Noah was my uncle, my father's brother. He's sort of the reason I'm here--- my Uncle Noah, I mean."

Seeing John's perplexed expression, Stephen said, "I got wind that a man by the name of Gideon Hamilton on Sandy Creek was in need of a miller. I knew it had to be the mill where my uncle worked before he was . . ."

John slapped Stephen's shoulder and said, "This is indeed good news, Stephen. Come to the house, and we'll find Gideon."

Ellie met them at the door and took Stephen's hat. Rachel and Sarah came from the kitchen to see who their visitor was.

Stephen quickly introduced himself with his infectious grin and warm handshake.

With his hand on Stephen's shoulder, John, smiling broadly, said, "Stephen's a nephew of Noah Walters, and he's here to see Gideon about milling flour."

Glancing at Sarah, John asked, "Can you tell us where we might find your husband, Sarah?"

"Yes, I can. He's in the mill with his son. I'll go with you and bring Phillip back with me."

Lottie had been outside stirring a load of bed linens in the iron wash pot, when Stephen rode up. Without seeming obvious, she watched as her father and the stranger went inside. When they disappeared into the mill, she went back to the hot task, wiping the sweat from her brow with her sleeve

Only a few minutes passed before John and Sarah, carrying a crying Phillip, came out of the mill, heading back to the house. As they passed Lottie, Sarah called out, "I'll be out to help you as soon as I feed Phillip and put him down for his nap."

Nodding, Lottie waved to Phillip and went back to stirring the boiling water. Ignoring sweat that escaped her mobcap to dampen a loose tendril of her hair, Lottie observed her brother and the stranger talking as they came outside and made their way to the mill dam. Neither looked her way, for which she was grateful.

Shading her eyes from the sun's brightness with her hand, she watched the two men continue their inspection of the mill until she lost sight of them when they turned a corner of the building.

Patting the sweat from her face with her apron, she wondered if this man would be the new miller. *Gideon should've asked*

Papa to interview the man, since neither of my brothers has any experience in the actual milling of grain.

With Sarah's help, Lottie finished the washing before supper. Feeling a trickle of sweat run down her back, she said, "Sarah, I'm getting a quick bath before supper, do you have time to wash the smell of smoke from my hair?"

"Of course, if you'll do mine afterwards."

After bathing, Lottie hurried back to her room to finish dressing so she could concentrate on drying her thick blonde hair.

She heard a light tap at her door, and Sarah entered the room. "I gave Phillip to his father, so I could come back and help with your hair."

Lottie looked at her sister-in-law's image in the mirror. "It doesn't have to be completely dry; I'm wearing a mobcap for the evening."

"Would you like me to do the back in a chignon? That's your most becoming style, especially sort of loose with a stray tendril at your ears."

Lottie's facial muscles tensed, hardening her features. "I'm not looking to attract a man, Sarah. I know there'll be a time when a man will come into my life, but now is too soon."

Holding up a white mobcap, she added, "With this cap and the blue dress I'm wearing, I'll be the very image of who I am—a backcountry farm girl."

Sarah pulled a chair beside Lottie. "I'm so very sorry if I've hurt you. Can you forgive me? I was only thinking of how beautiful your hair is and how lovely you look in a chignon."

Leaning to hug her sister-in-law, Lottie said, "I know you were. You didn't hurt me—you really didn't—so there's nothing for me to forgive. I feel the warmth of your love every day."

CHAPTER THIRTY FIVE

FAMILY PLANS

That evening, Rachel served a platter of fried venison to go with the biscuits and gravy and baked sweet potatoes. Before she sat down, Rachel took a heavy cloth and removed the last of two pecan pies from the hearth oven.

The family united in a clasping of hands, and John asked for the blessing of their food. Conversation swirled smoothly around the table, and Stephen, with his infectious grin, fit in as if he was an old friend of the family.

John could feel the warmth of love in the voices of his family. He wondered if Stephen could feel it. *This young man comes from a part of North Carolina that's known Loyalist country. Maybe we assume too much because his Uncle Noah was a Patriot.*

Stephen's voice broke into his thoughts. John looked around the table; his family's eyes were locked on the young man as he talked. The question of politics hadn't surfaced in the time since Stephen arrived, but John knew he must find out where Stephen stood.

A lull in the conversation gave John his opportunity. "Stephen, I heard you mention that your parent's home is in the Salisbury community of our neighboring state."

"Aye, Mister John. That's the place of my birth and where I grew to become the man you see today."

John could see he had the attention of everyone at the table. From the expressions on their faces, he knew both his sons understood the implication that the Salisbury area of North Carolina was well known as Loyalist country.

"I'm sure you know the Salisbury area—"

Interrupting, Stephen said, his grin waning, "—is a hotbed of Loyalist activity? I know you must be concerned about my politics. Salisbury's my heritage, sir. I cannot deny it, but I haven't lived there for four years—since I was eighteen."

Everyone sat in rapt attention, their eyes never left Stephen.

John's expression was passive as he leaned back and steepled his fingers. "It's not my desire to cause you any discomfort, Stephen, but I must know where your loyalty lies."

Shaking his head, Stephen replied, "No offense taken, sir. I will say it plainly, so there's no misunderstanding. I'm a patriot of the United States. I served three years in our army, mostly in the north under Generals Greene and Arnold."

From an inner pocket of his waistcoat, Stephen withdrew a folded paper that Gideon took and passed on to his father. Everyone's eyes followed the paper to John's hands and looked on as his eyes scanned the page.

When he'd finished reading, John looked up and smiled. His eyes went around the table. "Stephen has contributed much to our cause," John said, passing the paper back to Stephen. "And he's conducted himself bravely in the battles at Saratoga. This letter, under the seal of General Washington, attests to his daring in routing Burgoyne's redcoats."

Relief was visible in the faces of the rest of the family. Rachel went to the pie safe and brought two pies to the table.

"Ellie, serve a slice of your pecan pie to Stephen, and I'll get some milk from the cellar."

Serving Stephen her pie, Ellie stood back, her arms crossed across her apron. Stephen could feel her eyes on him as he took his first bite.

"Ummm, this is better than my mother's pecan pie," he said, his grin spreading across his face.

Ellie breathed a sigh of relief and felt a blush bloom on her face. Her eyes met Daniel's, and she could see he was proud for her. The pies made their way around the table, and the conversation picked up naturally as though it had never stopped.

After the dessert, the men were about to take their coffee outside when Daniel pushed his chair back and stood. Ellie's eyes watched him closely.

"Uh, I uh—," he cleared his throat, and smiled weakly at Ellie, "I have an announcement to make. It uh—it shouldn't come as a surprise to anyone, but Ellie and I want very much to be married as soon as we can."

The table was abuzz with congratulations and congeniality. Daniel sat down and put his arm around Ellie. She returned Daniel's gaze. Her heart was so warm knowing he was willing to show his affection publically, something few men would do. His awkwardness only made her love him more.

The men went outside, and Rachel began making more coffee. "Lottie, get the coffee server out and fill it when the coffee is done and take it out to the men."

Lottie's eyebrows arched. "Me? Why do you ask me to take coffee to the men? Ellie's man is out there. Sarah's man is out there, and your man is out there. Why ask me?"

Without turning from her task at the wash basin, Rachel said, "I thought you might want to spend some time with your father before he leaves again."

Lottie's eyes grew wide, the news her father was leaving threw her off guard. Rachel went still; she could almost feel the heartache in her daughter's clear, blue eyes. A mother's compassion filled her.

"Papa's leaving again—where? I thought the fighting was over after Cowpens," Lottie demanded, "Nobody tells me anything around here."

Dear Lord, Rachel thought. *We haven't told her. She'll use this as another reason to shut herself away from her family.*

Rachel dropped the bar of soap in the basin of water and wiped her hands on the front of her apron. "Well, actually, it's not settled yet, but John is pretty sure he and the boys will have to help Colonel Pickens run Lord Rawdon back to Charleston."

Frustration bathed Rachel's heart as she studied the scowl on her daughter's face. *It's not her fault; we should have told her, but then I'm probably the only one to feel this way.*

Lottie's eyes cast a withering glance at Ellie and Sarah. "I suppose the both of you know about this?"

The stabbing question took both women by surprise, and neither could think of a response. Rachel's heart was to the point of breaking. Somehow, she felt responsible for Lottie's anger and purposeful isolation from the rest of the family. Lottie was clearly wounded and angry with the whole lot of them.

Without waiting for either of the women to respond, Lottie swirled around and stalked out of the kitchen.

Lottie's outburst left the women speechless for a moment. Rachel's thoughts were in a whirl, and her heart ached for her daughter. She could see the hurt and affront in Ellie and Sarah's faces. Over the past year and some months, Rachel had come to take these young women as her own daughters. *Have I neglected them in favor of Lottie*, she thought. *Where are you, Lord when I need you so?*

"It seems that Lottie isn't getting over Robert's death," Rachel said. The words coming out terse, much more than she intended.

"She's not eating, and she mopes a lot. That's not like Lottie. She and Daniel have always been the lively ones in our family."

Ellie, untying her apron, glanced at Sarah. "We're a close knit family, Mama Rachel, and it's obvious to us all that Lottie's still hurting. If we can, we've got to get her mind off Robert, but I've no idea how to do that."

Shaking her head, Sarah said, "Maybe we *can* come up with some way to help her, but Lottie will have to want to get better. When a person comes out of mourning, they've decided to shed the past and embrace the present, and Lottie must want to do that for herself."

"I must want to do *what* myself, Sarah?" Lottie had returned to the kitchen unnoticed.

Thinking her sister-in-law was upstairs in her bedroom, Sarah was taken aback by the sound of her voice. "Uh—w-we were just—"

"Your attitude is unacceptable, Lottie," Rachel said, cutting Sarah off, "the conversation we were having was about how to help you, nothing more. Whatever is spinning through your head, you must know we all love you and want to do everything we can to bring back the Lottie we know you to be."

Silence hovered over the room, as dark and heavy as a moonless night. No one dared speak until Lottie voiced the reason she had returned. Forcing herself to end this standoff, she said in a mock self-effacing tone, "I came back, Mama, to tell you I'd be happy to take the coffee out to the men. I want to talk with Papa about some things important to me."

Seeing through her daughter's insincere act, Rachel sighed heavily and took a dishcloth to pick up the pot of coffee and pour it into the server.

⸻ ⸻ ⸻

Outside, the men had made their way along an old, worn trail leading down to the creek. Easing their way past the undergrowth, they soon came to the edge of the water. The creek narrowed here, and the current was flowing fast. Finding no place to sit, the men stood around where they found firm ground.

"Pa, since the season is almost on us, I hired Stephen before we came in for supper," Gideon said. "And we talked about his loyalty while we were in the mill, but I didn't speak up at supper because I thought it best to let the family hear from Stephen himself. I hope I did the right thing."

"Neither of us did wrong, son. It's the mark of our unsettled times, when men expect to be questioned about their loyalty. Stephen understands this."

Nodding his head in assent, Stephen agreed, "Aye Mister John, 'tis a mark of the times."

Watching his brother, Daniel could see the satisfaction and confidence Gideon felt about the mill, and now with Stephen to help him, there was an added promise of success. Daniel was proud for his brother, but he was anxious to marry Ellie, set out on his own, and raise his own family. Maybe the war wasn't quite over, but after Cowpens, it was obvious the British were running out of fight. From Georgia to North Carolina there was now only a smattering of British strongholds left.

The sound of someone coming down the trail brought a pause in the conversation. It was Lottie, with an intricately woven shawl around her shoulders, carrying a copper and tin coffee serving pot. Grasping the wooden handle tightly, she cautiously made her way toward the group of men, when suddenly a limb from an overhanging walnut sapling caught her bonnet and snatched it from her head.

"Oh!" she cried, as her hair spilled over her neck and shoulders in a cascade of blonde curls.

The sight of Lottie striding toward them had halted Stephen's conversation with John. He'd already noticed her during dinner, but she seemed distant and unresponsive to his attempt to draw her into a conversation.

In his travels around the backcountry, he'd not found any young females that could match the visage standing before him. She wore a plain homespun dress with a sky-blue pelisse and until a moment ago, a matching bonnet with a pink bow. He wondered if her lips, now pursed in annoyance, could form a smile.

Surely, the sound of her laughter would be music more beautiful than anything I've ever heard.

Stephen suddenly came alive, stepped past John, and was at her side before her brothers could move. His near frantic move startled Lottie. It seemed her bonnet had just taken flight when he was standing beside her, looking down at her with his now familiar grin. Their eyes met, and she could feel her cheeks redden. She thought he was the tallest man she'd ever seen, much taller than the men in her family. His beardless face was tanned—more so than she would expect from a man who claimed to be a miller—and accented with a firm jaw and straight nose. Instantly, she felt an attraction that was unnerving to her.

Leaning forward, Stephen felt her hair brush against him as he deftly fetched her cap. He caught the fresh scent of lilacs when he stepped back.

This was the first time she'd been this close to a man since Robert had held her in his arms, and it made her uncomfortable. Their eyes met again, and then remained fastened together for the briefest moment of hesitation before she turned away, but in that moment, Stephen caught a glimpse of pain on her face and it sent a chill through him.

"Thank you," she muttered, relieved he'd stepped back. Lottie moved quickly, before the notion struck him to speak to her.

Her father was grinning as she reached him. Tossing the cold remains of his coffee, he took the server and filled his cup. "Thank you, Princess, for bringing our coffee, I imagine we all would like a refill."

Lottie gave him the little girl smile she knew he expected. She wasn't feigning a smile like she so often did when she had to pretend to take part in family gatherings. It was real and reserved only for her Papa.

Keeping her voice low so the others couldn't hear her words, Lottie said, "Mama told me that you'll be leaving again soon, Papa."

Lottie's question struck a nerve, and John's grin tightened. Usually before these campaigns, he and Lottie would have some quiet time together.

How could I do such a thing . . . anything that would bring her more pain? Every day, I see sadness in her face, even when she smiles, even when she laughs . . .

"Maybe in the next day or two, Princess, your brothers and I'll be joining up with Colonel Pickens to challenge Lord Rawdon. I thought you knew, but you and I can still have our time together this evening or tomorrow, for sure . . . will that be all right?"

Continuing to speak in a low whisper, she replied, "Yes, Papa, that will all right." Standing on tiptoes, she kissed him on his cheek. "I love you, Papa."

Turning to leave, she saw that Stephen was still holding her bonnet and now he also held the near-empty serving pot. He was standing where she'd lost her bonnet and grinning from ear to ear. Lottie would've thought he was a comical sight with her bonnet in one hand and the server in the other, but he had the most beautiful eyes of any man she'd ever seen.

This is absurd! I'm behaving like some silly girl, and I do believe he's the most shameless man in South Carolina. The man is actually flirting with me in the presence of my father and brothers.

Stephen waited patiently for Lottie's conversation with her father to end. He wasn't able to hear what the two of them were saying, but just watching the animated expressions of her face and the movement of her lips as she spoke was enough for the moment. Her father's pet name for her was certainly fitting. She looked younger than twenty and was approaching full bloom, and she was of average tallness with a slender waist and filling out very well in her figure.

Whoa! You've seen attractive women before, a few just as beautiful as Lottie. What's got into you? He chided himself silently. *No doubt, she's on a quest for a husband, and I shouldn't be so obliging.*

Lottie stopped where Stephen was waiting and forced a benign smile. "Thank you for retrieving my bonnet, Mr. Walters, I'm in your debt, sir."

Their eyes met ever so briefly, before she dropped her eyes, but it was enough—enough for him to know Lottie was hiding something.

Stepping ahead of her to hold back an overhanging limb, he said, "Maybe I should walk with you . . . as far as the clearing, at least."

"No thank you, I'll manage quite well," she said crisply, "it's not that far."

Daring not to pursue the issue with her father and brothers standing so near, he stood aside and she strode to the house, her dress swishing around her ankles.

Lottie hurried back to the house. She wanted to put some distance between herself and the tall young man who, just with his deep brown eyes, drove her to distraction.

Stephen's gaze lingered a moment, as she made her way up the trail, but John's voice snapped him back to reality, and he swallowed. His throat suddenly seemed very dry when he saw John's eyes fixed on him.

"I feel I must warn you, Stephen, my daughter's a handful under the best of circumstances, and she's only recently come out of mourning."

Stephen wanted to choose his words carefully before he responded. He didn't want to put ideas in John's head about his intentions toward Lottie—mainly because he wasn't sure himself where this light flirtation was heading.

With the lingering memory of her scent still wafting around him, Stephen said, "I appreciate your being straightforward, Jo—Mister Hamilton. I shall keep that in mind—about her coming out of mourning, I mean."

⸺⸻⸻

"Is that you, Lottie?" Rachel called from the kitchen, as the front door closed.

Lottie crossed the kitchen and placed the coffee server in the washbasin. "It's me," she said, with a tone of detachment.

Rachel turned from the hearth and untied her apron, and then she walked over to the doorway. With her hands resting on her hips and a grim expression etched on her face, she said, "Go to our room and wait for me and your father," Rachel snapped, "It's time the three of us talked."

Rachel knew this wasn't going to be easy for her husband, since he doted on his daughter, but she knew he would agree it was time for Lottie to grow up.

Lottie was sitting on the edge of the bed when they entered her room. She looked first at her father, then at her mother. Both wore a similar grim expression. Rachel began first with words of assurance that they both loved her, and standing with his wife, John added his counsel, which at first, struck at the core of her heart. Lottie, in all of her years, had never heard her father's words of reprimand directed at her. She'd witnessed his discipline of her brothers, but those powerful arms that delivered whippings to her brothers, and the deep, angry sounding voice that he sometimes used with them, had always been gentle instruments of love when directed at Lottie.

Lottie listened and there was a reflection of pain in her eyes, and she fought back tears. Her mind was whirling with unhappy thoughts of the past year. *Oh God, I've been so mean to the people who love me. How can I ever make it up to them? How could I have thought no one understood what I've endured?*

John sat beside his daughter and swallowed hard, trying to keep the tears from his eyes. He squeezed her hand gently with his massive grip, and feeling his touch, Lottie couldn't keep herself composed any longer. Tears spilled freely down her face.

Rachel came to sit on her other side, and a silence fell over the room that was almost palpable.

Finally, Lottie raised her head and said, "I can only hope you believe me when I say thank you for loving me so. All my life, I've known nothing but love from my father and mother, and I feel it most warmly now."

Taking her mother's hand, she added, "My rudeness and shabby treatment of Sarah and Ellie, both whom I consider to be my sisters, is unforgivable . . . and I'm guilty of the same with both of you and my brothers."

Rachel felt a burden lifted from her heart. There was no ignoring the candor of Lottie's expression, and the glow on her face. Gone were the tense lines of pain on her face.

"I've hidden away long enough," Lottie said, "It's time for me to venture back into the world, into life."

Again, Lottie broke down, weeping. "Oh Mama, I can't remember Robert's face, anymore, and that's been eating away at my heart for a while," she said through her sobs. "It's killing me a little every day."

Rachel tucked her finger under Lottie's chin and raised her face. Her voice was just above a whisper. "Lottie, it's been four years since Robert stayed with us on his way to join the army, and it's perfectly normal for a person to forget someone's likeness, over time. But what you won't forget is the essence of

Robert—who and what he was—and how he loved you. Those memories will never leave you. You'll have them for the rest of your life."

⟵⟶ ⟵⟶ ⟵⟶

The next morning when Sarah came into the kitchen, she found Lottie lighting the kindling to start the oven fire. "Lottie, you're up so early! Did you have a fidgety night?"

Lottie, smiling brightly, looked up at her. "No, Sarah, I slept very soundly—for the first time in a long while, and I think I will from now on."

Tying her apron, Sarah looked at her and grinned widely. "Welcome back, sister. Welcome back!"

END

Epilogue

John and Rachel sat in two ornate lawn chairs under one of the stately live oaks while their grandchildren played around them. Today was a beautiful day for celebration. It was the United States' thirtieth birthday.

The family had just gotten back from nearby Camden where the men were part of the veteran's parade through town. The grand finale at the end of the parade was the community exhibition of fireworks and firing of the town's cannon.

Tables were set up under the tree and very soon would be laden with an abundance of food for the growing family.

Noisy and boisterous, the children encircled their grandparents until Lottie rushed over to quiet them.

"You children go play in the orchard. You're making Grandma and Grandpa nervous!"

John sat up straight, his voice strong, "Let them play, daughter! This is a day of celebration!"

Turning aside to Rachel, he looked at her smiling at him. At sixty-two, her chestnut colored hair had yielded to only scattered strands of silver. His gaze brought a warm feeling of love to her heart and she felt young and beautiful once more.

The children rushed to their grandpa, crowding around him. Ellie and Daniel's ten-year-old daughter, Liza, climbed onto John's lap. "It was me, Grandpa and I'm sorry if I made you and

Grandma nervous. Daddy says I can be louder than thunder, sometimes."

Stretching his arms to take in the others hovering nearby, John said, "I love each one of you more than I could ever say, and I'm happy for all of you. Go on and play as you were doing before, because today we're having a celebration. Today is the 4th of July, our country's thirtieth birthday, and it's a good day to run and play and to be loud if you want. Now hug your Grandma and go play."

John leaned back in his chair; his thoughtful eyes followed his grandchildren as they played noisily around him. Rachel, sitting close by, watched as the children climbed over him and clung to him shouting at the top of their lungs.

The youngest grandson, Jonathan, was wearing his grandpa's old militia hat and was carrying a stick for his saber. He had taken charge and was directing the others.

"That boy reminds me of myself when I was that age," John said smugly.

Rachel chuckled. "I think you're right. It's plain to see Jonathan's your grandson. Have you noticed how he pouts until he gets his way?"

⸙ ⸙ ⸙

The day of celebration came to a close as the last rays of the setting sun disappeared behind the treetops. Parents rounded up their children for baths and bed. By dark, John and Rachel were in bed themselves, while their three children, with their spouses, gathered on the veranda. After the last lamp had been extinguished, the house soon quietened until the only sound came from the ticking from the downstairs hall clock as the pendulum swung back and forth.

"Are you awake, Angel?" whispered John.

Drowsily, Rachel answered, "Yes. What is it?"

Turning toward her, John clasped her hand in his. "I was thinking of all the ways God has blessed us and our family. Eleven grandchildren who are all healthy is one of the very special gifts to us . . . my heart is so full sometimes, I can barely hold it in."

Not answering him right away, Rachel pulled their hands to her chest and said, "I know that feeling. It's as if Heaven opened its gates before us."

They lay there for a while listening to the faint sounds of the hall clock.

John caressed her face. "And blessings continue to fall from Heaven; Ellie and Lottie are both expecting."

Rachel giggled, and said, "We mustn't forget Phillip and his new bride. I imagine it won't be long before we'll have our first great-grandchild."

John bolted upright. "Do you realize, when that happens, I'll be married to a great-grandmother?"

Pulling him back down, Rachel purred, "You'll search far and wide to find another great-grandmother like me."

Holding her close to him, John replied, "Mm hmm, and who's searching?